Matt stared at her. This was a new twist. "Are you asking me if I'm passionate?"

Although the thought amused him, he just didn't see Kendra putting that sort of question to him. It didn't jibe with her personality—at least, not the way he perceived it.

Was he wrong? And if so, about what, exactly? Less than twenty-four hours in the woman's company and she was becoming one huge, intriguing enigma. A puzzle he found himself wanting to solve.

"No," she contradicted, a flash of embarrassment over the misunderstanding sending heat up her neck to her cheeks—as did the unbidden thought of his being passionate. "What I'm asking you is if your fellow coworkers know the first thing about what makes Matt Abilene tick," she asked. "Or do they know only what you want them to know?"

MARIE FERRARELLA

This *USA TODAY* bestselling and RITA® Award-winning author has
written more than two hundred books for Harlequin Books and Silhouette
Books, some under the name Marie Nicole. Her romances are beloved by
fans worldwide. Visit her website, www.marieferrarella.com.

MARIE FERRARELLA

Cavanaugh Rules

HARLEQUIN®

entertain, enrich, inspire™

Recycling programs
for this product may
not exist in your area.

ISBN-13: 978-0-373-27785-8

CAVANAUGH RULES

Copyright © 2012 by Marie Rydzynski-Ferrarella

CAVANAUGH REUNION

Copyright © 2012 by Marie Rydzynski-Ferrarella

www.Harlequin.com

Printed in U.S.A.

CONTENTS

Dear Reader,

Welcome back to the Cavanaughs. We continue to explore this latest branch that has recently come to light. This time, we peek into the life of Kendra Cavelli aka Cavanaugh, who, when her fiancé dies, distances herself from personal relationships, avoiding them like the plague.

For his part, her new partner, Matt Abilene, liked relationships just fine. The more, the merrier—and the lighter, the better. He'd learned to keep any sort of commitment out of the picture by watching the way his mother, desperate for someone to love, had been taken advantage of over and over again. He wanted to keep her safe and swore to himself that he would never follow in her footsteps.

But love, Kendra and Matt come to learn, is a very hard thing to shut the door on when it comes knocking. Come watch it unfold with me.

As ever, I thank you for reading and from the bottom of my heart, I wish you someone to love who loves you back.

All the best,

Marie Ferrarella

Cavanaugh Rules

To Nik

Hearts really do heal,

If you let them

Chapter 1

Detective Kendra Cavelli remembered reading somewhere that life was a series of leavings. At the time, she'd thought this was a very pessimistic point of view. But, she realized now, she'd been a lot younger and full of hope then.

Granted, no one would consider her old by any standards, except for maybe when measured against the life cycle of an everyday fruit fly. But the truth of it was, these days she felt a great deal older than what the age indicated on her birth certificate.

And who knew? Maybe the year that was written down wasn't as accurate as she'd once thought. Certainly the last name had turned out not to be.

She'd spent more than twenty-six years thinking she was a Cavelli, only to be told that she wasn't, that she and her brothers and sisters were actually Cavanaughs because her father was really a Cavanaugh. Thanks to a distraught maternity nurse who had been enveloped in grief the day her father and the *real* Cavelli baby were born, the two infants had accidentally been switched before either was a day old.

Former police chief Andrew Cavanaugh had done some research into the matter once it had come to light. It seemed that a nurse on the maternity floor, a Jane Allen, had just been told that her fiancé, Private First Class Wade Johnson, had been killed in some unnamed battle halfway around the world. Grief-stricken, Jane had gone through the paces of her job, utterly dazed and confused.

And because of that, Kendra's father and his subsequent offspring had lost their identities. Her father was taken home by the Cavellis while the real Sean Cavelli had been claimed by Seamus Cavanaugh and his wife.

And now, several months into what she and her siblings referred to as the "great revelation," she was still having trouble centering herself. She felt trapped between the past she'd *thought* was hers and the completely new present that loomed before her.

Maybe she'd have less trouble adapting, Kendra thought now as she cut across the hall of the second floor of One Police Plaza, if this name thing had not been tangled up with the loss of her own fiancé and now, on top of that, the sudden exit of her partner.

The first had all but destroyed her when he had deliberately blown himself away to the next world, and the second had just recently—and voluntarily—retired. The upshot was that both had left her to deal with things as best she could on her own.

She doubted that either one of them had given her

so much as a thought when making their final decision. God knew that Jason hadn't because if he had, he'd still be alive today. And they'd be married.

Instead, here she was, feeling incredibly isolated and alone. Alone even though her immediate family, counting her father, Sean, and her brothers and sisters, came to a grand total of seven people—plus her. At this point, Kendra didn't know if she was even allowed to count the family members she was no longer actually related to.

As for the "family" she was suddenly *supposed* to be part of, she hadn't gotten around to doing a successful head count there. All she knew was that, when gathered together, they could probably fill up half a stadium. God knew they filled a great deal of the Aurora Police Department, of which she was a proud part.

At least that hadn't changed.

At least, she now amended silently, she *assumed* that wouldn't change, even though she'd just been summoned by the chief of detectives, Brian Cavanaugh, who, along with the former chief of police, was one of her two "newfound" uncles.

Walking into the chief of detectives' outer office, she stopped at the desk positioned just in front of the door to the man's inner sanctum.

The entrance was guarded by a very capable-looking young woman in her late thirties. As Kendra crossed to her desk, the woman raised her eyes to Kendra's and quietly waited for her to say something.

"Detective Kendra Cavel—Cavan—" Kendra stumbled, not having decided which name she was going to use now that she was aware of the whole story. It wasn't as easy a decision as some might have thought.

Thomas and Bridget had already both opted to go with *Cavanaugh,* as had her father, but she wasn't sure if she wanted to abandon the name she'd used for more than a quarter of a century.

The decision to do so was particularly difficult for her in light of the fact that she already felt as if *she* had been abandoned. If she abandoned her name and the people she'd once regarded as family, what did that say about her?

Tabling her unsettling thoughts for a moment, Kendra said, "I'm here to see Chief Cavanaugh."

Lt. Reta Richards, the chief's administrative assistant for over ten years, smiled at her and nodded knowingly, as if she understood and sympathized with the dilemma Kendra was facing these days.

"The chief is on the phone right now," the lieutenant told her. "But he said to tell you that he'll see you as soon as he's through. Please have a seat." She indicated the chairs to the right against the opposite wall. "It shouldn't be long."

With a preoccupied nod, Kendra crossed to the chairs and took a seat.

That was when she noticed that she wasn't the only one waiting to see the chief of detectives. Occupying one of the other chairs was a tall, dark-haired, strikingly handsome man who despite his athletic build seemed to fill the room with his presence.

Making eye contact with her, the room's other occupant flashed her an easy smile. The kind of smile that said he was comfortable in his own skin and welcomed visitors regularly.

Kendra was well acquainted with the type. Not a serious thought in his head, except for having fun. Her engagement to Jason had rescued her from men like that.

Or so she'd thought at the time.

Instead, her engagement to the late firefighter had introduced her to a world of devastating grief and heartache.

She nodded absently at the man, acknowledging his silent greeting, and then took her seat. She was not about to start a conversation with him; she fixed her eyes on the inner door.

Kendra was torn between hoping the chief's door would open immediately, separating her from the possibility of having to make small talk with a man she didn't know who most likely just wanted a receptive audience, and hoping that Brian Cavanaugh would take his time getting to her because she had no idea what to expect.

The problem was, she had trouble waiting. Her father had commented affectionately, more than once, that she was not one of his more patient children.

It was hard not to shift restlessly in her seat. The man to her right occupied his chair as if he didn't have a care in the world. And when he smiled at her, all it seemed to do was increase her restlessness, although she couldn't explain why.

As it turned out, Kendra didn't have all that long to wait. Less than five minutes later, Reta saw the light go out on the phone's multiline keyboard and looked up. "The chief will see you now."

Since there were two of them and the lieutenant hadn't specified which of them she was speaking to, Kendra heard herself asking, "Which one?"

"Why, both of you," Reta replied pleasantly.

The man to her right was already on his feet. God but he was tall, Kendra thought as she rose from her chair. He had to be almost a foot taller than she was and she stood close to five-seven in her stacked heels.

For some reason she couldn't pinpoint, she felt a strange ripple of foreboding in her stomach.

She had a bad feeling about this.

Kendra walked in first, whether because she was just a little faster, or because of some latent gallantry on the man's part, she wasn't quite certain. Not that it mattered all that much, she supposed. What mattered was why she'd been sent for in the first place.

Old-school all the way, Brian Cavanaugh rose from his chair and leaned forward over his desk. He shook Kendra's hand warmly, as if they had known each other all her life instead of just a little while.

Oh, she'd known *of* him, and the chief had been the one to give her her gold shield at the ceremony when she'd been made a detective just shortly after she'd become engaged. But she hadn't actually known *him* until the "great mixup" had come to light. After that, there had been a slew of miscellaneous invitations—both for actual occasions and for no reason at all—to attend family gatherings, usually at retired police chief Andrew Cavanaugh's house, but not always.

Not everyone attended each gathering, but she'd seen the chief at these unofficial parties often enough. He'd worn the very same smile then as he was wearing now. Did that mean that she should relax?

Or was he just trying to soften the blow that was about to come?

She'd been born suspicious and while that was helpful in her line of investigative work, it did wreak havoc on her personal life.

"How's everything going, Kendra?" the chief asked her as he silently indicated the chair to the left of his desk.

By *everything,* she assumed he meant work. Her partner had retired two weeks ago and she was alternating between missing the man's grumpy countenance and being summarily angry at him for his abrupt retirement. Never mind that Det. Joe Walsh was approaching almost seventy and had well earned this retirement. The widower had led her to believe that he was planning to work forever. She'd allowed herself to get comfortable with the idea that she could count on seeing Joe's hangdog frown facing her each morning across their desks.

"I'm managing," she answered in a pleasant voice that neither confirmed nor denied her statement. Until she knew what was going on, her guard was going to remain up.

"And you, Detective Abilene?" Brian asked, looking at the tall, rangy man who'd stretched his long legs out before him the moment he'd sat down.

From this angle, the man seemed to be all leg, Kendra caught herself thinking.

"The same," the detective replied, nodding toward Kendra as if that meant he was echoing her assessment.

Brian smiled then and Kendra's uneasiness grew.

Part of the reason she disliked departures so intensely was because they were wrapped up in change. She'd never cared for change. It was a very real fact of life, but that didn't make it any easier for her.

Lately there'd been so many changes, she couldn't keep track of them all.

Brian laughed softly, causing both of the other two people in the room to look at him curiously.

"I'm getting ahead of myself," Brian said to them. "Introductions are in order. Detective Matthew Abilene, meet Detective Kendra—"

He paused then, realizing that he hadn't been apprised of her official decision yet. Each of the Cavellis, like the four stepchildren who had come with his marriage to his former partner, Lila, and the triplets from his late brother Mike's hidden family, had been given the option of changing their surnames and officially becoming Cavanaughs if they so chose.

So far, the family name was batting a thousand, but he was not about to jump the gun with the few who were still undecided.

"Have you made a decision about your last name yet?" he asked her.

Because the chief was being thoughtful rather than pushy, she offered the man a grateful smile. "I'm still working on it, sir."

He nodded understandingly. "I understand. It's a big step to take," he agreed. "Let me know what you decide." His intent was to let her know that while he was interested in the final outcome, he refused to apply any undue pressure on either side of the argument. "Anyway," he continued briskly, "it's come to my attention that the two of you have both recently lost your partners for one reason or another. Yours took his long overdue retirement," he said to Kendra, then turned to Matt. "And yours—"

"—picked up and left the state when his girlfriend decided she wanted to live somewhere where it's always raining," Matt commented. Glancing toward Kendra, he added, "They moved to Seattle."

Her eyes narrowed as she looked at the handsome face. Was he talking down to her? The man might be good-looking enough to have his own fan club, but she took offense. "I figured that part out on my own," she told him coolly.

"Sharp," Matt murmured. Whether he was just making an offhanded comment or being sarcastic, she wasn't sure. But she leaned toward the latter—in which case he needed to be taken down a few pegs even if she never saw the man again.

"Yes, she is," Brian replied in no uncertain terms. "Which is why I've decided to partner the two of you up."

Kendra frowned. She'd had a vague, uneasy feeling that this was coming but somehow, hearing it caused a jolt. She didn't want this. She knew she couldn't just pick a new partner, but this man was as far from her first choice as humanly possible. Any man *this* handsome would be trouble. She could feel it in her bones.

"Are you in Homicide?" she heard herself stiffly asking the other detective.

Because if he was, he and the partner who'd been dragged to Seattle had to have been next to invisible. She didn't recall seeing either one of them around and, annoying though he promised to be, Abilene was *not* the kind of man who blended into the woodwork. Once upon a time, before she'd been so terribly disillusioned, she might have even felt a flutter—or three—

in Abilene's presence. But those days were long gone. Still, she would have taken note of him—had he been there to take note of.

"Major Case Squad," the other detective corrected her.

Major Case? That didn't make sense. Why was the chief pairing her up with a detective from another division? Kendra turned to look at the man she was supposed to regard as her uncle.

"Then how—"

Brian anticipated the rest of her question and spared them both by answering, "I've decided to switch Detective Abilene to Homicide."

"You're taking me off Major Case?" Matt asked, surprised. Why? What had brought this on? His record was clean, exemplary even. He would have been aware of any complaints from his captain.

"Just for the time being," Brian told him mildly.

It was his way of helping his people adjust to new circumstances. He allowed them to believe that a change was temporary while they did their best to fit in. After the initial period of adjustment, he'd discovered that most times getting the same people to transfer back out—and leave their new partner—in order to go back to their old division required the assistance of a crowbar.

He was counting on that here.

"There's not that much to do, even with Seth gone," Brian pointed out to Matt. "Until it picks up, we could use a mind like yours over in Homicide." And then he instinctively turned toward Kendra and added, "And that in no way was meant to be a negative reflection on the caliber of your work. It's just that with Joe retired, you need a new partner."

Kendra knew that. And she knew that the chief was only trying to be helpful, even though she didn't want any help. But the only time detectives went solo was when their partners were either in court, testifying, out sick or on vacation. Otherwise, if detectives left or asked to be transferred out, the resulting gaps were filled as quickly as possible.

This was just a little faster than she'd expected. Or liked. Even if change hadn't made her feel uneasy, Abilene, with his perfect smile, did.

Joe's chair was still warm, she thought ruefully. She hadn't thought she would have to get used to someone new for at least another week. Maybe longer.

So much for longer.

She was well aware of procedure, but that didn't mean that she liked it. And she had the uneasy feeling that she'd just been partnered with a hotshot who got by on his looks. Granted, she was going by a gut feeling, but her gut had always been fairly accurate.

Kendra made up her mind to ask around about Abilene. Or maybe she would have Tom do it for her. Her older brother had a way of finding things out that didn't rub people the wrong way, while she, well, she hadn't quite managed to successfully develop that talent yet. At least not when she found herself heavily invested in something. Such as now.

She slanted a glance at the man sitting beside her. He seemed to be fine with the arrangement. Or at least he wasn't protesting it. But then, there were many ways to protest something, not all of them vocal. Abilene's expression gave her no clue as to what he was thinking even as, for one unguarded moment, it seemed to ripple directly into the pit of her stomach.

Definitely needed to have Tom ask around, she decided firmly.

Right now, she needed to know one thing. Taking a breath, Kendra asked the man sitting across from her, "Is this permanent, sir?"

Uncle or not, she knew that her family connection didn't figure into this right now and she didn't want him to think she was questioning his judgment. On the other hand, she really needed to know what she was facing here. Forewarned was forearmed.

Brian smiled and looked at the two people sitting before him, one at rigid attention, the other in a seemingly relaxed mode. He had a positive feeling about this. Although probably not immediately evident to either one of them, pairing these two was a good thing.

"We'll see," he answered. Turning his attention to Abilene, he gave the man an opportunity to voice any protest, although he had a feeling that there would be none forthcoming. It wasn't that Abilene was a dutiful "good soldier," but he rolled with the punches and took whatever came his way. But by no means was he a pushover. This would be a healthy blending of styles.

"So, unless you have any objections, Detective Abilene, you'll be moving your things over to Homicide, effective immediately."

Matt nodded. His expression remained the same, even while his eyes swept over the woman to his left, as if taking measure of her. If there was a verdict one way or another, he kept it to himself. There was neither eagerness nor covert annoyance in his voice. "I'll get right on it, sir," he promised.

Let the adventure begin, Brian thought.

Like a mechanic with an ear for the machines he worked with, Brian liked hearing the sound of a well-tuned engine. He had a feeling that was what he had here. Kendra would just have to get over the initial period of adjustment. But it would be worth it.

"Well, unless there's anything else," Brian said, a note of finality in his voice, "you're dismissed." And then, as the two rose to their feet, he added with a smile, "Make me proud."

"Yes, sir," Kendra replied, forcing a smile she didn't feel to her lips.

"Do my best, sir." Matt fired off the casual promise as he turned to leave. He caught the dark look that his new partner shot him.

The woman was very attractive, but she didn't know it. He'd never had a female partner before. This was going to be interesting. *Very* interesting.

Kendra strode out of the inner, then outer office ahead of him, putting distance between them quickly. She didn't bother to pretend to want to talk—because she didn't. She was busy dealing with this latest curve that Fate had tossed her.

Matt merely stretched his legs and shortened that distance to nothing in a matter of a few steps.

He caught up to her way before the elevator, but she kept on walking, not acknowledging his presence. It was as if she'd been encapsulated in a world all her own.

If only, she thought.

"So what do I call you?" Abilene asked as he reached

over her head and pressed the Up button on the wall before she could.

Forced to acknowledge him, she had a feeling her best bet was to put him in his place right from the very beginning. If she was wrong about him, there would be time enough to soften her approach.

Kendra looked up at him—she was going to need to get higher heels, she decided, then almost instantly rescinded that thought. A little distance between them might be a good thing. Being too close to him might blunt the edge she would need. There was no getting away from the fact that he *was* bone-meltingly good-looking and close proximity might cause her to forget.

"Good at my job," she answered.

Matt considered her reply for a second and then nodded. "Okay, but that's a little long. How about I just call you 'Good'?"

The elevator arrived and she turned her back on him as she entered, silently cursing Joe for having left her to undertake a life revolving around fly-fishing.

Chapter 2

When Abilene got off behind her, Kendra turned around to look at her new—and hopefully very temporary—partner. Why was he following her?

"Shouldn't you be going up to your floor to get your things?" she asked him.

Just for a moment, he'd allowed himself to watch her walk, appreciatively taking in the way her hips swayed ever so slightly. Her question pulled him back to reality. He nodded toward the squad room just behind her. "I thought I'd see where my desk is first."

"And what?" she asked. "If it doesn't meet with your standards, you'll stay where you are?"

Abilene grinned, amused. "Is that a hopeful note in your voice I hear?" He studied her for a moment, looking beyond her high cheekbones and her fascinating eyes. "You don't do change very well, do you?"

The last thing she wanted to put up with was being

analyzed. Kendra's eyes blazed as she tossed her head. "What I do or don't do is none of your business," she informed him.

The way he saw it, that wasn't quite true. "Some of it will be. And I want to see where my desk is so I don't have to wander around aimlessly when I come down with an armload of my stuff." He looked at her with eyes that seemed earnest. "Does that meet with your approval?"

Rather than answer him, she merely sighed and beckoned him to follow her through the door. Crossing the floor, she stopped at what seemed to be the center of the room.

"This is yours," she told him, gesturing toward the cleared expanse of desk that butted up against hers.

A greater contrast between the two areas would have been difficult to find. One desk was the picture of virgin territory without so much as a scrap of paper on it, while the other desk bore silent testimony to a very cluttered style. There was a computer off to one side, its keyboard stretched out before it rather than neatly tucked out of sight. The rest of the desk was buried beneath files and a snowstorm of scattered, interweaving papers. Not so much as a square inch of desktop was visible.

Matt made no verbal comment, but the way his mouth curved seemed to say it all. At least, she read a great deal into it.

Kendra took umbrage at what she perceived as criticism from her new, God-help-her, partner. Periodically, she went through everything on her desk and cleared spaces, trying her best to organize the raft of papers into some sort of a system, but inevitably, the stacks would bleed into one another again, merging and creating a chaotic pile.

"I've got a system," she retorted defensively in response to the amusement in Abilene's liquid-green eyes.

"I'm sure you do." To the untrained ear, Abilene's mild tone sounded completely agreeable. Why, then, did it make her want to scratch his eyes out or at least challenge him to a weapons proficiency contest on the gun range?

Absently, Matt opened the center drawer of his new desk, then checked, one by one, a few of the other drawers. Like the surface of the desk, they were all pristinely clean.

He shut the last drawer. "Your old partner did a thorough job cleaning things out. He didn't leave anything behind."

"Not even any hope," Kendra murmured under her breath. The amused sound coming from her new partner told her that her voice hadn't been quite as low as she'd thought.

Great, Pretty Boy has hearing like a bat.

Stepping back, Abilene pushed his chair into his desk. "I'll go get my stuff now."

"I can hardly wait," Kendra deadpanned, pasting a pained smile on her lips.

Matt paused for a moment, his eyes slowly sliding down the length of this sharp-tongued woman. Thanks to his chaotic upbringing, he was basically nomadic in his lifestyle and his relationships. It gave him the ability to take whatever came down the road because, good or bad, he knew it was only temporary and would eventually change.

"You know," he told her, "I'm really not such a bad guy to work with. Not as good as some, but better than most. You might want to put the pitchfork down, Good, and reserve judgment for a while."

The fact that Abilene wasn't heaping endless laurels on himself surprised her. Someone like him, who exuded sensuality with his every movement, ordinarily had the inside track on vanity, possessing an ego that made passage through narrow doorways an ongoing challenge.

She supposed she could be wrong about Abilene, but she didn't care to debate it with herself right now, one way or the other. She wasn't feeling all that magnanimous or friendly.

"The jury's still out on that one," Kendra informed him.

Matt supposed that was the best he would get for now. And maybe that was good because he could see himself being attracted to her, but that might complicate matters. And all he was interested in for now was a truce while he got his bearings. Later might prove to be another story, he mused, but right now, he just wanted to settle in.

He flashed an easy smile. "Sounds fair enough," he replied.

Turning on his heel, he was about to leave. All his things could be packed up and transported in one trip. Unlike his new partner, once he closed a case, he didn't hang on to the papers that went with it. Instead, he placed everything onto a flash drive and preserved the information that way. It took up a great deal less space. And it made for a neater desk. He worked better that way.

Matt got exactly three steps toward the squad room door when he heard his name being called.

"Hey, Abilene!"

When he turned around again, Matt found himself looking down at an older man with thick silver hair and a far thicker waistline. Rather than hiding the latter behind the all-forgiving folds of a jacket, the older man had left his jacket in his office and was wearing just his shirt. The sleeves of his slightly rumpled shirt were rolled up and his tie appeared to have been hastily loosened, as if leaving it in its initial position would have eventually wound up choking him.

"Abilene?" the older man repeated, this time turning the last name into a question.

From the looks of the man, this had to be his new boss, Matt thought. He doubled back in long, loping strides.

"Yes, sir," he responded easily, extending his hand to the other man, who stood only slightly shorter than he did. However, his slumped shoulders gave the impression that he was shorter than he was.

After a beat, the older man took Abilene's offered hand. The handshake was surprisingly hearty. "I'm Lt. Holmes," Isaac Holmes told his newest detective. "You're just in time."

Abilene cocked his head, the very gesture a query. "For?"

"You and Cavelli—you're still Cavelli, right?" Holmes asked Kendra, sparing her a quick glance, then turning away before she had a chance to answer. "Just caught a case," he concluded.

Matt jerked his thumb in the general direction of the hall—and the elevator. "I was just about to bring down my stuff," Matt told him.

"Your stuff can wait. It's not going anywhere. But you are." Tearing off the top page from his pad where he'd written down the incoming information, the lieutenant pressed the paper into Kendra's hand. "Super found a dead body. Not the one he expected to." Glancing over toward Abilene, he added, "Welcome to Homicide."

Kendra glanced at the paper Holmes had handed her, then tucked it into her pocket. "The Super *expected* to find a body?" she questioned.

"Not expected-expected," Holmes clarified. "Guy who lives there hasn't been seen for three days, so his boss sent someone to his apartment. When he didn't get an answer, the kid got the super."

"And they found a dead body in the apartment who wasn't the guy who lived there," Kendra guessed.

Holmes nodded. "I want you to find out whose body's in the apartment and see if you can get a handle on where the guy who pays the rent is. Apparently, he's still missing."

"You got it, boss," Abilene promised as he fell into step beside Kendra.

"Jump right in, don't you?" Kendra commented as she increased her pace. But even so, Abilene more than kept up. Man had legs that belonged on an ostrich, she thought darkly.

"Isn't that what I'm supposed to do?" he asked innocently as they went into the hall. If this wasn't going to be an all-out territorial war, he needed to do what he could to put her mind at ease. He was definitely not out to become king of the hill—at least, not this hill. "Look, I'm not trying to snag your territory, if that's what you're worried about. From what I hear, there's more than enough work to go around for everyone. This isn't a competition."

He was analyzing her again. Kendra gave him a cold look as she yanked open the door to the stairwell. She *hated* being analyzed. "Nobody said it was."

Abilene stopped short. Was she taking the stairs? "Hey, aren't we supposed to be taking the elevator down?" he asked.

"Go ahead," Kendra tossed over her shoulder. "Nobody's stopping you."

Like a door to a tomb, the stairwell door all but thundered as it closed behind her.

Peace at last.

Kendra's heels met the metal steps, emitting a quick, rhythmic staccato sound as she hurried down to the first floor. She was only halfway down the first flight with three more to go when she heard the stairwell door above her opening again. She didn't have to look to know that Abilene was now behind her—and catching up fast.

Couldn't she get at least a couple of minutes away from this man? She wanted to be able to clear her head and having him around was not at all conducive to that.

He had no idea how the woman's mind worked. Was she intent on trying to ditch him, or make him fail in front of the boss? Was she just playing some sort of a game where only she knew the rules? He wasn't about to take a chance on being left behind on the first assignment that he—that *they*—had just caught.

He was a firm believer that you never got to redo a first impression—and he knew that they were the ones that tended to last.

Shadowing his new partner's every step, Matt was half a beat behind her as they came to the bottom of the last staircase. She'd just reached the door when he stretched his hand over her head and pushed it open as she turned the doorknob.

Kendra bit back an annoyed retort. She felt as if she was almost encompassed by the man's long arms. He seemed to take up all the space around her, she thought grudgingly. *And* all the air. There was no other reason why, just for a second, she'd felt so hot and so light-headed.

"I can push open my own door, Abilene," she informed him crisply. Out of the stairwell, she took the opportunity to pull fresh air into her lungs. The feeling of heat began to recede.

"Nobody said you couldn't, Good," Abilene replied mildly. "Just doing what I can to help. It's a heavy door."

It *was* a heavy door, but she wasn't about to say anything to that effect. She didn't need some hotshot thinking he was her knight in dented armor.

Muttering a couple of choice words under her breath, Kendra all but marched into the parking lot. She went straight for her old Crown Victoria. Number 23, the one she used to share with Joe, before the man had been seduced by the idea of retirement.

"I've got the address, I'm driving," she crisply informed Abilene.

Wide shoulders rose slightly, then lowered again in what seemed like the most careless of fashions, as if the matter of who drove was the last thing on her partner's mind.

"Fine with me," he told her. "I like riding shotgun anyway." Opening the passenger door, he folded his long, lanky frame into the seat, then pulled out the seat belt and secured it. "Never cared much for driving in traffic."

Kendra frowned as she started up the vehicle. So far, Abilene seemed to be going out of his way to come across as agreeable. But she wasn't about to be lulled into a false sense of security. Joe had tripped her up several times before they'd found their work rhythm. Since he was her first partner after she'd been awarded her gold shield, she had nothing to compare the older man to and assumed that all male partners were going to challenge her straight out of the box until she proved herself capable.

After being on the job for over two years in the Homicide Division, she found it more than a little annoying to be sent back to square one. But that was the price she had to pay for being a woman—and for being related to the brass. Because her father was head of the CSI lab, she was acquainted with accusations of nepotism. But now that she was connected to the Cavanaughs, she had a feeling that she would never know a peaceful moment again.

She spared Abilene a glance as they took off. *Nope,* she thought. *Never again.*

* * *

The five-story apartment building where Lt. Holmes had sent them was located in the more well-off— although by no means rich—section of Aurora. Leaving the unmarked Crown Victoria parked in a space intended for deliveries, Kendra made sure that the police light was visible before she and Abilene went up the four flights in the elevator to the scene of the crime.

"What, no stairs?" Abilene asked, amused when she opted for the elevator.

"I thought I'd let you save your energy in case there's a need for some heavy lifting," Kendra told him without missing a beat.

"Thoughtful," he quipped as they got off.

The forced smile came and went in a blink of an eye. "I try."

"Yeah, me, too," he said, looking at her significantly.

Something in her gut undulated for half a heartbeat. She banked it down and walked faster.

The apartment in question wasn't hard to find. The immediate area directly before the crime scene was crowded with curious people. Apparently people from the building's other apartments, as well as an influx of others drawn by word of mouth, were gathered about the hallway in clusters like bees circling a hive.

The yellow tape strung across a doorway must have attracted them, Kendra couldn't help thinking.

The superintendent, when they finally located him, appeared rather young, inexperienced, and seemed completely distraught. Every few minutes he kept nervously repeating that this was his "first dead body" and that viewing it wasn't nearly as "cool" as he'd thought it would be. He seemed genuinely disappointed about that.

Kendra called the slight man a few choice names in her head, but for now kept them to herself. She glanced in Abilene's direction and guessed by his expression that perhaps a few of the same names for the super had occurred to him as well.

Maybe they weren't that different after all, she mused.

Getting down to business, Kendra went directly toward the body. Lying facedown in the middle of the living room, the victim was completely covered with a king-size blanket that appeared to have been taken from the lone bedroom. No limbs were peeking out at either end, but a pool of angry dark red blood haloed the blanket, bearing silent testimony to the fact that someone had indeed died in this apartment. No one ever lost that much blood and survived.

Squatting down beside the victim, Kendra raised a corner of the blanket and got her first view of the dead woman. Her reaction was always the same. Her heart would feel as if it was constricting in her chest as sympathy flooded through her.

The victim, a woman most likely in her twenties, was lying facedown on what had been a beige rug. The back of her head had been struck hard and was apparently the source of all the blood on the floor. Kendra's first guess was that the blow to the head appeared to be the cause of death.

Dropping the blanket back over the dead woman, Kendra rose carefully to her feet, ignoring Abilene's extended hand, offering her aid.

"Our killer knew the victim," she commented, more to herself than to Abilene. She wasn't quite ready to talk to him just yet, at least not in the role of her partner. She regarded him more as a casual observer. Baby steps, she counseled herself. "And apparently he felt remorseful enough to cover her up so he wouldn't have to look at her after he'd ended her life."

"Or she," Abilene interjected.

Caught off guard, Kendra stopped and looked at him quizzically. "What?"

"Or she," Abilene repeated. "The killer could have been a woman. Doesn't take much to pick up that statue and swing it hard enough to do some major damage at the point of contact."

Abilene nodded toward what appeared to be a rather cheap bust of Shakespeare lying on the floor not that far from the prone body.

Kendra stared down at the faux bronze bust. Shakespeare, no less.

You just never knew, did you?

Her first thought would have been that someone who'd gone out and bought something like that would have been mild-mannered and cultured. So much for being a profiler.

"No, it doesn't," she agreed.

Moving over to the bust, she squatted down for a better look at it. It was the murder weapon, all right. There was a thin red line of blood at one corner. The killer had obviously come up behind the victim and hit her when she hadn't been looking.

A lovers' quarrel? Or calculated, premeditated murder?

Too bad the bust couldn't talk.

More than four hundred years after the fact and the bard was apparently still killing people off, Kendra thought cynically. Except now they didn't get up for a final bow once the curtain fell.

With a suppressed sigh, Kendra rose to her feet again.

And then, just as she turned back to look at the prone figure lying on the floor beneath the ginger-colored blanket, one of the crime scene investigators who had arrived earlier came over to bag the ancient-looking bust.

"That comment about the killer knowing the victim," Abilene began.

For one tension-free second, she'd actually forgotten about him. Too bad that second couldn't have lasted a bit longer.

Abilene's remark, hanging in midair like that, had her looking at him sharply, anticipating some sort of a confrontation regarding her thought process.

Was he going to challenge something else she'd said? Already?

Kendra eyed the man she knew her sisters would have thought was a living, breathing hunk, trying to see past his chiseled exterior. She waited for the verbal duel to begin.

"Watch a lot of procedural television, do you?" he asked.

"I don't have to." Although she did, she silently admitted. The shows intrigued her. But he didn't have to know that. She debated saying anything further, then decided to go ahead. "My father's the head of the Crime Scene Lab."

"Boy, you sure have every angle covered, don't you, Good?" he laughed.

Kendra bristled. "I really wish you wouldn't call me that."

Now that was definitely amusement in his eyes. "Would you rather I called you Bad?" It was clearly a teasing remark and perhaps under other circumstances—before life had trampled all over her heart—she might have picked up the banter, even enjoyed it. But she was what she was and there was no going back.

Still, it didn't stop her from noticing that the man had the kind of smile a woman could get lost in—even a sensible woman.

But not her, of course.

Still, she wished the chief hadn't picked him to be her partner. Going it alone—even with an increased workload—would have been better for her in the long run.

"What I'd rather was that my old partner was still around."

He surprised her by leaning in and whispering, "Lemonade, Good. When life throws lemons at you, you make lemonade."

Her eyes held his for a long moment. Until she found herself sinking into them. She backpedaled quickly. "I don't like lemonade."

He laughed, shaking his head. "Why doesn't that surprise me?" he murmured before turning back to the murder scene.

Chapter 3

"Hey, Abilene, what do you—"

Kendra stopped abruptly. She'd assumed that the detective was behind her, but when she turned around, she only saw the crime scene investigators in the room.

"Great," she muttered. "Now he's wandering off." Biting off a few ripe words, she went to look for him.

She found her new partner in the bedroom. Abilene stood before the narrow mirrored closet. The sliding door was in the open position and he was staring into it.

Glancing over his shoulder, Kendra saw nothing that would have captured his attention so intently. Was she missing something, or was he one of those people who stared off into space as he pieced things together in his mind?

"So, what do you think?" she finally asked him.

If she'd surprised him by coming up behind him,

Abilene gave no indication. Turning from the closet, he looked at her as he lobbed her question back to her.

"You're the expert."

Did that mean he was unwilling to state an opinion, or that he was giving her her due? So far she really had no idea how to read this man and that bothered her. More than that, it annoyed her.

Hell, everything about this man annoyed her, not the least of which was that he seemed to be getting under her skin and this was only day one of their temporary partnership. What was she going to be like a month into this ordeal? She didn't want to think about it.

Kendra was aware that learning to pick up signals from this man would take time, but she'd gotten more impatient in this difficult past year and it made her less willing to wait. Jason's accident and subsequent suicide had made her want to seize things immediately, solve crimes yesterday. It was hard regaining her stride when all she wanted to do was run, not walk and certainly not stroll.

Abilene was still looking at her. Waiting for her opinion—or at least pretending to. Either way, she gave it to him.

She glanced back toward the living room, then said, "Looks to me as if Ryan Burnett and his girlfriend got into a fight—cause unknown at the moment—and in a fit of temper, he hit her with that bust. When he realized what he'd done—and that she was dead—he apparently got scared and took off."

"Stopping to pack?" Abilene asked.

He indicated the cluster of bare hangers in the closet. Off to one side of the tasteful, small bedroom was a black lacquered bureau. Several of its drawers were hanging open. From the disarray left behind, it was obvious that some items had been hastily grabbed from there, too.

She shrugged, amending her theory to fit the scene. "Maybe Ryan decided to take off permanently. Man's going to need more than a toothbrush if he's starting a new life somewhere else."

"That shows clear thinking," Abilene protested.

"It doesn't jibe with a supposed crime of impulse," he pointed out.

Kendra saw no contradiction. "The man's an accountant. He's supposed to be a clear thinker. It's the nature of the beast." She glanced at the bed. It had no comforter or blanket over its crisp, coordinated navy blue sheets. That confirmed her initial theory that the blanket in the other room, now spread over the murder victim, had come from here.

That brought her back to the theory that Ryan hadn't meant to kill the woman. Things had gotten out of hand for some reason. But what had triggered the argument? And why now, at this particular point? The answers to that might explain everything.

Seeing one of the two officers who had called in the homicide, she crossed to the man and asked, "Do we have an ID on the victim yet?"

The officer nodded and offered her the wallet he'd gotten from the dead woman's purse.

"Her name's Summer Miller," he told her. He handed over the wallet, exposing the driver's license for her benefit.

Kendra looked down at the small picture on the license. She'd seen a larger, framed photograph of Summer in the bedroom on the bureau. She was standing in front of a smiling young man. His arms were wrapped protectively around her. The two appeared very happy, as if they didn't have a care in the world between them.

They did now, Kendra thought grimly. She assumed that the man in the photograph was the missing accountant, Ryan Burnett.

"Well, at least we have a name for his girlfriend," she said quietly, closing the wallet for now.

Spying a pile of plastic sealable bags used for evidence, she picked one up and slipped the wallet inside. She closed the seal before tucking the wallet into her pocket. She wanted to hand-carry this piece to her father personally. There were questions she wanted to ask.

And then she turned toward Abilene. "You up for some canvassing of the neighbors on the floor, see if anyone heard or saw anything that might prove to be useful?"

"Lead the way," he said, gesturing toward the doorway. "But—"

Kendra crossed the threshold, then looked at him over her shoulder. "But?" she echoed.

"Shouldn't we inform her next of kin first before we start canvassing and flashing her picture around?" he asked.

"Since we're here, we'll canvas the floor first." Kendra didn't like wasting time and she sincerely doubted that word of the young woman's murder—as well as her name—would get out in the next hour. "She'll still be the victim of a homicide—and dead—in an hour," she assured Abilene. "Plenty of time to break her family's heart in an hour instead of now," Kendra added with a resigned sigh.

That was the worst part of the job as far as she as concerned. Informing the family of a death, then watching the light go out of a parent's or a spouse's eyes. They should have a special group of trained professionals who only did that—and rendered grief counseling while they were at it.

"I suppose you're right," Abilene murmured in a deep voice under his breath.

She knew he didn't mean it, but she took it as a token victory. In response, she paused to flash a quick, satisfied smile in his direction.

That he smiled back pleased her more than she was happy about.

They wound up canvassing the apartments on the crime scene floor. All the people who had been milling around the hallway had mysteriously disappeared when they came out, going back to their lives and choosing not to communicate with the police.

It turned out that only a few people—three, to be exact—were in their apartments to answer their doorbells when Kendra and Abilene came around.

The first was a young woman with a brand-new baby. The baby looked to be less than a month old. The new mother had all but physically dragged them into her apartment when they rang her bell. It was obvious that she was desperate for adult companionship, even companionship that involved being questioned about a murder.

It was clear that while she loved her infant son, the

woman was more than ready to return to work—or at least to be in the company of human beings who knew how to do more than spit up, cry, wet and sleep.

Moving like a woman who was sleepwalking, she admitted to not having heard anything out of the ordinary that day: no sudden shouts, no raised, angry voices, no loud crashing sounds.

They thanked her and left as soon as they could extricate themselves.

Two doors down, a night watchman finally opened the door after Abilene had given up ringing the doorbell and resorted to knocking—hard. Rumpled and bleary-eyed, the man appeared none too happy to be woken up. He was no more helpful than the new mother had been, shaking his head in response to the same questions.

"No, man, I didn't hear anything. I took a sleeping pill," he explained, then whined, "Only way I can get some sleep. It's just not natural to have to try to sleep during the day," he grumbled.

"Maybe you should try getting another job," Kendra suggested tactfully.

Her words brought an instant, almost malevolent look into the man's dark eyes. "Don't you think I would if I could?" he snapped at her. "I was a damn aerospace engineer before all those useless companies started to bail and move out of the state. This damn night watchman job was the only thing I could find after looking for five months." He glared at her accusingly. "Now I probably won't be able to get back to sleep because of you."

She was about to say something placating and apologetic to the belligerent watchman when she noticed Abilene shifting beside her. The next thing she knew, he was placing himself between her and the man in the doorway.

"Take it easy, man," Abilene advised, his voice mild. "Might help you fall back to sleep if you calm down a little."

By his subdued expression, it was obvious that the night watchman had become aware of the rather pronounced differences in height between him and the detective. Rather than say something sarcastic or cynical, the man nodded and backed up into the security of his apartment. The next moment, he'd shut the door.

For a second, Kendra was stunned. Turning, she was all set to tell Abilene that she didn't need him to run interference for her or play the big, bad guardian, but then she decided to let the matter drop. Maybe Abilene, in his own clumsy, heavy-handed way, was trying to be helpful. Even, perhaps, protective.

The last thought shimmied through her, creating a shiver she managed to tamp down. Maybe she was just working too hard. But she couldn't stop now.

Two doors away from the crime scene they found their third person to interview. Unlike the other two tenants, he was neither half-asleep, nor bleary-eyed and belligerent. Tyler Blake, a "currently" out-of-work actor according to his own description, was both friendly and more than willing to answer questions without seeming desperate for company.

And, also unlike the other two tenants they'd interviewed, Blake admitted to having heard something earlier that day.

"It sounded like two people arguing, but I just thought that someone had their TV turned up loud," he admitted ruefully. "I didn't pay attention and then it was quiet again. Sorry," he apologized, flashing a contrite smile at Kendra.

"Nothing to apologize for, Mr. Blake. You couldn't have known what was going on," she told him. Another question occurred to her and she asked, "Were you by any chance friendly with Mr. Burnett?"

The out-of-work actor shrugged. "Just small talk at the elevator and the mailbox. You know, 'Just another great day in Paradise,' that kind of thing. We never talked about anything personal, anything that mattered," he clarified.

"Did you know his girlfriend?" Abilene asked out of the blue. Up until now, he'd been rather quiet, letting her take the lead and choosing to listen rather than to question.

Tyler looked surprised at the question. "You mean to talk to, or by sight?"

"You tell us," Abilene replied, leaving it up to the actor to fill in the blanks.

"Well, I saw them leaving his apartment a couple of times, but I never had any conversations with her, if that's what you mean." A self-deprecating laugh escaped his lips. "Fact is, I'm not sure if I could pick her out of a lineup if I had to."

"Well, lucky for you that won't come up," Abilene told him. "Burnett's girlfriend was found dead in his apartment this morning."

Tyler's eyes widened in absolute shock. Perfectly round and black like small marbles, they gave the impression that they would fall out of his head at any minute.

"He killed her?" he asked in disbelief, his voice trembling.

"Right now, that seems to be the working theory," Abilene told the actor. "Unless you know something different." He paused, giving the actor a moment for the information to sink in. "Any thoughts on that?" he prodded.

Tyler *really* looked surprised then. "Me? No. No," he assured Abilene while trying to suppress a shiver of his own. "Just all sounds kind of creepy, that's all. When I did see them together, they looked happy—I guess," he tagged on with a shrug.

"You guess," Abilene repeated slowly, watching Tyler's eyes.

Tyler drew himself up to be a little taller, a little straighter. Abilene still towered over him. "Well, yeah. I didn't stare at them or anything. I've got my own life," he said. "And my own girlfriend," he added with pride. "She's my fiancée, actually," he clarified. "And she doesn't like me staring at other women," he added with a grin.

"I hear you," Abilene said with a conspiratorial laugh. "They can get really jealous on you for just being yourself. Nothing wrong with a guy just looking."

"If you think of anything else," Kendra said, interrupting what looked as if it had the makings of a guy fest and taking a card out of her pocket, "call this number." She tapped the phone number beneath her name. "Ask for Detective Cavelli."

"So, is that the name you're going with, Good? Cavelli?" Abilene asked as they walked away from the actor's apartment.

Why did his questions immediately get her back up? It was, after all, a legitimate question. But coming from Abilene, it got under her skin.

Just as he did.

She supposed she was being unfair—but that still didn't change her reaction.

"It's the name on the card," she told him. They stopped at the crime scene one last time. The crime scene investigators were apparently wrapping things up, she thought. That was their cue to leave. "I didn't want to confuse him. So far, this actor's our most lucid witness."

"Or at least he's playing the part of one," Abilene commented as they walked over to the centrally located elevator. His comment had her looking at him quizzically and he shrugged. "Hey, he's an out-of-work actor—they need audiences like most people need air."

"Speaking from experience?" she asked.

"In a way," Abilene admitted. "I dated an actress once." And then he laughed. He'd dated several of them, actually. At different times. Beautiful women with beautiful faces, all clamoring to be used—finding a personal hell on the other side. "Hard not to in this state."

"Dated an actress," Kendra repeated. Probably a whole bunch of them, possibly at the same time. He had the charm to pull it off, she decided. If you liked that sort of thing, she couldn't help adding. "How nice for her," she commented dryly.

"Nice for both of us," he said, then added with a smile, "Short and sweet."

Something in his voice caught Kendra's attention—

and, though she wouldn't have admitted it in so many words, it also aroused her curiosity, among other things she chose not to explore.

"Is that a requirement with you? 'Short and sweet'?" she repeated when he just looked at her.

His mouth curved devilishly. "As a matter of fact, yes, it is."

She'd been right about him, she thought as she got in behind the wheel of the Crown Victoria. Abilene was a player, trading on his exceedingly good looks and satisfying his appetite whenever the spirit moved him. She bet it moved him a lot.

"Where to now?" he asked as he buckled his seat belt.

"Back to the precinct to see what kind of information we can find about the late Summer Miller." She turned on the ignition. "By the way, what was that back there? With the actor," she specified.

"It's called being a detective and gathering information. Also questioning a witness. Why?" he asked her. "Wasn't I supposed to do any talking? Am I just supposed to be your strong, silent backup?"

She sincerely doubted the man *knew* the meaning of the word *silent*. For now, until she got used to him, she just wanted him to stay out of the way, not suddenly step up and take the lead. She had no problem sharing that position if the person she was sharing it with had respect for her. But Abilene wasn't giving off any of those vibrations. At least none on a frequency she was receiving.

"I only thought, this being your first case, you'd just observe," she told him.

"This is my first *homicide,* not my first case," he corrected. He wasn't some wet-behind-the-ears rookie to stand in awe of her. If that was what she wanted, she should have gone with one of the department's newly minted detectives, not him. "The actor just brought up some questions for me. Sorry, was I supposed to clear them with you first before asking him?"

It wasn't exactly a belligerent question, at least not in tone. But she could feel him challenging her nonetheless. Rules and boundaries needed to be established, here and now. Or maybe she was just reading too much into it. These days, she wasn't sure of anything anymore.

Maybe she just needed to unwind. Find a way to relax a little. She wondered what her sisters were doing after work tonight. Bridget was usually all caught up in her fiancé these days, but that still left Kari.

Maybe she'd give Kari a call—after she called Thomas to ask him to look into her new partner's background. She'd feel a lot better if she knew the kind of person she would be working with. Hotshots and red-hot investigators tended to come across the same way sometimes. It would be good to have a second opinion on what, exactly, she had on her hands here.

"Well, was I?" Abilene pressed.

Kendra blinked, then realized that she'd lost the thread of the conversation. She needed to ask for clarification—and that annoyed her.

"Were you what?" she asked, sparing him a quick glance as she eased the car to a stop at a red light.

Abilene suppressed an impatient sigh. "Was I supposed to clear it with you first before I asked the actor any questions?" This time, there was an edge to his tone.

That would be nice.

She knew the detective was being sarcastic. She supposed, in his place, she would have felt the same way.

Okay, so she was being testy. But that was because she didn't like change and she didn't like the fact that he had a way of looking at her that made her stomach muscles cramp up.

Kendra did her best to temper her own voice. "Of course not. I was just surprised to hear you asking questions, that's all."

Matt decided to give her the benefit of the doubt. Shrugging, he stood down and relaxed again. Maybe the woman wasn't a class-A pain in the butt. She just came across like one. But maybe she had a reason to— one that he intended to find out, provided there *was* a reason.

"Look," he said amicably, "there's going to be a period of adjustment. I get that. If we're going to make this work, then we need to get things out in the open."

She was on her guard again. "What things?" she asked.

"Things that bother us about the other person."

She could feel his eyes on her. It made her feel like squirming. So much for a truce. She would still hang on to the hope that this collaboration of theirs *was* only temporary.

Kendra made a right turn at the next corner. "I've got a better idea."

"Okay, I'm game."

Pushing down on the gas, she flew through the next

light just as it was turning red. She wanted to spend as little time in close quarters with this man as possible. For some reason, he seemed to deplete her oxygen supply. "Why don't we just see if we can find out who killed Summer Miller and just where Ryan Burnett ultimately ran off to."

He laughed shortly. Yeah, that was definitely another option. "You mean just work the case."

Kendra continued to look straight ahead as she drove. "I mean just work the case."

Abilene tempered the sarcastic retort that rose to his lips. "It might surprise you to know, but that was what I was doing when you asked me what I was doing," he told her.

Kendra blew out a breath. Maybe the key to surviving this union was to exchange as few words as possible—and to keep to well-ventilated areas. "Point taken. Okay, Abilene, as you were."

He grinned. "Wouldn't have it any other way."

Kendra wondered just how long she had to wait before she could officially request a change of partners without having the chief think that she was being unreasonable.

Chapter 4

Utilizing a couple of prominent social networks, a little more than an hour into her internet search, Kendra discovered that Summer Miller had no immediate family in the state.

The only listed relative turned out to be a distant cousin, someone named Sandra Hill, who lived in Springfield, Illinois.

But even that proved to be a dead end. When she tracked down the cousin's phone number and tried it, she was informed by an automated voice that the number she had dialed was "no longer in service."

Dropping the handset back into the cradle, Kendra sighed and shook her head.

Abilene looked up from the list of newly accumulated phone numbers related to the case. "Something wrong?"

"Just hit a dead end, that's all." Her frown deepened

as she stared at the last site she'd pulled up. "Hopefully not the first of many," she commented. In response to the questioning rise of Abilene's eyebrow—the extraneous thought that her partner had incredibly well-shaped eyebrows for a man floated through her head out of nowhere—Kendra filled him in. "The victim's cousin's phone is currently disconnected and I can't seem to find anyone else to call."

Although relieved not to have to notify a grieving family member of the young woman's untimely death, she felt sad to think that no one was there to make funeral arrangements for Summer Miller.

"Maybe there's a roommate or a best friend who can supply us with the names we need," Abilene suggested. "We can go check out where she lived. You still have her license, right?"

She'd almost forgotten about slipping that into her pocket. Her intent had been to drop the wallet off with her father at the crime lab—it would give her an opportunity to ask him some questions about the body—but then she'd gotten sidetracked. "Right."

"All right, then. Let's go," he said, already on his feet. "We've got the address, let's see if there's a roommate or a talkative neighbor."

Before she could rubber-stamp his suggestion, Abilene's cell phone rang. He paused, digging it out of his shirt pocket. Glancing at the caller ID, it was his turn to frown. Without thinking, he dropped back into his chair and turned it almost 180 degrees, deliberately cutting himself off from his partner.

When he spoke, his voice dropped down a couple of decibels.

Either action would have aroused Kendra's curiosity. That he did both increased her curiosity a hundredfold. Ever since she could remember, she'd always had this almost overwhelming desire to know—*every*thing—to get to the bottom of any matter.

This was no different.

As she pretended to write out her notes and some of the points she wanted to touch on later, Kendra listened intently, taking in what Abilene was saying to whomever was on the other end of his call. Lucky for her, Kendra had excellent hearing because her partner's voice was so low, it almost could have qualified for mental telepathy.

"No, I can't right now." He sighed, like a man searching for the right words and the strength not to raise his voice and yell in utter frustration. "You knew that this was going to be just temporary. Yes, you did," he insisted. "You're smart enough for that. No," he said in a firmer voice. Then, in the next moment, as Kendra continued to eavesdrop, she heard her partner relent. "All right, all right, don't cry," he told the person on the other end—obviously a woman. She could tell from his tone that he was a man who really hated tears. "Okay, I'll see you after work," he agreed. "We'll go out." Abilene paused, listening. As did Kendra, trying to piece together what was going on without being obvious about it. "It's the best I can do."

With that, he terminated the call. Dropping the cell phone back into his pocket, Abilene blew out a frustrated breath. As he glanced toward his partner's desk, it took him less than a second to come to the conclusion that she'd been listening in on his half of the conversation. Given her nature, it didn't surprise him.

His eyes met hers and he waited. He wasn't about to say anything unless she was.

He didn't have long to wait.

"Former girlfriend you dumped?" she asked, nodding toward the pocket with the cell phone in it. Getting up, she pushed in her chair.

"No," was all he said. They went into the hall together.

The single word vibrated with finality and an entire collection of No Trespassing signs.

So be it, she felt in a moment of empathy. If the tables had been turned, she wouldn't have wanted to be quizzed, either. She thought back to a little more than eighteen months ago. There'd been some really intense, poorly muffled conversations with Jason in the days before his suicide that she wouldn't have wanted to repeat, either.

"Sorry," she apologized, hitting the Down button for the elevator. "None of my business."

He hadn't thought that she was capable of an apology—at least, not one to him. Not when it came to something like this.

Because she had backed off, Matt found himself loosening up just a little.

"That was my mother," he told her.

Kendra looked up at him sharply. That wouldn't even have been her tenth guess.

"Your mother?" Kendra replayed the short conversation in her head, viewing it in a completely different light. She was still convinced that the other woman had been crying. Compassion flooded through her, not to mention a new, warm feeling as she regarded the man who'd been sitting across from her.

"You need to see her, I can cover for you," she offered.

Matt shook his head. Running to his mother's side wasn't going to help anything—or change anything. "Thanks, but no. This isn't anything new, even though she never seems to see it coming." The elevator car arrived and they got in. He paused for a second, debating whether or not to say anything else, then shrugged. It wasn't all that much of a big deal, he told himself. "My mother's got a habit of getting mixed up with the wrong kind of men."

Kendra thought of her desk and the brand-new notes she'd just written that now rested like so many new snowflakes on top of her other, older notes. Who knew—maybe that was ultimately Summer Miller's story as well. "A lot of that going on lately."

"Yeah, except that at her age, you would have thought my mother would have developed a little common sense and learned not to be charmed and taken in by some con artist's smooth line."

Rarely did the heart listen to reason. If it did, Kendra would have known enough to back away, to insulate her heart right after Jason's accident. That way his suicide wouldn't have almost destroyed her when it had happened.

"The heart wants what the heart wants," Kendra replied simply. The elevator doors opened and she led the way out. "Besides, it's a misnomer."

He caught up to her in less than one stride. "What is?"

"That bit about common sense." God, this man *really* had a long stride. She would never be able to beat him in a race. The realization annoyed her even though the need to outrun him would most likely never come up. "Sense isn't common. At least not when the heart is involved."

"You speaking from experience?" he asked her, moderately intrigued.

She was, but she wasn't about to go there. Not with someone she didn't know. It was hard enough to talk with her family about Jason and how she'd failed him— not that she actually did. For the most part, she avoided the subject altogether, even when one of her siblings— or her father—prodded her to go out socially again. She hadn't been out on anything even vaguely resembling a date since Jason had put that gun to his chin and put himself out of his misery—and greatly intensified hers.

"No," she replied with studied casualness. "Just a general observation."

She'd paused, Matt noted. Paused just long enough to make him think that his question had a positive answer, one that she was unwilling to talk about. Why? Had a relationship of hers gone sour?

Whoever it was probably never stood a chance against that tongue of hers, he surmised. It would take a hell of a man to go toe-to-toe with her and survive, Matt reasoned.

He tucked away the thought for future review. Right now, they had a job to do. No one had to tell him that he had to make a good first impression. That meant not just solving the case, but solving it as quickly as possible.

Coming up to the Crown Victoria, he opened the passenger door automatically. She seemed to enjoy driving and he enjoyed not having to bicker with her. As far as he was concerned, it was a win-win situation. He'd been the one to suggest going to Miller's apartment, but he recalled that this had all started when Ryan Burnett had been reported missing. Maybe they should go back to that salient point and begin the investigation from there.

"You want to check out the victim's place of residence, or where our missing accountant-slash-suspect worked?" he asked her.

"Let's go there first," she agreed. "Get a little more insight into what this guy is capable of." About to get into the car, she paused and looked at him over the roof of the car. "You sure you don't want to go see your mother? My offer to cover for you still stands."

He shook his head, although he appreciated the offer. Appreciated, too, the way her features seemed to have softened just now. He felt something distant stir inside him.

"I'm sure," Matt said as he got in.

There was a pattern to his mother's behavior. A well-worn pattern. For the next couple of hours, his mother would cry, long and hard. Cry as if her world was literally coming to an end and she didn't know how to go on. But, eventually, when her entire body would be drained of any and all moisture, she'd sink into a peaceful, albeit reluctant, acceptance of the events and begin the arduous task of trying to rebuild her life.

But first she would consume a half gallon of rum raisin ice cream.

It never ceased to amaze him, how his mother could remain as thin as she did. Most people who consumed that quantity of ice cream—especially with the regularity that she did—would eventually begin to tip the scales to an ever-increasing number.

But his five-foot-three mother had always been a size six. He supposed it was nature's way of compensating for allowing her to drag her heart through the prickly briar patch time and again.

"Your mother been divorced long?" Kendra asked casually as she pulled out of the parking space. She guided the car carefully to avoid hitting anything.

He glanced at her, then decided not to ask the obvious: what made her think his mother was divorced? Divorced or widowed, the upshot was the same. His mother had no permanent man in her life—other than him. There were times when the weight of that felt almost overwhelming.

"Yeah," he answered absently. *More like forever.*

She prodded him a little more. "How long is *long?*"

"I don't remember ever meeting my father," Abilene said after a beat that had gone on way too long.

His answer made her understand why he had almost not said anything. "I'm sorry," she said with genuine feeling.

Her father had *always* been there for her. However, in her case it was her mother who was missing from her life. And had been ever since she was a little girl, when her mother had lost her battle against cancer. She and her siblings had grown up with their father doing double duty as both mother and father to them. He'd more than held his own in both capacities and she loved him dearly for it. But she knew what it meant to miss a parent deep in the confines of her heart.

"No need to be," Abilene told her offhandedly. "All in all, it wasn't a bad life. A little nomadic, maybe," he allowed, "but not bad."

She spared him a glance as she continued down the main drag, away from One Police Plaza. "Nomadic?"

He couldn't think of a more descriptive word for a lifestyle that involved picking up in the dead of night and vacating the premises—quickly. "I figure that would be the best term to use for sneaking out in the middle of the night—ahead of the landlord—when my mother couldn't pay the rent."

She could feel her heart going out to the boy he had been. A life of being one step ahead of the creditor was no life for a child. Had he been afraid? Ashamed? It took her a moment to reconcile the man who projected such a laid-back exterior with the person she now believed was buried inside.

That was the moment, she later realized, that he stopped being this annoying man she was forced to put up with and started becoming her partner.

"Did that happen often?" Kendra asked, not bothering to mask her sympathy.

His shrug was dismissive. "Often enough, or at least it felt like it when I was a kid. Back then, I thought it was a big adventure," he confessed. "Until I was old enough to realize that you're not supposed to run off without paying. Sometimes," he recalled, "when she found a decent-paying job—or a guy who initially spent money on her before he took her for everything she had—my mother would send money back to the landlord she'd skipped out on. She'd send it in an unmarked envelope so he couldn't trace it back to her."

His mother had always had good intentions—just not such good luck when it came to choosing men.

"She really didn't like not paying," Matt explained. It was impossible to miss the fondness in his voice when he spoke of her—even if she had made him sigh before. "More than that, I think she was afraid I'd turn out to be a thief if she didn't make me understand that you had to take responsibility for your life—or at least your bills," he said with a quiet laugh.

Taking it all in, Kendra nodded now. "Sounds like a decent woman who just wanted to be loved," she said.

Abilene shrugged again and stared out the window. He'd said too much. Since when was that a failing with him? It wasn't like him to talk this much. He was going to have to police himself a little more around this woman—no pun intended, he added with a bemused smile.

"Yeah, maybe that's it," he agreed dismissively. And then he looked at her. His partner had subtly pulled all this out of him. Why? Was she going to use it against him somehow? She seemed and sounded sympathetic right now, but he didn't trust her yet. That was going to take a little time. *If* it happened at all. "What does this have to do with the case?" he asked, the edge back in his voice.

"Nothing," she told him honestly. "I'm just trying to get a handle on the guy I'm working with."

"You could get that out of my file."

She didn't bother telling him that she didn't have enough clout to have his file pulled—yet. The chief, of course, had access to it and probably so did her father, but she didn't try to pull strings like that. If she did, then she would deserve all the unflattering terms that were tossed her way by people who didn't know any better, who didn't know *her* better. Shortcuts were for emergencies, not to satisfy your curiosity or for some self-serving purpose.

But for now, she said none of this. If, for some reason, they remained partners after this case was over, he'd find out what she was like on his own.

The thought didn't bother her nearly as much as it would have initially.

"Won't tell me as much as you would. I'm not interested in You the Professional. I want to know what kind of *man* I'm trusting my back to. I already figured you were a decent enough detective or the chief wouldn't have transferred you down to Homicide."

"Why? Is that where the elite go?" he asked. The amusement in his voice hid the slight chip that had emerged on his shoulder.

"That's where the best are needed," she informed him. "I'm told that the chief tends to view this not as a job, but as a mission to protect his city. He wants to keep the people who live here safe. That's done by keeping killers off the streets and putting them behind bars. And *that's* done by putting the best detectives on the job."

He laughed shortly as she made a sharp right. "Now you're beginning to sound like a city council poster trying to get people to move here."

That was the *last* thing she would have wanted, to have more people move to Aurora.

"God forbid. Aurora's got enough people here already. Any more and it's going to get way too crowded for the people who initially moved here to get away from the big cities."

Her father would tell her stories about the city when the main thoroughfare had only two lanes, one in each direction, and there were only three traffic lights between the two freeways that buffered Aurora. That was when the developments could be counted on one hand and there were almost as many cows and horses as people living here.

Those days were far in the past, but somehow, Aurora had managed to maintain its small town *feel* even if it was far more "city" than "town" these days.

Silence descended over the vehicle and continued to travel with them for a couple of miles until Kendra decided to tender an invitation to Abilene or, actually, to his mother.

Even as the idea formed in her brain, she had a hard time believing that she would say this. But people in pain had a way of getting to her and from what she'd overheard earlier—and what he'd just told her now—Abilene's mother was in pain. Decent people shouldn't have to be in pain if there was any way around it.

"Look, I'm still just getting used to this whole deal about actually being a Cavanaugh and not who I thought I was—"

"A last name doesn't change who you are," he pointed out. "Although," he added with a touch of whimsy, "saying that you're a Cavanaugh might make things a hell of a lot easier for you."

"Or harder," she countered. "A lot of people think that just because I'm related to a Cavanaugh, I'm getting a free ride, that I don't have to work as hard as the next guy—I work twice as hard as the next guy."

"Unless the next guy happens to be me," Abilene said, his mouth curving.

Damn but he had a sexy-looking mouth, even when what came out of it annoyed her. "I work twice as hard as the next guy," she repeated with feeling. "No matter *who* the next guy is."

"The lady doth protest too much." The way he said it, it was more of a question than a statement.

It still wasn't received well. "The 'lady' is busy working her tail off to prove she can do the job each and every time," she said with feeling.

He seemed willing to take her at her word. With a casual shrug, he said, "Okay, we got that out of the way. Now, where were you going with all this before we got sidetracked?" he asked with a grin.

Right, the invitation. For a second, she felt awkward about extending it. After all, he might get the wrong idea—that she was interested in him. Which she wasn't. This wasn't for Abilene, she reminded herself. This was for his mother.

"That the former chief of police, Andrew Cavanaugh, likes to have people over for breakfast—or any meal. He sets a really good table and, personally, I have no idea how the man does it, but there always seems to be food ready. A battalion could come by and I think that he would have enough to feed them until their sides ached." She'd been present a couple of times when the man had juggled fifty guests and never broke a sweat. She found that incredible. "What I'm getting at is maybe you and your mother might want to drop by some morning, like on a Saturday," she suggested. "More specifically," she continued, suddenly remembering that her father had said something about there being a party of some sort at the former chief's house this weekend, "*this* Saturday."

"As your guest?" he asked.

She was about to say no, afraid he'd read into that, but then she relented. After all, it might make things easier all around if that was the initial invitation.

"Yeah. Sure. Why not? As my guests," she agreed. "It might just do your mother some good," she added so that there wouldn't be any misunderstanding about why she was suggesting this in the first place. If he thought she was interested in him, their budding working relationship would get shot to hell. "There's a lot of warmth and love coming from that group." She could testify to that firsthand. "Gives a person a feeling of well-being."

Abilene liked to keep his private life just that, private. But he needed help here. So he rolled her offer over in his mind. He loved his mother dearly and while he wouldn't have traded her in for anything in the world, what he *would* have changed about her was her emotional neediness.

She'd always been there for him and had done the best she could to raise him so that he wanted for little. If he had one wish in the world, it would be to see her finally happy—and secure.

Maybe she'd learn how by associating with people like the Cavanaughs.

"Sounds good to me," he finally told his partner. "Count us in."

She nodded. Now all she had to do was ask her father if she'd overstepped her bounds. She made a mental note to talk to him tonight.

The list of people she wanted to touch base with once she was off duty was growing.

Chapter 5

"No, I've never had any trouble with Ryan Burnett." The man they were talking to looked surprised to even be asked such a question. "If I had, I would have fired the guy, not sent someone to look for him when he didn't turn up at work or call in. Why?" he asked suspiciously, looking from one detective to the other. "What's going on?"

Lou Maxwell was the senior accountant and founder of the company that boasted a number of celebrity clients as well as doing the accounting for a large number of small corporations in the area, all of which he'd parlayed into a thriving business. The man had a booming voice, which was in complete contrast to his rather small, thin frame. Expensive clothes hung on his body like suits on a hanger, waiting to be pressed into service by an actual live person.

If Maxwell was aware of the shadow he cast—or didn't cast—he gave no indication of it.

When neither of the two detectives who had come into his spartan office to question him about his missing accountant answered his question, he went on to ask another.

"Kennedy said he saw a dead body on the floor," he said, referring to the junior accountant he'd sent in search of his missing employee, "but that it wasn't Burnett's. Whose was it and where the hell is Burnett?" Maxwell demanded.

Kendra shook her head. "We really can't discuss an ongoing investigation, Mr. Maxwell."

"You people wouldn't *have* an 'ongoing investigation' if I hadn't sent Kennedy to find out what was going on. Now I'm down two men instead of just one because Kennedy is still throwing up in the men's room and you won't tell me anything." He glared at the detectives when they still wouldn't tell him anything. "Look, someone on one of the news channels or one of the millions of blogs on the internet is going to find a way to ferret out the information and splash it all over the airwaves, so you might as well tell me now. I have a right to know."

Maxwell had a point. She could see by the look that Abilene gave her that the other detective thought so, too. She was surprised that Abilene was leaving it up to her rather than just stepping in and taking over. Maybe he did respect protocol—in his own way. He was turning out not to be such a bad guy after all. Then she cautioned herself to continue reserving judgment. After all, she didn't exactly have a sterling track record when it came to being right about men.

Determined to control the amount of information that came out, she kept it short and precise.

"We found a woman in Mr. Burnett's apartment. We didn't find him. Would you know where he would be inclined to go if he couldn't stay at his apartment?"

Maxwell shook his head. "Not a clue," he confessed. "Nice guy, but he kind of kept to himself. That's why I liked him," Maxwell underscored. "Worked hard from the minute he came in until the minute he left. No goofing off, no internet surfing on my time." He paused for a moment, thinking. "About a couple of weeks ago, I heard him mention he was going to get engaged."

"Who did he mention it to?" Abilene asked before Kendra could. It was a natural assumption that the woman was the same one found on Burnett's floor, but there was always an outside chance that it wasn't.

"Kennedy. That's why I sent him," Maxwell added. "Thought maybe they were friends." The small, deep-set brown eyes narrowed further, appearing to grow even smaller. "You telling me that you think Burnett killed the girl?"

"I'm not telling you anything," Kendra reminded the man tactfully. "Right now, we're just asking as many questions as we can think of, trying to see what we can find out. See what flies," she added, borrowing some of the accountant's short, clipped terms.

Maxwell snorted. "Well, if he did kill her, then I'm a rotten judge of character." It was evident by his demeanor that he didn't believe he was.

Kendra, however, wasn't as sure as he was. "Let's

hope you're not, Mr. Maxwell. Do you mind if we talk to your people? See if perhaps they might have anything to add?" They could do it with or without his permission, but with was always easier.

"Do I mind?" Maxwell echoed. "Yeah, I mind. If they're talking, they're not working. But go ahead," he concluded, waving them on to the outer office where the accountants who worked for him were all seated. "Get this over with. The sooner you do, the sooner you're gone and they get back to doing what I'm paying them for."

"Don't think anyone's going to be nominating him for Boss of the Year any time soon," Abilene commented under his breath as he and Kendra closed the door to Maxwell's office.

"Could be worse," Kendra deadpanned. When Abilene raised an eyebrow, she said, "He could have told us to come back and talk to the other accountants after hours."

Abilene took a chance that she was being serious and said, "Maybe he knew he'd be overridden and didn't want the hassle. Guys like that only pick fights they figure they'll win."

Guys like that in this case meant guys in control. Was Abilene referring to himself as well? She took it as another possible small piece of insight into the man assigned to work with her.

"I'll keep that in mind."

Abilene heard something in her tone and deduced the rest. Partnering with her would be a constant, ongoing battle of wits. He found himself kind of liking that. It would keep him on his toes.

"Not all guys," he interjected.

Okay, he's exempting himself, she thought, amused. She looked at Abilene for a long moment—and just for a second, caught herself thinking things that had no part in the investigation.

Doing an abrupt mental about-face, she murmured, "Good to know."

They both turned their attention to the accountants, taking them aside one by one into one of the small private offices meant for client-accountant interviews, and asked their questions.

The accountants were all of the same opinion. Talking to them just reinforced the initial impression of a hardworking, affable young man who was willing to pitch in when necessary but for the most part, kept to himself. No one had a bad word to say about him.

What Kennedy, the accountant who'd gone to Ryan's apartment, had seen had already made the rounds at the firm and to a person, they were convinced that Burnett couldn't have killed the girl. What they did believe was that the missing young man was perhaps in trouble or even imminent danger.

"Maybe somebody broke into his apartment and kidnapped him," said Gina, the accounting firm's one administrative assistant, a very young-looking blonde who seemed to favor braids as a hairstyle, her blue eyes wide and earnest.

Kendra decided to make the young woman work to put over her theory. "Then how do you explain the dead woman on his floor?"

Gina didn't even hesitate or need time to think. She'd

obviously figured out the kinks in her theory while waiting her turn to be questioned.

"She walked in on it and the kidnapper was forced to kill her because he couldn't take them both prisoners." Having advanced her theory, Gina seemed exceedingly pleased with herself. The next moment, she was looking to Abilene, rather than to the woman questioning her. She definitely looked interested in *his* reaction.

He didn't disappoint her. Instead, he nodded. "We'll take it under advisement," he told her in a quiet, thoughtful voice.

In response, the young woman lit up like a Christmas tree.

Her reaction was not lost on Kendra. *And another one bites the dust*.

Since this was the last interview, Abilene followed Kendra's lead and started to rise. He felt the administrative assistant place her hand on top of his, meaning to momentarily detain him.

"You'll let me know if that was what happened?" she asked hopefully. "That poor Ryan was kidnapped?"

"You'll be one of the first to know," Abilene assured her with solemnity.

"Laying the groundwork for a future conquest?" Kendra asked in a quiet, unfathomable voice as they left the outer office.

"Letting her think she said something important and useful," Abilene corrected. "And who knows? That woman's theory makes about as much sense as anything else right now."

Kendra relented. She supposed she had to agree at this point.

"One thing does seem to be clear right about now," he continued.

She would have been lying if she had said that she hadn't braced herself before gamely asking, "And what's that?"

"The guy who worked shoulder to shoulder with those other accountants in that office wasn't the kind of guy to kill his girlfriend in cold blood."

No, not according to the way they had perceived him. But there was also another explanation for what had happened in the small apartment. "How about in the heat of an argument?"

They stepped into the elevator. Abilene shook his head. "Didn't sound like a very passionate guy to me, either."

"How about you?" she asked without any preamble. She pressed for the first floor.

Abilene stared at her. This was a new twist. "Are you asking me if I'm passionate?"

Although the thought amused him, he just didn't see Kendra putting that sort of question to him. It didn't jibe with what he knew of her personality.

Was he wrong? And if so, about what, exactly? Less than twenty-four hours in the woman's company and she was becoming one huge, intriguing enigma. A puzzle he found himself wanting to solve.

"No," she contradicted, a flash of embarrassment over the misunderstanding sending color up her neck to her cheeks—as did the unbidden thought of his being passionate. "What I'm asking you is if your fellow co-workers know the first thing about what makes Matt Abilene tick," she asked. "Or do they know only what you want them to know?" Which was the more logical conclusion.

After a moment, Abilene nodded his head. They reached the first floor and he waited for her to step out first, then darted out just before the doors closed on him.

She didn't tell Abilene he looked rather adorable just then, even though the thought flashed through her mind.

"I see where you're going with this," he told Kendra.

She laughed, waving away his words. "I wasn't trying to make it a mystery—unlike who killed Summer and where our missing accountant is at the moment."

"Right now, I'd say the key is in their relationship," he speculated.

She seemed a little uncertain, even as she said, "Right now, I tend to agree."

Right now. Abilene smiled knowingly. "Don't commit fully, do you?"

She couldn't make up her mind whether she liked his smile—or found it distractingly annoying, not to mention unsettling.

"Not easily," she admitted when he was obviously waiting for her to say something.

He nodded. "Me, neither."

Tell me something I don't know. But out loud, she said, "I already figured that part out," all while sporting a pleasant, completely unreadable smile.

Abilene followed her out to the street. "Where to now?"

It was getting late. Shadows had begun to form, tagging one another on the ground. "I think you put in enough time on a first day," she told him.

He hadn't expected that. She reminded him of someone who pushed, who worked into the small hours and
expected no less from those who worked with her. "I'm
not a novice," he reminded her.

"No," she agreed, "but you do have a mother who's
waiting to see you. And we're not about to solve this
thing in a few extra hours tonight. Go, see your mother,
Abilene," she urged. "Make her feel better." She thought
of how much, after all these years, she still missed her
own. "You only get one mother."

He snapped his fingers. "And here I was, getting
ready to swing by the Mother Store to see if I could
trade mine in for another model."

Sarcasm was a weapon—and a defense mechanism. Which was he using? "You always crack wise
like that?" she asked.

"Not always," he admitted, his voice even, giving
nothing away. And then he looked at her significantly.
"Only when I'm inspired."

They'd come up to the car and she pressed the lock
release. A small *click* had all four locks opening and
standing at attention.

"C'mon." She opened the driver's-side door. "I'll
drop you off at the precinct."

"Okay. I owe you a drink."

That stopped her for a moment. She glanced at him
over the hood of the car. "How do you figure that?"

He dropped down into his seat, then waited for her
to do the same before continuing. "Isn't the new guy
supposed to buy drinks at the end of his first day?"

Buckling up, she shut the door. Kendra shook her

head just before turning on the ignition. "I was the last 'new guy' in our squad and they bought *me* drinks."

His laugh seemed to fill the interior of the vehicle and rippled along her skin.

"That works, too," he answered with an agreeable nod.

Kendra had a feeling that he would hold her to that drink.

They parted in the parking lot, with Abilene going his way and Kendra, supposedly, going hers. She watched his car pulling out of the lot in the distance. Only then did she get out of her vehicle and go back upstairs.

Tom was waiting for her. By request.

Taking the elevator to the Missing Persons squad room, she got out, entered the room and crossed to Tom's desk. Wearily, she dropped down into the chair positioned next to it.

"What do you know about him?" she asked. "My new partner," she added for clarification. And then, because it occurred to Kendra that she wasn't being at all clear, she backtracked and said what she should have mentioned in the first place: her new partner's name. "What do you know about Matt Abilene?"

The wide, muscular shoulders rose and fell in a minor, offhanded movement. "Off the top of my head—nothing," Tom admitted. "But I can ask around if you'd like." He looked carefully at Kendra, as if trying to discern if everything was all right. "I heard that the chief gave you a new one," he confirmed. "Is he giving you a hard time?"

She didn't want to answer that one way or another. To say yes would get her brother's protective side up and Abilene wasn't actually being condescending or disrespectful toward her, which meant that she couldn't say that he was giving her a hard time. It was more that he was irritating her—mostly in ways she couldn't talk about or explain, even to herself. Besides, knowing the way Tom thought, he just might interpret her words in a completely different and unwelcome way.

So, for now, she remained evasive. "I just like to know the kind of person I'm working with, that's all," she said in the most innocent voice she could muster.

"Wouldn't you figure that out after a few days of interacting with him?" Tom asked, putting the logical assumption out there.

For that, at least, she had an answer. "You know I'm the impatient type."

Tom grinned. "Which is why this new partner of yours gets more of my sympathy than you do," her brother told her.

Kendra eyed him impatiently. "So you're not going to help?"

"I didn't say that."

No, she had to admit that he hadn't. And that relieved her. For a second. "You just like to yank my chain."

Tom didn't bother suppressing the laugh. "Something like that."

Nothing new there, she thought. And then she remembered something else. Something she had jumped the gun on. Was this going to create problems now, she wondered uncertainly.

Kendra took a breath, then said, "Mind if I ask you a question?"

"Go ahead."

She pressed her lips together, then pushed ahead. "Think that the chief would mind my bringing two guests with me to his Saturday brunch thing this week?"

"Which chief?" he asked for form's sake, although only one of them really cooked. Brian just put up the tables. "We've got two of them in the family now," he reminded her, tongue in cheek. "It might be clearer if you refer to them as Uncle Andrew and Uncle Brian."

She couldn't bring herself to do that just yet. They were people she respected and in Brian's case, was honored to work with. But they weren't her uncles. Maybe in time they would be, but not yet. Not now.

"Doesn't feel right, yet," she told her brother. "And you know I'm talking about the brunches the former chief has in his house—Andrew, all right?" she tagged on, exasperated as she used the man's name.

Tom ignored her irritated tone. There was a more interesting question here than why her temper kept spiking. "What guests?"

She would rather not have said anything until later, but since he asked, she had to tell him. There was no easy way around it. "Abilene and his mother."

"So you're getting along with him, then," Tom assumed.

She wasn't about to launch into any long explanations right now. "One thing doesn't have anything to do with the other," Kendra countered.

Tom crossed his arms and leaned back in his chair. "All right. Educate me."

She sighed. "Abilene got a call at the office from his mother today. She was upset. From what I could gather, her boyfriend walked out on her. Abilene said it wasn't the first such occurrence. That it's a pattern." She recited the facts as she recalled them. "She sounds like a good woman who's made a lot of bad choices because she's afraid of winding up alone. Apparently, there's no other family. I just thought…"

Kendra let her voice trail off. Tom was the smart one here, she let him fill in the blanks.

"—that being subjected to the Cavanaugh family might help her feel less alone?" he guessed.

"Something like that," she acknowledged. "But I don't want to do something that'll make the chief think that I'm taking advantage of the so-called family connection."

Tom shook his head. "It's not a 'so-called' family connection," he corrected her. "It *is* a family connection. *Our* family connection. Like it or not, Kenny, Dad's a Cavanaugh. And so are we."

"Yeah, I know. But—" She paused for a moment, searching for words that didn't seem to want to materialize. "What do we do about…you know…the *other* family?"

"We don't 'do' anything about them. The way I see it, Kenny, we just got more family, we didn't trade one bunch in for another. You can't close your eyes to over twenty years of life and pretend it never happened. We thought they were our aunts and uncles, *they* thought they were our aunts and uncles. No reason for anything to change."

He was missing the huge elephant in the room—and

she knew he was too smart not to see it. So why was he taking this stand?

"Except that they're *not* our aunts and uncles," she insisted.

"Just a technicality, Kenny. Finding out about the hospital mix-up doesn't suddenly erase them, or make all those memories of Christmases past disappear. It sure doesn't erase them from our lives. They wouldn't want it and *we* wouldn't want it." He leaned forward in his chair, his voice gaining enthusiasm. "Life just got better, Kenny. And you don't have to choose between one camp or the other. This is one of those times when you can have it all and it's really okay."

He smiled at her as he rose. When she did as well, Tom gave her a quick, hard hug. "Give yourself permission to be happy again, Kenny. The rest of us are worried about you." And then he glanced at his watch. "Now, if you'll excuse me, I have a very sexy lady waiting to light up my life and I don't want to keep her waiting any longer."

That would be the detective who'd transferred from New Mexico after working with her brother on her niece's kidnapping case. Kaitlyn Two Feathers. Their family would become larger by one very soon. Kendra was happy for Tom, even as she felt an unexpected pang in her heart for what she no longer had. And maybe never did. Jason's suicide, despite all her efforts to help him, was evidence of that.

"Say hi to Kait for me. Tell her to treat my big brother well."

He grinned. "Will do."

She stood there, watching her brother leave and then,

quietly, she doubled back to the Homicide squad room. She made her way through the nearly deserted room until she reached her desk.

Taking a deep breath, Kendra sat down and started to go over all her notes on the current case from the beginning.

Again.

Chapter 6

Sabrina Abilene's impressively unlined, heart-shaped face lit up when she saw her son walking toward her booth.

She'd been sitting there for the last half hour and was thinking about leaving. She knew that Matthew's career didn't always remain between the lines. Sometimes he was forced to work around the clock. And while she worried about him a great deal because of his chosen career, she was also incredibly proud of him.

"You came," she cried once Matt was within earshot. Surprise and pleasure were evident in equal parts in her voice. "I didn't think that you were going to."

Matt slid into the seat opposite his mother. This was where they came whenever they wanted to celebrate an occasion. Or just to get away and talk.

It was the latter he was faced with now.

Somewhere along the line, their roles had gotten reversed and he'd become the parent while she was the child, at least when it came to matters of the heart.

"When have I not come?" he asked. Then, before she could reply, he said quietly, "You're getting me confused with all those other men in your life, Mom. The ones who keep disappointing you and running out on you."

"No, I'm not," she protested with a sad smile. "I just expect you to get fed up with holding my hand whenever I wind up having this happen to me," she told him honestly. Her eyes smiled as she looked at him. "I'd never confuse you with anyone else." Sabrina looked down at the one glass of wine she allowed herself to have whenever she came here. There were no answers in the light pink liquid. "Why do they keep running out on me, Matthew? What's wrong with me?" she asked in a very small, defeated voice.

Matt didn't bother with the menu. He knew what the restaurant had to offer by heart. The people who ran Haven knew when not to mess with a good thing and had left it unchanged for the past few years.

When the waiter approached their table, Matt ordered the lemon chicken. His mother echoed, "Make that two." Once the waiter retreated, only then did Matt answer his mother's question.

He hated seeing her like this. And hated what he had to tell her, even though they both already knew this. "You have lousy taste in men," he told her honestly. "And a good heart," he added to temper the harsher remark. "No matter how many times this happens to you, no matter how many men take everything you have to give and then disappear, you just can't seem to make yourself believe that not everyone is like you, that someone could actually be cruel on purpose."

His mother laughed shortly. "I guess that makes me a sucker."

"No," he told her carefully, "just a good-hearted person who really needs to be a little more cautious about opening up."

She began to speak, then waited until the waiter who'd returned with the basket of lemon chicken pieces that was to be their dinner left again.

"It's just that I get so lonely sometimes," she confessed quietly. Bright blue eyes looked up at him. "I miss your father."

"I don't think he'd be too happy about what you're going through, either, Mom," Matt pointed out patiently. "Listen, I have an idea. Why don't you do some volunteer work at the local hospital?" he suggested. "They could use the help and it'll make you feel as if you're doing something useful for people. That's a plus. You also might run into a better class of people than you do at your present job. Definitely another plus."

But Sabrina shook her head. "I can't do that and work," she protested. "My job takes up a great deal of my time."

The place where she worked—a bar named Sparky's—was not the place where he wanted his mother. It was the last in a long line of less than A-list places where she'd worked.

"Waiting tables at that...club—" he finally settled on the word rather than calling it a bar "—also puts you right out there with a whole unsavory class of people. Men just looking for women to take advantage of."

She pressed her lips together. "Meaning me."

"Listen." He leaned in closer. "You can quit that job. I have some money put away—"

"No, no, no, that's out of the question." She was his mother, Matthew wasn't supposed to have to take care of her. "I won't have you spending your hard-earned money on me—"

"My money, Mom," he told her. "I get to spend it the way I want to." He smiled at her, remembering the good times—and there had been good times. She'd tried very hard to give him a decent upbringing and he'd never doubted that she loved him. The rest of it was hard to take. "Can't think of a better way than helping you out."

"I can," Sabrina told him firmly. She placed her hand over his and patted it. "Your taking time out of your busy day to see me is all I want from you. That's already more than a lot of sons would do," she insisted. And then she forced a smile to her lips, putting up a brave front for him and trying at the same time to convince herself that from now on, it was going to be different. "I'll try to do better," she promised.

He nodded and pretended as if he believed her, but this was nothing new. His mother had made the same promise before, time and again, and she'd meant it.

But each and every time she'd wind up losing her soft heart to the first charismatic con man who crossed her path.

It was as if there was some kind of electronic bulletin board with her picture on it. The note beneath it urged anyone with larcenous tendencies to come find her because she was the perfect mark.

His mother had good intentions, but this pattern of

hers wouldn't change unless he found a way to do something about it.

What he needed, Matt told himself, was to find a way for his mother to mingle with a better element of people, he thought. That was when he suddenly remembered the invitation his partner had tendered. He had his doubts if the cocky detective actually meant it once she had the time to think it over, but whether or not she meant it, he decided he needed to take her up on it.

Or rather, his mother needed him to take her up on it.

"By the way," Matt said casually as he selected another piece of chicken from the basket—he favored drumsticks—"we've been invited to the former police chief's house on Saturday."

Sabrina's light green eyes widened in surprise. "Why? Is something wrong?"

"If something was wrong," Matt answered, doing his best not to laugh at his mother's dazed expression, "we'd be going to the precinct, not his house. Turns out that my new partner's one of his nieces and the former chief of police has a real penchant for having a lot of people over to his house for brunch and other get-togethers. Word has it that the man's one hell of a cook." A deep fondness filled his eyes as he grinned at his mother. "He probably can't hold a candle to you, but we might as well give the guy a chance. So what d'you say? Will you go with me?"

When Sabrina didn't answer right away, he prodded her a little. "Could be a lot of fun, being around a house full of honest people for a change—and me, of course," he winked.

As if he had a dishonest bone in his body, Sabrina

thought with a gentle laugh. She was and always had been very, very proud of him. Matthew was the very best part of her.

Sabrina leaned over the table and their basket of communal chicken and kissed his cheek. "You always could make everything all better just by talking to me, Matthew."

"Maybe I should tape-record my voice, leave you with that to listen to when I'm not around."

The smile on her lips was also reflected in her eyes. When she looked like that, his mother was downright beautiful. But, beautiful or not, she didn't deserve to be taken advantage of the way she was. And she certainly didn't deserve to have it happen to her over and over again. Maybe some time with the Cavanaughs would help her break that pattern, let her see the way decent people treated one another. Who knew—it might even help to build up her confidence.

"It's worth a try," she laughed, referring to the tape.

"Yeah, maybe it is, at that." Matt was only half kidding.

"'Morning, Good," Abilene said cheerfully as he slid into his chair and took his place behind his desk. "By the way, my mother says thank you for the invitation. She'll be very happy to attend the chief's brunch this Saturday."

About to get started with the files he'd left on his desk last night, Abilene took a sip of his coffee. That was when he took a good look at his partner for the first time.

He wasn't much on noticing a woman's clothes, but

he was fairly certain that he'd seen his partner wearing this same outfit yesterday. In his experience, most women didn't wear the same thing two days in a row unless they hadn't been home the night before.

He eyed her over the rim of his container. "Did you go home last night?"

Kendra looked up ruefully. It wasn't something she was happy about acknowledging. Sleep last night had come when she'd least expected it and she'd wound up with her head on the desk, getting about four hours, perhaps less. It hadn't been restful. Her neck was killing her this morning and she was pretty sure that beneath her sandy bangs was the imprint of a staple.

None of that put her in a good mood, or even a tolerable one. The edges of her temper were already pretty frayed. And it was still early.

"Let's get one thing straight. You're my temporary partner, not my guardian angel," she told him.

"Temporary, huh?" he repeated. "Is that what you think?" If it was, that explained a lot, he reasoned.

She shrugged, not about to discuss it when she felt so overwhelmingly underarmed. Her mind fuzzy, she was still having trouble focusing.

"Everything's temporary one way or another. Who knows?" She threw the ball into his court. "Things might not work out and you might be the one asking for another partner."

She was a Cavanaugh. He wouldn't jeopardize his career like that. You didn't get very far by complaining about the chief's niece.

"Or you might." And that, he knew by the way she'd

said the word *temporary,* was a far more likely scenario in this case.

"There's that, too," Kendra agreed with a dismissive sigh he couldn't quite interpret. "What was that you said about your mother?" she asked, looking for a way to change the subject.

"I said she wanted me to thank you for the invitation to the chief's house." Had the woman been here all night? he wondered. Working on the case? She certainly didn't look as if she'd found anything for her trouble. He doubted she'd be quite this surly if she had.

Why was it so hard for her to think clearly? Kendra wondered, annoyed with herself and the fog that had set in on her brain. She used to be able to get by on four hours' sleep—just not four hours grabbed on top of a desk, she reminded herself.

What had Abilene just said about his mother? Oh, right. That the other woman had extended her thanks. She stitched together the rest of the conversation, then, just to be clear, asked, "Then she's coming?"

"Took a little persuading—my mother really doesn't like to feel as if she's imposing—" he explained, to forestall any further misunderstanding.

"Trust me, from what I know about Andrew Cavanaugh's get-togethers, she's not," Kendra assured him.

"But she is coming," he said, finishing his sentence despite the fact that they seemed to be talking over one another here. He paused for a second, then asked, "You were serious, right?"

"Absolutely."

Right now, given her present state of nonclarity, she wondered what had possessed her to invite Abilene, but then she recalled that he'd told her about his mother's penchant for getting taken by the men she let into her life. She supposed, in a way, Abilene's mother and she had something in common. The men in their lives had ultimately disappointed them.

Except that in her case, it wasn't so cut-and-dried. She was disappointed because, on some existential plane, she had failed Jason. If she hadn't, she would have been able to make him come around and renew his hold on life. Instead, he'd gone ahead and romanced a gun, using it to end his life, rather than fighting his way back from the depths of the black hole he'd slipped into.

"So how do you want to work this?" he was asking as she distanced herself from Jason and the memory of that awful day, of finding him like that, lifeless and bleeding.

She took a breath, then focused her attention back on the case. "Well, right now I'm having a lot of photos of Burnett printed up so that we can show it around in all the train and bus stations and at all the airline terminals at the local airport. This way, if he's leaving town any other way than by car, we've got him."

"Great." He nodded, but that wasn't really what he was asking. "But I meant on Saturday. At your uncle's house." She really wasn't here, was she, he thought, looking into her eyes again. He couldn't help wondering what was going on in her mind.

Kendra blinked. It took her a second to refocus her thoughts, shifting them away from the case and reluctantly onto her personal life. She almost corrected him about Andrew being her uncle—except that, when she came right down to it, she really couldn't. He *was* her uncle. Not in name only, but in actuality.

It was just going to take a lot of getting used to.

"Oh, that. Well, I could meet you at your place, or you could—"

She was about to say that he and his mother could meet her at her place, but then that meant she'd have to give him her address and she wasn't in a place emotionally where she was willing to give out that kind of information to him just yet. She preferred doling out personal information slowly. When she knew Abilene better—*and* he was her partner of record for a while—*then* she'd let him know where she lived.

Maybe.

"Why don't I swing by your place, pick you and your mother up and we'll go from there?" she suggested pleasantly.

"All right." He wasn't about to ask her why she'd doubled back so abruptly. He had a feeling he knew. The woman was very guarded and she didn't immediately "work well and play well with others," as they used to say on grade-school report cards from decades gone by. "Give me an approximate time so I can pick up my mother first and have her back in time for when you do your 'swinging by,' Good."

She could feel her temper shortening drastically. She wished he wouldn't call her that, but obviously the more she asked, the more he seemed to "forget." The only way to deal with this was to ride it out.

For some reason, while Abilene wasn't being exactly sarcastic outright, it was pretty damn close, she realized. Why? Kendra silently demanded. Was he reacting to something she'd said, or—?

She was overthinking again. Her brothers and sisters always said that was her biggest fault. Thinking things to death. She hadn't always been like that. But having a fiancé kill himself on what was to have been their wedding day sent ripples through a person's life. Big ripples.

There were times, in the very beginning, when she'd secretly marveled that she was simply putting one foot in front of the other and not just huddled somewhere in a fetal position.

After that horrible accident, which had claimed the lives of four of his fellow firefighters, when Jason lay there in the hospital bed, so much of his body scarred by the fire, she'd come to see him every day. She and her family had been his cheering section and she had sworn to him that it didn't matter to her if he had one leg or two, didn't matter if he met her at the altar in a wheelchair or on crutches, just as long as he was there.

She loved *him,* she'd insisted, not just some part of him, or, in this case, a missing part of him.

It had gotten to the point where she thought he believed her, but obviously she'd failed somehow, failed to convince him, failed to save him. He hadn't believed her when she'd told him that she loved him, that she would be there for him and that she wanted to help him regain his enthusiasm for life.

If he'd believed her, wouldn't he still be here?

The thought vibrated in her brain. Tears gathered in her eyes.

"Hey, you okay?"

Abruptly, Kendra came back to her surroundings.

She noted the concern in Abilene's voice. She also realized that in her momentary lapse, his butt had somehow gotten planted on her desk. Obviously, he'd come around when she hadn't answered him and had sat on her desk to look down into her eyes.

Not only that, but he had one of her hands in both of his and she *knew* he wasn't just trying to shake it.

Something warm and unbidden rose up in response within her. Startled, she was quick to shut it down and pulled her hand away.

"I'm fine," Kendra retorted.

Ordinarily, he would have retreated and said "the hell with it." But something in her expression caught his attention. And captured his concern. Something was out of sync.

"Yeah," he agreed. "For a woman who's a million miles away."

Damn but having him as a partner had a definite downside. During the past couple of years, she could count on Joe dozing at his desk half the time. He certainly didn't play Twenty Questions and probe her like this.

"I was just thinking," she tossed off carelessly.

He laughed shortly. "I kind of figured that."

"Good for you." Rising abruptly, Kendra pushed her chair in. The armrests banged jarringly against the desk. "Let's see if the people where Summer Miller worked know if her boyfriend was hot-tempered enough to kill her."

Sounded like as good a place to start this morning as any. Abilene gestured toward the doorway. "Lead the way."

Her eyes narrowed. Did he think she was waiting for his permission?

"Thanks," she said frostily. "I will." Lengthening her stride, she walked out of the office quickly.

"Hey, Good," he called after her, increasing his own stride. It didn't take much to catch up to her. He saw her shoulders tense in response to the name he called her, but pretended not to. "Did I say something to set you off?" he asked.

You mean today? Or just in general? "Yes."

"What?" he asked, curious.

"Everything," she fired back at him, stabbing at the Down button on the wall between the two closed elevator doors.

"In other words, you don't want me to talk?"

She came very close to saying yes, but she knew damn well that she was being unfair to him. Just because she had issues didn't mean that she should take it out on him. Or chew him out.

It wasn't his fault she wasn't woman enough to save Jason.

"Sorry," she apologized with a heartfelt sigh. "I get crabby when I don't get enough sleep. I didn't mean to make you feel I was chewing you out."

"You want to go home and catch a couple of hours?" he offered. "I can handle questioning Summer's employer and coworkers," he told her, then added, "The lieutenant doesn't need to know," in case she thought he was planning on telling their boss.

"I can handle my own problems," she informed him.

Talk about being touchy, he thought. "Didn't say you

couldn't. Just thought you might handle things better with a couple of hours' sleep under your belt."

She had to admit the offer was exceedingly tempting. Every fiber in her body suddenly begged her for the opportunity to just curl up on a soft surface and shut her eyes. But there was no way she had any intention of shirking her duties.

"Thanks, but no. I'll manage," she insisted.

"If you say so," he answered glibly.

"Yes, I do."

Kendra's tone was firm even if her resolve wasn't quite there yet.

Chapter 7

When questioned about Summer Miller, the heavy-set man with the curly, faded yellow-white hair sadly shook his head.

"No, I had to let her go. PartyTyme! is owned by this family-run corporation and they have very strict rules," he told them solemnly. He paused for a moment to reengage in his ongoing battle with his ever-sinking trousers, pulling them up to just beneath his expanded waistline. Temporarily, they hung on his hips before once again beginning a slow descent. "There's zero tolerance for drugs. Summer failed the last random test we had and bam, she was out the door."

"Summer had a drug habit?" Kendra asked. According to the M.E., the first tox screen had been negative. Maybe further testing was in order.

Harvey Abernathy raised his seriously sloping

shoulders in a hapless shrug that seemed over before it started.

"I never saw any evidence of it in her work, but, yeah, I guess she had to," he concluded. "Otherwise, she would have passed the test. But there are no second chances here. So I had to let her go, even though I didn't want to. She was a good worker."

"When was this?" Abilene asked.

"A week ago last Monday. My guess was that she had to have been partying all weekend for it to still be in her system like that. But I don't really know," he quickly added, his small eyes darting from one face to the other. "I don't do things like that myself." His voice was breathless and almost wistful as he told them this.

"Was she close to or friendly with anyone here?" Kendra asked. She glanced over her shoulder at the cubicles scattered about the floor. There was a person within each enclosure, manning a phone. Planning parties, she imagined.

"You could try talking to Suzanne Del Vecchio," he said, pointing to a cubicle on the left. A thin brunette was seated at the desk there. Unlike the others, she wasn't on the phone. She was typing something on the keyboard. "I saw them going out to lunch a few times." Abernathy shook his head again. "Too bad Summer had a drug problem," he said with real feeling. "She really *was* a good worker when the chips were down and we had a deadline to meet."

Kendra forced a smile to her lips. "Thank you for your help, Mr. Abernathy." She closed her notepad and tucked it back into her pocket. "We'll just go have a few words with Suzanne and maybe a couple of your other employees, if it's all right with you."

The sloping shoulders rose a little and collapsed again. "Have at it," he told them, gesturing vaguely toward Suzanne's cubicle and beyond. He watched them as they left his cluttered, claustrophobic office.

"Drug problem?" Abilene questioned somewhat skeptically the moment they left the supervisor's office. The idea seemed rather clichéd, but then, clichés existed for a reason.

"The M.E. didn't find any needle marks on her," Kendra offered.

"Lots of ways to take drugs," he reminded her.

She glanced at him. What was this, Rookie 101? "Thank you, I did not know that," she said, enunciating each word.

Rather than retreat because he was obviously rubbing her the wrong way—again—Abilene grinned and inclined his head.

"Glad to help." He saw his partner's lips move, but whatever she was saying, it was too low for him to hear. He had a feeling that it was probably better that way—for both of them.

"Yeah, we hung out together sometimes," Suzanne Del Vecchio told the two detectives who'd entered her cubicle and asked about Summer Miller. "Whenever her boyfriend was working overtime," she qualified. "Otherwise, she was always with him. They were going to get married, at least that was what she kept telling me."

"You didn't believe her?" Abilene questioned.

The brunette shrugged. "I figure men tell you a lot of things they don't mean just to get their way."

Amen to that, Kendra thought. "You never met him?" she asked the other woman.

"Once or twice," Suzanne allowed. "He seemed nice enough, I guess. Why? You think that he's the one who killed her?" she asked eagerly. When neither of the two detectives answered her, she told them, "The story's all over the office. Personally, he didn't look like a killer. But then, you never can tell."

Kendra was tempted to ask the woman what she thought a killer was supposed to look like, but that was only being testy, so she kept the question to herself. Instead, she focused on the new piece of information they'd just discovered.

"Your supervisor said she was fired for having a drug problem. What do you know about that?"

Suzanne blew out an impatient breath and snorted contemptuously. "Summer didn't have a drug problem. *He* has the drug problem," she accused, her brown eyes momentarily darting in the direction of Abernathy's glass-enclosed office. "Always watching people like some card-carrying Nazi."

"Your company has a strict no-drug policy," Abilene pointed out.

"Well, maybe it shouldn't," Suzanne said defiantly. "Besides, Summer didn't have a drug problem, she *did* drugs."

"The difference being?" Kendra asked.

A slight look of condescension entered Suzanne's brown eyes. "The difference being was that Summer did drugs socially. Like once in a while. She wasn't an *addict,*" Suzanne said with feeling. "She could take them or leave them. Her boyfriend was strait-laced so she made sure she never had any on her around him."

"And when she was doing these drugs 'socially,'" Abilene began, using Suzanne's terminology. "Where did she get them?"

Suzanne frowned and looked at the corner of her desk. "I don't know," she said, annoyed at being asked the question.

"You're lying," Abilene told her, his voice mild. When the girl glanced up at him sharply, a denial ready to burst from her lips, Abilene went on talking. "CSI 101: you just said that without making eye contact. If you were telling the truth, you wouldn't have stared at your desk. Now why don't we save everybody a whole lot of time, and you tell me who Summer's drug contact was."

When Suzanne's look turned defiant with an underlying element of fear, Kendra set her mind at ease the best she could. "We're not out to make a drug bust, Suzanne. All we want to do is find out who killed Summer. This dealer who provided her with happy pills might be able to point us in the right direction. Don't you want whoever did this to Summer to pay?"

Torn, the brunette began to waver. "Well, yeah, sure. Oh, okay," she finally relented, exasperated. Opening her purse, she pulled a card out of her wallet and handed it to Abilene, then belatedly said, "I was just holding that card for her."

Abilene exchanged looks with his partner. *The hell she was,* he thought, even though he nodded solemnly at her statement. "Lucky for us you were." He indicated the card. "Mind if we take this?"

Relieved not to be arrested, Suzanne merely waved the card away. "No, keep it for as long as you want. Keep it forever. I don't have any need for it now that Summer's gone." The last word echoed of sadness as the reality of the situation finally began to penetrate.

Abilene glanced at the card before tucking it into his shirt pocket. He frowned. "This is the address of a pet store."

"Yeah. It's his day job," Suzanne told them. "That's his name on the bottom."

"'John Smith,'" Abilene read out loud. There was no missing the sarcasm in his voice.

"Original," Kendra commented dryly.

"Probably all he could come up with while on his designer drugs," Abilene speculated. He looked at the young woman who'd given them the card. "We'll be in touch if we have any more questions." He could have sworn the brunette cringed a little.

The pet store on "John Smith's" card was located at the end of a strip mall in one of the older sections of the city. The entire block had seen better days and most of the businesses that had been here then had gone off in search of those days, leaving behind empty windows and emptier stores. The pet store had once been next door to a video rental store. The only thing left to testify to this was an old poster for *The Lord of the Rings* that had been abandoned in the window and was now burned by the sun and curling away from the glass. The glue on the tape used to keep the poster in its place had long since dried up.

The pet shop itself, while still operational, was a rather sad-looking place. There were no energetic little puppies or kittens or rabbits to snare the attention of people passing by. For the most part, there were no people passing by and that was just as well. Rather than pets looking for a good home, shredded newspaper remained as the makeshift bathroom for whatever small animals had once been in the window.

Looking through the dirty glass, Kendra scanned the interior. "Looks like it's closed."

"No, I see some movement," Abilene contradicted. "There, in the back. Next to that rear door."

As he said it, the tall, somewhat scruffy-looking thin man who had caught his attention bolted through the same door.

"Guess he's not interested in making new friends," Kendra quipped as they quickly rounded the building to the back of the store and the alleyway that ran the length of the strip mall.

"Maybe he's just shy," Abilene responded dryly.

When they reached the alley behind the pet store, there was less than a beat before someone started shooting at them.

The moment he heard the sound of the first gunshot, Abilene yanked Kendra's arm and pulled her to the ground, throwing himself on top of her to shield her from the bullets. Discarded large cartons that had once contained giant supplies of pet food provided partial shelter.

Despite the dire situation, Abilene was not unaware

of the feel of her body beneath his. Nor was he oblivious to the very strong reaction he was having to her.

Forcing his mind back to the immediate problem, Abilene scanned the area to see where the gunfire had originated. His body still pressed completely over hers, he pulled out his own weapon and returned rapid fire.

"I'll cover you," he told her. "You get back into the building."

"The hell I will. But you can get off me," she ordered. She couldn't breathe with his weight on her and more than that, she didn't like the reaction she was having to his body aligned with hers this way. Every inch of her body was aware of his. Big-time.

The sudden guttural scream told them that despite all odds and very poor visibility, Abilene had somehow managed to hit the fleeing suspect who was firing wildly at them.

"You shot me!" The bewildered, belligerent accusation echoed in the empty alley. "I'm bleeding!" the dealer cried in panic. "Help me! I'm dying!"

"That's one hell of a drama queen," Abilene commented.

"You're still on top of me," Kendra pointed out through clenched teeth.

"So I am." Abilene drew back slowly. On his feet, he offered her a hand, which she ignored.

"If that's a chuckle," she warned as she scrambled to her feet, "you're a dead man."

"Just clearing my throat," her partner told her innocently.

Kendra gave him a dirty look, then turned her attention to the man who was still screaming that he was dying.

"We can get you to a doctor," she called out, raising her voice above the panicked dealer's cries. "But you have to throw out your gun."

"John Smith" was all but sobbing now. "Okay, okay, okay, here it is." He tossed it out then came out himself from behind the Dumpster he'd used for cover. "Now get me some help before I bleed to death!"

On her feet, she was about to take the lead and was utterly surprised when Abilene caught her arm again. But this time, rather than pull her down to the ground, he merely switched places with her, going first.

She knew what he was doing—putting himself in harm's way instead of her, just in case the man had another weapon hidden somewhere. While a part of her appreciated the fact that he was trying to protect her, that was *not* the way a partnership like theirs was supposed to work.

What was with this man, anyway? Were his testosterone levels off the chart?

"What?" she demanded, trying to pull him back—it was like trying to move a mountain, something else to annoy her about him. "Are you suddenly bulletproof?"

"Didn't you know that?" he deadpanned. "It's right there in my résumé. Page two: Bullets just bounce off me without leaving a dent."

"Must have missed that part." Her own weapon drawn, they approached Summer's alleged recreational drug supplier, watching for any sudden moves. But the part-time pet store employee had morphed from preening drug supplier to a frightened stuck pig. All he wanted was to have the bullet removed from his arm and the bleeding stanched.

"Can you stop the bleeding?" she asked Abilene. Her plan was to extract information from the man in exchange for taking him to the hospital—but she wanted the information first, because she knew if it was the other way around, the drug dealer would renege and give them nothing.

"You mean like putting my finger in the hole?" Abilene asked innocently. "Yeah, I can do that."

Even as he said it, Abilene placed his thumb over where the bullet had entered the dealer's shoulder. The man let loose with a blood-curdling scream.

"I need to get to a hospital," he cried. "You gotta get me to a hospital." The man was practically begging now.

"As soon as you tell me why you killed Summer Miller," Abilene told him.

The man stared at him, bewildered. "Who?" he cried, shaking his head at the same time to actively deny any wrongdoing.

"Summer Miller." Kendra dug into her back pocket and pulled out the photograph of the dead woman that the M.E. had given her. Summer was lying on the autopsy table, waiting to be taken apart bit by bit. "You supplied her with drugs."

Squinting, the man finally nodded, obviously recognizing the dead woman. "Yeah, I supplied her, but I didn't kill her." His head jerked up as he demanded wildly, "Why would I kill her? That's bad for business." Hysteria punctuated his words. "I'm bleeding to death here. You don't get me to that hospital, I'm gonna die!"

"If you didn't kill her, then maybe you can tell us

where you were three days ago, say all day?" Abilene asked him.

The dealer shook his head, the ends of his dirty hair swinging about like stretched-out commas. "I don't know," he wailed.

It wasn't easy, since at bottom she was a caregiver, but Kendra remained firm. "Not good enough," she told him with a shake of her head. She looked at her partner and asked, "You have a Band-Aid on you, Abilene? I'm fresh out."

"Sorry, never carry any," he told her, playing along for the dealer's benefit.

The latter was becoming genuinely panicked. "Wait, wait, I do know. I remember. I was in San Francisco," the man cried. Relief flooded his expression because he remembered. "At this big party."

"San Francisco," Kendra echoed somewhat skeptically. "And you can prove this?"

He looked at her wild-eyed, sweating profusely and seemingly light-headed.

Kendra knew they only had a couple of minutes left, if that much, before they lost their advantage and had to take the man to the nearest E.R. He was losing blood and at this rate, he would pass out on them.

"I got money from the ATM down the block from the party. I had to make change for this big ape who only had hundred-dollar bills on him. He was showing off for this skanky-looking girl he was with." The man was babbling now. "They've got cameras, right? The ATMs, they've got cameras? You can see it's me on the camera. I wasn't anywhere near that dead girl."

Abilene was as calm as the other man was agitated.

"They're supposed to. You'd better hope that yours was working."

The next moment, he was forced to catch the dealer as the man's eyes rolled up in his head and, passing out, he pitched forward.

Holding him upright, Abilene looked at Kendra. "Get enough?" he asked.

"Provided he was telling the truth and the camera was working, yes, we've got enough to either clear him or put him closer to the scene," she answered. And then her eyes narrowed as she saw a bright streak of red across the back of Abilene's shirt. It was dripping down his sleeve. "What's that?" she asked, even though, as far as she was concerned, it was a rhetorical question. When Abilene turned his head and looked at her quizzically, she pointed to the back of his arm.

Craning his neck, Abilene glanced at it and then shrugged off her question and the streak. "The guy's blood."

The hell it was. "I don't think so," she said flatly. "Not at this angle." Inspecting his upper arm quickly as Abilene held onto the drug dealer to keep the unconscious man from sinking to the pavement, Kendra bit off half a curse. "Dammit, you're hit. He shot you, probably while you were playing at being a bulletproof shield and draping yourself over me."

Abilene grinned broadly at her, despite the stinging sensation that was beginning to penetrate his consciousness. "Was it good for you, too, Good?" he cracked.

"Abilene—" There was a warning note in her voice that told him to back off. She didn't consider this a laughing matter. And she definitely didn't want to revisit that one flash of heat she'd felt when his body had pressed into hers.

Again he shrugged in response, but this time there were consequences to the action. She saw the wince he tried to cover up.

"All in a day's work, Good," Abilene told her cavalierly.

"Yeah, if you're working as a superhero," she countered, her temper fraying. He could have been killed, playing the hero. And it would have been her fault, she thought with a twinge of guilt. She couldn't have been able to handle that, having Abilene die because of her. "You didn't have to throw yourself over me like that," she insisted angrily. "I have a gun and I know how to use it."

Rather than argue with her—something Matt was quickly learning just led to nothing but one dead end after another—he caught her off guard by quietly saying, "You're welcome."

The two simple words stopped her cold in her tracks even though she continued to glare accusingly at him. She knew damn well that she would probably have been the one with the bullet in her if he hadn't played the hero.

And who knew? That bullet could have gotten lodged in a fatal place. In effect, he could very well have saved her life, even if she was having trouble admitting that fact.

"Yeah," Kendra finally acknowledged with more than a little reluctance, all but spitting the word out as if it had turned bitter on her tongue. "Thanks."

He laughed. "Sugar and spice" was definitely not a

description that could easily have been applied to her. She was more like hot sauce and wasabi.

"Don't worry, Good. I'm not about to say that your life's mine now or anything like that just because I saved you." Moving quickly despite his wound, he cuffed the unconscious dealer's hands behind his back. "I just didn't want to disappoint my mother and tell her that the invitation was canceled." With that, he hefted the skinny man up over his good shoulder, ready to transport him into a vehicle.

"Get in the car," she ordered, pointing to their un-marked vehicle. "I'm driving."

The second he did, after depositing the unconscious drug dealer in the back, Kendra took off.

Abilene braced his one good arm against the dash-board, thinking that perhaps the invitation would have to be canceled after all. Dead people didn't attend brunches.

Chapter 8

"Who taught you how to drive?" Abilene asked less than ten minutes later as they peeled into the hospital's E.R. parking lot.

The entire trip whizzed by in a blur with his partner going way over the speed limit and flying through yellow lights less than a beat away from turning red. He'd white-knuckled it all the way, wondering if they would make it to the hospital in one piece or if her driving would land them in the morgue instead.

"My brother, Tom." Kendra brought the car to a jarring stop. "Why?"

Abilene silently released the breath he'd been holding for the last nine and a half minutes. "By any chance does your brother have anger issues?"

Kendra shot him a warning look. "No, but I do."

Jumping out of the car, she rounded the hood before Abilene could get his door open and was at his side as he slowly rose from his seat. She saw that he needed to hold on to the side of the vehicle to do it. The whole side of his sleeve was now crimson.

This was not good, she thought, concerned and disturbed by what she saw. "Dammit, Abilene, you could have been seriously hurt!"

He forced a smile to his lips. "Ah, Good, I didn't know you cared."

"I don't, wise guy," she bit off. "I just hate filling out reports in triplicate—and God only knows who they'd give me as a partner this time around, seeing as how they're already scraping the bottom of the barrel." She looked at him accusingly.

"Stop, you're making me blush," Abilene protested, pretending to hide his face.

"You wish," she retorted. In contrast to his shirt-sleeve, he looked exceedingly pale. "My God, Abilene, right now it looks like all your blood is draining out of your body."

"My body's just fine," he assured her, then made her an offer, smiling weakly. "Care to check it out for yourself?"

"I'll pass, thanks." She hoped her flippant retort would hide her concern. "Stay here, I'll get someone to bring a gurney for our friendly neighborhood dealer," she told him, nodding at the unconscious suspect in the back seat.

"You know where to find us," Abilene called after her as she hurried away. Still holding on to the side of the vehicle, he lowered himself back into the passenger seat.

Kendra returned quickly, leading an orderly and a

nurse back to the parked car. Between them they were pushing a gurney.

"Stayed right where you told me to," he declared, trying to sound cheerful and carefree. Watching Kendra approach, Matt pulled himself back up to his feet again. It took more energy this time.

"Good, looks like you're finally learning how to listen, Abilene," she quipped, doing her best to hide how worried she was. She came around to his side as she got out of the orderly's way. "Now if only—Abilene?" she said uncertainly as she saw the towering man swaying ever so slightly.

When he turned his head to look at her, Matt felt his knees start to buckle. He did his best to stiffen them and remain standing.

Seeing him begin to sink, Kendra reacted instinctively. She pushed her shoulder under his arm and turned herself into a human crutch. Holding on to his arm, which she'd leveraged around her neck, she braced her partner against herself and struggled to keep Matt upright. Her free arm immediately tightened around his waist as she felt his weight begin to shift.

"A little help here," she called out to the orderly. The other man had his hands full transferring the unconscious drug dealer to the gurney.

But it was Abilene who answered her. "You're doing just fine," he drawled. There was the hint of an amused smile in his voice.

She looked up at her partner suspiciously, wondering if he was doing this on purpose, but something in her gut told her that he wasn't. He was just reacting to losing so much blood.

"I need another gurney for my partner," she called over to the nurse, who was already helping the orderly guide their prisoner back through the hospital's electronic doors. "Now!" she ordered.

"I love it when you throw your weight around," Abilene muttered, his words tumbling into one another.

"Shut up, Abilene," she warned.

"Right away," the nurse was saying, responding to the request for another gurney. "We just need to get this one inside the hospital."

"I don't need a gurney," Abilene protested with what he thought was feeling, but he was just short of slurring his words. "You're doing just fine propping me up like this, Good."

She slanted a look at him. "Don't tempt me to drop you." Dammit, didn't he realize how serious this could get?

Just then, Abilene gazed down into her face, his eyes on hers. Something inside her warmed and sent out pulses through her whole body. She couldn't begin to describe the feeling it generated—or maybe she could, but thought it best not to.

"You wouldn't do that," he told her in response to her threat.

He wasn't baiting her, daring her or even teasing her. He was telling her what he knew to be true. That even though their partnership was still in its infancy, he absolutely *knew* beyond a shadow of a doubt that she had his back and that he could count on her not to let him down no matter what.

Kendra chose not to respond, not because she felt he was putting undue pressure on her with his assumption but because she struggled with the implications of his statement. It took the partnership out of the realm of the temporary, which she considered nice and safe, and tossed it into the dependable and permanent, which, given her track record with permanent, scared her.

She preferred looking to the future in terms of day by day, not with any sort of a permanent plan. It was far safer that way.

"Just shut up and try to keep upright until they come back with a gurney for you," Kendra instructed him testily.

"Yes, ma'am," he murmured.

She could feel him growing more lax, could feel his limbs growing heavier. She wasn't sure how much longer she was going to be able to sustain him in his present vertical position.

"C'mon, Abilene, stop playing around," she ordered, doing her best to sound really annoyed.

She knew he wasn't playing around, that he was doing what he could not to collapse against her completely. But berating him might get Abilene to rally faster than merely tossing encouraging words at him. The man responded to a challenge, she thought.

The nurse, followed by two orderlies and an E.R. doctor, returned just in the nick of time. The moment they did, Kendra felt Abilene go completely limp. Another second and they would have both been on the ground with her finally succumbing to Abilene's lax body and sinking under his weight.

"We'll take it from here," the physician told her as he and an orderly each took one side of Abilene to ease him onto the gurney.

"But we were doing so well," Abilene protested dryly.

"Shut up, Abilene," she ordered.

She heard him suck in a lungful of air before being able to make any sort of a response. "Yes, ma'am."

Stopping before an empty trauma room, the doctor turned to her as the orderly and a nurse pushed the gurney and her wounded partner into the room.

"Do you have a number where we can reach you?" he asked her.

"Lean out of the room and shout," she told him. "I'm not going anywhere."

"He's not in any immediate danger," the doctor assured her, apparently thinking that might be why she wanted to stay.

"I'm not going anywhere," she repeated.

"Don't argue with her," Abilene advised the E.R. doctor weakly just before the door closed. "You'll never win."

"Jerk," she muttered under her breath as she stood outside the room, hating the fact that she was left out in the corridor to pace and wonder and worry—almost against her will—until someone came out to talk with her.

Because she didn't want to dwell on what was happening behind closed doors, Kendra took the opportunity to make a few calls. She called her lieutenant and filled him in on everything that had happened, including the fact that they had a drug dealer in custody at the local hospital. *And* that Abilene was being stitched up.

"Does the dealer look good for the murder?" the lieutenant asked.

"Well, he *says* he was in San Francisco at the time and took some cash from an ATM at approximately the time of the murder. I need to get a look at the footage from the ATM camera to confirm his alibi."

"I'll turn you over to Wong," the lieutenant told her. "He can check it out for you. Let me know how Abilene's doing," Lt. Holmes tacked on just before he terminated the phone call.

"Most likely I'll find him flirting with a nurse once they've got him all stitched back together," she prophesied.

But she was talking to dead air. With a sigh, she closed her cell and put it away.

She went back to waiting.

Impatiently.

But when it was over, she didn't find Abilene flirting with the nurse in attendance, even though she was rather cute. Kendra couldn't help wondering if they'd stitched up his libido as well.

The E.R. physician had paused to give her a quick update on Abilene's condition when he was finished with the minor surgery. Abilene's wound had turned out to be just a flesh wound. The reason he had lost more than the usual amount of blood was because he'd been popping aspirin to help ease the pain of an old knee injury. The aspirin, in turn, had rendered clotting generally elusive, thus contributing to the inordinate amount of blood flow and his weakened state.

Given the go-ahead, when Kendra walked in on her partner, Abilene was already sitting up on the gurney, struggling to put his shirt back on over the rather bulky bandage.

"Doctor said it was 'much ado about nothing,'" she told him dryly as she walked into the small recovery area where they had placed her partner after his surgery.

His back to the entrance, Abilene twisted around slightly to look at her. "Here, give me a hand with this, will you?" he requested. "My arm's a little sore from being used as a pin cushion."

"Your arm shouldn't be 'a little sore,'" she informed him, picking up his casual shirt and easing one of the sleeves over his arm and shoulder. "It should be in a sling."

His expression told her what he thought of that suggestion. "The bullet just nicked me." He said it as if it was an everyday occurrence.

"Tell that to all the blood you lost." And then her agitation and exasperation got the better of her. "Don't you know better than to pop aspirins like they were candy?"

He paused to smile at her. "That's what I have you for. To be my nagging Jimmy Cricket."

"Jiminy," she corrected. "I think you might mean Jiminy."

He'd never been up on all those kids' movies. Beyond the fact that Snow White knew seven dwarfs, the extent of his knowledge was rather limited.

"Whatever." He waved away the correction. Leaning forward, he felt Kendra slide on the other sleeve. *Houston, we have liftoff.* "I could have just slapped a couple of butterfly Band-Aids from my medicine cabinet on it and been okay."

"The doctor told me that you had to be given a pint

of plasma as well. Got that in your medicine cabinet, too?" she queried innocently as she flagged down a nurse who, it turned out, had Abilene's discharge papers ready for him to sign.

The man signed the papers in just under the speed of light. He was more than ready to go. The plasma must have given him a boost of energy because he was feeling more like his old self. And that old self was definitely reacting to the volatile little firecracker giving him all this lip. The woman aroused him.

"You always like to have the last word, don't you, Good?" he asked mildly as they stepped out into the E.R. parking lot.

She made him stay where he was—the car was only a short distance away and she brought it back to the entrance to pick him up.

"When I'm right—which I usually am," she said, picking up the thread of the conversation again as if there had been no long pause between sentences, "then, yes, I like having the last word."

Abilene deliberately eschewed her offer of help—it was a matter of male pride—and lowered himself into the passenger seat as smoothly as he could.

"I'm honored to be driving around with a saint," he told her evenly.

Having rounded the hood and gotten in on the driver's side, she glared at him as she buckled her seat belt again. The car hummed to life. "Now, I didn't say I was that, did I?"

Their eyes met for a very long, electricity-filled second and he murmured, "Oh, God, I hope not." Because saints didn't do the kind of things that just being around this woman seemed to keep conjuring up in his mind.

Kendra slowly released a breath, wishing she could steady her pulse as easily. Why she felt suddenly enveloped in a blast of heat she had no idea, especially since not a single other factor around her had changed even minutely.

Talk, idiot, before he thinks you've been struck dumb. "Do you want me to take you home?"

The smile on his lips unfolded slowly. Sexily. "Is that a proposition, Good?"

She didn't bother trying to get him to stop calling her that. Apparently, it was a useless exercise.

"No," Kendra replied as evenly as she could, "that's a question related to your so-called flesh wound. After losing all that blood, I thought you might want to go home and rest instead of going back to the precinct and all that paperwork."

Well, maybe he wasn't chomping at the bit to get to the paperwork, but the rest of it sounded pretty good to him. This case had become almost personal for him. Maybe because it was his first in Homicide, but he was determined to solve it, to close it. And that meant being there, not going home and lying down. He needed to prove himself to her, to show that he had something to contribute to this partnership, other than just being a human shield.

"Nope. I'm definitely good to go," he told her solemnly. His eyes never left hers as his mouth curved teasingly. "And I'm pretty much ready to work, too," he added.

Why did she feel as if he was propositioning her?

And why in heaven's name did she want to take him up on it? What was wrong with her? Was it just a matter of her not having been with a man for over eighteen months? The last time had been just before Jason had been so badly burned. After he'd killed himself, her heart had just slipped into solitary confinement and she'd withdrawn from everyone but her family.

These days, she still didn't mix work with her personal life beyond grabbing an occasional drink at the local hangout with some of the people she worked with.

So why the change now?

Maybe because your last partner looked like an aged lawn gnome and this one could raise the body temperature of a dead woman.

Snapping out of it, she slid the key into the ignition.

"Okay, Wong is checking out 'John Smith's' story about using that ATM in San Francisco at the time of Summer's murder. Let's get back to the office and you can write up your notes."

"Notes?" he echoed.

Had he taken notes? And where was his notepad, anyway? His brain still felt a little fuzzy and unfocused. The only thing that seemed to be coming in loud and clear was his reaction to Kendra. Ever since his body had pressed hers to the ground, he'd detected a low-grade hum running through it.

Celebrating.

"Yes, notes. You're right-handed, right?" Kendra glanced at his hand resting on his knee.

"Right, but I think it's experiencing sympathy pains for my left arm," he told her solemnly. To "prove" it he held up his hand and pretended to try to flex his fingers. Under his watchful eye, they moved stiffly, like sticks bowing one by one. "See?"

"I see, all right. I see a fraud. Now, you can't have it both ways. You can't go back to work and then milk everyone for sympathy and not do anything," she pointed out.

Because it amused him, he played the game a few minutes longer. "Wow, they didn't tell me you were this hard-hearted."

She doubted if anyone even had any sort of opinion about her. "You just didn't ask the right questions," she countered flippantly.

"Apparently not," he agreed. His voice was lofty again and seemed to be regaining some of its former volume, along with a little wry humor.

"Seriously," she told him, her expression reflecting how she felt about his almost getting killed protecting her. It was what partners were supposed to do, watch one another's backs, but had he been killed, she would have had a great deal of trouble coming to terms with that. "I don't want you doing that kind of thing again, all right?"

"Okay," he responded glibly. "Next time I see someone pointing a gun at you, I'll just let them go ahead and do what comes naturally." He looked at her pointedly. "Happy?"

"Happy" would have come with another partner. One who didn't constantly keep stirring her up this way, Kendra thought.

"You know what I mean," she bit off.

"Sadly, most of the time, no," he confessed with a sigh. Shifting in his seat, he looked forward. His body started to ache something fierce. Whatever effects the local anesthetic had had on him began to vanish, leaving behind a light residue of pain and exhaustion.

"It's been a long day, Good, and it's not nearly over yet. Tell you what, just let me close my eyes for a minute and you just drive us to the precinct." Matt glanced at her to see if she had any objections. "Is that okay with you?"

She didn't answer. Instead, she pointed out what he'd neglected to do. "You forgot to buckle up."

"It's a little awkward, reaching for the seat belt from this angle," he confessed.

"You're a detective. You're supposed to set a good example."

"For who? You march to your own drummer anyway. As far as I see, you're the only other person in this car, Good."

With a sigh, she leaned over him and grabbed hold of his seat belt, then pulled it across his body and slid the metal tongue into the groove. Though she tried to avoid it, that involved getting very close to him and all but brushing against his torso. Granted, it was not nearly as close as he had gotten earlier, pressed against hers, but it was still something that didn't exactly go unnoticed by either one of them.

"Thanks," he murmured when she was finished.

"You're welcome," she answered, doing her best to sound casual even as a warm blush crept up her cheeks. Backing out of the spot, she put the car in gear and drove.

And pretended she didn't hear him laughing softly to himself.

Chapter 9

At first, Matt thought it was his imagination. But it only took the short ride from Sabrina Abilene's apartment to his own to convince him that something was off with his mother. He needed to find out what before his partner showed up to take them to the former chief's house.

"Everything all right, Mom?" he asked as he studied her.

Over the years, he'd become pretty much of an expert when it came to reading her. Sometimes he got more out of observing her than talking to her.

Sabrina raised and lowered her shoulders in a vague, dismissive way, trying to tough it out for a second. Failing, she blurted out, "Are you sure I won't embarrass you?"

Since when was his mother this insecure? That last guy had really done a number on her by walking out,

Matt thought. Maybe it was lucky for him that the bastard had vanished the way he had, because if he had the man in his sights right now, he might not be responsible for his actions.

"Why?" he asked, feigning amusement. "What are you planning on doing?"

Sabrina gazed down at her freshly polished pink nails, acting unusually flustered. "Nothing," she declared breathlessly. "But, well, these are people you work with, right? People whose opinions you probably value?"

"Right. These are down-to-earth people," he emphasized. "Not born-with-a-silver-spoon-in-their-mouths, critical-of-everyone-who-breathes Southampton people." He paused for a moment, ignoring the doorbell that had just begun to ring. "You're a survivor, Mom." He gave her hand a squeeze. "You could never embarrass me."

But his mother apparently remembered it differently. "How about the time you came home early from school and walked in on me and—"

He was *not* about to go there. It had taken him a while, all those years ago, to purge from his brain the compromising sight of his mother and her then "boyfriend" in bed.

"Okay," he allowed, "maybe that one time. But I've never been embarrassed by you, the person." He gave her forehead a quick kiss. "Ready?"

Sabrina took a deep breath and smoothed down the skirt of her yellow-and-white sundress, even though it was lying perfectly flat.

Swallowing, she nodded. "Ready."

Ushering her gently over to the door, Matt opened it. Kendra was standing in his doorway, her hair pulled back in two short, sassy pigtails. She was wearing a white peasant blouse that ran out of material just shy of the top of the waistband of her frayed, faded denim cutoff shorts.

Matt certainly hadn't been prepared for this. He all but did a double take at the expanse of tempting, creamy skin.

"You look like a teenager, Good," he told her. "A *young* teenager."

She cocked her head. "I don't know if you just complimented me or put me down." Ignoring any further exchange with her partner, Kendra put her hand out to the slender, petite strawberry-blonde woman standing next to him. "Hi, I'm Kendra, Abil—Matt's partner," she introduced herself, smiling warmly.

"I'm Sabrina Abilene," the woman said, flashing Abilene's smile at her. They had the same slightly tilted curve of the lip on one side, Kendra noted. "Did my son just call you 'Good'?" the woman asked her, slightly confused.

"That he did," Kendra answered, then realized that, from a mother's point of view, that "name" might be misconstrued. "It's a long story."

Sabrina smiled brightly. "I'd love to hear it sometime."

Backed into that one, Kendra thought. "If there's a lull at the barbecue," she promised, then glanced at her watch. "In the meantime, I think we'd better get going."

Abilene waited for his mother to cross the threshold,

then following, he turned to lock the door behind him. "You didn't tell me we'd be punching a time clock."

"We don't," Kendra answered. "But if you want to park somewhere relatively close to the house, it pays to show up early. Depending on how many people are coming today, any latecomer might have to walk about half a mile or more to get to the house."

Sabrina looked from her son to his partner, waiting for some punch line.

"You're kidding, right?" she asked as she got into the passenger seat in Kendra's car.

Kendra glanced at her partner. "Have you warned your mother how big the family is?" Not waiting for a response, she continued. "And that doesn't begin to touch on any friends who might have been invited." Her focus was back on his mother as Kendra pulled her vehicle away from the curb. "I know this word tends to get overused, but the chief's parties are *legendary*. The food is fantastic, and the people—" she smiled at the woman "—well, they have a way of making you feel glad you're alive."

"Is it that way for you?" Abilene asked from the backseat.

Kendra fully expected to see a smirk or a cocky half smile on Abilene's lips, but when she spared him a glance over her shoulder, he actually seemed serious. As if he'd just asked something he wanted answered, not eventually, but now.

"Sometimes," she allowed cautiously, again addressing her words to his mother. For some reason she couldn't explain, saying that to him would have felt way too personal. "Anyway, I think you'll have a great time, Mrs. Abilene."

"Oh, call me Sabrina," the woman told her with feeling, then tagged on an emphatic "please."

Kendra didn't ordinarily feel comfortable calling someone's mother by her first name, but this woman seemed exceedingly youthful. She made a guess that Sabrina Abilene had to have been awfully young when her son was born.

"All right," she said to his mother, "if you insist."

"I do," Sabrina told her with a soft little smile. She seemed to relax a little for the first time since before her son had come to pick her up.

"Your mother's very nice," Kendra said, tossing the words over her shoulder to the man sitting directly behind her. "What happened to you?"

"The 'nice' gene made a U-turn and doubled back when it realized it was going into my body," Abilene quipped without hesitation.

"That's not true," Sabrina protested. "You're a very good son."

But Kendra nodded as if Abilene had just recited chapter and verse of what she'd already suspected.

"That would go a long way toward explaining things," she murmured under her breath, even as she smiled broadly at the passenger to her right and said, "I'm sure he is, Sabrina."

"Come in, come in!" Andrew Cavanaugh greeted them warmly less than a beat after Kendra rang the doorbell. Because they were guests, the former chief of police and acting patriarch of the family first shook

Sabrina's hand and then her son's. "Good to see you again," he told Abilene.

Turning toward Sean's daughter, Andrew embraced Kendra. Her immediate reaction was to stiffen. The next moment, she forced herself to relax. She wasn't entirely successful.

"Better," Andrew said, laughing as he released her. "We'll get you into this hugging thing yet. It's an acquired taste." There was a twinkle in his eye as he said it.

Even back during his hectic days as chief of the Aurora police department, Andrew Cavanaugh was nothing if not a devoted family man first, a servant of the people second. Nothing and no one was ever more important to him than family. He was a firm believer in "the more, the better." Kendra's slight resistance to being absorbed by the family was nothing new to him.

He was accustomed to reluctance. It had taken patience to bring around some of his late brother's children. Until a couple of years ago, he hadn't even known of the triplets' existence and they—Ethan, Kyle and Greer—had believed themselves to be the children of a dead war hero, not the illegitimate offspring of a policeman shot in the line of duty. And there'd been the four stepchildren—Zack, Taylor, Riley and Frank—that his younger brother Brian had brought into the family fold when he'd married his former partner, Lila McIntyre.

But all that paled in comparison to the eight new members they had uncovered when the hospital mixup had come to light.

They were all trying to work out the emotional logistics. But, for the most part, Andrew felt that it was coming along rather nicely, all things considered. Sean Cavanaugh had already been embraced as the long-lost brother. Even their father, Seamus, had left his idyllic life in Florida, pronouncing it "boring," and had returned to Aurora to meet the son he'd never known. The reunion had gone so well, that the once-vibrant police officer who'd fathered them all made up his mind that he would stay.

Their numbers were growing by leaps and bounds and Andrew, for one, couldn't be happier about it.

"Why don't you grab something to drink—or eat—and introduce Sabrina around?" Andrew suggested to his niece.

Kendra glanced into the living room and the family room beyond. She was still trying to get everyone's names straight herself.

"I didn't bring my player's handbook," Kendra confessed wryly.

Andrew didn't see that as a deterrent. "No shame in asking. Sometimes I forget a name, too," he confided with a wink.

"Must be your advanced old age," Seamus said to his son as he came up behind him. He clamped a hand down on Andrew's shoulder.

Andrew laughed as he half turned to look at his father. "Careful, old man, or I'll hide your teeth," he warned.

"These are all mine," Seamus assured Kendra and her partner and especially Sabrina as he pulled at a couple to show how solidly embedded they were. "You must have me confused with yourself." And then he bowed gallantly, although not as low as he once could have, before Sabrina. "Tell you what, why don't I do the honors for this pretty lady?" he suggested. Straightening, he gallantly offered Sabrina his elbow. "Let's go dazzle the natives, shall we?"

"He's some character," Abilene commented to Kendra as he watched his mother be whisked off by the oldest of the Cavanaughs.

"You'll get no argument from me on that score," Andrew agreed.

Matt hadn't thought that the chief could hear him. He didn't want the man to think he was being flippant about his father. "I'm sorry, sir, I didn't mean—"

Andrew waved the apology away. "Sure you did. And you're right. Dad *is* a character. And a handful." He watched as his father seemed to disappear into the crowd with his newfound charge. "Brian and I still haven't figured out how to handle him."

"You don't 'handle' a man like that," Sean told his newly discovered older brother as he joined the small circle, finding a place beside Kendra. He brushed a kiss against his daughter's cheek by way of a greeting, never missing a beat of the conversation. "You just get out of his way before he mows you down. It's what you do with a force of nature."

Approaching from the family room, Brian Cavanaugh laughed as he overheard Sean's assessment of their father. "You're a fast learner," he commented with approval. "But then, you *are* a Cavanaugh." He patted Sean on the back.

"No self-esteem issues in this crowd," Lila Cavanaugh laughed as she slid in beside her husband. She smiled at Matt. "Hi, you must be Kendra's partner, Matt Abilene."

"I must be," he agreed affably, shaking the woman's hand. He'd been here perhaps a couple of times before, invited by a friend of a friend of one of the Cavanaughs. Once had been for a Christmas party. The family was even warmer than he remembered. "And you're—"

"Hungry," Lila confided, looking at Andrew. "Isn't it almost about time that you fired up the grill, Chief?" she asked.

"Just waiting for someone to suggest it, Lila," Andrew told her. For Matt's benefit, he nodded his head toward the still very pretty blonde and said, "And she's Lila, who's much too good for Brian but she sticks by him anyway. She used to be his partner, you know. Back in the day. I figured she was way too good for him even then." Before Brian could utter a comeback, Andrew took charge of both his brothers. "C'mon, you two, you can help."

"I can't cook," Sean protested, falling into place beside Brian and behind Andrew.

"Okay, but you can lug, can't you?" Andrew asked as they went out.

"Lug?" Kendra asked uncertainly, looking to Lila for a possible explanation.

"He's probably referring to the propane tank for the grill," Lila guessed.

"That he is. Andrew likes to make people feel useful," Rose, the former chief's wife, told the two newcomers as she drifted by them with a tray filled with tiny smoked-cheddar cheese stuffed mushrooms. "Have a couple," she offered, holding the tray lower so that

Kendra and Matt could make their choices. "Hopefully it'll tide you over as you find your way around this maze," she told them. "There's always a lot of smoke when Andrew barbecues. I think he does it on purpose. It's almost like watching a magic act. Just follow your nose and you can't go wrong."

"Well, they certainly are a friendly bunch," Kendra commented just before she took a bite out of the stuffed mushroom she'd selected.

Matt regarded her for a long moment. She was a complicated piece of work. In his partner's place, he would have welcomed being part of this forceful family.

"You don't sound as if you know whether that's a good thing or not."

"I do know that it's pretty overwhelming," she freely confessed.

By now she should have gotten somewhat used to it, he thought.

Looking around, he could see his mother in the center of a small cluster of people. Even at this distance, he could see how wide her smile was. She was enjoying herself. He felt a sense of relief.

"My mother seems to have taken to it like a duck to water," he observed. And then he surprised Kendra by shifting gears. "Why's your guard up?"

She had a choice of denying his observation, ignoring it or telling him the truth. Caught off guard, she went with the truth.

"I find it hard to get close."

"Because they won't let you in?" Even as he asked, he knew that couldn't be it. The Cavanaughs were family-oriented to a fault—and for them, "family" included the men and women of the department as well.

"Because *I* won't let me in," she told him simply.

She'd told him this much, so Matt decided to dig a little further. "Why? You don't strike me as the naturally shy type."

Finished eating, she balled up the napkin in her hand. "No, just supercautious."

"Why?" he asked again. "Have you been burned?"

The choice of words was enough to startle her. She covered it quickly, but he'd seen the sudden wariness, the quick intake of breath, the single second of pain in her eyes to know that somehow, without meaning to, he'd managed to strike a nerve.

"Want to talk about it?" he asked quietly.

There was no way she wanted to talk about it, especially not with someone she would have to see day in, day out, at least until this case was solved. After that, maybe one of them could get a transfer.

"No."

He knew when to push, and when to back away. "Okay. I can respect that. Me, I don't get close because I've watched my mother do it for most of my life and all she ever managed to get for it was kicked in the teeth."

To him, it was a simple object lesson. You put yourself out there, as his mother did, you were asking to have your heart tossed into a shredder. He figured that relationships, if they had a prayer of working, developed slowly, over time. They didn't burst upon you like fireworks on the Fourth of July.

She felt as if she was looking at him for the first time. He'd suddenly become more than simply two-dimensional. "So you've made up your mind that it wasn't going to happen to you."

Shrugging, he looked away, pretending as if something else had caught his attention—rather than her. "Something like that."

"How's that going for you?" she asked, curious. Tom hadn't had much to tell her about Abilene. Maybe she could find out from the horse's mouth.

"For the most part, okay." He looked back at her. Nope, no doubt about it. He was attracted to her. More than just a little. And seeing her like this, with so much skin to peruse, just brought this fact home to him that much faster. "But there's this one woman who's really driving me crazy. It's like she's gotten under my skin. You know," he continued in a lower voice, "like an itch I just can't scratch."

Had it suddenly gotten warmer in here? Had to be the press of all these bodies milling around, using up the oxygen, she told herself. "What'll happen if you do scratch it?"

And hadn't he been asking himself that same question since he'd first laid eyes on her? "Most likely it'll be like nothing I've ever experienced before—and quite possibly mark the end of civilization as we know it."

"Then maybe you shouldn't scratch that itch," she told him. Because, tempting though it seemed right at this moment, they *were* partners and things could get very awkward if they did give in to the moment. "If it means saving the world, and all."

"Maybe," he conceded loftily. Then he went on to admit, "But I have been thinking about scratching an awful lot lately."

That was the exact moment that she felt her lips go dry. Which made talking more difficult. She had to all but push out the words.

"Keep me posted on that." She tried clearing her throat and even the sound seemed to get stuck.

"Don't worry," Abilene promised her quietly, "you'll be the first to know." Without thinking, he put his hand lightly against her back, meaning to guide her into the living room.

Kendra fought hard not to shiver in response to the single stroke she could have sworn she felt against the small of her back.

Served her right for not wearing enough clothing, she silently chided herself. But then, she had a feeling that she would have felt that—whatever *that* was—even if dressed in a heavy suit of armor.

The next moment, another group of Cavanaughs— this particular one composed of twenty to twenty-eight-year olds—converged and surrounded her partner and her. Within less than a heartbeat, it felt as if they were assimilated into the group's collective.

Like the classic science fiction line, resistance was futile. She'd discovered that the last couple of times she'd been invited to one of Andrew's "unofficial" parties. Not only that, she always seemed to leave the party a couple of pounds heavier and with a slightly shifted perspective on at least one if not more things.

Since this was a more structured party, she had a feeling she had even less of a chance of remaining on the outside, looking in.

And the thing of it was, she was surprised to realize, that she had less and less of a desire to *be* that outsider.

Chapter 10

Close to ten hours into the party and the crowd had only thinned out slightly.

Some of the younger Cavanaughs with very small children had said their good-nights and then gone home. But a lot of the others with sleepy children had availed themselves of portable cribs or one of the beds that had been left standing in rooms that Andrew's five adult children had long since vacated.

This way, tired grandchildren and grand-nephews-and-nieces had somewhere to lie down and, most likely, recharge their batteries. It was an exceedingly family-friendly house, Brian had told her during one of her first visits, and always had been.

Right now, she found it difficult to move around without tripping over some member of the family, or, in some cases, a member-to-be.

And everyone, apparently, seemed to be in excellent spirits. There were no arguments, no nasty flares of temper over some sensitive subject. As a general rule, everyone within the Cavanaugh domain seemed to get along.

She supposed, if she had to be part of a larger family than the one she'd been born into, this one wasn't all that bad.

And she'd never seen her father looking happier. It was as if he'd finally found that "missing piece" of himself he'd once told her about. That missing piece that made him feel so restless sometimes. Maybe somehow subconsciously, he'd felt he wasn't where he was supposed to be when he was growing up in the Cavelli household.

Not that he had cut that family off when his real identity had come to light. That wasn't her father's way and it wasn't theirs, either. She and her siblings still touched base with the aunts, uncles and cousins they'd known all their lives.

Their family had just expanded, her father had told her more than once.

But watching him tonight, Kendra knew that this was where her father felt he belonged. And that was good enough for her. She made up her mind then and there to change her name to Cavanaugh.

Permanently.

"Do you think that maybe we should get going?" Abilene suggested, coming up behind her. The barbecue had been over for quite a while now. Everyone was stuffed to the gills and while it wasn't late, it had been a very long day. He looked at her, waiting for her reaction. "What do you think?"

Kendra was surprised that he'd left the decision up to her. Maybe the man wasn't such a knuckle-dragging Neanderthal after all. And she could see that he did genuinely care about his mother. She'd already given him points for that.

"I think maybe you're right," she agreed. Then, scanning the immediate area, she asked, "Where's your mother?"

Abilene realized that he'd gotten so caught up with both Kendra and the Cavanaughs, he'd lost track of his mother.

"I don't know," he admitted, looking around. He thought for a minute. "I haven't seen her since just after we sat down to eat."

"Which time?" Kendra asked.

There had been wave after endless wave of food. If she continued attending these little impromptu feeding fests, she would either have to have all her clothes let out or her mouth sewn up.

He was still scanning the area for his mother. Her particular color of strawberry-blond hair tended to stand out. So far, though, he hadn't seen her. "The first time," he told Kendra.

"Well, don't worry, your mother has to be around here somewhere. Nobody could have possibly made off with her in a house full of cops," she assured him.

It took a little while, weaving their way through the various clusters of family members and gently extricating themselves from conversations that threatened to draw them in, but they finally found Sabrina. She was in the backyard, several yards past the patio. She was sitting on the porch swing, rocking.

And Matt immediately saw that his mother wasn't alone.

"My father seems to be bending your mother's ear," Kendra observed as they came closer to the couple.

"She doesn't look like she seems to mind," Matt noted.

Sean and Sabrina appeared completely oblivious to their approach. Despite the swirling din of noise coming from the house and other parts of the yard, the two single parents might as well have been alone.

From where they stood, Kendra thought, Abilene's mother gave the impression of hanging on her father's every word and he, in turn, looked as if he was trying very hard to entertain her.

Was this the start of something? Or just an evening's interlude? She knew which side she was rooting for. Her father had been very vocal about getting her "back on the playing field," but deliberately deflected any of her comments about the fact that he had *not* done the same after her mother died. He merely shrugged and said that once was enough for him.

Maybe that had changed, she thought, watching as Sabrina threw her head back and laughed at something her father had said.

"Think they might need a chaperone?" Matt asked her. She couldn't quite tell if he was kidding.

Kendra smiled. "This might be the best thing for both of them," she commented with growing enthusiasm. "My dad's certainly not going to make off with any of your mother's money or things, and she might just remind him that he's more than simply an active part of the police department and a father."

When Abilene looked at her quizzically, she elaborated. "When my mother died, a side of him seemed to just vanish. But obviously, it just went into hiding," she said with a satisfied smile. "It's nice to see him embrace that part of himself again—even for a little while."

She missed hearing her father whistle. He always used to whistle when her mother was alive. When she died, he just stopped, as if he didn't have anything that happy, that carefree to whistle about any more. And the light had gone out of his eyes.

"I hate to break this up, Mom," Matt said as they reached the couple, "but Good here wants to get going."

Sean looked up at his daughter. "'Good'?" he questioned, more amused than confused.

She instantly thought of the way her father might have interpreted the nickname. Horrified—this wasn't the kind of thing adult children shared with their parents even if they *were* very close—she was quick to offer up a denial.

"Oh, no, it's not what you think—"

Sean stopped her before she could get wound up, holding his hands up in front of him as if to block the onslaught of words. "I'm not thinking a thing," he told her innocently. "And don't worry, Matt, I can take your mother home." He flashed a smile at his companion on the swing who appeared contented enough to begin purring. "Most likely it's on my way."

"Actually, it's not—" Kendra began, then stopped abruptly. She didn't want to throw cold water on whatever it was that her father was planning. "—Unless you take the scenic route," she amended. She looked at her new partner. "Okay, Abilene, I guess it's just you and me in the car. Just like every other day," she added with a deliberately weary sigh.

Apparently, Abilene couldn't help himself. His eyes skimmed along her torso and Kendra could have *sworn* she felt his gaze touching her bare skin. Touching her in places that definitely increased the heat level.

"I don't know about that," Abilene commented. "I don't remember you *ever* coming into work dressed— or undressed—like that." Appreciation resonated in his voice.

"It's a barbecue," she told him. "Not a spring formal."

"Definitely nothing formal about what you're wearing," he agreed. Turning back to his mother, he grinned. "See, I told you that you'd have a good time. Next time, you'll know not to doubt me." Leaning down, he gave her a quick kiss to the cheek. "Don't stay out too late."

Sabrina shook her head. "Last time I looked, I was the parent, you were the child."

"Look harder," Matt advised, the grin on his lips widening. Turning away, he began to walk toward the house with Kendra. "Your father going to be all right?"

That was *not* the question she thought he would ask. "Your mother's not exactly a femme fatale out to bilk him of his life savings," she pointed out.

"No, but she does tend to respond to kindness rather quickly." He laughed under his breath. "She might have them going steady before the morning light."

Kendra found the old-fashioned term almost sweet. This man definitely had layers to him. "It's nice of you to be concerned, but my dad could really use a little ex- citement in his life that doesn't involve piecing together dead bodies or reconstructing homemade bombs. I think it's kind of nice, really," she told him.

Entering the house through the sliding-glass door, she looked around for the chief. Family or no family, she wouldn't feel right about leaving without thanking him first.

"What do you think is kind of nice?" Matt prodded when she just left the sentence hanging there.

"Flirting at their age. Or whatever the current term is for what they were doing." She shrugged, feeling a little self-conscious. "I'm a little out of practice these days."

"Right." There was no missing the sarcastic tone surrounding the single word. It all but vibrated and was a total match with the smirk on his lips.

"I am," she protested.

Finding Andrew, Kendra wove her way over to that side of the living room. The former police chief and all-around amazing chef was sitting back on an overly large sofa, his wife nestled beside him, and both were engaged in a conversation with half a dozen other members of their family.

"A hottie like you?" Abilene mocked in a low voice only she could hear.

"—who's consumed with her work," Kendra tagged on.

They both thanked their host and then withdrew, promising to be at the next gathering which, according to what Andrew called after them, would be there "before you know it."

"Only if you want to be," Abilene said, picking up the thread of their conversation the second they turned away from Andrew and the others. "Why do you want to be consumed by your work to that extent?"

The night air was cool in comparison to the way it had been earlier that day. The lack of humidity at this hour made it feel rather pleasant. It was a good night for a walk, Kendra thought. But, because they had arrived fairly early, the car was parked not too far down the street.

Kendra walked quickly, as if to distance herself from his question.

As if that was possible.

Abilene was waiting for an answer. She didn't have to look at him to know that he was.

She tried to go on the attack. "Aren't you getting a little too personal here?" she countered.

"Personal is if I asked you what you weighed or what you had under those short-shorts besides an incredible pair of legs." His eyes seemed to be gleaming as he allowed himself to envision her wearing even less. "*This* is taking an active interest in my partner's psychological profile."

She laughed shortly. "Oh, is that what it is?"

"Yes," he answered, as somber as if he was stating his case before a judge. "If somewhere down the line, something suddenly makes you snap, I need to know if I should be prepared for that burnout mode—or not."

She didn't take offense at his scenario. He was just trying to rattle her cage—and that was rarely done these days.

"You could always change partners," Kendra said.

He inclined his head, as if to acknowledge changing as a possibility—if he wanted it to be.

"Let's say I don't want to," he told her.

Releasing the locks on the car, she opened the car door on her side.

Well, that was a surprise. She'd just assumed that he wanted to be away from her as much as she told herself she wanted to be away from him. Who knew?

"You're not going to drop this, are you?" she asked him.

Abilene got in on his side and watched her for a long moment before answering. "What do you think?"

She blew out a breath. "I think I should have told you I was dating someone exclusively."

He shook his head. "I already know you're not."

About to turn the ignition, her eyes opened wide. "You asked around about me?" There were few things she hated as much as someone prying into her background. That she had tried to do the very same thing with Abilene was beside the point.

He saw the quick flash of temper and did what he could to head it off and set her straight. "No, but if you were 'dating someone exclusively,' he would have been here and the *two* of you would have been by to pick my mother and me up."

She snapped her fingers as if that was a stunning revelation. Actually, it *was* a pretty clever deduction on his part—especially considering that she'd expected not all that much from him.

"By George, you *are* a real detective, aren't you?" she cracked.

He took the comment, as he took everything else, in stride. "Told you I was." He waited a beat as she began to drive down the street, then continued with his mission to unravel his partner. "So?" he prodded.

She sat up a little straighter, bracing her shoulders as if the words she was about to say wouldn't relax her. When she spoke, it was in a slow, hoarse whisper, as if her voice would break at any moment.

"My fiancé killed himself on the day we were supposed to get married." She couldn't bring herself to refer to it as their wedding day, but it would have happened had Jason not been trapped in that awful fire.

"What?" He needed details and did his best to try to coax them out of her. "Wouldn't it have been easier just to cancel the wedding? Just as quick and a lot less messy?"

She wasn't saying anything. *Maybe his comment had been too flip.* He debated retreating and decided that this would always be out there until she told him the whole story. They had to deal with it and then sweep it away. Curiosity didn't motivate him. He wanted to help. For the first time since he'd met her, she wasn't the feisty little powerhouse, plowing over him. She was a woman who had been badly wounded.

"There's more to it," he told her simply. "What aren't you telling me?"

Her eyes were stinging badly. She didn't know how much longer she could keep the tears at bay. She didn't want to cry in front of this man, and yet, there was nowhere to go inside her.

"What I'm not saying is that Jason was a great guy. We'd dated all through high school and all he ever wanted to be was a fireman," she said, remembering the young man he had been. The one who had captured her heart so completely.

"So he became one." And with that, she thought, his fate had been sealed. "He went at his job each and every day like the hero that he was." She pressed her lips together, searching for strength to continue, to finish the story. "On what turned out to be his last day on the job, four of his buddies were trapped on the third floor of a crumbling apartment building. Jason had just come out with this old man he'd rescued. He didn't even stop to catch his breath, he just went charging back into the building."

She stopped for a moment, afraid her voice would crack. Abilene waited, instinctively knowing that his silence was all she could handle right now.

"The floor beneath them collapsed. His friends died, burned almost beyond recognition. The other firemen managed to save Jason, but he had burns over 85 percent of his body." Remembering those awful days, waiting for him to wake up, she had to take a shaky breath. Tears began to slide down her cheeks but she pushed on. "Eventually, he lost a leg. I kept trying to tell him that he was lucky to be alive, but he'd look at me with those dead eyes and tell me that he didn't feel so lucky.

"Every day he slipped away a little more. There was no way I could reach him, no matter what I said or how hard I tried." That was what hurt even more than seeing him like that. That she couldn't help the man she loved. "I just couldn't get through to him.

"He had God knows how many skin grafting operations—they had to scrape away all his burned skin and replace it. In between, the hospital tried to get him to work with a team of physical therapists. He tried in the beginning, but then he'd just tell them to leave him alone. That he was useless.

"I was there every morning, every evening. The moment I was off duty, I went to the hospital to be with him, to offer my support. But it didn't do any good." The tears were coming faster now. She wiped them away with the back of her hand. "He just lost his will to live. And then, on the day we'd set to get married, someone—and we never found out who—managed to bring him a gun despite all the security measures in place at the hospital."

Kendra was talking in short bursts now, as if she couldn't draw enough air into her lungs to speak in long sentences.

"And he put that gun to his temple—and he pulled the trigger. And then he didn't have to be that broken man in the hospital bed anymore. He found his peace— and all the rest of us—his family, his friends, me—we were left in hell."

She was crying now, almost uncontrollably, hating herself for allowing this breakdown in front of a witness.

"Pull over," Abilene ordered.

They were still a couple of miles from his apartment complex. Maybe she hadn't heard him correctly. She felt shell-shocked. "What?"

"Pull over," he repeated in a firmer voice.

When she did, pulling up the hand brake and turning off the engine, he leaned over and put his arms around her. Kendra struggled for a second, not wanting his pity, but he remained firm, holding her despite the awkward angle.

And then whatever was left of her strength broke down completely and she just cried. Cried so hard that her entire body shook.

He said nothing, letting her cry it out as he continued to hold her.

Chapter 11

Kendra cried for several minutes, cried, despite struggling hard not to, as if her heart had just broken into tiny little pointy pieces inside her chest.

And then she stopped.

Abruptly.

Finally pulling herself together, Kendra blew out a long sigh that shuddered through her body. Lifting her head from her partner's shoulder, Kendra used the heel of her palm to wipe away some of the damp streaks along the length of her cheeks—she couldn't begin to erase all of them.

She was torn between lashing out at him because he'd been a witness to this breakdown, had drawn it out by his kindness, and apologizing for letting her emotions get the better of her around him.

Pressing her lips together, Kendra looked at Matt's

shoulder again. There was almost an oblong-shaped wet mark on the light blue material.

Her tears.

"Sorry," she murmured, then cleared her throat, attempting to negate the raspiness that came out when she tried to speak. "I didn't mean to get your shirt soggy like that."

A soggy shoulder was so far down on the list of his concerns, it didn't even begin to register. He laughed shortly.

"It'll dry," Matt told her, dismissing the unnecessary apology with a shrug. "Want me to drive?" he offered, thinking that, after crying so hard, perhaps she was exhausted and didn't feel up to driving.

To her, the question had pretty much come out of the blue. Her ability to navigate a vehicle had nothing to do with the temporary breakdown of emotions she'd just suffered.

"Why would I want you to drive?" Kendra asked. "I didn't short-circuit my wiring by crying. Just give me a second."

She paused, taking in a deep breath, as if that somehow helped her to center herself. To put this break from her customary closemouthed approach behind her and forget about it.

And she's back, he couldn't help thinking after her flippant comment. *Shields up and all.*

Although Matt liked Kendra's bravado, he had to admit that the vulnerable woman he'd just glimpsed did appeal to the protector in him. He supposed that was because he had never quite gotten over his Eagle Scout training as a boy. Damsels in distress—any kind of distress—had always been a weakness of his.

"Take all the time you want," he urged. "The evening's not going anywhere."

She meant to say something flippant about his comment. Instead, what came out went back to her emotion-fueled moments where she'd bared her soul to him. She really should have held it together instead of falling apart like that, she silently chided.

What was she thinking?

"I'm sorry."

"For what?" he asked. "For being human? I kind of already suspected that you might be, except that I didn't have any proof."

She wiped away another stray tear. "And now you do." It was part question, part assumption.

Matt inclined his head magnanimously. "And now I do," he agreed.

"It shouldn't have happened. My breaking down like that," she said, trying very hard to distance herself from the event by viewing the whole thing in a clinical light. Was this going to make working together harder, now that he knew about her pain? "That's why I never talk about Jason and what happened."

"Not with anyone?" he asked, surprised. Even without the Cavanaughs, she had a pretty big family and from what he'd seen and heard, they were a tight, close-knit bunch. They had to have known what happened to her fiancé.

In answer to his question, Kendra shook her head. Taking another long, deep breath, she turned the key in the ignition, then put her hands on the steering wheel and started to drive again.

"No," she finally said.

Okay, he was no psych major, but anyone with an

ounce of common sense could see what was coming down the road in that sort of a situation.

"You know, keeping that kind of thing bottled up inside you can make a person just explode at the worst possible time," he told Kendra.

The wording struck her as funny, though she suppressed the laugh. But not the laughter in her eyes. "There's a good time to explode?"

Abilene inclined his head in agreement. Poor choice of words, he told himself. "Point taken."

He didn't strike her as the type to spread rumors. But the truth, well, he just might be willing to pass that along if he perceived it as an amusing true anecdote. She didn't want to take that chance. Would asking him to keep silent about what had just happened make him refrain from talking about it—or just encourage him to tell anyone who would listen?

Like everything else, she decided, it was a gamble.

"Look, what I just told you," Kendra began haltingly, "I'd rather you didn't talk about it with anyone."

Matt snapped his fingers, as if he'd just lost out on something big. "Well, I guess there goes my blog post for today."

He said it so matter-of-factly, for a split second Kendra actually thought he was being serious. Slanting a look at her partner, she asked cautiously, "You're kidding, right?"

"I am definitely going to have to work on my delivery," he murmured, as if to himself, then said, "Yes, I was kidding. I don't have this driving need to share every little thing I hear with the immediate world. Let the world entertain itself some other way," he told her, hoping to put her mind at ease.

Or as at-ease as someone as wired as Kendra Cavelli/ Cavanaugh could be, he amended.

They had reached his apartment complex and within another minute or so, Kendra brought her car to a stop in a guest parking space that was only a few feet away from the door of his ground-floor apartment.

Instead of saying good-night and getting out, Abilene turned toward her and said, "I appreciate your inviting my mother to the party. I think she really enjoyed herself. It was just what she needed to feel better about herself."

He meant every word. Why did he suddenly feel so awkward saying this? And why the hell did he feel like some gangly teenager who didn't know where to put his hands? What was it about this woman that kept rubbing away his guard?

And then, having absolutely no intention of extending any sort of an invitation, Matt still heard himself saying, "Would you like to come inside for a minute?" as he nodded toward the apartment door behind him. "I don't have anything fancy to drink," he warned. "But I do have a couple of beers with a foreign-sounding label slapped on the bottle."

Kendra laughed. Was that meant to impress her? Or did he think she was some sort of a snob? God, nothing could be further from the truth.

"I don't need anything 'fancy,'" she assured him. "And I drink beer, even without foreign-sounding names written on the label."

"So that's a yes?" he asked, his hand on the handle of the passenger door, waiting.

After purging her soul, she didn't want to be alone, at least, not right now. Talking about it to her partner had unearthed just too many memories, memories she didn't know if she could handle in her present frame of mind. So, accepting the lifeline he'd just tossed her, she shrugged in response to his question.

After all, she had to keep in character. Otherwise he might suspect just how very vulnerable she actually was.

"Sure, why not?"

"Can't remember when I've had a more eager acceptance," he said wryly, getting out. He came around quickly to the driver's side and opened the door for Kendra before she could do it herself.

Ignoring the hand he offered, Kendra swung her legs around and got out. "I'll just bet," she answered with a short laugh.

He looked at her for a moment. "Meaning?"

"Just that your reputation precedes you."

"I don't have a reputation," he informed her mildly. "Unless you're referring to the one about my caseload." It was her turn to look confused, so he elaborated. "I led my division in the number of cases I closed," he said.

"And in the number of short-term relationships you amassed," Kendra interjected. That was what she'd initially been referring to when she'd mentioned his reputation.

"All amicably ended," he was quick to point out. "No promises of a rose garden or happily-ever-afters. Just a good time to be had by all. And then we went our separate ways."

"Your mother's influence?" she guessed. It didn't take much to put two and two together.

"Maybe," he allowed as he unlocked his front door

and let her walk in ahead of him. "Or maybe I'm just not built for a long-term relationship."

"Maybe," she echoed. Some people weren't. She now thought that she belonged in that group as well. "If you never make a promise, you can't break it." *And then your heart doesn't get scarred.*

"Exactly," he agreed, closing the door.

They were standing inside his apartment now, with only the single low light that he always left on illuminating the immediate area and holding the darkness at bay.

Was that what made her appear particularly appealing to him? That illumination whispering of things not seen?

But then, he'd found himself attracted to her off and on—mainly on—since they'd first been paired together. The pull had only grown stronger, and right now, he was having a really hard time resisting it. A larger and larger part of him didn't even want to continue resisting. If there was fallout because of it, he'd deal with that later.

"So," he said in a low, deliberate voice, "I guess we both know where we're coming from."

"I guess we do," she agreed, never taking her eyes off his.

Suddenly, this was not just a philosophical exchange about the nature of relationships and how to avoid disappointment. There was an underlying current pulsing between them and she would bet anything that he was as aware of it as she was.

"Want that beer now?" he asked, nodding toward the darkened kitchen on his left and the refrigerator that was there.

Suddenly mesmerized, Matt couldn't seem to draw

his eyes away from her lips, watching them move as she answered, "Not particularly."

"Then what would you like?" he asked, every syllable undulating seductively along her bare throat and shoulders.

Kendra didn't answer. At least, she didn't say anything out loud.

But he could have sworn that somehow between them, the word *guess* vibrated, sending off shock waves. Tempting him to take her.

He gave up the pretense of resisting.

Like a man walking on a beach for the first time after a particularly cold, desolate winter, Matt tested the incoming waters slowly.

Taking her face in his hands, he framed it gently, then, almost in slow motion, he lowered his mouth to hers. Their lips touched lightly, then pressed.

Then kissed.

The kiss deepened and grew, taking them both to a high, sharp edge neither one of them had even been sure existed.

And then he kissed her again.

And again.

Until they lost count and lost their sensibilities as well. What began in slow motion suddenly grew and multiplied in speed and urgency.

As pulses and heart rates sped up, so did the tempo of their needs. Hands flew, caressing here, tugging there, learning, absorbing, reveling.

Bringing unbridled pleasure with every stroke, every touch.

She'd purged herself of all her tears and found that she needed to somehow fill the emptiness that had been left behind within her, the emptiness that had been haunting her these last eighteen months.

Needed, ever so desperately, to feel *alive* again.

She needed to *feel* like a woman, to be *regarded* as a woman.

And his hands, as they passed over her body worshipfully, made her want things she thought she'd never want again.

The more he kissed her, the more he touched her, the more she wanted him to. On some logical plane, Kendra knew she should be backing away, calling a halt to this before it went too far. Before she couldn't control what was happening inside her.

Abilene was her partner, a man she would be working with for at least a while and this might create some awkwardness between them.

But she didn't care.

Didn't care because what she was feeling right now was absolutely *wonderful,* like attending her own rebirth, with heat, stars, sunshine and explosions of happiness all rolled up into one, lighting her up like a Roman candle.

It had taken less than two minutes to undress her.

Kendra pulled away his shirt, tugged at his belt, desperately wanting him to be as naked as she was, as vulnerable as she was.

Now.

It took longer to undress him than it had her, but that was because her fingers seemed to be fumbling. And he had more on to begin with.

When his belt became stuck, she yanked at it in frustration and heard Matt laugh softly. Her eyes darted up to his face, but the amusement in his eyes wasn't at her expense. Instead, it seemed to give her a sense of sharing. Like they were laughing at something *together*.

"I'll do it," he told her, stilling her hands.

And then, just like that, there were no more barriers in the way. Just like that, she found herself on the sofa, expecting the next moment to bring with it fulfillment—and an ending.

She was only half-right. There was fulfillment as he pleasured her in ways that took her breath away, even as they brought a shower of stars swirling about in her mind's eye, but there was no ending.

Instead, the climax she experienced dovetailed into another wild, skyrocketing ride, leaving her to hang on for dear life.

To her unsuspecting delight, she quickly discovered that droll words were not the only things that could roll off Abilene's tongue. He could all but make it do tricks.

She felt it, and his lips, passing along her skin, drawing in closer and closer to its target and then suddenly, as he thrust into her extremely sensitive core, there was an avalanche of stars and sensations shooting all through her.

Kendra caught herself digging her fingernails into the cushions, arching up into him as she tried to absorb every nuance, every wondrous feeling that this man was capable of creating within her.

Breathing hard, she pulled his face up to hers. Drawing as much air into her lungs as she could, Kendra pressed her lips to his, determined to at least partially affect him. Trying to make him feel as helplessly exhausted and crazy as he had just made her.

With her hands, her lips and her tongue, mimicking his style, she managed to bring Matt figuratively to his knees.

A long breath shuddered through his aching body.

Matt stared at her in wonder. She was one hell of a fast learner. He didn't know how much longer he could hold himself in check, not when his entire body begged him to let go, to enjoy the wild sensation that had so swiftly built up within him, demanding to be released.

But Matt wanted to be certain that he had taken her up as far as she was capable of going, wanted to be sure that she bordered on exhaustion and had no resolve left.

He couldn't put it into words that made sense, even to himself, but he felt a kinship with this woman to whom life had been so subtly cruel. Felt a kinship and at the same time felt a need to somehow make it all up to her, even though none of it was his fault.

Who knew—maybe his early nomadic life with his mother had somehow fried his circuits so that he was incapable of thinking clearly.

He didn't know.

All he knew was that once he and Kendra had begun making love, he became determined that this was the experience she would remember no matter how many years she lived.

Because God knew he was going to remember it even with his dying breath.

That was the surprise of it. Wanting to pleasure her, he'd uncovered a world of pleasure himself. So much so that part of him wanted it to continue and stretch out as long as humanly possible.

But he knew his limitations, his boundaries. He had reached the end of his tether and it was time for the final volley.

Shifting his body over hers, Matt drew her into his arms, kissing her over and over again and then he began the final phase.

A new wave of passion washed over him as he entered her.

One was made out of two.

And then, with swift, sure movements, the upward ascent began, growing quicker and quicker in tempo. As they clung to each other, both scrambled to the highest point on the peak before them.

Eighteen months of celibacy exploded within Kendra the moment she and Matt reached that much-desired plateau together.

Euphoria embraced her as hard as Abilene did, holding her tightly in its grasp as her heart hammered wildly.

She was panting as if she'd just sprinted the last mile of a twenty-six-mile marathon.

Kendra clutched on to the moment—and the man—knowing in her heart that both would be gone from her life all too soon.

But they were here now, in the moment, and that was all that mattered to her.

Tomorrow was still an eternity away.

Chapter 12

"You know what this means, don't you?"

Abilene's question broke the silence that had been hanging between them these last few minutes as euphoria receded and the world came back into focus.

Kendra slanted a wary glance at him. Instinctively, she braced herself, although exactly for what she was unable to say.

She could feel her body tensing anyway.

"What?" she asked, her voice toneless. If he was going to say something flippant, she was determined to be blasé.

"Well, the way I see it," Matt began slowly, struggling to keep the grin out of his voice. It was a short battle and he lost. "We're going to have to change your name from *Good* to *Fantastic.*" He shifted so that he was able to face her now. "Or maybe some word that's even better than that. What's better than *fantastic?*" he asked her.

"Your ability to spout absolute nonsense," she told him, shaking her head.

She was doing her best to look irritated, but there was no denying that inwardly, she was grinning fit to kill. Matt was teasing her, but also telling her that he had enjoyed their interlude just as much as she had.

"I beg to differ," he contradicted. "You were not on the receiving end of you." He grinned as he wound a long, blond strand of her hair around his finger, absently noting how soft and silky it felt. Just the way she did. "I was."

Kendra could never really handle genuine compliments of any sort for more than a second—and this was a whole new level of compliment—without blushing or feeling awkward. Or both.

"Kendra," she blurted out. "My name is Kendra. You can call me Kendra, or, on a good day—and if I let you—you can call me Kenny. Or you can call me Cavanaugh if you want to keep it strictly business."

"Only when we have our clothes on," he told her, teasingly referring to the "strictly business" comment she'd just made. And then he replayed her words in his head. "Wait. What? Back up a minute. You said I could call you *Cavanaugh?*"

She sighed. Now where was he going with this? "That's right."

Curious, Matt propped himself up on his elbow and looked down into her face. "When did you make up your mind about that?"

She supposed she owed him an explanation—and

if she withheld it, he'd poke and prod at her until she told him. Might as well get it over with now and spare them both.

"When I saw how happy my father was today. He looked as if he'd finally found his niche." Her father was very dear to her and it was nice seeing him like that. God knew he deserved all the happiness he could find after struggling to be both mother and father to all seven of them.

"And he hadn't before?" Matt asked, curious. As he spoke, he slowly drew his fingertips along the inviting curve of her hip, skin against skin. Seemingly oblivious to the effect he was having on her.

But she knew better.

"Not entirely," Kendra admitted. She was trying to appear aloof, but it was difficult to concentrate on what she was saying. Her body began to vibrate in anticipation again.

"The Cavellis are all good, decent people, but I always had the impression that Dad felt kind of out of sync around them." She tried to give him an example. "You know, like when you have a pair of shoes that don't quite fit, even though they're the right size— Will you please stop that?" she finally said, unable to pretend that she was unaffected any longer. "I can't think straight when you do that."

"And do you want to?" He shifted again, this time his body provocatively touching hers. "Think straight?" he asked innocently—but there was definite mischief in his eyes.

"Yes, of course I want to think straight— Oh, the hell with it," she cried, giving up.

And with that, she wound her arms around his neck and kissed him, surrendering any and all pretense of indifference to the magic that this man conjured up whenever he so much as touched her.

"My sentiments exactly," he echoed with a laugh. The next second, Matt lost himself within her.

The body wash she'd used that morning still managed to linger along her skin and it was filling his head, effectively adding to the heat swirling through his veins.

Although she would have never suspected it, making love the second time with Matt was even better than the first time. The stakes had become even higher, the need to pleasure, to excite, even greater.

There was nothing "business as usual" about this second trek through the fiery regions of Matthew Abilene's lovemaking.

He surprised her in a hundred different ways.

She was surprised by her own wild desire, by the ever-shifting newness of his techniques and by her own unbridled responses to what he was doing to her.

And she was equally surprised by her almost fierce desire to bring this man with the fabulous lips and tongue up just as high, making him just as mind-numbingly delirious as she was.

And the most frightening part of this second encounter with Matt was that it only made her want more. Made her want to do this heated, frenzied meeting of bodies and spirits again and again to the exclusion of absolutely everything else.

This lovemaking came before eating, sleeping, *breathing*.

Before everything.

She wanted this passion, this insatiable desire to continue forever, without end. Logic, something she'd always bowed to, dictated otherwise. But she had no use for logic—not tonight. Not here, not now.

But eventually, despite their youth and their stamina, sheer exhaustion caught up to them both. It had already made away with their ability to think or make any sort of decisions.

They fell asleep in each other's arms. Kendra had absolutely no memory of when.

The gleeful noises of raised voices followed by the sound of water being splashed penetrated Kendra's subconscious a number of times, going deeper each time.

It finally roused her and she had no choice but to reluctantly wake up and open her eyes.

Kendra's first bewildered thought was that she had no idea where she was.

But then the weight of the very masculine, very muscular arm lying across her chest caused her memory to return.

Abilene.

She'd slept with Abilene.

Over and over again.

Each thought, coming on the heels of the last, alarmed her more and more.

Oh, God, what had she done in a moment of absolute weakness and insanity? Was she completely out of her mind?

Not that it hadn't been wondrous. Even looking back, in a growing state of panic, she still had to admit to that. The man had a fabulous technique—she had to give him his due.

An extraordinary technique learned and perfected, no doubt over a period of time, on heaven only knew how many willing young women who had passed through the man's life and through his bedroom sheets. Sheets that they'd moved to at some point during the night and that were now wrapped around her.

But what was going to become of their working relationship now that they'd been this intimate? Was he going to expect to "grab a little loving" as Jason used to call it, whenever the spirit moved him?

When they were going over a crime scene and were left on their own, would he suddenly have an itch he wanted scratched?

She would have to set Abilene straight about that right up front. Otherwise, this just wasn't going to work.

Okay, that was the plan, she told herself. The minute he woke up, they were going to talk.

"So who won?"

Startled, she almost yelped. Instead, she pressed her lips together, shifted and saw that Abilene was looking at her.

Grinning.

The big dumb lug was awake. For how long? Had he been staring at her the whole time? Why hadn't she known that?

Her brain felt like a briar patch, all tangled up and thorny.

And what the hell was he talking about, anyway? "What?" she asked, confused.

"Who won?" he repeated. "You had this look on

your face like you were conducting some sort of an argument in your head. I was just wondering which side won, that's all."

When had she become this transparent, and to him of all people?

"Nobody 'won,'" she retorted.

What did he think, that she heard voices?

Well, don't you? Sometimes? Just calm down, she schooled herself.

Taking a breath, Kendra was just about to tell her partner about the ground rules she felt needed reinforcing, but she never got the chance. He interrupted her again.

"Oh, good, then you're not renouncing or denouncing anything that went on last night," Abilene concluded, pleased.

That made her stop for a moment.

"Does that happen often for you?" she asked. What kind of a woman made love with him and then turned around to revile him about it? Maybe he was so lighthearted in his relationships because he was afraid that something might set her off.

Stop defending the man. Sometimes a wolf is just a wolf, not an enchanted prince, she reminded herself sternly.

"Nope." It didn't happen at all, because the women he picked all knew the rules ahead of time. "But then, I have to admit, you're not like the rest."

Right, I'm "special." And if I believe that, you have a bridge you want to sell me—retail.

"Nice platitude," she quipped out loud. "Is that supposed to make me breathe a sigh of relief and then, out of gratitude, issue you carte blanche so you can feel free to do anything you want with me once we're outside of work?"

He knew if he laughed, she was liable to haul off and hit him. Getting annoyed at her sarcastic tone would probably get him the same reaction.

So he held the laugh in check and tried honesty.

"No, that's supposed to let you know that I think you're unique right down to your toes." He could see that she was tensing, as if she expected some kind of a confrontation on some level. "Easy, Cavanaugh, I wasn't planning on another go-round, at least, not without an invitation." Although, God knew, just looking at her had him ready and able. "Now, since this is my place, what would you like for breakfast?"

"My clothes."

Matt never missed a beat. "Boiled, scrambled, sunny-side up?" he asked as if she were talking about eggs and hadn't just requested the shorts and shirt that had heated him up so much in the first place. "By the way, you're welcome to stay just as you are for as long as you'd like."

In response, she slid off the bed, tugging the sheet around her as she went. Somehow, she managed to do it regally, looking like a displaced Greek goddess in search of a private section of heaven for herself. As far as he was concerned—at least for this morning— heaven was right here, held captive in Kendra's eyes.

She still hadn't said anything about what she wanted to eat. And she definitely wasn't taking him up on his suggestion that she remain just as she was.

"Okay, be that way," he said good-naturedly. "Since

you made no requests, I'm making a Denver omelet," he informed her.

Instead of putting on any of the clothes that had been haphazardly discarded on the rug, Matt stood up, incredibly oblivious to his naked state, and walked over to the small bureau. Opening a drawer, he took out a pair of washed-out denim shorts that were badly frayed along both cuffs and pulled them on.

Kendra chastised herself for not being able to tear her eyes away. He really was a magnificent specimen of manhood.

"Don't you want to put on underwear first?" she heard herself asking.

He shrugged dismissively. "I'm just throwing something on to make breakfast. I'll get more formal after my shower," he promised.

Breakfast. Abilene'd been serious about his offer, then. Now *that* was surprising. "You really cook?" she asked.

"Haven't killed anyone yet," he told her matter-of-factly.

Which brought her back to the amount of traffic this apartment had to have seen in the last few years. That should keep her grounded, she thought. She was just one of many.

"So it's a package deal?" Kendra asked him flippantly. "You serve up a hot night and then a hot meal in the morning?"

"You make it sound like a bed-and-breakfast pamphlet," he said, amused. "And to answer your question, no, it's not a package deal. At least, not usually," he amended because, after all, wasn't that what he was doing right now? "Let's just say that you bring out the best in me."

She didn't understand. "But you just said you've never managed to kill anyone with your cooking—if you weren't talking about women who've spent the night with you, who were you talking about?" she asked. It was obvious that she didn't believe him and was just curious to see how Abilene intended to wiggle out of this.

"My mother," he told her simply. By the way she was staring at him, he knew she hadn't been expecting that for an answer. But it was true. "When I was growing up—and there wasn't some guy she'd opened up her heart to lying in bed next to her—she'd hold down sometimes two, three part-time jobs, trying to make ends meet for the two of us. That left her pretty tired. So on Sundays, I'd get up early, sneak into the kitchen and make her breakfast with whatever I could find in the refrigerator."

For a second, Matt had left her almost speechless. But she rallied quickly enough.

"My God, you sound like some kid in one of those after-school specials that they used to love to air on the Family Channel," she told him, getting somewhat accustomed to the plaintive puppy-dog eyes he had turned her way.

"Too tame?" Matt asked, amused, as he began to walk out of the bedroom and into the small kitchen.

Kendra trailed after him, still wearing the sheet around her like a flowing toga. She moved more slowly than she liked, careful not to trip over the excess material. That would have been all she needed, to fall flat on her face in front of him. With her luck, the sheet would somehow unravel, leaving her far more exposed than she would have liked.

Kendra paused to awkwardly pick up her discarded shorts, top and the undergarments that went with them. Clutching them against her, she followed Matt the rest of the way into the kitchen.

She was having trouble reconciling what he'd just told her with the image she had of him. "That helpful little wide-eyed boy doesn't really jibe with what I know about you."

He opened up a cabinet and took out a heavy iron skillet, placing it on a burner adjacent to another, smaller pan. Watching him, she decided that maybe the man actually did know his way around a kitchen.

"You mean with what you *think* you know about me," he corrected.

Oh, now he was going to tell her that he was a closet saint? "What? What I saw in public is just your secret identity and this is the real you? You're a master chef who perfected his skills making Sunday brunch for his mother?"

"It was breakfast, not brunch," he corrected. "And I didn't claim to be a master—at least not at cooking," he said, looking at her over his shoulder. The sexy grin on his lips went straight to her gut as if it was mounted on an arrow that he'd just shot. "People are complex, Cavanaugh." Opening the refrigerator, he began to take out what he needed. Unlike when he'd been a boy, this refrigerator was well stocked and had a lot for him to choose from. "You ought to know that."

The last remark had her radar going up. Was that

a crack? About what, exactly? "What's that supposed to mean?"

Did she want to pick a fight? he wondered. Why? Because she'd enjoyed herself too much and was now waiting for him to disappoint her somehow, the way her fiancé had? Or was she just plain ornery?

He had a feeling it wasn't the latter.

"That you're not the only one with several layers," he answered simply. "Why don't you take a shower while I make breakfast?" he suggested, his voice mild, completely nonconfrontational. And then he grinned wickedly as he added, "Unless you want to wait until I'm finished out here and then we can take a shower together."

"Worried about conserving water?" she asked. California had its share of droughts off and on and they were never completely out of the woods.

But to her dismay, rather than take the bait, Matt wound up disarming her again with another sensual grin.

"Conserving energy was the very *last* thing on my mind when I suggested showering together."

Meaning she would have found out what it was like to make love in a shower stall while her body was being pelted by water.

Why did that sound hopelessly erotic to her? It was just water, for heaven's sake. What was it about this man that just a simple suggestion from him could cause her breath to literally back up in her lungs like that?

Hell, he could achieve the same result with just a look, a phrase with a double meaning.

After all, it wasn't as if she was some untried, vestal

virgin. Granted, she hadn't made love in a year and a half, but whatever pent-up energy, emotions and combustible feelings she'd been harboring all these months had all emerged, exploding out and making their presence—and exodus—known in a glorious shower of fulfillment.

So how could she be thinking about going to bed with this man all over again as if last night had never taken place?

Or was that because last night *had* taken place and she was desperate to re-create it?

She just didn't know.

But Matt did.

She had a gut feeling that Abilene knew exactly what was going on in her head. He *had* to. There was no other reason why he was looking at her so knowingly right now.

"Bathroom's right back there," he told her, pointing toward the bedroom again. "You'll find fresh towels in the linen closet on your way there. Breakfast will be ready soon. Don't take too long," he warned. "Or I'll be forced to come looking for you."

"Wouldn't want that," she quipped.

He merely smiled. "That remains to be seen," he said under his breath.

But she heard him.

Kendra hurried away, giving herself a mental count of ten minutes to shower, dress and be back in the kitchen. Eleven, tops. Otherwise, she had absolutely no doubt that Abilene would make good on his promise to come looking for her.

The trick, she thought as she stepped into the light

beige tiled shower, was not to allow herself to dawdle because that would mean that she *wanted* him to come into the shower with her.

And if that happened, she knew damn well that neither one of them would have any interest in the hot meal he'd have left waiting on the stove.

Chapter 13

Forcing herself to hurry through her shower, Kendra was just about to turn off the water when she became aware of the noise.

Knocking?

No, more like pounding. Impatient pounding. The noise sounded like a woodpecker trying to penetrate a petrified tree.

Abilene.

But why was he pounding? Was this some Jekyll/Hyde thing? What did she really know about this partner of hers, anyway?

Thinking that any second the man who had made the very earth move last night would just barge in, she grabbed a towel and wrapped it around herself.

"Hey!" she heard Abilene call through the door. "We finally got lucky!"

Lucky? Was he actually saying what she *thought*

he was saying? Denigrating the whole interlude from last night by describing it with the crass term of *getting lucky?*

She felt a hot flash of anger.

"'Lucky'?" she echoed, securing the towel around herself as best she could. "How can you say that?" she demanded.

"Well, what the hell would you call it?" he asked, mystified by her reaction. He'd thought she'd be happy. "Wong just called, said we got a hit on Burnett's ATM card."

The last part of his sentence dribbled from his lips in slow motion because she'd pulled open the door, her eyes flashing, obviously ready to confront him and give him a piece of her mind. Why, he didn't know. What she gave him instead was an eyeful.

Never mind that he'd already seen every inch of her unclothed. This was somehow even sexier. The towel was barely large enough to cover the essentials. Had she been a woman with a longer torso, she would have had to make a judgment call as to which part of her she wanted to protect more from being exposed to appreciative eyes.

Coming to, Matt held up a piece of paper with the information he'd just hastily jotted down while on the phone with the other detective.

"I've got a location, but it's Sunday. Nobody's going to be at the bank to help us." And then he grinned at Kendra. "God, you smell better than what I'm cooking."

"I'm not sure if that's a compliment or not," she retorted. Though she could have gotten sidetracked more easily than she was happy about, Kendra forced herself to focus on the paper in Abilene's hand. "We can get the name of the bank manager, have him come down to the bank and let us watch the footage on the surveillance camera," she said. He'd been staring at her with a strange expression on his face the entire time. Impatient curiosity finally got the better of her. "What?"

"Why did you get so mad when I knocked on the door just now?"

"First of all, you didn't knock, you pounded. And second, to answer your question, it was because I thought—I thought—" If she admitted to her mistake, he'd think that *she* thought there was something more to last night than just casual sex. Kendra decided that it was a subject better left untouched. "Well, never mind what I thought—"

The moment she stopped talking about it, the answer suddenly dawned on Matt. His grin was back, broader than before, if that was possible. "Oh, you thought I meant the other kind of lucky."

"We don't have time for this," she informed him primly. "This is the first lead we've had on our suspect since we found that woman's body. We need to follow it up. And I need to get dressed."

She could all but feel his eyes raking up and down along her body. If there was more time…

But there wasn't and she had to remember that. She was a police detective *and* a Cavanaugh now. That meant she had a great deal to live up to. That didn't involve grabbing a little morning delight before going after a murder suspect.

"You might get more cooperation if you don't," he told her.

Kendra frowned, waiting for him to leave before she discarded the towel and started getting dressed. "I'll chance it."

Matt nodded toward the kitchen. "I'd better go turn off the stove."

She could feel her stomach begin to growl. The prospect of a long morning loomed before them. "Wrap the breakfast up to go," she called after him. "Shame to see it go to waste."

Matt looked back at her over his shoulder, his eyes taking one final tour over her wet, barely covered body. "My sentiments exactly," he confessed with a sigh he didn't bother to suppress.

She forced herself to cross to the door and then shut it, leaving Abilene on the other side of it. Otherwise, with only a towel acting as a barrier, she wasn't sure just how long she would be able to resist her very sexy partner and his bedroom eyes. Especially when she knew exactly what the man was capable of doing to her.

C'mon, Kenny. Focus, focus, focus, she ordered herself, moving as quickly as she could.

"You come here from a picnic?" Detective Alexander Wong asked her when she first walked into the squad room just ahead of Abilene.

For a couple of minutes back there, she'd thought about making a quick run home to change into something a little less skimpy, but she didn't want to waste the time. She was too eager to see if this lead did *lead* somewhere. And, since she was fairly certain that the squad room would be mostly empty, she thought she could get away, just this once, with wearing something that made the usual casual clothes seem formal in comparison.

"Long story," she told Wong with a dismissive wave of her hand. She shot Abilene a warning look in case he had any ideas about picking up the narrative for the other detective's sake.

For now, Abilene was humoring her.

"Hey, I've got time. Fill me in," Wong all but begged.

"Some other time, Wong," she told him, "when this case is behind us."

Along with about fifty years or so, she added silently.

She wouldn't dare admit to *anyone* that she'd spent the night in Abilene's apartment. Not that she was ashamed of what had happened last night—she was, after all, an adult—but neither did she want it broadcast on the morning news. What she did and who she did it with after hours was her business and she intended to keep it that way.

"Spoilsport," Wong complained, all but pouting. It still didn't prevent him from sending long glances her way.

"Yup, that's me," she admitted cheerfully. "Now that we have that out of the way, where are we on getting the bank manager to come down?"

"Still trying to track him down," Abilene told her, chiming in. Getting the name and contact number for the bank manager had been his assignment the second they had set foot in the squad room. He held up the telephone handset that he'd been on. "All the calls keep going to his voice mail."

There could be more than a dozen reasons for that. But right now, Kendra zeroed in on only one. The reason she *didn't* like and hoped wasn't true. "Think he could be dead, too?"

"Could be," Matt allowed, hitting the Redial button on the keypad again. "But let's not get ahead of ourselves," he cautioned.

"That would have been a good rule to go by last night, too," she murmured under her breath as she sank down in her chair to check out something on her monitor.

"Guess we've got a basic difference of opinion on that," Abilene told her.

She flushed, then quickly struggled to get herself under control. She hadn't thought he'd hear her, what with the air-conditioning unit struggling to come on and making rumbling noises.

Clearing her throat, she became all business. "Do we know where Mr. Bank Manager lives?" she asked. In response, Matt held up a piece of paper with the man's home address on it. Leaning over her desk, she took possession of it. "Okay, let's go."

Abilene looked at her as she rose behind her desk. "Go?"

"Yes, 'go,'" she repeated. As lead on the case, she didn't owe him any explanations, but because he was looking at her, waiting, she said, "I'm feeling antsy and this is our only lead. Let's see if Mr. Bank Manager is home and just not answering his cell phone. He might think he deserves some time off because it's Sunday."

"Poor delusional fool," Abilene quipped, seeing the look in Kendra's eyes. He quickly rose and followed her out. The bank manager had no idea what he was in for, Abilene thought with a grin.

* * *

This time, they did make a quick stop at her apartment. If she was going to be questioning a bank manager, she needed to have on something a little less casual than a pair of frayed shorts and a blouse that only came halfway down to her midriff.

Leaving her partner in the kitchen, she dashed into her bedroom to change. She opted for a black sleeveless pullover and a pair of jeans that had taken on her shape even when she wasn't in them. The transformation took her exactly five minutes, counting entry and exit.

"Let's go," she declared as she sailed by him and out the door.

Matt took a long look at her as they hurried back to his car. "I dunno. Maybe the manager'd be more inclined to talk to you if you stayed dressed the way you were," he speculated.

Getting in the car, she secured her seat belt. "If it's all the same to you, I didn't want him thinking I was going to trade a lap dance for a confession," she told him as he got in on his side.

"You know how to give a lap dance?" he asked, intrigued. The car rumbled to life and they quickly pulled out of the development.

"Eyes on the road, Abilene—" She struggled not to let on that the gleam in his eye secretly pleased her. "And as for your question, giving a lap dance can't be all that hard."

"Well, then, you'll have to show me sometime," he told her.

She laughed shortly. "In your dreams, Abilene." Kendra couldn't help thinking that her words would have held a great deal more weight if they hadn't just spent the night together.

Matt spared her a lingering, appreciative glance. "There, too."

"The road, the road, watch the road," she ordered. If the grin on his face was any wider, she couldn't help thinking, it would have probably split his face right in half.

Kendra turned out to be right. The bank manager, a Howard Hanna, had turned his cell phone off because it was Sunday and he was trying to spend some uninterrupted quality time with his family.

Politely apologizing for separating him from that same family, Kendra explained that it was an emergency. The person they were looking for had most likely killed his girlfriend. And, as luck would have it, he'd used his ATM card to access his savings account at Hanna's location. They needed to see last night's tapes from the surveillance camera.

The bank manager seemed hesitant. "Can I see your IDs again?"

Kendra and Matt both took out their wallets and let him examine each in turn.

"Satisfied?" Kendra asked.

"Well, you know those can be faked," Hanna said, still not looking completely convinced.

"You're welcome to call the chief of detectives with our shield numbers," Kendra told him.

"He doesn't like to be disturbed on a Sunday," Abilene told him matter-of-factly. "But he'll talk to you and back up our story."

Hanna appeared torn for a moment, then shrugged. "No need to disturb him. I guess you're on the level. I'll take you to the bank," he agreed.

He accompanied them on the short run to the bank, but he was still uneasy about surrendering the surveillance tapes.

"I'm usually supposed to clear this with the corporate offices," he explained. "Technically, the video feed belongs to them, not me."

"Well, you can call them," Abilene agreed. "But remember, by the time your request goes through all the proper channels, Mr. Hanna, our suspect could very well kill another woman—or just disappear. And that would be on you," he added seriously, wielding guilt like a sharp scalpel.

"We really do need your help," Kendra told the manager, trying to appeal to his sense of decency.

They were playing good cop/bad cop, Abilene mused. And watching Kendra, he had a feeling the woman was appealing to the man's other senses as well. He'd already noted the way the manager kept looking at her—like a hungry stray mutt wanting to steal a bone from beneath another dog's nose.

Not that he blamed him, Abilene thought.

Hanna's dark eyes seemed to dart back and forth as he thought things over. It was a short battle.

"All right, wouldn't want him killing someone else because I couldn't get you a release fast enough through channels," the manager told them—mainly Kendra.

They arrived in front of the bank branch where Burnett had used his card. Hanna took out an impressive set of keys and selected a key from among them to open the outer door, then quickly fed the security code into the keypad, disarming the alarm.

The inside of the bank was eerily quiet and the dormant air was stifling. No doubt eager to have the whole thing behind him, Hanna hurried over to the small room where the ATM video feed was recorded and stored.

The room could barely accommodate the three of them, especially since the manager was more than a little overweight.

"Now, when did you say this was?" Hanna asked.

Matt glanced down at the notes he'd made right after Wong had called this morning. "Early this morning. According to the hit that came up, Burnett withdrew two hundred dollars from his savings account."

Hanna fast-forwarded through the videotape from the first half of that day. "Just two people used their ATM cards this morning," he said. He stopped the tape, rewound it and started it again so that they could see for themselves that he hadn't missed anything. "One of our senior citizens took out eighty dollars from her savings account," he narrated as he played the image for them on a small flat screen. "And a teenager wearing his cap backwards like some would-be punk was the only other customer to use the ATM." He turned from the monitor. "He took out the two hundred dollars you were talking about. Is he your killer?"

"No," Kendra cried, frustrated. She knew what Burnett looked like. There'd been a couple of framed photographs of the man with his now-dead girlfriend in the apartment. Under no lighting and under no circumstances was the man in the photographs the teenager on the tape.

"Are you sure those were the only two people at the ATM this morning?" Kendra pressed.

"I can play it again for you," Hanna offered. "But I've already gone through it twice, so unless your guy's invisible—"

Matt could feel Kendra's frustration mounting, not to mention his own. He pointed to the screen image of the teenager. "Can you get a close-up of the name on the account he's accessing?" It wasn't a request, but a politely worded order.

"Sure." Since this *was* his home turf, the manager seemed confident. He centered on the desired documentation, then enlarged it several times over, each time doubling it in size. "But you just told me that this isn't—"

"'Ryan Burnett,'" Kendra read the name out loud. "That kid has Burnett's ATM card and he's obviously got the password." She looked up at her partner and could see that Abilene was thinking the same thing. "The kid had to have somehow gotten his hands on the card."

"Maybe even killed Burnett to get it," Abilene speculated. "Hell, maybe he's the one who killed Summer in the apartment." Instead of answers, they just had more questions.

Kendra looked back at the teenager's face. She shook her head. Something in her gut was telling her no. "I don't know, Abilene. He doesn't look like a killer to me."

"That's what they said about Baby Face Nelson, too," he pointed out, mentioning a romanticized gangster from the late twenties and early thirties.

She had no idea who he was talking about, but his tone clued her in. "Just when I think there's hope for you, you turn cynical on me, Abilene," she couldn't help commenting.

While he couldn't deny the charge, he could amend it. "Only sometimes, Cavanaugh. Only sometimes."

She was surprised that she liked the sound of that. She could feel a mellowness returning, something that had been absent from her countenance for too long a time. For eighteen months.

Maybe she'd been fighting everything too hard, including the circumstances that had recently arisen. Up until now, she'd felt that if she accepted the fact that she was part of such a large law enforcement family, she was somehow being disloyal to the people she'd always believed were her extended family.

Now's not the time for philosophical ruminations, she upbraided herself. There was a case to solve and apparently more than one person to bring to justice.

Or so it seemed.

Damn, there was nothing simple about this so-called simple case.

Their first step had to be to find out who this teenager was and how he was mixed up in all this.

"Okay, how do we find this kid?" she asked Abilene, thinking out loud. Before her partner could say anything, she turned to the manager and asked the man a very obvious question. "Mr. Hanna, have you ever seen this teenager before?"

The bank manager shook his head adamantly. "No. I don't recognize him."

"Are you sure?" Matt pressed.

The man remained firm. "Positive."

Kendra sighed. "Can't ask for more than that."

Playing a long shot, Kendra and Matt went back to Ryan Burnett's apartment building and questioned all his neighbors. When they showed the photo of the teenager lifted from the surveillance tape, no one could recall ever having seen him around.

"I suppose we could get a court order to confiscate the ATM and bring it to the lab to check the outside for fingerprints," Kendra said halfheartedly an hour later as they faced each other across their desks in the squad room.

"Half the city's fingerprints might be on that keypad," Matt pointed out.

"Yeah," she said with a sigh. "So near and yet so far."

"Speaking of near, how about grabbing a bite to eat and heading back to my place?" he suggested.

They were alone in the squad room. Wong had gone home half an hour ago and he'd been the last one there with them. There was no longer a reason to keep her voice low the way there had been earlier—Wong had ears like a bat and he also loved gossip.

"Look, just because I spent one night with you doesn't mean that I'm going to hop into bed with you every time you smile," she informed Matt.

"I know that," he told her solemnly, then asked, "So, how does pizza sound?"

She hadn't been able to resist him when she'd been operating on all four cylinders. In her present condition, she knew damn well that she didn't stand a chance and was only going through the motions of holding him at arm's length for form's sake. She didn't want to appear supereasy.

The truth was that spending another night with him sounded incredibly appealing.

"Perfect," she told him with a tired sigh. Switching off her computer, she rose to her feet. "As long as you promise no anchovies."

He pretended to sigh as he followed suit. "You drive a hard bargain."

Kendra laughed shortly as she crossed the empty squad room. "Hey, I'm a Cavanaugh. We're supposed to be born tough."

"So the legend goes," he agreed, letting her walk out first. "Okay, no anchovies."

Once she crossed the threshold into the hallway, he hit the light switch. The squad room fell into darkness, except for a single light left on in the lieutenant's office. Lately, everyone had been reminded to do their part to conserve energy.

He intended to follow the letter of the request—at least at work. In his apartment, though, it was a whole different story—and he couldn't wait to get there to watch it unfold.

Chapter 14

Several days went by, shrouded in frustration. Their investigation had ground to a complete standstill. There were no more sightings of the teenager using Ryan Burnett's ATM card and no one had seen Ryan himself, not anyone in his building nor at his workplace. They had left instructions at both places to be called immediately if the man turned up.

The phone, in that respect, remained exasperatingly silent.

In the interim, Matt ran off copies of the teenager's photo that they had lifted from the initial bank surveillance tape and then had them distributed to all the other bank branches in the county as well as the surrounding counties. They were hoping that greed could prompt the teen to tap into a second ATM.

After a week had gone by, there still hadn't been any new hits.

They were swiftly running out of innovative ways to approach the problem.

"Damn!"

The softly muttered curse had Kendra looking up from the papers on her desk and at her partner. Despite everything, her expression instantly softened. Their case might not be going anywhere, but it seemed as if they were.

Not that she had the slightest idea *where* it was that they were headed, but for now, the holding pattern they were currently engaged in had her waking up with a smile each morning despite the frustration she was professionally encountering.

When it came time to leave the precinct for the day, it made no difference if they walked out together or separately and at different times—they still wound up together that evening.

In each other's arms.

And neither one of them minded.

Kendra refused to explore what was happening, refused to think beyond the moment because she knew from experience that the next moment could bring with it devastation and events that could very well blow her life apart. So she told herself she wasn't invested, that she was simply enjoying the moment and the very steamy, teeth-jarring fact that the good-looking man seated across from her in the squad room was one incredible lover.

And that, she told herself over and over again, was enough for her.

If at times she wondered how he felt about what was happening between them, she forced herself to block the questions and think of something else. *Anything* else. In this particular situation, ignorance *was* bliss—because knowing, most likely, would bring with it some sort of excruciating pain and if she could avoid it, even by simply sticking her head in the sand, she was going to do it.

Besides, she reminded herself, there was no basis to believe that anything of a permanent nature would ever be in the offing. The man had a history of loving 'em and leaving 'em. Fruit flies had longer relationships with one another than Matt Abilene had with the women who passed through his life, and she was vaguely aware that she was already pushing the time limit.

But if she pretended oblivion and said nothing, maybe he wouldn't notice and this moment they were sharing would continue a little while longer.

It was the only plan she had.

"Another dead end?" she asked, nodding at the phone.

Coming to, he replayed her question in his head and had no point of reference. "What?"

"You just said 'Damn,' so I'm asking you if that's another dead end. Our case," she prompted when he looked at her quizzically. "You remember, dead body in bachelor's apartment. ATM hits by a third party." She cocked her head, looking up at the face that had already turned up several unnerving times in her dreams. "Any of this ringing a bell for you?"

"Yeah, yeah." For now, he waved away her question and her reference. This wasn't about their case, but something far more personal. Something that caused him worry and concern on a regular basis. Why couldn't he have a normal mother who went off on tour buses with her friends and gambled twice a year in Vegas? "She's still not answering," he said in frustration.

It was Kendra's turn to be confused. *"She?"* She was only focused on one *she* right now. "The dead woman?"

"No," Matt bit off, exasperated not so much with her as with who he was trying to reach—and couldn't. "My mother." In an effort to make more sense, he back-tracked and said, "I keep leaving messages on her phone and she's not picking up or returning my calls."

That didn't sound all that unusual. After all, he and his mother had separate lives to live. "Maybe she went away for a while."

He shook his head. "Not without telling me."

She laughed softly, wondering if he knew what that sounded like. "You realize that you're making noises like a parent."

He couldn't remember a time when he wasn't the responsible one, the one who watched out for his mother instead of the other way around.

"With her I always have been." He dragged his hand through his wayward dark hair and looked accusingly at the telephone handset again. "Other than one message on my voice mail in which she said all of two words, I haven't heard from her all week."

Kendra humored him and asked for more details. "And those two words were?"

"Thank you. She said, 'thank you.'" He said the words as if they held some hidden insult.

Kendra smiled and nodded knowingly. "Ah."

She had his attention immediately. "What do you mean, 'ah'? Was that some form of female-speak that I'm not getting?" he asked.

This was a side of the man she found amusing. And strangely endearing, although there was no way she would ever say that to him.

"In a way," she admitted, and then she decided to clue him in, at least in the way she interpreted it. "I think your mother was thanking you for taking her to the gathering at the chief's house last weekend."

"Okay." He continued looking at her, waiting for further enlightenment. He didn't see any reason for his mother to simply say that and nothing more. "Okay," he repeated, this time with a touch of frustration because Kendra was obviously seeing something that he didn't. "Fill in the blanks for me. What is it that I'm not getting?"

"That your mother probably hooked up with my father."

He could feel his protective side rising up. There was an edge to his voice as he asked, "*Hooked up* in the old sense or in the new sense?"

That was a subject she neither wanted to explore nor talk about at length.

"Either way, I think your mother's happy. And I caught my father humming the other day when I came down to the lab with our possible suspect's photo. My father doesn't hum," she told him, in case the significance of that escaped him. "At least, he hasn't since my mother died."

Matt was still stuck at the starting gate as the significance of what she was saying began to sink in. "Meaning your father and my mother—"

"Had a good time," Kendra said euphemistically. And then, because she wasn't really able to read her partner's expression, she continued in their individual parents' defense, "Hey, they're both consenting adults…." Not wanting to go into any sort of detail, Kendra deliberately let her voice trail off.

"My mother's been through the ringer emotionally," Matt protested. He definitely didn't want to see that happening to the woman again. Didn't want her taken advantage of again, even unintentionally.

Kendra did her best not to take offense and just focused on the fact that her partner was worried about his mother—not that Abilene was inadvertently insulting her father.

"And my dad's not the kind of guy to just have a fling without any thought to possible consequences— not like some people."

That brought the conversation to a skidding halt. Her partner's vivid green eyes narrowed as he looked at her. "Was that meant for me?"

Denial at this point would have been useless, so rather than retreat or pretend that he'd misunderstood her, she stuck by her words. "I don't see anyone else in this conversation."

And that was when the alarms went off in her head. What the hell was she doing? Since when did she behave like a "typical female," to use one of her brothers' labels, acting as if she wanted to know "where this relationship is going"? That wasn't her. At least, that wasn't her anymore, right? Because she didn't want a relationship, just something casual, nothing more, she silently insisted.

"Sorry, forget I said anything," she told Abilene with a dismissive wave of her hand. "I'm just punchy, that's all. The important thing is, don't worry about your mother. If my dad's spending time with her, then she is definitely in safe hands. He's the old-fashioned type—chivalrous to a fault," she added with emphasis, because Abilene still looked pretty unconvinced.

The phone rang on his desk just then, preventing her partner from responding to her assurances about her father and his mother.

"Abilene," he snapped impatiently into the handset.

Kendra watched him and decided that it wasn't his mother finally returning his calls. An alert expression had come into his eyes. This had to be about the case.

"We'll be right there," he promised, hanging up. Matt looked at her. "We've got a hit."

She was on her feet immediately, grabbing what she needed and shoving it into the pockets of her jacket. "He showed up at another branch of the bank? Is he still there?" she asked eagerly.

Matt shook his head. "The bank security guard saw the kid through the glass doors, apparently making a withdrawal. By the time he got outside, the kid had driven away."

Kendra blew out a breath. "Terrific," she bit off in frustration.

"Actually, yes."

"Go on," she prompted.

"The guard got a partial plate number," he explained as they hurried out of the squad room.

"You could have led with that," she told him in exasperation. "Well, every little bit helps." She tried not to allow herself to get too excited. This could lead to just another dead end—then again, maybe they had gotten a little closer to finding their perpetrator.

Instinctively, Matt knew that she'd want to take the stairs rather than wait for the elevator, so he headed in the opposite direction of the elevator banks, toward the door to the stairwell.

When he was directly behind her, Kendra smiled to herself. The man was learning.

"I'm sorry," the security guard, a retired former patrolman with the Aurora P.D., apologized for the third time in as many minutes. "I was on my break and coming in through the other entrance when I spotted the kid you're looking for. He was just finishing up and by the time I got over to that side of the building, he was driving away." The guard had already given them the paper with the partial license plate he'd managed to copy down. "It was one of those little cars, you know, looks like it belongs in a toy box."

"A smart car?" Abilene guessed. It was the smallest-looking vehicle that he knew of.

The man shook his head. "No, it's a mini-something-or-other."

"A Mini Cooper?" Kendra asked.

"Yeah, that's the one. Mini Cooper," he repeated, relieved to get that off his mind. "It was navy and white," he described.

Kendra nodded. Finally, they were getting some pieces to work with. "We're going to need to see the surveillance tape," she told him.

"Sure, I already told the assistant manager you'd be asking," he informed them, then added, "The bank manager's out today," as he led them inside the bank to speak to the woman.

They got luckier.

The teenager's car was parked directly behind him as he'd made the withdrawal and the rest of his license plate was visible after the in-house tech at the police station worked her magic for them and removed the glare from an adjacent window.

From there, the steps became easier.

"Hello, Scott Randall," Abilene declared as he pulled up the Mini Cooper's registration. Armed with the teenager's name, they pulled up his driver's license.

Which was where it looked as if their streak of luck ran dry.

The man whose name was on the registration for the car looked like—and was, according to his date of birth—a senior citizen.

"If that's a teenager, then I belong in nursery school," Kendra commented as she came around to her partner's side of the desk and looked over his shoulder at the photo on the driver's license he'd pulled up on the screen.

"Maybe it's the kid's father," Matt speculated.

"More like his grandfather, is my guess," she said, shaking her head. "Either that or there are a hell of a lot of people involved in this case." Going back to her side of the desk, she sighed, took out her weapon and holstered it. "It's all we've got. Let's go pay Mr. Randall a visit and ask him if he knows who's been using his car." She rolled her eyes, thinking of worst-case scenarios as she walked out of the room. "And I swear, if he tells us his car was stolen and he was just getting around to reporting it, I'm going to scream."

She probably would, too, Matt thought. "Just give me fair warning, that's all I ask," he said to his partner as they went toward the stairwell again.

The car in question was not parked in front of the house listed on the DMV registration.

Big surprise, Kendra thought, getting out of the Crown Victoria. She braced herself for the disclaimer she anticipated coming from the man they were about to question.

Matt pressed down hard on the doorbell. When the door opened a couple of minutes later, a rather befuddled, somewhat overweight man with flyaway white hair looked at them over the tops of his rimless glasses.

"Can I help you?" he asked, one hand still on the door. It was obvious he was prepared to swing it shut at a moment's notice.

"We certainly hope so, Mr. Randall," Kendra said in her most soothing voice. "Do you by any chance own a navy-and-white Mini Cooper, license plate number—"

The man held up his hand, stopping her before she could launch into the sequence of numbers. "Don't read the numbers to me. Waste of time," he informed her. "I can't picture them in my head. I've got to see the numbers written on a piece of paper or something."

Perfectly happy to play along, Kendra handed the man the paper and Scott Randall peered at it very carefully, blinking his eyes several times.

And then he raised his eyes to hers. "What about the car?" he asked cautiously.

"Then you *do* own it," Matt said, wanting to establish that fact first.

"And if I do?" Randall's small brown eyes went from Kendra to Matt like tennis balls moving in slow motion. "Who's asking?"

"Detectives Abilene and Cavanaugh," Kendra said, nodding toward her partner as she held up her identification for the man to see. Abilene took his out and did the same.

For form's sake, Randall studied one, then the other. And then sighed deeply. "What's he done now?"

"'He'?" Kendra echoed.

"Yeah. Scottie. My grandson." Each word sounded as if it weighed more than a ton on his tongue before he uttered it.

Kendra took out the photo she and Abilene had been showing around for the past few days.

"Is this your grandson?" she asked, mentally crossing her fingers. She held her breath, waiting for the man to answer.

He did reluctantly after a beat. "Yeah, that's Scottie."

"Does Scottie by any chance live with you?" Matt asked.

The old man laughed. "Does he live with me? Ever since he was three days old and his mother, my daughter, left him on my doorstep and took off." He shrugged haplessly. "Just as well. That girl could never take care of any living thing. All her pets always died. She kept forgetting to feed them," he confided. And then he grew very serious. "What's this all about?" Randall asked, growing somewhat distressed. "Scottie's a good boy," he assured them. "He just can't seem to get his act together."

Kendra felt sorry for the older Scott Randall, but there were rules about discussing ongoing investigations, namely: don't. So her hands were tied and she was forced to ignore his question.

"Where can we find Scottie right now?" she asked the old man.

He thought for a moment. "At Fashions for Less on Windom and Halladay. He's a stock boy there. It's not that he doesn't work hard," the man quickly added. "He just can't seem to hold on to anything. This is Scottie's fifth job since the beginning of the year," he confessed, embarrassed. And then he looked at them again. "Please, what's he done?"

Kendra threw him a crumb—it was the best she could do. "Hopefully something minor."

"Have him call me when you find him," Scottie's grandfather called after them as they walked away from the house.

Kendra raised her voice. "We'll do our best," she promised, fervently hoping she could keep her word. "Poor guy," she murmured under her breath as she and Abilene walked back to the unmarked vehicle they'd left parked at the curb.

Her partner paused and looked at her over the roof of the car. "You know, you act tough, but you're pretty softhearted," he noted.

She didn't want him extrapolating from there and going in directions she wasn't comfortable with.

"Depends on the situation," she said crisply. She got into the car on the driver's side. "I just felt sorry for the old man." In her opinion, it was hard not to. "He does a good deed, takes in his daughter's kid—a kid she thought nothing of abandoning," she added with a shake of her head. "And now his payback might be that he raised a killer." Although she still had a long way to go before she was convinced of that.

"Maybe not," Matt speculated. "Nothing about this case is cut-and-dried," he pointed out. "For all we know, this kid could be an innocent dupe in all this."

Now *that* surprised her. She spared him a glance at the next light just to be sure he hadn't morphed into someone else.

"Well, look at you, Mr. Optimist." She grinned. "Nice to know there's a streak of optimism buried in there somewhere."

He shrugged off her words and said flippantly, "I guess maybe you're contagious. I should have gotten my shots first before we got…'started,'" he finally concluded.

"Maybe you should have," she agreed.

And while they were at it, she added silently, she should have gotten hers—against him. Because God knew he was definitely getting to her. Here they were, on the cusp of possibly catching a break in the case, and all she could think of was being alone with Abilene tonight.

Something was definitely wrong with this picture. And she was really going to get hurt if she wasn't careful.

Chapter 15

"Murder? What murder? Whose murder?"

Scottie Randall croaked out the questions, his voice getting higher and reedier with each panicked syllable he uttered. His head looked as if it was on the verge of spinning around like some character in a grade B horror movie.

Kendra and Matt had found the nineteen-year-old exactly where the teen's grandfather had said he would be, working in the back room of Fashions for Less, stocking the shelves. They took Scottie back to the precinct with them for questioning and at the time, he seemed happy enough to get away from the airless stockroom and go with them.

But once the tone changed and the questions began coming, his affable smile melted into confusion and then shock.

"I didn't kill nobody," he protested again, genuinely frightened. His eyes were pleading. "You gotta believe me."

Any second now, their suspect was going to get hysterical on them, Matt thought. Time to change tactics. He spoke to the teen slowly, calmly, doing what he could to soothe him and distance Scottie from any possible breakdown. A breakdown wouldn't help them or answer any questions that needed answering.

"We'd really like to believe you, Scottie, but that account you've been taking money out of, that's not your account."

He shook his head and for just a second, it occurred to Kendra that she was looking at someone incapable of lying to save his life. "No, it's not."

"It belongs to someone who's currently missing," Kendra told him. She'd come up on his other side so that between them, she and Matt had become the teen's human bookends.

"He's not missing, he's right there," Scottie cried, his head swiveling to look from one detective to the other and then back again. "In his apartment." He ran his hand along the back of his neck. "Jeez, he said there wouldn't be any trouble."

"Hold it," Matt held up his hand. "In his *apartment?* You took the money back to his apartment? What's the address?" he asked.

Scottie rattled off the address of the building where Summer's body had been discovered. Ryan Burnett's apartment building.

The superintendent had been instructed to call them, night or day, if the man returned. So far, that call hadn't come in.

"And you didn't think it was odd that Burnett was sending you to withdraw money for him?" Kendra asked the teenager.

The thin shoulders rose and fell haplessly. "He said he was real busy and that if I got the money out for him, he'd give me a—a—he called it a service charge," Scottie remembered, brightening as he repeated the phrase.

Like a frantic puppy, eager to please his master and not quite sure who that master was, he looked from Kendra to Matt and then back again. "And he was alive when he took the money from me," he said adamantly.

"And when was that?" Matt asked.

"Today," Scottie cried. "Right after I took out more money for him." He lowered his voice, as if to share a confidence. "I said it would go faster if he just went in and took the money out himself, but he said this was just fine for him." He shrugged. "I guess he knows what he's doing."

"And this is the address you went to?" Kendra turned the paper she'd written the address on around so that Scottie could see it.

He gazed at it intently, then looked up at her. "Yeah."

"You're sure?" Matt pressed, his eyes pinning the teen down.

"Yeah." This time there was less confidence in his voice. He was growing nervous again. "Why?"

Instead of answering, Kendra took out the folded photograph of Burnett that she had in her pocket. "And this is the man you gave the money to?"

He stared at the photograph as if he was waiting for it to do something. But it didn't. Finally, he looked up. "No, that's not Ryan Burnett," he told her.

"What apartment number did you go to?" Kendra asked.

"Better yet," Matt interjected, "why don't you just take us there?"

Scottie shook his head. "I can't."

Uh-oh, here it comes, Kendra thought. Maybe he was a far better liar than she'd thought and this innocent, wide-eyed thing was just an act. "And why is that?" she asked.

"You left my car in the parking lot," Scottie whined.

Kendra exchanged looks with Matt. It was obvious her partner was thinking the same thing she was. That this particular teen was not the brightest bulb in the ceiling fixture.

"We'll drive," Kendra told him, gently placing her hand against the back of his shoulder and giving him a slight push toward the door. "You just lead us to the apartment."

The teen was agreeable to that. "Okay, but then can you take me back to work? This is my first week and I don't want them to fire me yet."

Yet.

The last word amused Matt. The teen obviously had a game plan that involved not working too hard. With that kind of attitude, Scottie was a perfect candidate for someone with a devious mind-set to use as his lackey and errand boy.

The question was, exactly *who* was pulling these strings?

"We'll have a patrolman bring you back after you take us to the apartment where you last saw Ryan Burnett," Kendra promised.

Though he continued to look a little uneasy, Scottie's panicky expression had disappeared. It was obvious that he took them at their word. Considering the kind of people she was accustomed to dealing with, Kendra decided that Scottie Randall was an exceedingly trusting soul—which, again, made her think of him as ripe for the picking for anyone who wanted to operate from behind the scenes.

Maybe they were finally on the right path to wrapping this up. God, she hoped so.

When they arrived at the apartment building where Summer Miller's body was first discovered, Scottie took them up to the third floor. Ryan Burnett's floor. But when she and Matt turned to go to the left, Scottie remained standing where he was and looked at them with curiosity.

"It's over this way," he told them, indicating an apartment down the hall on the opposite end of the hallway.

Definitely not Burnett's apartment, Matt thought. The last time they were here, canvassing the floor, this was the young, friendly actor's apartment.

Were the twists and turns in the case *ever* going to lead them to a conclusion?

Scottie rang the doorbell at the apartment in question. The noise coming from inside the apartment was rather loud and had most likely drowned out the sound of the doorbell.

"We'll take it from here," Matt told him.

Moving the teenager aside, Matt fisted his hand and pounded against the door. When there was no response, he pounded even louder.

"I can get the super," Kendra offered, raising her voice to be heard above the blaring music inside.

Who listened to that kind of stuff without going deaf? she couldn't help wondering.

"Might not be a bad idea," Matt agreed, raising his voice as well.

"Can I go back to work now?" Scottie asked them hopefully.

Kendra nodded at the patrolman who'd arrived at the scene. "Take him where he needs to go. And Scottie," she added as a footnote, as she turned to look at him, "don't leave town."

Scottie bobbed his head up and down vigorously and seemed rather excited about the standard warning she'd issued.

"Cool," he pronounced, then turned to go with the patrolman.

"Cool," she repeated under her breath. Kendra shook her head. It took all kinds.

In the interim, Matt had given pounding his fist against the door one more try. This time, he was successful and it opened.

A man somewhere in his mid-thirties or so who appeared to be feeling very little pain stood in the doorway, using the doorknob to help him maintain his vertical position. He squinted at them—predominantly at Kendra.

"You the entertainment?" he asked. It was obvious that the idea pleased him.

"Detectives Cavanaugh and Abilene," Kendra informed him, holding up her badge as Matt held up his.

The man grinned. "Yup, you're the entertainment,"

he declared, weaving just a little as he backed up and held the door all the way open for them. He leered at her in anticipation as she passed him. "Guess it's going to take you a while to get out of all those clothes, isn't it?"

"Longer than you could possibly imagine," she answered crisply.

"Hey, Tyler, who hired your strippers?" their doorman asked, tossing the remark back over his shoulder into the general throng.

"What?" Tyler Blake worked his way to the front door. Kendra noted that the genial smile on his lips faded just for a moment before he brightened and said, "Detectives, have you come to do me the honor of staying for my bachelor party? I'm getting married Saturday," he told them, repeating a fact that he had already mentioned in the last interview he'd had with them. "You're welcome to come to the ceremony, but right now, I've got to get back to the party. My best man went through a lot of trouble throwing this together at the last minute and it wouldn't be polite not to enjoy myself."

Matt placed a hand on the actor's shoulder, stopping him in his tracks as the latter began to retreat.

"We'll write him a formal apology," he promised. "Right now, my partner and I have a few more questions for you."

Tyler turned around slowly and looked at Matt. "It can't wait?"

"It can't wait," Kendra assured him firmly. "You need to come down to the station with us."

With a resigned sigh, he said, "All right." Tyler latched onto another man who appeared more intoxicated than the one who had opened the door. "Jeffrey,

I've got to go talk to these people. Don't let the party die down."

"No chance, Ty-man," his friend promised with a wide, silly grin.

As they left, Kendra could foresee the neighbors calling the police about the noise shortly—if they hadn't done so already.

"What is this about?" Tyler asked once they were at the precinct and he was seated in one of the interrogation rooms.

During the entire short ride to the station, the out-of-work actor had said nothing, as if gathering his thoughts together and deciding how he wanted to play the scene. When he finally opened his mouth, he sounded unbelievably calm in Matt's opinion.

"I think you already know the answer to that," Matt said quietly, his eyes riveted to Tyler's very blue orbs—contacts?

Matt gave the impression of looking into the other man's mind and after a few moments, it seemed to work because Tyler's carefully reserved facade abruptly began to crack.

Tyler did not appear to be able to sustain the performance he had wanted to render.

"Just for the record, why don't you tell me?" he finally said.

"Okay, 'just for the record,'" Matt obliged him. "Why do you have Ryan Burnett's ATM card and password and why are you emptying out his bank account?"

Tyler sat up straight, indignation suddenly emerging from every pore. "Who told you that?" the man demanded angrily.

"Scottie Randall," Matt said matter-of-factly. Then, for leverage, he added, "We caught him on the bank surveillance tape making the withdrawals. He said you gave him the card and he seems to think that you're Ryan Burnett."

Unprepared to have it all unravel right in front of him so quickly and without a prepared script at the ready, Tyler panicked.

"He's lying!"

Kendra shook her head. "Scottie's not clever enough to make up a lie. His brain works on a much less complicated level than yours," she told him. "Now, why don't you save us all some time and just tell us the truth? Where is Burnett?"

Stalling, Tyler looked from her to Abilene, then finally said, "Ryan's in Costa Rica. I'm supposed to wire him the money as soon as I get it. I forgot because of the party, but I'm going to do it tomorrow morning. I swear it."

"You know what I think?" Matt said, shifting so that he was directly in the man's line of vision despite Tyler's attempts to turn away from him. "I think you're lying, Tyler."

"No, I'm not," the other man insisted fiercely. "Ryan asked me to do this for him and then he just took off."

Matt leaned in closer, eyeing him. "The police department was pretty good about installing a first-class air-conditioning system at the precinct for days just like today. It would take about three hours to defrost a bag of frozen peas—but you're sweating," he pointed out. "Why is that?"

"My body rhythm's out of sync," Tyler answered, a note of mounting desperation entering his voice. "I've always been like that. Drives my fiancée crazy."

"That happens when a person's nervous," Kendra said, joining in on the psychological attack. "Especially when they're lying."

Tyler's voice rose half an octave as he insisted again, "I'm not lying."

"Aren't you?" Kendra probed, maintaining eye contact just as Matt had. "If I call all the airlines, I'm going to find out that Ryan never booked a flight to Costa Rica, aren't I?"

"Private plane," Tyler blurted out. "Ryan was on a private plane. It belongs to a friend of his. I don't know the name."

"Not necessary," Kendra told him. "But just so you know, there would be a flight plan filed with the control tower," she said mildly.

"Easy enough to find out," Matt agreed.

It was all blowing up in front of him. A drained Tyler dragged both hands through his hair, looking as if his head had suddenly become too heavy for him to hold up any longer.

His breathing grew heavier, more labored. And then he cried out, "Dammit!"

"Yes?" Kendra moved her chair in closer. "Are you asking to revise your story?"

"It wasn't supposed to get out of hand like this. It was supposed to be so simple." He looked now like a frightened man who was watching his future, his entire life slip through his fingers. "If she'd just married me a little sooner, none of this would have happened. It wouldn't have been necessary. But she said she wanted to be 'sure.' I didn't have time to wait for 'sure.' I needed to get the money *now*."

"Necessary?" Kendra repeated in disbelief as she stared at the man. Was he serious? "Since when is murder necessary?"

"Since it had to look as if Ryan killed his girlfriend and then, overwhelmed and afraid of the consequences of what he did, fled the country."

Matt closed in on the man. "Burnett didn't kill her, did he?" When Tyler didn't answer, he repeated more sternly, "Did he?"

Tyler stared down at his fingertips. "No," he said in a quiet whisper.

"But Burnett is dead, isn't he?" Matt pressed. Tyler continued to avoid looking at either one of them and just stared vacantly at the top of the table before him. "Isn't he?" Matt repeated, raising his voice harshly. He was losing patience.

Suddenly, the actor's head jerked up, a naked, desperate look in his eyes.

"I didn't *want* to kill him. You've got to believe me," he cried. "But I had to. They were going to kill me if I didn't come up with the money and Burnett was the only one I knew—besides my fiancée—who had any real money in the bank."

"Back up," Kendra interrupted. "*Who* was going to kill you and *what* money?" she asked Tyler.

The sigh came out more like a shudder. The actor's

shoulders seemed to cave in on him. He looked every bit the broken man.

"The money I owed this loan shark. He called himself a 'money facilitator,' but he's a freakin' loan shark, all right." Misery filled his eyes as they began to tear up. "I never gambled before. Suddenly, I couldn't stop. It was like this rush, this high. At first, I couldn't lose—and then, I couldn't win."

The story was so stereotypical, Kendra found it hard to listen. How could people just throw their lives away like that?

"It's all I thought about," Tyler was saying, wringing his hands now. "I didn't want to eat, I didn't want to act. I just wanted to *win.*"

"But you just kept losing," Matt guessed. The gambling bug had bitten him once or twice while he and his mother had lived in Vegas, but he knew enough to steer clear and not start what he might not be able to finish.

"Yeah," Tyler said wistfully. "That winning hand, the one that was going to turn everything around for me, that was out there, just out of reach and no matter how much I tried, I just couldn't wrap my hands around it." He looked up at Matt. "I bet everything I had—and everything I didn't have—until I was in just too deep to get out."

"Why didn't you just try to borrow the money through regular channels?" Matt asked.

Tyler laughed. "If you were a bank, would you lend me money? Besides, it was too big a sum to even apply for. I owed almost half a million dollars. I couldn't ask anyone for that kind of money."

"So you killed him for it instead?" Kendra asked incredulously.

Tyler didn't answer. It was as if he just couldn't bring himself to form the words.

"Where's the body now?" Matt asked.

"At a construction site. That big mall where the physical fitness chain is going to be building their latest franchise. I buried him there." An extremely sad, ironic smile played on his lips. "He was always into physical fitness. I thought it would be a good final resting place for him. They're going to be pouring cement tomorrow morning."

"No, they're not. Their work plans just got delayed," Kendra said, picking up the telephone handset. She intended to call the chief of Ds. If anyone could get a temporary stop-work order issued, it was the chief.

"Look, I get why you might have killed Ryan. You were desperate and he looked like your only way out," Matt said, trying to get answers while the actor was still volunteering them. "But why kill his girlfriend? Was she there in the apartment at the time? Did she walk in on you when you were killing Burnett?"

He shook his head. "No, she came in later, looking for him. I had to make it look as if he had a reason to just disappear. I wanted to make it look logical. If he killed Summer, he wasn't going to hang around until someone put two and two together."

Matt shook his head. It took all kinds to make a world, but it still never ceased to amaze him how very different people could be.

"Maybe you should have followed that advice yourself," Matt suggested as he took out his handcuffs.

"Stand up." When the actor did, Matt cuffed him. "Tyler Blake, you're under arrest for the murders of Summer Miller and Ryan Burnett…" he began, reading the out-of-work and definitely out-of-luck actor his rights.

Glancing over, he saw Kendra hanging up the phone. "The chief's going to get the construction company to back off until we can locate Ryan Burnett's body." She looked at Tyler. "Any helpful hints to follow?"

The actor appeared to be slipping into a world of his own. Before he made the transition, he said, "Look for suitcases."

Terrific, Kendra thought grimly. *The body was in pieces.*

Chapter 16

"God, this is one day I just want to put behind me," Kendra said late the next day.

Not only was she struggling to get her exhaustion under control, but her sense of revulsion as well. That morning, armed with a temporary stop-work order and with the help of two cadaver dogs, Kendra, Matt and two other detectives working with them, plus several patrolmen recruited to do the initial digging, were able to go over the grounds and locate the suitcases. In all there were four—four suitcases each stuffed with some part of Ryan Burnett's decomposing body.

All four suitcases were photographed in the exact place where they were found, carefully documented, and then sent over to the medical examiner. The body of the missing accountant then became one giant jig-saw puzzle until it could be verified that they did indeed find all of him.

They had.

The horrible stench, when she and Matt had witnessed the opening of the first suitcase, was still with her, despite the fact that the last of the suitcases had been opened over five hours ago.

"I don't think I'm ever going to be rid of that smell," she told Matt wearily. It seemed to hover around her no matter which way she turned.

Matt wasn't experiencing the same reaction, but he could understand hers. "Right now, it's just all in your head," he assured her.

"It feels more like it's all in my nostrils," she complained.

Matt smiled at her across the desks. "That's because you have a vivid imagination. It'll pass," he promised her with a certainty that was meant to comfort her. "In the meantime, I'll see if I can find some vanilla candles for you when we leave here. What?" he asked, when he saw the bemused expression on her face.

Kendra shook her head. "I just can't picture you picking up scented candles, that's all." He'd struck her as way too macho to even *know* that vanilla-scented candles existed.

"Is that your way of saying you think I'm insensitive?" His voice gave nothing away. She had no idea if she'd insulted him or he was just baiting her.

Kendra winged it. "No, that's my way of saying I can't picture you doing typical 'girlie' things. Hell, I don't do typical 'girlie' things," she admitted. She'd never even lit one scented candle in her life, thinking of it more in terms of a fire hazard than something needed to create a romantic mood.

"Then maybe you need lessons," Matt teased. And then he shrugged. "It was just something I read in a magazine article while trapped in a dental office, waiting for a root canal." Stretching, Matt pushed back from his desk. "You ready to call it a night?"

Oh, so ready, she thought. Instead of answering his question directly, Kendra pretended to take him literally and announced, "Night," then rose to her feet.

"I guess you are," he murmured under his breath. Pushing his chair in against his desk, Matt was all set to walk out of the squad room when his cell phone began to ring. With a sigh, he looked down at it to check the caller ID.

Kendra saw his eyebrows rise in a silent question, as if he was surprised to be on the receiving end of a call from whoever was on the other end.

"Who is it?" she asked.

He looked at her as he opened the phone and raised it to his ear. His expression told her that he had no idea what this was about. "Your father."

"We didn't find Burnett?"

It was the first thing that occurred to her. She couldn't think of another reason why her father would call Abilene—but then, he knew she was acting as primary on the case. Why wasn't her father calling her if there was some news? It didn't make any sense.

Listening closely to the limited exchange between Matt and her father gave her no further clues.

"Yes, sir," Matt said, ending the call. He closed his phone and slipped it back onto his belt. Seeing the unanswered question in her eyes, he said, "He wants to see us."

But the case was all but wrapped up, wasn't it? Why the eleventh-hour call?

"What's wrong? Wasn't that Burnett in the suitcases?" she asked as they headed out toward the bank of elevators.

Matt shook his head. "He didn't say. Just that he wanted to see us. We'll find out soon enough."

She sighed as she pressed the Down button beside the elevator. Within less than a minute, the elevator doors were opening on their floor, ready to take them to the basement and the CSI lab.

She got on and pressed B. "I don't think I can stand one more twist in this case, at least not tonight. I don't remember when I've felt so drained." Did that sound as whiny to him as it did to her?

The half smile that curved Matt's sensual mouth told her that he could remember a time.

She knew immediately what he was thinking of. "Not a word," she warned.

She didn't trust the utterly innocent look on his face one bit.

Getting off the elevator, she marched ahead of him to the lab.

"Well, we're here," Kendra announced to her father as she pushed the door open. From the looks of it, the day shift had all left and the night shift hadn't arrived to take their place. Either that, or they were all out on a call. In any case, that didn't concern her. Her father's summons, however, did. "Okay, tell me. What's wrong?" she asked.

Her question took Sean by surprise. "Since when have you become such a pessimist?"

That was easy. Kendra could document the exact time and place for this last wave of uncharacteristic dark outlook on her part.

"Since a seemingly perfectly affable man took it upon himself to hack his trusting neighbor into four pieces in order to keep a loan shark from possibly doing the same to him."

"If you put it that way, it's understandable, I suppose. I'm just not used to your being so bleak in your outlook." Sean moved aside what he was working on and came around the steel table to join the pair he had sent for. "But this isn't about the case," he told her.

It was her turn to be caught by surprise. "Then what is it about?" Kendra asked uncertainly.

Rather than answer her, Sean Cavanaugh directed his words to her partner. "I thought that you should be the first to know—" And then he stopped. For the first time in a long time, he felt somewhat uncomfortable. Shaking his head, Kendra's father laughed to himself. "I'm really out of practice here," he confessed almost sheepishly to them.

Though Matt looked puzzled, it took Kendra less than a second to put all it together. Ordinarily, her father was quiet confidence personified. She could only think of one thing that would strip him of that confidence.

She stared at her father, stunned. "Are you trying to ask Abilene's permission to date his mother?"

"No," Sean answered honestly, then explained, "We're already doing that." Taking a deep breath, he started again. "I just wanted you to know that it's becoming serious."

"How serious?" Matt asked. There was no indication in his low, monotone voice how he felt about the matter.

Sean's eyes looked directly into Matt's. "Serious," he repeated, as if the word was enough to convey it all. And then he ratcheted it up several notches. "If it continues this way, I'm thinking of asking your mother to marry me."

Kendra's mouth dropped open. For a moment, she didn't know whether to congratulate her father or hint that he was out of his mind. Wasn't this going too fast?

"You're kidding."

"No, I'm not," he assured her solemnly.

She knew he had as much of a right to happiness as anyone. More. But he was a novice here, as far as she was concerned. "Don't you think you're rushing things a little?"

Her choice of words made her father laugh softly. "At your age, I'd be rushing it. At mine, *time* is what's rushing. I don't have as much of it left as I once did. And as you do," he told them, looking from his daughter to Sabrina's son. "I just wanted to make sure that you didn't have any major objections," he told Matt.

"And if I did?" Matt asked.

Sean gave him an honest answer. "I'd hear you out and then we'd discuss them."

At least the man wasn't trying to snow him—and he wasn't backing off, either. Apparently, his partner's father had the courage of his convictions. He liked that.

"Can't ask for anything more than that," he told Sean with an understanding smile. "I just want my mother to be happy."

Then they were on the same page, Sean thought, relieved to have this over with.

"So do I, Matt. So do I. Well, that's all I had to say," Sean told them, rounding the table again to his original side. He began locking down his station. "I didn't mean to keep you," he apologized. Sean glanced at his watch. "Hey, I've got to get going myself. I told your mother I'd meet her for dinner tonight at that little Italian restaurant she likes." Sean smiled broadly at them as he shed his lab coat and hung it up on the back of the door. "See you both at the next family gathering."

Kendra suddenly came to. "And you don't have anything new to tell us about the man subdivided in the suitcases?" she called after her father as he started to walk out.

"Only that it's the man you were looking for," he said just before the door closed in his wake.

Her father was serious about Abilene's mother. The words swirled about her head like a news headline.

She was vaguely aware that her partner was wordlessly ushering her out of the lab.

Was this relationship between their parents going to change things between them? she wondered. Matt seemed to like her father, but there was a world of difference between liking the head of the day shift CSI unit and liking the man who was dating his mother.

It occurred to her—not for the first time—that she didn't want things to change between them. Not for any reason. She didn't want this interlude they found themselves in to end, even though she'd been preparing herself for just that eventuality since the moment it had begun. Status quo had suddenly become very important to her.

The silence between them was deafening. They'd been driving in it for the past five minutes. Finally, she couldn't stand it any longer. "Are you angry?"

Matt continued watching the road. "No, why would you think that?"

Wasn't it obvious? "Well, you're not saying anything."

Her logic escaped him. "That doesn't automatically mean I'm angry."

She was willing to accept that, as long as he explained the silence. Why wasn't he talking to her? "Okay, then what are you?"

"Thinking," he answered.

About the case? About their parents? He had to give her more of a hint than that. "About?" she asked impatiently.

She was definitely not prepared for what Matt said next. "Us."

"Us?" she echoed. Was she right? Was he looking for a way to end this? Her mouth felt sandpaper-dry as she asked, "What about 'us'?"

"What your father said back there started me thinking," he began, then glanced at her. "I realized that I still don't know where 'this' is going," he confessed, referring to what was happening between them, "but I'm beginning to think I know where I want it to go."

Why did that spark such a sense of panic within her? Panic no matter how this played itself out. If Matt told her he wanted to take their relationship to the next level, she was terrified of being disappointed in the end, the way that Jason had disappointed her. But if Matt told her he wanted his space, then the disappointment she lived in fear of would be right there.

There was no winning in this.

"Oh?" Kendra did her best to sound cavalier. "Care to share?"

This time the look Matt spared her was longer. And penetrating. "Do I have to?"

She took his words at face value. "Well, it'd be nice to know what you have in mind."

Matt shook his head as he turned left at the light. She didn't understand. "No, I meant I don't think I have to say it out loud—because I think that you already know where I want this to go."

It didn't change a thing. Either way made her nervous. She didn't want to pin down what was going on between them, didn't want to give it a name—because things with names tended to disappoint you in the long run. And she'd already had her heart ripped out once.

"Let's just table this for now, okay? Please?" she asked.

He *knew* she was going to say that. It still didn't make it any easier for him to hear. He kept his disappointment to himself. "You don't have to run from this, you know."

Oh, yes, I do. Because you're only going to hurt me. Big-time. She'd never thought she'd ever fall in love again, but she had. It had snuck up on her and knocked her knees out from under her.

Because she loved him, because she didn't want either of them to be hurt, she did her best to try to make him understand. "Look, I've already been there once, had it blow up in my face once—"

She'd given him the opening he wanted and he seized it. "Right. *Once,*" he emphasized, interrupting her. "When you were engaged to Jason. But newsflash, Cavanaugh," he said, deliberately using her last name, reminding her of how things did change in life, "I'm not Jason. I don't have a hero complex with unrealistic expectations for myself. And I don't have any unrealistic expectations for you, either."

"Nice to know." There was a tinge of sarcasm surrounding her words.

Matt continued as if he hadn't heard her or picked up on her tone. What he had to tell her was too important to get sidetracked by minor details and wounded pride.

"Hell, you've already exceeded any expectations I might have had beyond my wildest dreams," he said with finality. "All I have to do is look at you and I find myself wanting you more than I even want to breathe."

"*Really* nice to know," she said, amending her original response and definitely eliminating the sarcastic tone that had come with it.

"My point was," Matt went on, "that I don't know where this is going, but I want to give it every chance to get to the right destination." They were at a red light and he looked at her intently. "I want to go the distance with you."

"I thought we already were."

She was being flippant. It was, he'd come to understand, one of her defense mechanisms.

"Not that distance," he laughed, and then he grew serious again. "The *big* distance—the kind of distance that your mother and father went. The kind," he said with feeling, "that your father is proposing to go with my mother."

Her mouth was now drier than dry. She was surprised she wasn't croaking as she asked, "Are you asking me to marry you?"

"Not yet," he told her honestly. "But there is a distinct possibility that we will be having that conversation in the not-too-distant future." Then, before she could protest, he assured her, "I know what you went through and I don't want to rush you. And I know how I felt about the thought of marriage—until I started dealing with you. Things change, and they don't always have to change for the worse." He waited for her to stay something. When she didn't, he prodded, "Well?"

"Drive faster," she said.

"What?"

"Drive faster," Kendra repeated firmly. "I want to carry on this conversation at my place, preferably without so many clothes in the way," she said, ending her statement with a wicked wink that had his stomach tightening, then flipping over.

"Kendra, I'm serious."

Yes, he was, Kendra thought. It was the first time she'd heard him say her name. "I know," she told him, her tone utterly subdued as she looked at him. Her smile was warm—and full of promise. "So am I."

Matt stepped on the gas and sped up.

Epilogue

The moment Kendra slammed shut the front door of her apartment, the blizzard of clothing began, falling on the floor, marking their path.

By the time Matt and she had gone the short distance from her door to her bed, there no longer remained anything between them except the very intense desire to share all the heated pleasures they had come to discover in each other's arms.

In the relatively short time they had been together, Kendra had learned an infinite number of ways to make love, to give, sustain and get the maximum thrill from intimate rituals and she was incredibly eager to revisit each and every method, each and every movement.

Her heart was pounding wildly as she found herself on the receiving end even as she made plans to reverse the tables on him.

The first spectacular climax occurred within less

than five minutes of her unlocking her front door. More followed, but by then she could no longer gauge time and space, only heat and exhilarating bursts of pulsating pleasure.

Exhaustion never felt so wonderful.

"No fair, no fair," she gasped in protest, "you're ahead."

"I'll let you catch up," Matt promised, murmuring the words against the sensitive skin along her throat. "I just wanted to prove to you that I'm serious."

"So am I," she breathed.

A salvo of energy infused her. In a moment she was switching positions with him and climbing on top, doing her best to at least partially drive him as crazy as he had already driven her.

And then, into this mutually acceptable madness, a jarring noise began to invade. It continued, taking on shape until she recognized it for what it was.

Ringing.

"Dammit, it's my cell phone," she cried in frustrated annoyance, not wanting to surrender a moment of what was happening. "I should have dropped it in a glass of water when we came in."

"You'd better take it," Matt recommended. His words would have had more conviction had he not been pressing his lips and other parts of his body against receptive parts of hers.

Delicious waves of heat and passion were licking at her as Kendra struggled to clear her head and reached for the phone she'd flung somewhere on the nightstand.

"Cavanaugh," she declared into the phone. It took more than a little effort and she struggled to try to keep that shred of her brain that was still functioning receptive. And then her eyes flew open. "Say again?" The next moment, she sighed. Resigned. "Damn. Okay, keep me posted if there's any more news. Thanks. I appreciate it."

Closing her phone, she let it slip from her fingers, already forgotten.

But she'd piqued Matt's curiosity. "What was that about?" he asked, even as he trailed his lips along her naked shoulder.

Another, more heartfelt sigh preceded her answer. "The actor escaped."

He raised his head to look at her. "What?"

She filled him in as best she could, given that her body was once again tingling in high anticipation of the magic she knew was to come.

"Wong just called. Somehow, Blake got his hands on a guard's uniform and walked right out of jail. Nobody knows where he is."

He asked because he knew procedure, not because he wanted to. "They want us to go after him?"

There they had lucked out. For now. "Wong and Ruiz already said they were on it, but they don't hold out much hope." She had to admit, though, if only to herself, that there was a part of her that felt they had not heard the last of Tyler Blake.

But, right now, none of that mattered. The only thing that did matter was the way that Matt made her feel: incredibly alive and hopeful.

"Then we can go back to what we were doing," he concluded, never really having stopped.

Every part of her smiled in response. "Absolutely."

"Good," he said, both to the situation and recalling the nickname he'd teasingly given her the first day they'd met.

In either case, it was the last thing either one of them said for the rest of a very long, inspired and delicious evening.

* * * * *

Cavanaugh Reunion

To
the wonderful Harlequin family,
and especially Patience Bloom,
who more than lives up to her name.
I thank you all for making my dreams come true.
And, to Pat Teal,
who started it all by asking,
"Would you like to write a romance?"
Thank God I said "Yes."
And last, but by no means least,
to you, beloved readers,
thank you!
I wouldn't be here without you.

Chapter 1

He smelled it before he saw it.

His mind elsewhere, Detective Ethan O'Brien's attention was immediately captured by the distinct, soul-disturbing smell that swept in, riding the evening breeze. Without warning, it maliciously announced that someone's dreams were being dashed even as they were being burnt to cinders.

Or, at the very least, they were damaged enough to generate a feeling of overwhelming sorrow and hopelessness.

Summers in California meant fires, they always had. Natives and transplants would joke that fires, earthquakes and mudslides were the dues they paid for having the best, most temperate overall weather in the country. But they only joked when nothing was burning, shaking or sliding away. Because during these catastrophic events, life proved to be all too tenuous, and there was no time for humor, only action. Humor was a salve at best, before and after the fact. Action was a way to hopefully curtail the amount of damage, if at all humanly possible.

But it wasn't summer. It was spring, and ordinarily, devastating fires should have still been many headlines away from becoming a very real threat.

Except that they were a real threat.

There were fires blazing all over the southern section of Aurora. Not the spontaneous fires that arose from spurts of bone-melting heat, or because a capricious wind had seized a not-quite-dead ember and turned it into something lethal by carrying it off and depositing it into the brush. These fires, ten so far and counting in the last two months, were man-made, the work of some bedeviled soul for reasons that Ethan had yet to understand.

But he swore to himself that he would.

He'd been assigned to his very first task force by Brian Cavanaugh, the Aurora police department's chief of detectives, and, as he'd come to learn in the last nine months, also his paternal uncle.

Knowledge of the latter tie had jolted him, Kyle and Greer the way nothing ever had before. He could state that for a fact, seeing as how, since they were triplets, there were times when he could swear that they functioned as one single-minded unit.

The three of them received the news at the same time. It had come from their mother in the form of a deathbed confession so that she could meet her maker with a clear conscience. She'd died within hours of telling them, having absolutely no idea what kind of turmoil her revelation had caused for him and his siblings.

Initially, finding out that he, Kyle and Greer were actually part of the sprawling Cavanaugh family had shaken the very foundations of their world. But in the end, once they'd gotten used to it and accepted the truth, the information had proven not to be life-shattering after all.

He had to admit, at least for him, that it was nice to be part of something larger than a breadbox. Back when his mother's death was still imminent, he'd anticipated life being pared down to it being just the three of them once she was gone. Three united against the world, so to speak.

Instead, the three of them were suddenly part of a network, part of something that at times seemed even greater than the sum of its parts.

Just like that, they were Cavanaughs.

There were some on the police force who were quick to cry "Nepotism!" when he, Kyle and Greer advanced, rising above the legions of patrol officers to become detectives in the department. But as he was quick to point out when confronted, it was merit that brought them to where they were, not favoritism.

Merit riding on the shoulders of abilities and quick thinking.

Like now.

On his way home after an extraordinarily long day that had wound up slipping its way into the even longer evening, Ethan had rolled his windows down in an attempt to just clear his head.

Instead, it had done just the opposite.

It felt as if smoke was leeching its way into his lungs and body through every available pore. The starless sky had rendered the black smoke all but invisible until he was practically on top of it.

But nothing could cover up the acrid smell.

In the time that it took for the presence of smoke from the fire to register, Ethan was able to make out where the telltale smell was emanating from. The building to his right on the next block was on fire. Big-time.

Ethan brought his lovingly restored 1964 Thunderbird sports car to a stop, parking it a block away so he didn't block whatever fire trucks were coming in. And truth be told, it was also to safeguard against anything happening to it. After his siblings, he loved the car, which he'd secretly named Annette, the most.

"I'll be right back, Annette," he promised the vehicle as he shut down the engine and leaped out. Despite the urgency of the situation, Ethan made sure that he locked the car before leaving it.

Where was everyone?

There were no fire trucks, not even a department car. People from the neighborhood were gathering around, drawn by the drama, but there was no indication of any firefighters on the scene.

But there was screaming. The sound of women and children screaming.

And then he saw why.

The building that was on fire was a shelter, specifically a shelter for battered women and their children.

Protocol, since there was no sign of a responding firehouse, would have him calling 911 before he did anything else. But protocol didn't have a child's screams ringing in its ears, and calling in the fire would be stealing precious seconds away from finding that child, seconds that could very well amount to the difference between life and death.

Out of the corner of his eye, Ethan saw several people gathering closer, tightening the perimeter of the so-called spectacle.

Voyeurs.

Disasters attracted audiences. This one time he used that to his advantage. Or rather the shelter's advantage.

"Call 911," he yelled to the man closest to him. "Tell them that the Katella Street Shelter's on fire." He had to shout the end of his sentence, as he was already running toward the building.

Turning his head to see if the man had complied, Ethan saw that he was just staring openmouthed at the building. Disgusted, Ethan reached into his pocket and pulled out his cell phone.

The fire couldn't be called an inferno yet, but he knew how little it took to achieve the transformation. It could literally happen in a heartbeat.

Raising the windbreaker he was wearing up over his head as a meager protective barrier against the flames, Ethan ran into the building even as he pressed 911.

The next moment, he stumbled backward, losing his footing as someone came charging out of the building. Springing up to his feet, Ethan saw that he'd just been knocked down by a woman. A small one at that. The blonde was holding an infant tucked against her chest with one arm while she held a toddler on her hip on the other side. A third child, just slightly older than the toddler, was desperately trying to keep up with her gait.

He was holding tightly on to the bottom of her shirt and screaming in fear.

Trying to catch his breath, Ethan was torn between asking the woman if she was all right and his initial intent of making sure that everyone was out of the building.

The once run-down building was spewing smoke and women in almost equal proportions. In the background, Ethan heard the sound of approaching sirens. It was too soon for a response to the call he'd made. It was obvious to him that someone else must have already called this fire in. There were two firehouses in Aurora, one to take care of the fires in the southern portion, the other to handle the ones in the northern section. Even given the close proximity of the southern-section fire station, the trucks had to have already been on their way when he'd first spotted the fire.

The woman who had all but run over him now passed him going in the opposite direction. To his amazement, she seemed to be running back into the burning building.

Was she crazy?

He lost no time heading her off. "Hey, wait, what about your kids?" he called out. She didn't turn around to acknowledge that she'd heard him. Ethan sped up and got in front of her, blocking her path. "Have you got another one in there?" Ethan grabbed the woman's arm, pulling her away from the entrance as two more women, propping each other up, emerged. "Stay with your children," he ordered. "I'll find your other kid," he promised. "Just tell me where."

"I don't know where," she snapped as she pulled her arm free.

The next moment, holding her arm up against her nose and mouth in a futile attempt to keep at least some of the smoke at bay, the woman darted around him and ran back into the burning building.

Ethan bit off a curse. He had a choice of either remaining outside and letting the approaching firefighters go in after her or doing it himself. Seeing as how they had yet to pull up in front of the building, by the time they could get into the building, it might be too late. His conscience dictated his course for him. He had no choice but to run after her.

Ethan fully intended to drag the woman out once he caught up to her. If she was trying to find another one of her children, he had the sinking feeling that it was too late. In his opinion, no one could survive this, and she had three children huddled together on the sidewalk to think about.

Mentally cursing the fate that had him embroiled in all this, Ethan ran in. He made his way through the jaws of the fire, its flames flaring like sharp yellow teeth threatening to take a chunk out of his flesh. Miraculously, Ethan saw the woman just up ahead of him.

"Hey!" he shouted angrily. "Stop!"

But the woman kept moving. Ethan could see her frantically looking around. He could also see what she couldn't, that a beam just above her head was about to give way. Dashing over, his lungs beginning to feel as if they were bursting, Ethan pulled the woman back just as the beam came crashing down. It missed hitting her by a matter of inches.

Still she resisted, trying to pull free of his grasp again. "There might be more," she shouted above the fire's loud moan. She turned away but got nowhere. Frustrated fury was in her reddened eyes as she demanded, "Hey! Hey, what are you doing?"

"Saving your kids' mother," Ethan snapped back. He threw the obstinate woman over his shoulder, appropriately enough emulating fireman style.

She was saying something, no doubt protesting or cursing him, but he couldn't hear her voice above the sounds of the fire. As far as he was concerned, it was better that way.

His eyes burned and his lungs felt as if they were coming apart. The way out of the building felt as if it was twice as far as the way in had been.

Finally making it across the threshold, he stumbled out, passing several firefighters as they raced into the building.

One of the firefighters stopped long enough to address him and point out the paramedic truck that was just pulling up.

"You can get medical attention for her over there," were the words that the man tossed in his direction as he hurried off.

"Let go of me!" the woman yelled angrily. When he didn't respond fast enough, she began to pound on his back with her fists.

For a woman supposedly almost overcome with smoke, Ethan thought, she packed quite a wallop. He was having trouble hanging on to her. When he finally set her down near the ambulance, Ethan instinctively stepped back to avoid contact with her swinging fists.

She all but fell over from the momentum of the last missed swing. Her eyes blazed as she demanded, "What the hell do you think you were doing?"

He hadn't expected a profusion of gratitude, but neither had he expected a display of anger. "Off the top of my head, I'd have to say saving your life."

"Saving my life?" she echoed incredulously, staring at him as if he'd just declared that he thought she was a zebra.

"You're welcome," Ethan fired back. He gestured toward the curb where two of the three children were sitting. The third was in another woman's arms. The woman was crying. "Now go see to your kids."

She stared at him as if he'd lost his mind. What the hell was he babbling about? "What kids?" she cried, her temper flaring.

"Your kids." Annoyed when she continued staring at him, Ethan pointed to the three children she'd had hanging off her as if she were some mother possum. "Those."

She glanced in the direction he was pointing. "You think—" Stunned and fighting off a cough that threatened to completely overwhelm her, Kansas Beckett found that she just couldn't finish her thought for a moment. "Those aren't my kids," she finally managed to tell him.

"They're not?" They'd certainly seemed as if they were hers when she'd ushered them out. He looked back at the children. They were crying again, this time clinging to a woman who was equally as teary. "Whose are they?"

Kansas shrugged. "I don't know. Hers, I imagine." She nodded toward the woman holding the baby and gathering the other two to her as best she could. "I was just driving by when I smelled the smoke and heard the screams." Why was she even bothering to explain her actions to this take-charge Neanderthal? "I called it in and then tried to do what I could."

Kansas felt gritty and dirty, not to mention that she was probably going to have to throw out what had been, until tonight, her favorite suit because she sincerely doubted that even the world's best dry cleaner could get the smell of smoke out of it.

Ethan gaped at what amounted to a little bit of a woman. "You just ran in."

She looked at him as if she didn't understand what his problem was. "Yeah."

Didn't this woman have a working brain? "What are you, crazy?" he demanded.

"No, are you?" Kansas shot back in the same tone. She gestured toward the building that was now a hive of activity with firemen fighting to gain the upper hand over the blazing enemy. "From the looks of it, you did the same thing."

Was she trying to put them on the same footing? He was a trained professional and she was a woman with streaks of soot across her face and clothes. Albeit a beautiful woman, but beauty in this case had nothing to do with what mattered.

"It's different," he retorted.

Kansas fisted her hands on her hips, going toe-to-toe with her so-called rescuer. She absolutely hated chauvinists, and this man was shaping up to be a card-carrying member of the club.

"Why?" she wanted to know. "Were you planning

on using a secret weapon to put the fire out? Maybe huff and puff until you blew it all out? Or did you have something else in mind?" she asked, her eyes dipping down so that they took in the lower half of his frame. Her meaning was clear.

He didn't have time for this, Ethan thought in exasperation. He didn't have time to argue with a bullheaded woman who was obviously braver than she was smart. His guess was that she probably had a firefighter in the family. Maybe her father or a brother she was attempting to emulate for some unknown reason.

Ethan frowned. Why was it always the pretty ones who were insane? he wondered. Maybe it was just nature's way of leveling the playing field.

In any case, he needed to start asking questions, to start interviewing the survivors to find out if they'd seen or heard anything suspicious just before the fire broke out.

And he needed, he thought, to have the rest of his team out here. While his captain applauded initiative, he frowned on lone-ranger behavior.

Moving away from the woman who was giving him the evil eye, Ethan reached into his pocket to take out his cell phone—only to find that his pocket was empty.

"Damn," he muttered under his breath.

He remembered shoving the phone into his pocket and feeling it against his thigh as he'd started to run into the burning shelter. He slanted a look back at the woman. He must have dropped it when she'd knocked him down at the building's entrance.

Kansas frowned. "What?"

Ethan saw that she'd bitten off the word as if it had

been yanked out of her throat against her will. For a second, he thought about just ignoring her, but he needed to get his team out here, which meant that he needed a cell phone.

"I lost my cell phone," he told her, then added, "I think I must have lost it when you ran into me and knocked me down."

Ethan looked over in the general direction of the entrance, but the area was now covered with firefighters running hoses, weaving in and out of the building, conferring with other firemen. Two were trying to get the swelling crowd to stay behind the designated lines that had been put up to control the area. If his phone had been lost there, it was most likely long gone, another casualty of the flames.

"You ran into me," she corrected him tersely.

Was it his imagination, or was the woman looking at him suspiciously?

"Why do you want your cell phone?" Kansas asked him. "Do you want to take pictures of the fire?"

He stared at her. Why the hell would he want to do that? The woman really was a nut job. "What would anyone want their phone for?" he responded in annoyance. "I want to make a call."

Her frown deepened. She made a small, disparaging noise, then began to dig through her pockets. Finding her own phone, she grudgingly held it out to him.

"Here, you can borrow mine," she offered. "Just don't forget to give it back."

"Oh, damn, there go my plans for selling it on eBay," he retorted. "Thanks," he said as he took the cell phone from her.

Ethan started to press a single key, then stopped himself. He was operating on automatic pilot and had just gone for the key that would have immediately hooked him up to the precinct. He vaguely wondered what pressing the number three on the woman's phone would connect him to. Probably her anger-management coach, he thought darkly. Too bad the classes weren't taking.

It took Ethan a few seconds to remember the number to his department. It had been at least six months since he'd had to dial the number directly.

He let it ring four times, then, when it was about to go to voice mail, he terminated the call and tried another number. All the while he was aware that this woman—with soot streaked across her face like war paint—was standing only a few feet away, watching him intently.

Why wasn't she getting herself checked out? he wondered. And why was she scrutinizing him so closely? Did she expect him to do something strange? Or was she afraid he was going to make off with her phone?

No one was picking up. Sighing, he ended the second call. Punching in yet another number, he began to mentally count off the number of rings.

The woman moved a little closer to him. "Nobody home?" she asked.

"Doesn't look that way."

But just as he said it, Ethan heard the phone on the other end being picked up. He held his hand up because she'd begun to say something. He hoped she'd pick up on his silent way of telling her to keep quiet while he was trying to hear.

"Cavanaugh," a deep voice on the other end of the line announced.

Great, like that was supposed to narrow things down. There were currently seventeen Cavanaughs on the police force—if he, Greer and Kyle were included in the count.

He thought for a moment, trying to remember the first name of the Cavanaugh who had been appointed head of this task force. Dax, that was it. Dax.

Ethan launched into the crux of his message. "Dax, this is Ethan O'Brien. I'm calling because there's just been another fire."

The terse statement immediately got the attention of the man he was calling—as well as the interest of the woman whose phone he was using.

Chapter 2

"Give me your location," Dax Cavanaugh instructed. Then, before Ethan had a chance to give him the street coordinates, he offered, "I'll round up the rest of the team. You just do what you have to do until we get there."

The chief had appointed Dax to head up the team. Calling them was an assignment he could have easily passed on if he'd been filled with his own importance. But Ethan had come to learn that none of the Cavanaughs ever pulled rank, even when they could.

Ethan paused for a moment as he tried to recall the name of the intersection. When he did, he recited the street names, acutely aware that the woman to his right was staring at him as if she were expecting to witness some kind of a rare magic trick. Either that or she was afraid that he was going to run off with her cell phone.

"You want to call the chief, or should I?" Dax was asking, giving him the option.

Ethan thought it just a wee bit strange that Dax was referring to his own father by his official title, but he supposed that just verified the stories that the Cavanaughs went out of their way not to seem as if they were showing any favoritism toward one of their own.

"You can do it," Ethan told him. "The chief's most likely home by now, and you have his private number."

Ethan shifted to get out of the way. The area was getting more and more crowded with survivors from the shelter and the firemen were still fighting the good fight, trying to contain the blaze and save at least part of the building.

"And you don't?" Dax asked in surprise.

Out of the corner of his eye, Ethan saw the woman moving in closer to him. Apparently, she had no space issues. "No, why should I?"

"Because you're family," Dax said, as if Ethan should have known that. "My father lets everyone in the family have his home number." To back up his claim, Dax asked, "Do you want it?"

Dax began to rattle off the numbers, but Ethan stopped him before he was even halfway through. "That's okay, I'm going to have my hands full here until the rest of the team comes. You can do the honors and call him."

The truth of it was, Ethan didn't want to presume, no matter what Dax said to the contrary, that he was part of the Cavanaugh inner circle. Granted, he had Cavanaugh blood running through his veins, but the way he came to have it could easily be seen as a source of embarrassment, even in this day and age. Until he felt completely comfortable about it, he didn't want to assume too much. Right now, he was still feeling his way around this whole new scenario he found himself in and wanted to make sure he didn't antagonize either Andrew or Brian Cavanaugh.

Not that he would mind becoming a real part of the family. He wasn't like Kyle, who initially had viewed every interaction with their newfound family with suspicion, anticipating hostile rejection around every corner. He and his sister, Greer, secretly welcomed being part of a large, respected family after all the years they'd spent on the other side of the spectrum, poor and isolated—and usually two steps in front of the bill collector.

But he wanted to force nothing, take nothing for granted. If Brian Cavanaugh wanted him to have his private number, then it was going to have to come from Brian Cavanaugh, not his son.

"Will do," Dax was saying, and then he broke the connection.

The moment Ethan ended the call and handed the phone back to her, the blonde was openly studying him. "You a reporter?" she asked.

Damn, she was nosey. Just what was it that she was angling for? "No."

The quick, terse answer didn't seem to satisfy her curiosity. She came in from another angle. "Why all this interest in the fires?"

He answered her question with a question of his own. "Why the interest in my interest in the fires?" he countered.

Kansas lifted her chin. She was not about to allow herself to get sidetracked. "I asked first."

Instead of answering, Ethan reached out toward her hair. Annoyed, she began to jerk her head back, but he stopped her with, "You've got black flakes in your hair. I was just going to remove them. Unless you want them there," he speculated, raising a quizzical eyebrow and waiting for a response.

Something had just happened. Something completely uncalled-for. She'd felt a very definite wave of heat as his fingers made contact with her hair and scalp. Her imagination?

Kansas took a step back and did the honors herself, carelessly brushing her fingers through her long blond hair to get rid of any kind of soot or burnt debris she might have picked up while she was hustling the children out of the building. She supposed she should count herself lucky that it hadn't caught fire while she was getting the children out.

"There," she declared, her throat feeling tight for reasons that were completely beyond her. She tossed her head as a final sign of defiance. And then her eyes narrowed as she looked at him. "Now, why are you so interested in the fires, and who did you just call?"

She was no longer being just nosey, he thought. There was something else at work here. But what? Maybe she was a reporter and that was why she seemed to resent his being one, as per her last guess.

If that was what she was, then she was out of luck. Nothing he disliked more than reporters. "Lady, just because I borrowed your phone doesn't entitle you to my life story."

She squared her shoulders as if she were about to go into battle. He braced himself. "I don't want your life story. I just want an answer to my question, and it's Kansas, not 'lady.'"

Ethan's eyebrows lifted in confusion. What the hell was she talking about? "What's Kansas?"

Was she dealing with a village idiot, or was he just slow? "My name," she emphasized.

Ethan cocked his head, trying to absorb this meandering conversation. "Your last name's Kansas?"

She sighed. She was fairly certain he was doing this on purpose just to annoy her. "No, my *first* name is Kansas, and no matter how long you attempt to engage in this verbal shell game of yours, I'm not going to get sidetracked. Now, who did you call, and why are you so taken with this fire?" Before he could say anything, she asked him another question. "And what did you mean by 'there's been another one'?"

"The phrase 'another one' means that there's been more than one." He was deliberately goading her now. And enjoying it.

She said something under her breath that he couldn't quite make out, but he gathered it wasn't very favorable toward him.

"I know what the phrase means," she retorted through gritted teeth. "I'll ask you one more time— why are you so interested in the fires?"

"What happens after one more time?" Ethan wanted to know, amused by the woman despite himself. Irritating women usually annoyed the hell out of him—but there was something different about this one.

She drew herself up to her full height. "After one more time, I have you arrested."

That surprised him. "You're a cop?" He thought he knew most of the people on the force, by sight if not by name. He'd never seen her before.

"No. I'm a fire investigator," she informed him archly. "But I can still have you arrested. Clapped in irons would be my choice," Kansas added, savoring the image.

"Kinky," he commented. Damn, they were making fire investigators a hell of a lot prettier these days. *If* she was telling the truth. "Mind if I ask to see some identification?"

"And just so I know, who's asking?" she pressed, still trying to get a handle on his part in all this.

It was a known fact that pyromaniacs liked to stick around and watch their handiwork until the object of their interest burnt down to the ground and there was nothing left to watch. Since she'd begun her investigations and discovered that the fires had been set, Kansas had entertained several theories as to who or what was behind all these infernos. She was still sorting through them, looking for something that would rule out the others.

"Ethan O'Brien," he told her. She was still looking at him skeptically. He inclined his head. "I guess since you showed me yours, I'll show you mine." He took out his ID and his badge. "Detective Ethan O'Brien," he elaborated.

Like his siblings, he was still debating whether he was going to change his last name the way Brian and his brother Andrew, the former chief of police and reigning family patriarch, had told them they were welcome to do.

He knew that Greer was leaning toward it, as were Brian's four stepchildren who'd become part of the family when he'd married his widowed former partner. Kyle was the last holdout if he, Ethan, decided to go with the others. But he, Greer and Kyle had agreed that it would be an all-or-nothing decision for the three of them.

As for himself, he was giving the matter careful consideration.

"*You're* a cop," she concluded, quickly scanning the ID he held up.

"That I am," Ethan confirmed, slipping his wallet back into his pocket. "I'm on the task force investigating the recent crop of fires that have broken out in Aurora."

"They didn't just 'break out,'" she corrected him. "Those fires were all orchestrated, all set ahead of time."

"Yes, I know," Ethan allowed. He regarded her for a moment, wondering how much she might have by way of information. "How long have you been investigating this?"

There was only one way to answer that. "Longer than you," she promised.

She seemed awfully cocky. He found himself itching to take her down a peg. Take her down a peg and at the same time clean the soot off her bottom lip with his own.

Careful, O'Brien, he warned himself. *If anything, this is a professional relationship. Don't get personally involved, not even for a minute.*

"And you would know this how?" he challenged

her. How would she know what was going on in his squad room?

"Simple. The fire department investigates every fire to make sure that it wasn't deliberately set," she answered him without missing a beat. "That would be something you should know heading into *your* investigation."

He'd never been one of those guys who felt superior to the softer of the species simply because he was a man. In his opinion, especially after growing up with Greer, women were every bit as capable and intelligent as men. More so, sometimes. But he'd never had any use for people—male or female—who felt themselves to be above the law. Especially when they came across as haughty.

"Tell me," he said, lowering his voice as if he were about to share a secret thought. "How do you manage to stand up with that huge chip on your shoulder?"

Her eyes hardened, but to his surprise, no choice names were attached to his personage. Instead, using the same tone as he just had, she informed him, "I manage just fine, thanks."

"Kansas!" The fire chief, at least a decade older than his men and the young woman he called out to, hurried over to join them. Concern was etched into his features. "Are you all right?"

She flashed the older man a wide smile. "I'm fine, Chief," she assured him.

The expression on the older man's face said that he wasn't all that sure. "Someone said you ran into the burning building." He gestured toward the blazing building even as he leaned over to get a closer look at her face. "They weren't kidding, were they?"

She shrugged, not wanting to call any more undue attention to herself or her actions. "I heard kids screaming—"

Chief John Lawrence cut her off as he shook his head more in concern than disapproval. "You're not a firefighter anymore, Kansas," he pointed out. "And you should know better than to run into a burning building with no protective gear on."

She smiled and Ethan noted that it transformed her, softening her features and in general lighting up the immediate area around her. She was one of those people, he realized, who could light up a room with her smile. And frost it over with her frown.

It was never a good idea to argue with the fire chief. "Yes, I do, and I promise to do better next time," she told him, raising her hand as if she were taking an oath. "Hopefully, there won't be a next time."

"Amen to that," the chief agreed wholeheartedly. He had to get back to his men. The fire wasn't fully contained yet. "You stay put here until things are cool enough for you to conduct your initial investigation," he instructed.

The smile had turned into a grin and she rendered a mock salute in response to the man's attempt at admonishing her. "Yes, sir."

"Father?" Ethan asked the moment the chief had returned to his truck and his men.

Kansas turned toward him. He'd clearly lost her. "What?"

"Is the chief your father?" The older man certainly acted as if she were his daughter, Ethan thought.

Kansas laughed as she shook her head. "Don't let his wife hear you say that. No, Captain Lawrence is just a very good friend," she answered. "He helped train me, and when I wanted to get into investigative work, he backed me all the way. He's not my dad, but I wouldn't have minded it if he were."

At least, Kansas thought, that way she would have known who her father was.

His curiosity aroused, Ethan tried to read between the lines. Was there more to this "friend" thing than met the eye? Lawrence was certainly old enough to be her father, but that didn't stop some men. Or some women, especially if they wanted to get ahead.

"Friend," Ethan echoed. "As in boyfriend?" He raised an eyebrow, waiting to see how she'd react.

She lifted her chin. "Unless you're writing my biography, you don't have the right to ask that kind of question," she snapped.

Ethan's smile never wavered. He had a hunch that this woman's biography did *not* make for boring reading. "I'm not writing your biography," he clarified. "But there are some things I need to know—just for the record."

She bet he could talk the skin off a snake. "All right. For the 'record' I was the first one on the scene when the shelter began to burn—"

He'd already figured that part out. "Which is why I want to question you—at length," he added before she could brush the request aside. "I need to know if you saw anyone or anything that might have aroused your suspicions."

"Yes," she deadpanned, "I saw the flames—and I instantly knew it was a fire."

He had nothing against an occasional joke, but he resented like hell having his chain yanked. "Hey, 'Kansas,' in case it's escaped you, we're both on the same team. It seems to me that means we should be sharing information."

She was sure that he was more than eager for her to "share" and doubted very much that it would be a two-way street as far as he was concerned. Until he brought something to the table other than words, she was not about to share anything with him.

"Sorry." With that, she pushed past him.

"I bet the box that said 'works and plays well with others' always had 'needs improvement' checked on it," he said, raising his voice as she walked away.

She looked at him over her shoulder. "But the box labeled 'pummels annoying cop senseless' was also checked every time."

Ethan shook his head. Working together was just going to have to wait a couple of days. He had a definite hunch that she'd be coming around by then.

"Your loss," he called after her, and turned just as he saw Dax Cavanaugh coming toward him.

Right behind him were Richard Ortiz and Alan Youngman, two other veteran detectives on the force who now found themselves part of the arson task force. Remarkably, none of the men seemed to resent his presence despite the fact that they were all veterans with several years to their credit, while this was his very first assignment as a detective.

There were times he could have sworn that his shield was still warm in his wallet.

"What have you got?" Ortiz asked him, looking more than a little disgruntled. "And it better be worth it because I was just about to get lucky with this hot little number."

"He doesn't want to hear about your rubber doll collection," Youngman deadpanned to his partner.

Ortiz looked insulted. "Hey, just because you're in a rut doesn't mean that I am," the younger man protested.

"Guys," Dax admonished in a low voice. "Playtime is over."

Youngman frowned as he shook his head. "You're no fun since they put you in charge."

"We'll have fun after we catch this arsonist and confiscate his matches," Dax replied.

Overhearing, Kansas couldn't help crossing back to the men and correcting this new detective. "He's not an arsonist."

Dax turned to her. His eyes, Ethan noticed, swept over the woman as if he were taking inventory. What was conspicuously missing was any indication of attraction. Brenda must be one hell of a woman, Ethan couldn't help thinking about the man's wife.

"And you would know this how?" Dax asked the self-proclaimed fire investigator.

"An angel whispered in her ear," Ethan quipped. "Dax, this is Kansas Beckett. She says she's the fire department's investigator. Kansas, this is Dax Cavanaugh, Alan Youngman and Richard Ortiz." Three heads bobbed in order of the introductions.

It was more information than she wanted, but she nodded at each man, then looked at the man conducting the introductions. "I didn't *say* I was the fire investigator. I *am* the fire investigator. And how did you know my last name?" she wanted to know. "I didn't give it to you."

"But remarkably, I can read," Ethan answered with an enigmatic smile. "And it was on the ID you showed me."

"How do you know it's not an arsonist?" Dax persisted, more emphatically this time.

She patiently recited the standard differentiation. "Arsonists do it for profit," she told him, moving out of the way of several firefighters as they raced by, heading straight for the building's perimeter. "Their own or someone else's. The buildings that were torched, as far as we can ascertain, have no common thread drawing them together. For instance, there's no one who stands to profit from getting rid of a battered-women's shelter."

Ethan turned the thought over in his head. "Maybe there's a developer in the wings, looking to buy up land cheap in order to build a residential community or a king-size mall or some vast hotel, something along those lines."

But she shook her head. "Too spread apart, too far-fetched," she pointed out. "It would have to be the biggest such undertaking in the country," she emphasized. "And I don't really think that's what's going on here."

Dax was open to any kind of a guess at this point.

"So who or what do you think is behind these fires?" he asked her.

She was silent for a moment. Almost against her will, she glanced in Ethan's direction before answering. "My guess is that it's either a pyromaniac who's doing it for the sheer thrill of it, or we're up against someone with a vendetta who's trying to hide his crime in plain sight with a lot of camouflage activity."

"In which case, we have to find which is the intentional fire and which were set for show," Ethan theorized.

Kansas looked at him. "I'm impressed. Chalk one up for the pretty boy."

He couldn't tell if she was being sarcastic or actually giving him his due. With Kansas, he had a hunch that it was a little bit of both.

Chapter 3

In all, twelve children and nineteen adults were saved. Because the firefighters had responded so quickly to Kansas's call—and despite the fact that several women and children wound up being taken to the hospital for treatment—not a single life was lost.

Tired, seriously bordering on being punchy, Ethan nonetheless remained at the scene with the other detectives, interviewing anyone who'd been in the building just before the fire broke out. It was a long shot, but he kept hoping that someone might have witnessed even the slightest thing that seemed out of the ordinary at the time.

Because she wanted to spare the victims any more unnecessary trauma, and since the nature of the questions that the police were asking were along the lines of what she wanted to ask, Kansas decided it was best to temporarily join forces with the Neanderthal who had slung her over his shoulder.

The women and children who'd been in the fire had her complete sympathy. She knew the horror they'd gone through. Knew, firsthand, how vulnerable and helpless they'd all felt. And how they'd all thought, at one point or another, that they were going to die.

Because she'd been trapped in just such a fire herself once.

When she was twelve years old, she'd been caught in a burning building. It occurred in the group home where she'd always managed to return. She'd come to regard it as a holding zone, a place to stay in between being placed in various foster homes. But in that case, there'd been no mystery as to how the fire had gotten started. Eric Johnson had disobeyed the woman who was in charge and not only played with matches but deliberately had set the draperies in the common room on fire.

Seeing what he'd done, Kansas had run toward the draperies and tried to put the fire out using a blanket that someone had left behind. All that had done was spread the flames. Eric had been sent to juvenile hall right after that.

Kansas couldn't help wondering what had happened to Eric after all these years. Was he out there somewhere, perpetuating his love affair with fire?

She made a mental note to see if she could find out where he was these days.

Kansas glanced at O'Brien. He looked tired, she noted, but he continued pushing on. For the most part, he was asking all the right questions. And for a good-looking man, he seemed to display a vein of sensitivity, as well. In her experience, most good-looking men didn't. They were usually one-dimensional and shallow, too enamored with the image in their mirror to even think about anyone else.

More than an hour of questioning yielded the consensus that the fire had "just come out nowhere." Most of the women questioned seemed to think it had started in the recreation room, although no one had actually seen it being started or even knew *how* it had started. When questioned further, they all more or less said the same thing. That they were just suddenly *aware* of the fire being there.

Panic had ensued as mothers frantically began searching for their children. The ones who hadn't been separated from their children to begin with herded them out into the moonless night amid screaming and accelerated pandemonium.

The chaos slowly abated as mother after mother was reunited with her children. But there was still one woman left searching. Looking bedraggled and utterly shell-shocked, the woman went from one person to another, asking if anyone had seen her daughter. No one had.

Unable to stand it any longer, Kansas caught O'Brien by the arm and pulled him around. She pointed to the hysterical woman. "She shouldn't have to look for her daughter on her own."

Busy comparing his findings with Dax and all but running on empty, Ethan nodded. "Fine, why don't you go help her." More than any of them, this impetuous, pushy woman seemed to have a relationship with the women at the shelter. At the very least, she seemed to be able to relate to them. Maybe she could pick up on something that he and the others on the task force couldn't—and more important, she could bring to the table what he felt was a woman's natural tendency to empathize. That would probably go a long way in giving the other woman some measure of comfort until they were able to hopefully locate her missing daughter.

Kansas pressed her lips together, biting back a stinging retort. She couldn't help thinking she'd just been brushed off.

Not damn likely, Detective.

Detective Ethan O'Brien, she silently promised herself, was about to discover that she didn't brush aside easily.

The moment she approached the distraught woman, the latter grabbed her by the arm. "Have you seen her? Can you help me find my Jennifer?"

"We're going to do everything we can to find her," Kansas told the woman as she gently escorted her over to one of the firemen. "Conway, I need your help."

"Anytime, Kansas. I'm all yours," the blond-haired fireman told her as he flashed a quick, toothy grin.

"This woman can't find her daughter. She might have been one of the kids taken to the hospital. See what you can do to reunite them," Kansas requested.

The fireman looked disappointed for a moment, then with a resigned shrug did as he was asked and took charge of the woman. "Don't worry, we'll find her," he said in a soothing, baritone voice.

Kansas flashed a smile at Conway before returning to O'Brien to listen in on his latest interview.

"Buck passing?" Ethan asked when she made her

way back to his circle. Curious to see what she did with the woman, he'd been watching her out of the corner of his eye.

"No," she answered tersely. "Choosing the most efficient path to get things done. Conway was part of the first team that made it inside. If there was anyone left to save, he would have found them." She crossed her arms. "He's also got a photographic memory and was there, helping to put the injured kids into the ambulances. If anyone can help find this woman's daughter, he can."

Ethan nodded, taking the information in. "You seem to know a lot about this Conway guy. You worked with him before?"

"For five years."

He was tempted to ask if she'd done more than just work with the man. The fact that the question even occurred to him caught him off guard. The woman was a barracuda. A gorgeous barracuda, but still a barracuda, and he knew better than to swim in the water near one. So it shouldn't matter whether their relationship went any deeper than just work.

But it did.

"How does someone get into that line of work?" he wanted to know.

He was prejudiced. It figured… "You mean how does a woman get into that line of work?"

Ethan knew what the sexy force of nature was doing, and he refused to get embroiled in a discussion that revolved around stereotypes. He had a more basic question than that. "How do you make yourself rush into burning buildings when everyone else is running in the opposite direction?"

It was something she'd never thought twice about. She'd just done it. It was the right thing to do. "Because you want to help, to save people. You did the very same thing," she pointed out, "and no one's even paying you to do it. It's not your job." She looked back toward Conway and the woman she'd entrusted to him. He was on the phone, most likely calling the hospital to find out if her daughter was there. Mentally, Kansas crossed her fingers for the woman.

"It's all part of 'protect and serve,'" she heard O'Brien telling her.

Kansas turned her attention back to the irritating detective with the sexy mouth. "If you understand that, then you have your answer."

Greer blustered through life, but Ethan's mother had been meek. He'd always thought that more women were like his mother than his sister. "Aren't you afraid of getting hurt? Of getting permanently scarred?"

Those thoughts had crossed her mind, but only fleetingly. She shook her head. "I'm more afraid of spending night after night with a nagging conscience that won't let me forget that I *didn't* do all I could to save someone. That because I hesitated or wasn't there to save them, someone died. There are enough things to feel guilty about in this world without adding to the sum total."

She didn't want to continue focusing on herself or her reaction to things. There was a more important topic to pursue. "So, did you find out anything useful?" she pressed.

What did she think she missed? "You were only gone a few minutes," he reminded her. The rest of the time, she'd been with him every step of the way—not that he really minded it. Even with soot on her face, the woman was extremely easy on the eyes.

"Crucial things can be said in less than a minute," she observed. Was he deliberately being evasive? *Had* he learned something?

"Sorry to disappoint you," Ethan said. "But nothing noteworthy was ascertained." He looked back at the building. The firemen had contained the blaze and only a section of the building had been destroyed. But it was still going to have to be evacuated for a good chunk of time while reconstruction was undertaken. "We'll know more when the ashes cool off and we can conduct a thorough search."

"That's my department," Kansas reminded him, taking pleasure in the fact that—as a fire investigator—her work took priority over his.

"Not tonight." He saw her eyes narrow, like someone getting ready for a fight. "Look, I don't want to have to go over your head," he warned her. He and the task force had dibs and that was that.

"And I don't want to have to take yours off," she fired back with feeling. "So back off. This is *my* investigation, O'Brien. Someone is burning down buildings in Aurora."

"And running the risk of killing people while he's doing it," Ethan concluded. "Dead people fall under my jurisdiction." And that, he felt, terminated the argument.

"And investigating man-made fires comes under mine," she insisted.

She didn't give an inch. Why didn't that surprise him?

"So you work together."

They turned in unison to see who had made the simple declaration. It had come from Brian Cavanaugh, the chief of police. When Dax had called him, Brian had lost no time getting to the site of the latest unexplained fire.

Brian looked from his new nephew to the woman Ethan was having a difference of opinion with. He saw not just a clash of temperaments as they fought over jurisdiction, but something more.

Something that, of late, he'd found himself privy to more than a few times. There had to be something in the air lately.

These two mixed like oil and water, he thought. And they'd be together for quite a while, he was willing to bet a month's salary on it.

His intense blue eyes, eyes that were identical in hue to those of the young man his late brother had sired, swept over Ethan and the investigator whose name he'd been told was Kansas. He perceived resistance to his instruction in both of them.

"Have I made myself clear?" Brian asked evenly.

"Perfectly," Ethan responded, coming to attention and standing soldier-straight.

Rather than mumble an agreement the way he'd expected her to, the young woman looked at him skeptically. "Did you clear this with the chief and my captain?"

"It was cleared the minute I suggested it," Brian said with no conceit attached to his words. "The bottom line is that we all want to find whoever's responsible for all this."

The expression was kind, the tone firm. This was

a man, she sensed, people didn't argue with. And neither would she.

Unless it was for a good cause.

Kansas stayed long after the police task force had recorded and photographed their data, folded their tents and disappeared into what was left of the night. She liked conducting her investigation without having to trip over people, well intentioned or not. Gregarious and outgoing, Kansas still felt there was a time for silence and she processed things much better when there was a minimum of noise to distract her.

She'd found that obnoxious Detective O'Brien and his annoying smile most distracting of all.

Contrary to the fledgling opinion that had been formed—most likely to soothe the nerves of the shelter's residents—the fire hadn't been an accident. It had been started intentionally. She'd discovered an incendiary device hidden right off the kitchen, set for a time when the area was presumably empty. So whoever had done this hadn't wanted to isolate anyone or cut them off from making an escape. A fire in the kitchen when there was no one in the kitchen meant that the goal was destruction of property, not lives.

Too bad things didn't always go according to plan, she silently mourned. One of the shelter volunteers had gotten cut off from the others and hadn't made it out of the building. She'd been found on the floor, unconscious. The paramedics had worked over the young woman for close to half an hour before she'd finally come around. She was one of the lucky.

Frowning, Kansas rocked back on her heels and shook her head.

This psychopath needed to be found and brought to justice quickly, before he did any more damage.

And she needed to get some sleep before she fell on her face.

She wondered where the displaced residents of the shelter would be sleeping tonight. She took comfort in the knowledge that they'd be returning in a few weeks even if the construction wasn't yet completed.

With a weary sigh, Kansas stood up and headed for the front entrance.

Just before she crossed the charred threshold, she kicked something. Curious, thinking it might just possibly have something to do with the identity of whoever started the fire, she stooped down to pick it up.

It turned out to be a cell phone—in pretty awful condition, from what she could tell. Flipping it open, she found that the battery was still active. She could just barely make out the wallpaper. It was a picture of three people. Squinting, she realized that the obnoxious detective who'd thought she'd needed to be carried out of the building fireman-style was in the photo.

There were two more people with him, both of whom looked identical to him. Now there was a curse, she mused, closing the phone again. Three Detective O'Briens. Kansas shivered at the thought.

"Tough night, huh?" the captain said, coming up to her. It wasn't really a question.

"That it was. On the heels of a tough day," she added. She hated not being able to come up with an answer, to have unsolved cases pile up on top of one another like some kind of uneven pyramid.

Captain John Lawrence looked at her with compassion. "Why don't you go home, Kansas?"

"I'm almost done," she told him.

His eyes swept over her and he shook his head. "Looks to me like you're almost done *in*." Lawrence nodded toward the building they'd just walked out of. "This'll all still be here tomorrow morning, Kansas. And you'll be a lot fresher. Maybe it'll make more sense to you then."

Kansas paused to look back at the building and sighed. "Burning buildings will never make any sense to me," she contradicted. "But maybe you're right about needing to look at this with fresh eyes."

"I'm always right," Lawrence told her with a chuckle. "That's why they made me the captain."

Kansas grinned. "That, and don't forget your overwhelming modesty."

"You've been paying attention." His eyes crinkled, all but disappearing when he smiled.

"Right from the beginning, Captain Lawrence," she assured him.

Captain Lawrence had been more than fair to her, and she appreciated that. She'd heard horror stories about other houses and how life became so intolerable that female firefighters wound up quitting. Not that she ever would. It wasn't in her nature to quit. But she appreciated not having to make that choice.

Looking down, she realized that she was even more covered with dust and soot than before. She attempted to dust herself off, but it seemed like an almost impossible task.

"I'll have a preliminary report on your desk in the morning," she promised.

Lawrence tapped her on the shoulder, and when she looked at him quizzically, he pointed up toward the sky. "It already is morning."

"Then I'd better go home and start typing," she quipped.

"Type later," Lawrence ordered. "Sleep now."

"Anyone ever tell you that you're a nag, Captain Lawrence?"

"My wife," he answered without skipping a beat. "But then, what does she know? Besides, compared to Martha, I'm a novice. You ever want to hear a pro, just stop by the house. I'll drop some socks on the floor and have her go at it for you." He looked at her. "I don't want to see you until at least midday."

"'O, Captain! my Captain!'" Throwing her wrist against her forehead in a melodramatic fashion, Kansas quoted a line out of a classic poem by Walt Whitman that seemed to fit here. "You've hurt my feelings."

He gave her a knowing look. "Can't hurt what you don't have."

"Right," she murmured.

She'd deliberately gone out of her way to come across like a militant fire investigator, more macho than the men she worked with. There was a reason for that. She didn't want to allow *anything* to tap into her feelings. By her reckoning, there had to be an entire reservoir of tears and emotions she had never allowed herself to access because she was sincerely afraid that if she ever did, she wouldn't be able to shut off the valve. It was far better never to access it in the first place.

Heading to her car, she put her hand into her pocket for the key...and touched the cell phone she'd discovered instead. She took it out and glanced down at it. She supposed that she could just drop it off at O'Brien's precinct. But he *had* looked concerned about losing the phone, and if she hadn't plowed into him like that, he wouldn't have lost the device.

Kansas frowned. She supposed she owed O'Brien for that.

She looked around and saw that there was still one person with the police department on the premises. Not pausing to debate the wisdom of her actions, she hurried over to the man. She was fairly certain that the chief of detectives would know where she could find the incorrigible Detective O'Brien.

"I could drop it off for you," Brian Cavanaugh volunteered after the pretty fire investigator had approached him to say that she'd found Ethan's cell phone.

She looked down at the smoke-streaked device and gave the chief's suggestion some thought. She *was* bone-tired, and she knew that the chief would get the phone to O'Brien.

Still, she had to admit that personally handing the cell phone to O'Brien would bring about some small sense of closure for her. And closure was a very rare thing in her life.

"No, that's all right. I'll do it," she told him. "If you could just tell me where to find him, I'd appreciate it."

"Of course, no problem. I have the address right here," he told her.

Brian suppressed a smile as he reached into his inside pocket for a pen and a piece of paper. Finding both, he took them out and began writing the address in large block letters.

Not for a second had he doubted that that was going to be her answer.

"Here you go," he said, handing her the paper.

This, he thought, was going to be the start of something lasting.

Chapter 4

Ethan wasn't a morning person, not by any stretch of the imagination. He never had been. Not even under the best of circumstances, coming off an actual full night's sleep, something that eluded him these days. Having less than four hours in which to recharge had left him feeling surly, less than communicative and only half-human.

So when he heard the doorbell to his garden apartment ring, Ethan's first impulse was to just ignore it. No one he knew had said anything about coming by at a little after six that morning, and it was either someone trying to save his soul—a religious sect had been making the rounds lately, scattering pamphlets about a better life to come in their wake—or the neighbor in the apartment catty-corner to his who had been pestering him with everything from a clogged drain to a key stuck in the ignition of her car, all of which he finally real-

ized were just flimsy pretexts to see him. The woman,
a very chatty brunette who wore too much makeup
and too little clothing, had invited him over more than
a dozen times, and each time he'd politely but firmly
turned her down. By the time the woman had turned
up on his doorstep a fifth time, his inner radar had
screamed, "Run!" Two invitations were hospitable. Five,
a bit pushy. More than a dozen was downright creepy.

When he didn't answer the first two rings, whoever
was on his doorstep started knocking.

Pounding was actually a more accurate description
of what was happening on the other side of his door.

Okay, he thought, no more Mr. Nice Guy. Whoever
was banging on his door was going to get more than
just a piece of his mind. He wasn't in the mood for this.

Swinging the door open, Ethan snapped, "What the
hell do you want?" before he saw that it wasn't someone looking to guide him to the Promised Land, nor
was it the pushy neighbor who wouldn't take no for
an answer. It was the woman he'd met at the fire. The
one, he'd thought, whose parents had a warped sense
of humor and named her after a state best known for
a little girl who'd gone traveling with her house and a
dog named Toto.

"To give you back your cell phone," Kansas snapped
back in the same tone he'd just used. "Here." She thrust
the near-fried object at him.

As he took it, Kansas turned on her heel and started
to walk away. *March away* was actually more of an accurate description.

It took Ethan a second to come to. "Wait, I'm sorry,"

he called out, hurrying after her to stop her from leaving. "I'm not my best in the morning," he apologized.

Now there was a news flash. "No kidding," she quipped, whirling around to face him. "I've seen friendlier grizzlies terrorizing a campsite on the Discovery Channel."

With a sigh, he dragged his hand through his unruly hair. "I thought you were someone else."

She laughed shortly. "My condolences to 'someone else.'" Obviously, it was true: no good deed really did go unpunished, Kansas thought.

But as she started to leave again, her short mission of reuniting O'Brien with his missing cell phone completed, the detective moved swiftly to get in front of her.

"You want to come in?" he asked, gesturing toward his apartment behind him.

Kansas glanced at it, and then at him. She was bone-weary and in no mood for a verbal sparring match. "Not really. I just wanted to deliver that in person, since, according to you, I was the reason you lost it in the first place."

Ethan winced slightly. Looking down at the charred device, he asked, "Where did you find it?"

"It was lying on the floor just inside the building." Because he seemed to want specifics, she took a guess how it had gotten there. "Someone must have accidentally kicked it in." She looked down at the phone. It did look pretty damaged. "I don't think it can be saved, but maybe the information that's stored on it can be transferred to another phone or something." She punctuated her statement with a shrug.

She'd done all she could on her end. The rest was

up to him. In any case, all she wanted to do was get home, not stand here talking to a man wearing pajama bottoms precariously perched on a set of pretty damn terrific-looking hips. Their initial encounter last night had given her no idea that he had abs that would make the average woman weak in the knees.

The average woman, but not her, of course. She wasn't that shallow. Just very, very observant.

With effort, she raised her eyes to his face.

Ethan frowned at the bit of charred phone in his hand. They had a tech at the precinct who was very close to a magician when it came to electronic devices. If anyone could extract something from his fried phone, it was Albert.

"That's very thoughtful of you," he told her.

"That's me, thoughtful," Kansas retorted. It was too early for him to process sarcasm, so he just let her response pass. "Well, I'll see you—"

Ethan suddenly came to life. Shifting again so that he was once more blocking her path, he asked, "Have you had breakfast yet?"

Kansas blinked. "Breakfast?" she echoed. "I haven't had *dinner* yet." She'd been at the site of the women's shelter fire this entire time. And then she replayed his question in her head—and looked at him, stunned. "Are you offering to cook for me, Detective O'Brien?"

"Me?" he asked incredulously. "Hell, no." Ethan shook his head with feeling. "That wouldn't exactly be paying you back for being nice enough to bring this over to me. No, I was just thinking of taking someone up on a standing invitation."

And just what did that have to do with her? Kansas

wondered. The man really wasn't kidding about mornings not being his best time. His thought process seemed to be leapfrogging all over the place.

"Well, you go ahead and take somebody up on that standing invitation," she told him, patting his shoulder. "And I'll—"

He cut her off, realizing he hadn't been clear. "The invitation isn't just for me. It applies to anyone I want to bring with me."

She looked at him. Suspicion crept in and got a toehold. Ethan O'Brien was more than mildly good-looking. Tall, dark, with movie-star chiseled features and electric-blue eyes, he was the type of man who made otherwise reasonable, intelligent women become monosyllabic, slack-jawed idiots when he entered a room. But she'd had her shots against those kinds of men. She'd been married to one and swiftly divorced from him, as well. The upshot of that experience was that she only made a mistake once, and then she learned enough not to repeat it.

Her eyes narrowed. "Excuse me?"

"It's easier to show you. Wait here," Ethan told her, backing into the apartment. "I've just got to get dressed and get my gun."

"Now there's a line that any woman would find irresistible," she murmured to herself, then raised her voice as she called after him, "If it's all the same to you, Detective—" not that she cared if it was or not "—I'll just be on my way."

Ethan turned from his doorway, still very much underdressed. It was getting harder and harder for her to focus only on his face. "The invitation's for breakfast at my uncle's house," he told her. "'Dozens of chairs, no waiting.'" The quote belonged to Andrew.

She had to admit that O'Brien had made her mildly curious. "What's he run, a diner?"

He had a feeling Andrew would have gotten a kick out of the question. "Very nearly. I've only been a couple of times," he confessed. "But the man's legend doesn't do him justice."

"I'm sure," she murmured. Ethan had the distinct feeling he was being brushed off. Her next words confirmed it. "But all I want to do right now is crawl into bed. If it's all the same to you, I'll just take a rain check."

Where this tinge of disappointment had come from was a complete mystery to him. He was only trying to thank her for reuniting him with his phone, nothing more. Ethan chalked it up to having his morning shaken up. "If I tell him that, he'll hold you to it. He'll expect you to come for breakfast sometime soon," Ethan added when she made no comment.

Like she believed that.

Kansas knew she should just let the matter drop, but it annoyed her that this walking stud of a detective thought she was naive enough to believe him. She deliberately pointed out the obvious.

"Your uncle has no idea who I am." And it was mutual, since she had no idea who this "Uncle Andrew" and his so-called legend were.

"Uncle Andrew's the former chief of police," O'Brien informed her. "He makes a point of knowing who *every-one* is when it comes to the police and fire departments."

This was something she was going to look into, if

for no other reason than to be prepared in case she ever bumped into Detective Stud again.

"I consider myself duly warned," she replied. "Now, unless you want me falling asleep on your doorstep, I'm going to have to go."

Maybe not the doorstep, Ethan thought, but he certainly wouldn't mind finding her—awake or asleep—in his bed. He had a hunch, though, that she wouldn't exactly appreciate him vocalizing that right now.

"Sure. I understand. Thanks again," he said, holding up the phone she'd brought to him.

Kansas merely nodded and then turned and walked quickly away before O'Brien found something else he wanted to talk about. She headed toward the vehicle she'd left in guest parking.

Closing his hand over the charred phone, Ethan watched the sway of the fire investigator's hips as she moved. It was only when he became aware of the door of the apartment catty-corner to his opening that he quickly beat a hasty retreat before his neighbor stepped out and tried to entice him with yet another invitation. Last time she'd come to the door wearing a see-through nightgown. The woman spelled trouble any way you looked at it.

Andrew smiled to himself when he looked up to the oven door and saw the reflection of the man entering his state-of-the-art kitchen through the back door.

"C'mon in, little brother." Andrew turned from the tray of French toast he'd just drizzled a layer of powdered sugar on. His smile widened. He knew better than anyone how hectic and busy the life of a chief could be.

"It's been a long time since you dropped by for breakfast." Maybe he was taking something for granted he shouldn't. "You *are* dropping by for breakfast, aren't you?"

Brian moved his shoulders vaguely, trying to appear indifferent despite the fact that the aroma rising up from his brother's handiwork had already begun making him salivate—and food had never been all that important to him.

"I could eat," he answered.

"If breakfast isn't your primary motive, what brings you here?" Andrew asked, placing two thick pieces of toasted French bread—coated and baked with egg batter, a drop of rum and nutmeg—onto a plate on the counter and moving it until it was in front of his brother.

Brian took the knife and fork Andrew silently offered. "I wanted to see if you'd gotten over it."

Andrew slid onto the counter stool next to his younger brother. "'It'?" he repeated in confusion. "Someone say I was sick?"

"Not sick," Brian answered, trying not to sigh and sound like a man who'd died and gone to heaven. His wife, Lila, was a good cook, but not like this. "Just indifferent."

Rather than being clarified, the issue had just gotten more muddied. "What the hell are you talking about, Brian?"

Brian's answer came between mouthfuls of French toast. He knew it was impossible, but each bite seemed to be better than the last.

"About not answering when someone calls to you." He paused to look at his older brother. The brother he'd idolized as a boy. "Now, my guess is that you're either going deaf, or something's wrong."

Andrew frowned slightly. None of this was making any sense to him. "My hearing's just as good as it ever was, and if there's something wrong, it's with this so-called story of yours."

Putting down his fork, Brian looked around to make sure that his sister-in-law wasn't anywhere within earshot. He got down to the real reason he'd come. Lowering his voice, he said, "I came here to tell you to get your act together before it's too late."

This was just getting more and more convoluted. "Explain this to me slowly," he instructed his brother. "From the top."

Brian sighed, pushing the empty plate away. "I saw you with that woman."

"Woman?" Andrew repeated, saying the word as if Brian had just accused him of being with a Martian. "What woman? Where?" Before Brian could elaborate, Andrew cut in, concerned. He knew how hard Brian worked. "Brian, maybe it's time to start considering early retirement. We both know that this job can eat you alive if you let it. You have a lot to live for. Lila, your kids, Lila's kids—"

This time Brian cut Andrew off. "This has nothing to do with the job, and I'm well aware of my blessings. I'm just concerned that maybe you're taking yours for granted." He hated being his brother's keeper. Andrew was always the moral standard for the rest of them. But after the other day, he knew he had to say something. "I know what I saw."

Andrew sighed. "And what is it that you *think* you saw?"

He's actually going to make me say it, Brian thought, upset about having been put in this position. "You, walking into the Crystal Penguin, with another woman."

"The Crystal Penguin?" Andrew repeated incredulously. The Crystal Penguin was an overpriced restaurant that didn't always deliver on its promises of exquisite dining experiences. "Why would I go to a restaurant? And if I did go to one, it certainly wouldn't be a restaurant that overcharges and undercooks."

That's what he would have thought if someone had come to him with this story. But he'd been a witness to this. "I saw you, Andrew."

Andrew didn't waste his breath protesting that it wasn't possible. "And just when did this 'sighting' occur?"

Brian had been sitting on this for several days now, and it was killing him. "Last Friday evening. At about seven-thirty."

"I see." His expression was unreadable. "Why didn't you come up and talk to me?"

He almost had, then decided to restrain himself. "Because you're my older brother and I didn't want to embarrass you."

And then Brian delivered what in his estimation was the knockout blow.

"Some of the others have mentioned seeing you around the city with this woman. I told them they were crazy, but then on Friday I saw you myself, and now I'm begging you," he entreated, putting his hand on Andrew's arm, "break it off before Rose gets hurt. You spent all that time looking for Rose when everyone else, including me, thought she was dead. Don't throw all that away because of some middle-aged itch you want to scratch."

"You done?" Andrew wanted to know.

"Yes," Brian said quietly. "Just promise me you'll break it off with her."

"It would seem like the thing to do." To Brian's surprise, his brother got off the stool, walked to the doorway between the kitchen and the living room and called out, "Rose? Would you mind coming here?"

Brian hurried over to him. "What are you doing?" he whispered into Andrew's ear. He knew that for some, the need to confess was almost an overpowering reaction, but he would have never thought it of Andrew. This had all the makings of a disaster. "Don't dump this on Rose. Don't tell her you've been cheating on her just to clear your conscience."

"Good advice," Andrew quipped.

Before Brian could ask if he'd lost his mind, Rose walked in. "Hello, Brian. Nice to see you." She turned toward her husband. There was no missing the love in her eyes. "You wanted me, honey?"

"Only every minute of every day," Andrew said, a gentle smile curving the corners of his mouth. He slipped his arm around her waist. "Rose, could you tell Brian where we were last Friday?"

Rose sighed, shaking her head. "Don't see why you would even want to admit to it."

He laughed, giving her a quick hug. "Humor me, my love."

"Okay." Rose turned toward her brother-in-law. "We

saw the most god-awful movie. *Heaven Around the Corner*. Quite honestly, I still can't figure out how the people behind that silly thing managed to get funding to produce it." Her eyes crinkled as she slanted a glance and a grin in her husband's direction. "Even Andrew could have written a better story."

"Thank you, dear," Andrew deadpanned. "I can always count on you to extol my many talents."

She laughed. Standing on her toes, she brushed a kiss against his cheek. "Don't worry, dear. No one can touch your cooking."

Still holding his wife to him, Andrew turned his attention back to his younger brother and Brian's allegations. "Satisfied?"

Rose looked from one man to the other, a curious expression filling her eyes. "Satisfied about what? What's this all about, Andrew? Brian?" She waited for one of them to enlighten her.

"Brian thought he saw me clear across town last Friday. At the Crystal Penguin. With another woman. I don't know which is more absurd, the restaurant part or the other woman part." He caught the look on Rose's face. "The other woman part. Definitely the other woman part," he assured her.

Amused, Rose laughed. "Not unless Andrew's suddenly gotten superpowers and found a way to be in two places at the same time."

Brian sighed with relief. "You don't know how glad it makes me to hear that." But then he frowned slightly. There was still a mystery to be unraveled. "But whoever I saw looked just like you, Andrew."

"Maybe it was one of the boys," Andrew suggested.

But Brian shook his head. He'd already thought of that. "Too old."

Andrew gave him a quick jab in the arm. "Thanks a lot."

He hadn't meant it as an insult. "You know what I mean. Around our age, not younger."

"Someone else out there with those handsome features?" Rose teased, brushing her hand across her husband's cheek.

"I know. Lucky dog," Andrew deadpanned. He grew a little more serious as he asked Brian, "And you're saying this isn't the first time this doppelgänger's been spotted?"

Brian nodded. "Jared's mentioned seeing 'you,'" he told Andrew, referring to one of his sons. "Said you ignored him when he called out to you. And Zack said he thought he saw you walking into the Federal Building about a month ago. Same scenario. He called out and was ignored."

Listening to this, Rose glanced at her husband. He'd become quietly thoughtful. "I know that look," she said. "You're working something out in your head."

"What's on your mind?" Brian probed.

Andrew raised his eyes to look at Brian. "That maybe Mom wasn't imagining things all those years ago."

Chapter 5

Still completely in the dark, Brian and Rose exchanged quizzical glances.

Brian was the first to speak. "Mom wasn't wrong about what?"

Andrew looked up as if he'd suddenly become aware that he wasn't alone and talking to himself. "That the hospital had given her the wrong baby." He doled out the words slowly, thoughtfully, as he continued sorting things out in his mind.

"The wrong baby?" Brian echoed, staring at Andrew as if his brother had just sprouted another head. This was making less sense now, not more. "Which one of us is supposed to have been this 'wrong baby'? Mike or me?"

Andrew took a deep breath before answering. It had been a very long time since the name he was about to say had been uttered. An entire lifetime had gone by.

It had become a family secret, known to only his late parents and him. Maybe it was time to air out the closet.

"Sean."

"Sean?" Brian repeated, more mystified than ever. "Andrew, maybe you've been standing in the kitchen too long and the heat's gotten to you. I know that there are a lot of Cavanaughs to be tallied these days, but there is no Sean in our family."

"I know." Andrew's eyes met Brian's. "That's because he died."

Brian shook his head as if to clear it. It didn't help. "Andrew, what are you *talking* about?"

In for a penny, in for a pound. He needed to get this whole thing out. It was long overdue.

"Something Mother and Dad never wanted to talk about." He looked from his brother to his wife. "Sit down, Brian. You, too, Rose."

Rose dropped onto the counter stool beside her husband. "I think I'd better. Is this where you tell me I'm married to someone who's descended from the Romanovs?" she asked, clearly trying very hard to lighten the somber mood that was encompassing them.

Maybe he should have done this years ago, after their parents were both gone. But he'd always felt it wasn't his secret to share. And he'd been so young when it was all going down. There were times he had almost talked himself into believing it had all been just a dream.

"No, love." He felt her slip her fingers through his, as if silently offering him her support, no matter what was ahead. God, he loved this woman. "This is where I tell Brian that there were actually four Cavanaugh boys, not three."

None of this was making any sense to Brian, and it was only getting murkier. And if this Sean person was supposedly dead, who was it that he had seen walking into the Crystal Penguin on Friday?

"So where is this Sean?" he asked, struggling with a wave of angry confusion that was totally foreign to him. "Did Mom and Dad decide they could only afford to keep three of us and made us draw straws to see who'd stay and who'd go? And why haven't I heard anything about this before?"

Andrew chose his words very carefully. "Because Sean died before he was a year old." He backtracked a little to give Brian a more concise picture. "He was born between Mike and you." Andrew closed his eyes, remembering the anguish on his mother's face. Everything about the day had left an indelible impression on his young mind. "One morning, Mom got up all sunny because Sean had slept through the night for the first time. She went into the nursery to get him and then I heard her start screaming." As he spoke, it all came back to him in vivid color. "I remember Dad rushing in and then coming out with the baby in his arms, trying desperately to revive him. But it was too late to save him. He was blue. Sean'd died somewhere in the middle of the night." He felt Rose tighten her grasp on his hand. "They called it 'crib death' back then."

"SIDS," Rose murmured. "Sudden infant death syndrome."

Andrew nodded. He noted that Brian still looked confused, and unconvinced.

"So this is what?" Brian pressed. "Sean's ghost walking the earth?"

"No," Andrew answered patiently. "But when she first brought Sean home from the hospital, I'd see Mom staring at him, shaking her head. Saying that she felt there'd been a mix-up in the hospital. That this baby didn't *feel* like *her* baby." He took a deep breath. "After Sean died, Dad told me that maybe some inherent, unconscious defense mechanism had made Mom find reasons not to get close to Sean. He said it was as if she'd subconsciously known that Sean wasn't going to live long.

"The very thought of losing Sean upset her so much, Dad told everyone at the time, including me, that we weren't to talk about Sean anymore." He looked at his youngest brother. "You were born less than a year after that. She went a little overboard and completely doted on you," he reminded Brian.

Brian shrugged, trying to lighten the moment for both his brother and himself. "I always thought it was because I was so adorable."

Andrew laughed shortly and snorted. "Not damn likely."

"So now what?" Rose prodded gently, looking from her husband to her brother-in-law and back again.

"Now," Andrew answered, "we go and find out who this guy who looks like me is—"

"And more important, exactly where and when he was born," Brian interjected. "That includes the name of the hospital."

Rose sighed. Shaking her head, she rose from the stool. "I've got a very strong feeling that I'm going to have to be buying more dishes soon." She looked at the table in the next room. "Not to mention more chairs."

Andrew laughed and gave her a one-arm hug while planting a quick kiss against her temple. "This is one of the reasons why I love you so much, Rose. You're always one step ahead of me."

"Only to keep from being trampled by the Cavanaugh brothers," she quipped just before she left the kitchen.

Since Andrew had dropped this bombshell on his unsuspecting brother, he knew that his wife had made a graceful exit so the two could talk in private. However, he had no doubt that she would ask her own questions later.

With almost five hours of sleep under her belt, Kansas was back at the shelter. Bypassing the yellow crime-scene tape that encircled the entire outer perimeter of what was left of the building, she made her way inside. Once there she began sifting through the rubble in an effort to piece together as much information as she could about what had gone on here less than a day ago.

She'd managed to find the fire's point of origin and also to rule out that the fire had been an accident. She discovered what was left of the incendiary device. It had a timer on it, which could only mean that the fire had been deliberately set, and whoever had done it had a definite time in mind. To kill someone specific? she wondered. If so, whoever had set it had miscalculated. No one had died last night.

The device wasn't a match for the M.O. of any of the known arsonists or pyromaniacs in the area. There was an outside chance that it could still be the work of someone belonging to one group or the other, someone who had managed to go undetected.

Until now.

It was frustrating, she thought. There *had* to be some kind of a connection, no matter how minor, if she was to believe that these weren't just random fires haphazardly set. But what connection? And why? Why these structures and not the ones down the block or somewhere else? What did these particular buildings that had been torched have in common—assuming, of course, that they actually *had* something in common?

Rocking back on her heels, Kansas ran her hand through her hair and sighed. It was like banging her head against a concrete wall. There were no answers to be found here.

"Penny for your thoughts."

Caught completely off guard, Kansas swallowed a gasp as she jumped to her feet. When she swung around, she found O'Brien watching her from a few feet away. She'd been so preoccupied, she hadn't heard anyone come in. She was going to have to work on that, she told herself.

"A penny?" Kansas hooted. "Is that all it's worth to you? I take it I'm in the presence of the last of the big-time spenders."

"I don't believe in throwing my money away," he told her matter-of-factly. "I also didn't expect to find you here."

"Oh?" She looked at him, perplexed. "Tell me, just where would you expect to find a fire investigator, Detective?"

He shrugged, joining her. He looked down at the

rubble she'd been sifting through. "I just thought you'd gotten everything you needed last night."

Maybe he was a little slow on the uptake, she thought. The good-looking ones usually were.

"If I had," she pointed out patiently, crouching down again, "I'd know who did it. Or at least why. Right now, I'm still trying to find all the pieces of that puzzle," she said under her breath.

Crouching down beside her, Ethan looked at what she was doing with interest. "Find anything new?"

Amusement curved her mouth as she glanced up for a moment. "Are you asking me to do your work for you, Detective?"

"No, I'm asking you to share," he corrected. He thought the point of all this was to find who was responsible, not participate in a competition. "We're both part of the same team."

He *couldn't* be that naive. "Detective, not even different divisions of the same department are on the same team, and in case you haven't noticed, you're with the police department and I belong to the fire department. Big difference," she concluded.

He followed her statement to its logical conclusion. "So to you, this is a competition?" He wouldn't have thought that of her, but then, he reminded himself, he really didn't know this woman. Chemistry—and there was plenty of that—was not a substitute for knowledge.

It wasn't a matter of competition, Kansas thought defensively, it was a matter of sharing information with someone she trusted. Right now, she had no basis for that. Moreover, she didn't trust this man any further than she could throw him.

"To me, Detective, you're basically a stranger—"

He finished the statement for her. "And your mother taught you never to speak to strangers, right?"

One would think, after all these years, the word *mother* wouldn't create such a feeling of emptiness and loss within her. But it did.

"I'm sure she would have if I'd had one," Kansas answered, her voice distant. He looked as if he was going to say something apologetic, so she quickly went on. "What I'm saying is that you're an unknown quantity and I haven't got time to waste, wondering if you have some kind of ulterior motive...or if I can confide in you because you're really one of those pure-hearted souls who believes in truth, justice and the American way."

"I think a red cape and blue tights would go with that," he responded drily. "Me, I'm not that noble. I just want to put this son of a bitch away before he hurts someone else—and if I have to work with the devil or share the stage with him to do it, I will."

There was only one conclusion to be drawn from that. For the second time, Kansas rose to her feet, her hands on her hips. "So now I'm the devil?" she demanded.

He looked surprised that she would come to that conclusion. "No, I didn't say that. You really are something," he freely admitted, "but *devil* isn't the word that readily comes to mind when thinking of you." He flashed a grin at her that shimmied up and down her spine and was totally out of place here. "I was just trying to let you know how far I'd be willing to go to catch this guy if I had to."

His grin, she caught herself thinking, had turned utterly sexy. And he undoubtedly knew that. She'd never met a handsome man who was unaware of the kind of charisma he wielded.

"So," Ethan was saying, "why don't we pool our resources and see what we can accomplish together? Bring your team over to the precinct," he encouraged.

It pained her to admit what she was about to say. "I *am* the team."

"Then you won't need to find a large car to drive over." Ethan put his hand out to seal the bargain. "What do you say?"

She looked down at the hand he held out to her. While she preferred working on her own, the point here was to catch whoever was setting these fires and keep him—or possibly her—from doing it again. The fire-bug needed to be caught as quickly as possible...before actual lives were lost.

She slipped her hand into his and shook it firmly. "Okay."

"Attagirl." He saw a look come into her eyes he couldn't fathom. Had she just taken that in a conde-scending manner? "Sorry, I didn't mean it the way it might have sounded. Just expressing relief that I got you to come around so quickly."

Okay, she needed to set him straight right from the beginning. "You didn't get me to 'come around so quickly,' Detective. It's just common sense. You have an entire task force devoted to tracking down this fire-bug." There was a safe expression, she thought. It didn't espouse any particular theory other than this unbal-anced person felt a kinship to flames. "That means you have more resources available to you than I do. We can hopefully move forward more quickly and put an end to this sick reign of fire before someone *is* actually killed."

Ethan nodded in agreement. "A woman after my own heart."

She paused to pin him with a look that spoke volumes. Mostly it issued a warning. "Not even in your wildest dreams, Detective."

Ethan smiled to himself. Nothing goaded him on like a challenge. Maybe, he thought, he'd get this strong-principled, "get the hell out of my way" woman to eat her words. He had a feeling that she could be a hell of a wildcat in bed.

"If you're through here," he said, "you're welcome to come back to the precinct with me now and take a look at the information we've got."

It was probably more than she had compiled. They had only recently been entertaining the idea that the fires were connected and the work of just one person or possibly one team.

Kansas nodded. "Okay, I just might take you up on that, Detective."

"I do have a first name, you know."

Kansas looked at him with the most innocent expression she could muster. "You mean it's not 'Detective'?"

"It's Ethan."

Like he was telling her something she didn't already know. She made it a point to access all the information she could about the people whose paths she crossed. "Yes, I know. What floor are you on, Detective?" She deliberately used his title.

Ethan laughed softly under his breath. She'd come

around in her own time. And if she didn't, well, he could live with that. She wasn't the last beautiful woman he'd ever encounter.

"Third," he answered. "Why?"

She packed up some of the tools she'd been using to collect evidence. "Well, here's a wild thought—so I know where I'm going."

He looked at her quizzically. "I thought I'd take you."

"Yes, I know," she told him. "I'd rather take myself if it's all the same to you. Besides, there's something I need to do first before going to the precinct."

He made an educated guess as to what that was. "You don't have to run this past your captain. The chief of Ds has already cleared it with him."

She didn't like being second-guessed. It made her feel hemmed in. "That's all well and good, but that's not what I need to do first."

She still wasn't elaborating. "You always this vague about things?" he wondered.

Her smile widened. "Keeps people guessing." *And me safe,* she added silently. Slipping the recorder she'd been using to tape her thoughts into her case, she snapped the locks into place and picked up the case. "I'll see you in a bit."

He had no idea if she intended to make good on that or if she was just saying it to humor him. All he knew was that he fully intended to see her again, fire or no fire.

Dax paced back and forth before the bulletin boards in the front of the room.

"There's *got* to be some kind of pattern here," he

insisted, staring at the three bulletin boards he'd had brought into the task force's makeshift squad room.

Each fire had its own column with as much information as they could find listed directly beneath it. The fires had all broken out in the past six months in and around Aurora. Other than that, there was nothing uniform and no attention-grabbing similarities about them.

And yet, he had a gut feeling that there had to be. What was he missing?

"If there is," Ortiz commented in a lackluster tone, "I can't see it." Rocking in his seat, Ortiz slowly sipped his extra-large container of chai tea. He drank the beverage religiously at least once a day, claiming it gave him mental clarity.

The others knew better. Especially after Ethan had pointed out that Ortiz liked to flirt with the cute dark-haired girl behind the counter who filled the detective's order as well as his less-than-anemic imagination.

"Maybe we're including too many fires," Ethan speculated, gesturing at the bulletin boards with its news clippings.

"Isn't that the point?" Youngman questioned. "These are all the fires that've taken place in and around Aurora in the last six months. If we don't include all of them, we might come up with the *wrong* pattern."

He knew he was playing devil's advocate here, but they had to explore all the avenues before they found the one that would lead them to the right answer. To the man or men responsible for all that destruction.

"But maybe they weren't all set by the same guy," Ethan insisted.

"But they *were* all set."

Ethan, Dax, Youngman and Ortiz all turned to see Kansas walking into the small, cluttered room that the task force was temporarily using to cut down on any distractions from the other detectives.

She walked as if she owned the room.

"And we won't come up with the wrong answer," she assured them with feeling. "If we just keep talking all this out long enough, we're going to either find the answer, which has been right in front of us all along, or stumble across something that'll eventually lead us to the right answer.

"But one way or the other," Kansas concluded, "we *are* going to get to the bottom of this."

Her eyes swept over the four detectives. There was no mistaking the confidence in her voice.

Ethan couldn't help wondering if she meant it, or if she was just saying that for their benefit, giving them a glimpse of her own version of whistling in the dark to keep the demons at bay.

It wouldn't be the first time that he'd encountered female bravado. Because of his sister, Greer, he'd been raised with it. He had a gut feeling that the two women were very much alike.

Chapter 6

Ethan was the first to break the silence.

"My money's still on an arsonist doing this," he said even though he knew that the new, adjunct member of the team vehemently disagreed with this theory.

Kansas thought about holding her tongue. She was, after all, the outsider here, and arguing was not the way to become part of the team. She'd stated her point of view and should just let it go at that.

But she'd never been one to merely go with the flow. It just wasn't part of her nature. The words seemed to come out almost of their own accord.

"Where's the profit to be gained from burning down a church and an abused-women's shelter that's already pretty run-down?" she challenged.

"Real estate," Ethan argued. "The places aren't worth anything as they are, and there might be little or no insurance on the structures, so there's definitely not enough money to rebuild. That would make whoever owns the property willing and maybe eager to sell." He shrugged. "Maybe they feel that they can start somewhere else with the money they get from selling the land the property stands on."

Kansas rolled her eyes at his explanation. "So, in your opinion, some big, bad CEO is paying someone to run around and burn down buildings in and around Aurora in order to put together a colossal shopping mall or something to that effect?"

Ethan scowled. He didn't care for her dismissive tone. "It sounds stupid when you say it that way," he accused.

"That's because it *is* stupid—no matter which way you say it," Kansas pointed out, happy that he got the point.

Dax literally got in between his cousin and the woman his father felt they needed to work with.

"Children, children, play nice," he instructed, looking from one to the other to make sure that his words sank in. "And in the meantime," he said, turning to another detective, "Ortiz, see if you can check with Records down at the civic center to see if anyone has put in for permits to start building anything of any consequence."

"If Ortiz doesn't find anything, it doesn't mean the theory doesn't hold up," Ethan interjected.

Dax crossed his arms before his chest, striking a pose that said he was waiting for more. "Go ahead. I'm listening."

"It just means that whoever it is who's doing this hasn't had time to properly file his intent to build whatever it is that he's going to build," Ethan explained. "The destroyed properties are far from desirable, so maybe he figures he has time. And the longer he takes to get to 'step two,' the less likely it'll be that someone will make the connection between the arson and the motive behind it."

Kansas supposed that O'Brien had a point. She wasn't so married to her theory that she would stubbornly shut her eyes to exclude everything else.

"Maybe we should check out whether anyone's bought any of the properties previously destroyed by the fires," she suggested.

"Then you're on board with this theory?" O'Brien asked. There was a touch of triumph in his voice that irritated her. It had her reverting to her original theory.

"No, I just want to put it to rest once and for all." Her eyes narrowed ever so slightly as she continued. "I'd stake my job that this isn't a fire-for-hire situation." She could feel it in her bones, but she wasn't about to say that out loud. She didn't know these people well enough to allow them to laugh at her, even good-naturedly. "It's some pyromaniac getting his high out of watching everyone scramble, trying to keep the fire from destroying another piece of real estate. Another person's hopes and dreams."

Dax was still open to all possibilities until something started to gel. "Okay, why don't you and Youngman go check it out," he instructed her. "Begin with the first fire on the list and work your way up."

But Youngman shook his head. "No can do, Dax. I've got that dental appointment to go to. Doc says it's going to take the better part of two hours to do the root canal." He cupped his right cheek to underscore his situation. "I'd cancel, but I already did that once, and this thing is just *killing* me."

Dax nodded. Youngman had already told him about the appointment this morning. Things were getting so hectic, he'd just forgotten. "Go. Get it seen to." Without missing a beat, Dax turned to his cousin. "Take his place, Ethan."

"In the dental chair?" Ethan asked hopefully.

"Very funny. You, her, go," Dax said, nodding toward the door. "See what you can come up with that might get your theory to float."

"An anchor comes to mind," Kansas muttered under her breath.

Grabbing his jacket and slipping it on, Ethan shot her an annoyed look. He was going to enjoy putting her in her place. And then, once the shrew was tamed, other possibilities might open up, he mused.

"I'll drive," he announced as they left the squad room. He punched the Down button for the elevator.

The statement was met with a careless shrug. "If it's that important to you, I wouldn't dream of fighting with you about it," she murmured.

The elevator car arrived and she stepped in. He was quick to get in with her, then pressed the button for the first floor.

"It's not important to me," he informed her, his irritation growing. Supposedly, the woman was agreeing with him. But it was the manner in which she was agreeing that he found annoying. "It's just that—"

She turned the most innocent expression he'd ever seen in his direction. "Yes?"

The woman was playing him. The second the steel doors parted, he all but shot out of the elevator, heading for the precinct entrance. "Never mind," he ground out. "You want to drive? Because if you do, we'll take your car."

She preceded him outside. There was a soft spring breeze rustling through everything, quietly reminding them that at any moment, it could pick up and fan any flames it encountered.

"You don't trust me with your car?" she asked. *Typical male*, she thought.

"I don't trust *anybody* with my car," he told her. "I spent too much time, effort and money restoring her to just hand the keys over to someone else."

Sounded like the man was obsessed with his car, she thought. The smile she raised to her lips was the embodiment of serenity. "You can drive," she told him. "It's okay."

She was yanking his chain—and a few other things, as well. He led the way to his car, parked over in the third row. "Why do I get the feeling that you're laughing at me?"

The woman looked as if she was seriously considering the question. "My first guess would be insecurity," she said brightly.

"Your first guess would be wrong," he retorted.

She paused before the cream-colored two-seater. She wasn't really up on cars, but she recognized it as a classic. "It really is a beauty," she told him.

The compliment instantly softened him. "Thanks." He pressed the security button on his key chain and released the locks. "You have the list of sites where the fires took place?" he asked. Since she'd already gotten in on her side, he slid in behind the steering wheel— and saw that instead of buckling up, she was holding up several sheets of paper. He presumed they were the list he'd referred to. "Okay, where to first?"

"How about MacArthur and Main?" she suggested after a beat. "That's the church," she explained, shifting as she buckled her seat belt. "That was the first fire," she added in case he'd forgotten.

He hadn't. "Where that firefighter rescued the visiting priest from Spain. The priest was sleeping in Father Colm's room," he recalled.

She vividly remembered all the details of that one. Daring, last-minute rescues like that always tugged on her heartstrings. "There was footage of the old priest being carried out of the burning building."

The media, always hungry for something to sink its teeth into, had carried the story for days, and the morning talk shows vied for the exclusive rights to being the first to interview both the firefighter and the priest, sitting in the studio side by side.

He thought of the theory that he'd espoused. It seemed rather shaky here. "I really doubt that the church is being put up for sale."

"I doubt it, too," she agreed. Since he'd backed off, she could afford to be magnanimous. "But we can still ask if anyone made any offers on the property since the fire." She shrugged again. "At any rate, it's better than nothing."

As he drove, he slanted a glance at her, looking for confirmation in her expression. "You're humoring me, aren't you?"

"No," she said honestly, sitting back in her seat, "what I'm trying to do is prove or disprove your theory once and for all so we can move on."

He knew which side of the argument she was on, and

he didn't care for being summarily dismissed. "What if it turns out that I'm right?"

"Then, most likely," she recited, "you'll be impossible to live with and I'll be happy that I'm not part of the police department, because I won't have to put up with it. But even if hell does freeze over and you're right, the upshot will be that we've caught the person or persons responsible for all this destruction, and that'll be a very good thing." And then the corners of her mouth curved in a forced smile. "But you won't be right, so there's no point in anticipating it."

The woman was being downright smug, he thought. Since when did he find smug so arousing? "You're that sure?"

She lifted her chin ever so slightly, making it a good target, he couldn't help thinking. Damn, his feelings were bouncing all over the place today. "I'm that sure."

The light up ahead turned yellow. In any other car he would have stepped on the gas and flown through. But this was his baby, and he eased into a stop at the intersection several beats before the light turned red.

"Tell me," he said, turning toward her, "do you walk on water all the time, or just on Sundays?"

"Mainly Sundays," she answered with a straight face. There wasn't even a hint of a smile. "There's the church." She pointed to the building in the distance on the right. "Looks like it's being rebuilt."

The light turned green. Ethan drove over to the church and said nothing as he pulled the vehicle into the parking lot. He brought his vehicle to a stop in front of the partially demolished building.

Kansas was out of the car before he had a chance to pull up the hand brake. For a woman who was wearing rather high heels, she moved inordinately quickly, he thought.

Kansas was more than several strides ahead of him by the time he got out.

"Father," she called out to the cleric, waving her hand to get his attention.

A white-haired man in jeans and a sweatshirt, its sleeves pushed all the way back beyond his elbows, turned around in response to her call. He was holding on to the base of a ladder that was up against the side of the church, keeping it steady while a much younger man stood close to the top, trying to spread an even layer of stucco.

Kansas flipped her wallet open to her ID and held it up for the priest to see as she approached. "I'm Investigator Kansas Beckett—with the fire department." Putting her ID away, she nodded toward Ethan. "This is Detective Ethan O'Brien with the Aurora P.D. We're looking into this awful fire that almost took down your church, Father."

"*Almost* being the key word," the priest responded with a pleased smile. He turned back to look at the church. His smile told her that he was seeing beyond what was currently standing before them.

"I see that you're rebuilding," Ethan observed.

"Not me," the priest answered modestly. "I'm just holding the ladder, stirring paint, that sort of thing. St. Angela's is blessed to have such a talented congregation." He beamed, looking up the ladder he was holding steady. "Mr. Wicks is a general contractor who, luckily for us, is temporarily in between assignments, and he kindly volunteered to give us the benefit of his expertise."

The man Father Colm was referring to climbed down the ladder. Once his feet were on the ground, he shook hands with Ethan and Kansas, holding on to her hand, she noted, a beat longer than necessary. But she did like the appreciative smile on his lips as he looked at her.

Flattery without any possibility of entanglement. The best of all worlds, she thought.

"By 'in between,' Father Colm means unemployed." Wicks regarded the older man with affection. "I'm just glad to help. It keeps me active and allows me to practice my trade so I don't forget what to do. It's been a *long* dry spell," he confessed.

"With so many of the parishioners volunteering their time and talent, it won't be long before we have the church whole and functional again," the priest informed them with no small amount of pride.

It was as good an opening as any, Kansas thought. "Father, right after the fire—"

"Terrible, terrible time," the priest murmured, shaking his head. His bright blue eyes shone with tears as he recalled. "I was afraid that the Vatican wouldn't approve of our being here any longer and would just authorize everyone to attend Our Lady of Angels Church on the other end of Aurora."

Kansas waited politely for the priest to finish unloading the sentiments that were weighing down on him. When he stopped, she continued her line of questioning. "Did anyone come with an offer to take the property off your hands? Or, more aptly I guess, off the Church's hands?"

"The only ones who approached me," Father Colm told her and O'Brien, "were Mr. Wick and some of the other parishioners. Everyone's been so generous, donating either their time, or money, or sometimes even both, to rebuild St. Angela's." He sighed deeply. "I am a very, very blessed man." There was a hitch in his voice and he stopped to clear it.

Ethan rephrased the question, asking it again, just to be perfectly clear about the events. "So, you're sure that no one offered to give you money for the property, saying you'd be better off starting over somewhere else from the ground up?"

"No, Detective O'Brien," the priest assured him. "I might be old, but I would have remembered that. Because I would have said no. I've been here for thirty-six years. I'm too old to start at a new location." And then he paused, looking from one to the other, before exchanging puzzled looks with the general contractor. "Why do you ask?"

O'Brien hesitated. Kansas saw no reason for secrecy, not with the priest. So she was the one who answered the man. "We're investigating the rash of recent fires in Aurora. Yours was among the first. We're attempting to find a common motive."

Father Colm looked horrified. "You seriously think that someone *deliberately* tried to burn down St. Angela's?"

"All evidence points to the fact that the fire here wasn't just an accident. It was set," Ethan told the priest.

"You're kidding," Wicks said, looking as if he'd been broadsided.

Father Colm shook his head, his expression adamant. "No, I refuse to think of this as a hate crime, Detective O'Brien. That's just too terrible a thought to entertain."

"I don't believe that it was a hate crime, either," Kansas assured him. Although, she supposed that would be another avenue they could explore if they ran out of options. "This is the only church that was burned down. If it were a hate crime, there would have been at least a few more places of worship, more churches targeted. Instead, the range of structures that were torched is quite wide and diverse."

The priest looked as if he were struggling to absorb the theory. "But the fires were all deliberately set?"

O'Brien looked as if he were searching for a diplomatic way to phrase his answer. Kansas took the straightforward path. "Yes."

The old man, a priest for fifty-one years, appeared shell-shocked. "Why?" The question came out in a hoarse whisper.

"That, Father, is what we're trying to find out," Ethan told him, thinking that they had just come full circle. He was quick to launch into basic questions of his own.

Again the priest, and this time Wicks, were asked if there was anything unusual about that day, anything out of the ordinary that either of them could remember seeing or hearing, no matter how minor.

Nothing came to either of the men's minds.

Kansas nodded. She really hadn't expected any earthshaking revelations. Hoped, but hadn't expected.

She dug into her pocket and retrieved two of her cards. "If either of you *do* think of anything," Kansas told the men as she held out her business cards, offering one to each of them, "please call me."

Ethan gave the priest and Wicks his own card. "Please call us," he amended, glancing in Kansas's direction and silently reprimanding her for what he took to be her attempt to edge him out.

"Right, us," Kansas corrected with a quirk of a smile

that came and left her lips in less than a heartbeat. "I forgot I'm temporarily assigned to Detective O'Brien's task force," she confided to the priest.

Father Colm nodded, apparently giving his whole-hearted approval to the venture. "The more minds working on this, the faster this terrible situation will be resolved."

She'd never gone to any house of worship. There'd been no one to urge her to choose one religion over the other, no one to care if she prayed or not. But if she were to choose a single place, she thought, it would be one whose pastor was loving and kind. A pastor like Father Colm.

Kansas flashed a grin at the cleric. "From your lips to God's ears," she said, reciting a phrase she'd once heard one of the social workers say to one of the other children in the group home.

Father Colm laughed warmly in response. Kansas found the sound strangely reassuring. "I'll be back," she promised.

The bright blue eyes met hers. "Feel free to stop by anytime," the priest urged. "God's house is always open to you."

Kansas merely nodded as she left.

O'Brien and she made no headway of any kind at the site of the second fire. The charred remains of the building were still there, abandoned by one and all and presently neglected by the city. Kansas made a mental note to look up the current status of the property and see who owned it.

The site of the third fire, a movie triplex that had gone up in flames long after the last show had let out, appeared to be suffering the same fate as the second site. Except that someone had put in a bid for it.

In front of the burnt-out shell that had once contained three movie theaters was a relatively new sign announcing that several stores were coming soon to that area. The name of the developer was printed in block letters on the bottom right-hand side of the sign. Brad McCormack and Sons.

Kansas wrote the name down in her small, battered notepad. "What do you say to paying Mr. McCormack a visit?" she asked when she finished.

"Sure," Ethan agreed. He glanced at his watch. "How about right after lunch?"

"It's too early for lunch," she protested. She wanted to keep going until they actually had something to work with.

"It's almost noon," he pointed out. "What time do you eat lunch?"

It couldn't be that late. Kansas glanced at her watch, ready to prove him wrong. Except that she couldn't. "You're right," she muttered.

"I know. I had to learn how to tell time before they'd let me join the police force," he told her drily.

She sighed, walking back to his car. "Did you have to learn sarcasm, as well? Or was that something you brought to the table on your own?"

"The latter." He waited until she got in. Because she'd leaned her hand on the car's hood for a moment, Ethan doubled back and wiped away the print with a handkerchief before finally getting in on his side. He didn't have to look at her to know that Kansas had rolled her eyes. "And speaking of table, where would you like to go for lunch?"

He wasn't going to stop until she gave in, she thought. That could start a dangerous precedent. *Where the hell had that come from?* she wondered, caught off guard by her own thoughts.

Out loud she asked, "What is it with you and food?"

"I like having it. Keeps me from being grumpy." He looked at her pointedly as he started up the vehicle. "You might want to think about trying it sometime. Might do wonders for your personality."

She let the comment pass. "All right, since you have to eat, how about a drive-through?"

He was thinking more in terms of sitting back and recharging for an hour. "How about a sit-down restaurant with tables and chairs?" he countered.

She merely looked at him. "Takes less than twenty minutes to start a fire."

Yeah, he thought, his eyes washing over the woman sitting next to him in the vehicle. *Tell me something I didn't already know.*

And then he sighed. "Drive-through it is."

Chapter 7

"Is it okay to pull over somewhere and eat this, or do we have to ingest lunch while en route to the next destination?" Ethan asked drily, driving away from the fast-food restaurant's take-out window.

The bag with their lunches was resting precariously against his thigh while the two containers of economy-size sodas were nestled in the vehicle's cup holders. The plastic lids that covered the containers looked far from secure.

Amused rather than annoyed by the detective's sarcasm, Kansas answered, "It's okay to pull over. I just meant that going inside a restaurant is usually a full-hour proposition, especially at this time of day. And if we're going to spend time together, I'd rather it was at one of the sites where the fires took place."

Driving to a relatively empty corner of the parking lot that accommodated seven different fast-food establishments, Ethan pulled up the parking brake. He rolled down his window and shut off the engine. Glancing inside the oversize paper bag he'd been awarded at the drive-through window, he pulled out a long, tubular, green-wrapped item and held it out to her.

"This is yours, I believe. I ordered the cheeseburger."

"I know. Not exactly very imaginative," Kansas commented, taking the meat-and-cheese wrap from him.

She tried not to notice how infectious his grin was. "Sue me. I like basic things. I'm a very uncomplicated guy."

Uncomplicated? Kansas raised her eyes to his. *Who does he think he's kidding?*

Drop-dead gorgeous men with their own agendas were generally as difficult to figure out as a Rubik's Cube. Definitely *not* uncomplicated.

"Yeah, I'll bet," she muttered audibly just before taking her first bite.

With a cheeseburger in one hand, he reached into the bag with the other and pulled out several French fries. He held them out to her. "Want some of my fries?" he offered.

She shook her head, swallowing another bite. She hadn't realized until she'd started eating just how hungry she actually was. If she didn't know better, she would have said her stomach was celebrating. "No, I'm good, thanks."

A hint of a smile curved his mouth. "I'm sure you are."

The low, sultry tone he'd used had her looking at him again, but she kept silent. She had a feeling that she was better off not knowing the explanation behind his words. No doubt, the path to seduction, or what he perceived as the path to seduction, was mixed in there somewhere.

Giving her full attention to eating the turkey-and-pastrami wrap she'd ordered, Kansas was in no way prepared for what came next.

"You never knew your mother?"

The bite she'd just taken went down her windpipe instead of her esophagus. She started coughing until there were tears in her eyes. Abandoning his lunch, Ethan twisted her in her seat and began pounding on her back until she held her hand up in surrender.

"It's okay. I'm okay," she protested, trying to catch her breath. When she finally did, her eyes still somewhat watery, she looked at O'Brien. "Where did that come from?"

He slid back into his seat. "From what you said earlier."

Her mind a blank, she shook her head. "I don't recall."

He had a feeling that she remembered but was dismissing the subject outright. "When I made that crack about your mother teaching you not to talk to strangers and you answered that you were sure she would have if you'd had one."

Kansas placed what was left of the wrap down on the paper it had come in and looked at him. "Where is this going?"

There was a dangerous note in her voice that warned him to tread lightly. Or better yet, back off. "I was just curious if your mother died when you were very young."

Her expression was stony as she told him, "I have no

idea if she's dead or alive. Now could we drop this?" she asked in the coldest tone she'd ever summoned.

It wasn't cold enough. "You didn't know her." It didn't take much of a stretch for him to guess that.

The first reply that came to her lips was to tell him to damn well mind his own business, but she had a feeling that the retort would fall on deaf ears. He didn't strike her as the type to back off unless he wanted to. The best way to be done with this was just to answer his question as directly and precisely as possible.

"No, I didn't know her." She addressed her answer to the windshield as she stared straight ahead. "All I know is that she left me on the steps of a hospital when I was a few days old."

Sympathy and pity as well as a wave of empathy stirred within him. There'd been times, when he was much younger, when he'd felt the sting of missing a parent, but his mother had always been there for all of them. What must it have been like for her, not having either in her life?

"You're an orphan?"

He saw her jawline harden. "That's one of the terms for it. 'Throwaway' was another one someone once used," she recalled, her voice distant, devoid of any feeling.

She wasn't fooling him. Something like that came wrapped in pain that lasted a lifetime. "No one ever adopted you?"

She finally turned toward him. Her mouth quirked in a smile that didn't reach her eyes. "Hard to believe that no one wanted me, seeing as how I have this sweet personality and all?" One of the social workers had called her unadoptable after a third set of foster parents had brought her back.

He knew what she was doing, and he hadn't meant to make her feel self-conscious or bring back any painful memories. "I'm sorry."

Her back was up even as she carelessly shrugged away his apology. "Hey, things happen."

"Do you ever wonder—"

She knew what he was going to ask. If she ever wondered about who her parents had been. Or maybe if she wondered what it would have been like if at least her mother had kept her. She had, in both cases, but she wasn't about to talk to him about it. That was something she kept locked away.

"No," she said sharply, cutting him off. "Never." Balling up the remainder of her lunch, she tossed it and the wrapper into the bag. "Now, unless you've secretly been commissioned to write my biography, I'd appreciate it if you'd stop asking me questions that aren't going to further this investigation." She nodded at the burger he was still holding. "Finish your lunch."

Not until he evened the playing field for her, he thought. He didn't want her thinking he was trying to be superior or put her down in any manner. That was not the way he operated.

"I never knew my father."

Oh no, they weren't going to sit here, swapping deep-down secrets that he hoped would ultimately disarm her so that he could get into her bed. It wasn't going to work that way. It had once, but she'd been very young and vulnerable then. And stupid. She'd grown up a lot since she'd made that awful mistake and married a man she'd thought could be her shelter from the cruelties of life. Grown up enough to know that there would never be anyone out there to love her the way she needed to be loved.

The way she so desperately wanted to be loved.

Like it or not, she'd made her peace with that and she wasn't about to suddenly grow stupid because the guy sitting across from her with the chiseled profile and the soulfully beautiful blue eyes was doing his best to sound "nice."

Kansas looked at him and said flatly, "I don't want to know this."

Ethan didn't seem to hear her. Or, if he did, it didn't deter him. He went on as if she hadn't said anything.

"My mother told us he died on the battlefield, saving his friends. That he was a hero." For a moment, a faraway look came into his eyes as bits and pieces of that time came back to him. "She told us a lot of things about our father, always emphasizing that we had a lot to be proud of."

She had no idea why he was telling her this. Did he think that sharing this was going to somehow bring them closer? "Okay, so you had a legend for a father and I didn't. How does this—"

She didn't get to finish framing her question. His eyes met hers and he said very simply, without emotion, "She lied."

That brought what she was about to say to a screeching halt. Kansas stared at him. "Excuse me?"

"She lied," he repeated, and then, for emphasis, said again, "My mother lied."

Despite her initial resolve, Kansas could feel herself

being drawn in ever so slowly. It was the look in his eyes that did it. She supposed, since O'Brien seemed so bent on talking, that she might as well try to gain a measure of control over the conversation. "About his being a hero?"

If only, Ethan thought. If it had just been that, he could have easily made his peace with it. But it went far beyond a mere white lie. And it made him slow to trust anyone other than Kyle and Greer, the only two people in the world who had been as affected as him by this revelation.

"About all of it. Everything she'd told us was just a lie."

Kansas felt for him. She would have been devastated in his place. *If* what he said was true. "How did you find out?"

"From her. On her deathbed." *God, that sounded so melodramatic,* he thought. But it was the truth. Had his mother not been dying, he was certain that the lie would have continued indefinitely. "She knew she didn't have much longer, and apparently she wanted to die with a clear conscience."

Kansas took a guess as to what was behind the initial lie. "She didn't know who your father was?"

"Oh, she knew, all right." An edge entered Ethan's voice. "He was the man who abandoned her when she told him she was pregnant. The man who bullied her into not telling anyone about the relationship they'd had. If she did, according to what she told us, he promised that he would make her life a living hell."

Kansas didn't know what to say. Going by her own feelings in this sort of a situation, she instinctively knew he wouldn't want her pity. She shook her head, commiserating. "Sounds like a winner."

"Yeah, well, not every Cavanaugh turned out to be sterling—although, so far, my 'father' seems to be the only one in the family who dropped the ball."

The last name made her sit up and take notice. Her eyes widened. "Are you telling me that Brian Cavanaugh is your father?"

He realized that he hadn't been specific. "No, it's not Brian—"

"Andrew?" she interjected. She'd never met the man, but the detective had mentioned him and she knew the man by reputation. The very thought that Andrew Cavanaugh would have a love child he refused to publicly acknowledge sounded completely preposterous, especially since he was known for throwing open his doors to *everyone*.

But then, she thought, reconsidering, did anyone really ever know anyone else? When she'd gotten married, she would have sworn that Grant would never hurt her—and she'd been incredibly wrong about that.

"No, not Andrew, either." He would have been proud to call either man his father, but life hardly ever arranged itself perfectly.

She frowned. *Was* he pulling her leg? "All the other Cavanaughs are too young," she retorted. The oldest was possibly ten or twelve years older than O'Brien. Maybe less.

"It was Mike Cavanaugh," he said flatly.

Mike. Michael. Kansas shook her head. "I'm afraid I don't know who that is."

"Was," he corrected her. "Mike Cavanaugh died in

the line of duty a number of years ago. Patience and Patrick are his legitimate kids—"

She stopped him cold. He was treading on terrain that encompassed one of her pet peeves.

"Every kid is 'legitimate,'" she said with feeling. "It's the parents who aren't always legitimate, not thinking beyond the moment or weighing any of the consequences of their actions. Allowing themselves to get careless and carried away without any regard for who they might wind up hurting—"

Ethan held up his hand to get her to stop. "I'm not trying to get into an argument with you," he told her. "I'm trying to make you see that we have more in common than you think."

Not really, she thought.

"At least you *had* a mother, a mother who tried to shield you from her mistake, however badly she might have done it. A mother who tried to give you something to believe in. Mine couldn't be bothered to do anything except to literally pin a name on me that would always make me the butt of jokes." She saw him looking at her quizzically and elaborated. "She pinned a piece of paper to my blanket that said, 'Her name is Kansas. I can't raise her.' That's it. Eight words. My entire legacy, eight words."

"At least she did give you a chance to live," he pointed out. "I've seen newborn babies thrown out in garbage cans, discarded by the wayside, like spoiled meat." He recalled one specific case that had taken him months to get out of his head.

Kansas sat silent in the car, studying him for a long moment. Just as the silence began to seem as if it was going on too long, she said, "You're a silver-lining kind of guy, aren't you?"

Kyle had been the last one to accuse him of that, except that the terminology his brother had used wasn't quite as squeaky-clean as what Kansas had just said.

"Once in a while," he allowed. "It does help sometimes."

Kansas didn't agree. Optimists tended to be stomped on. She'd been down that route and learned her lesson early on.

"Being a realist helps," she countered. "That way, you don't wind up being disappointed." Her mouth feeling exceptionally dry, she stopped to drain the last of her soft drink. "What do you say we get this show on the road and go talk to Mr. Silver, the owner of that discount store that burned down?" In case he'd forgotten, she prompted, "It was the fourth fire."

He nodded, recalling the notes he'd written beneath the photos on the bulletin board. "That was the fire that led the chief of Ds to believe that there was just one person setting all of them."

"Right." Captain Lawrence had mentioned that to her in passing.

O'Brien turned the key in the ignition and started the car. Just as he was about to shift out of Park, she put her hand on top of his, stopping him. He could have sworn he felt something akin to electricity pass through him just then. Masking it, he looked at Kansas quizzically.

"This all stays here, right?" she questioned sharply. "What we just talked about, my background, it stays here, between us. It goes no further. Right?" This time it sounded more like an order than a question. Or, at the very least, like a sharply voiced request for a confirmation.

"Absolutely," he assured her immediately. Pulling out of the spot and then merging onto the street, he slanted a glance in her direction. "But if you find you ever want to just talk about it—"

She cut him off before he could complete his offer. "I won't."

The lady doth protest too much, he thought. "Okay," he allowed. "But should hell begin to freeze over and you find that you've changed your mind, you know where to find me."

"Don't worry," Kansas assured him. "I won't be looking."

She bottled things up too much, he thought. He'd had one of his friends, a firefighter at another house, discreetly ask around about this woman. She didn't go out of her way to socialize and definitely didn't hang out with the firefighters after hours. She was, for all intents and purposes, a loner. Loners tended to be lonely people, and while he had no illusions or desires to change the course of her life, he did want to offer her his friendship, for whatever that was worth to her.

"Ever heard that poem about no man being an island?" he asked.

She could feel her back going up even as she tried to tell herself that O'Brien didn't mean anything by this. That he wasn't trying to demean her.

"Yeah," she acknowledged with a dismissive tone. "It was about men. Women have a different set of rules."

He doubted that she really believed that. She was just

being defensive. She did that a lot, he realized. "Underneath it all, we're just human beings."

"Stop trying to get into my head, O'Brien," she warned. "You'll find it's very inhospitable territory."

He debated letting this drop and saying nothing. The debate was short. "You're trying too hard, Kansas."

God, she hated her name. It always sounded as if the person addressing her were being sarcastic. "Excuse me?"

"I said you're trying too hard," he repeated, knowing that she'd heard him the first time. "You don't have to be so macho. This isn't strictly a man's field anymore. Trust me, just be yourself and you'll have the men around here jumping through hoops every time you crook your little finger."

Was he serious? Did he actually think she was going to fall for that? "I don't know if that's insulting me or you. Or both."

"Wasn't meant to do either," he said easily, making a right turn to the next corner. He slowed down as he did so and gave her a quick glance. "You really are a beautiful woman, you know."

She straightened, doing her best to look indignant even as a warmth insisted on spreading through her. "I'd rather be thought of as an intelligent, sharp woman, not a beautiful one."

He saw no conflict in that. "You can be both," he answered matter-of-factly, then added more softly, "You are both."

Kansas frowned. Oh, he was a charmer, this temporary partner of hers. He was probably accustomed to women dropping like flies whenever he decided to lay it on. Well, he was in for a surprise. She wasn't going to let herself believe a word coming out of his mouth, no matter how tempting that was or how guileless he sounded as he delivered those words. She'd had the infection and gotten the cure. She was never going to allow herself to be led astray again. Ever.

"Don't you know that ingesting too much sugar can lead to diabetes?" she asked sarcastically.

"I'll keep that in mind," he promised, not bothering to keep a straight face. "Were the cross streets for that discount house Culver and Bryan?"

"Culver and Trabuco," she corrected.

As soon as she said it, he remembered. "That's right." He laughed shortly. "After a while, all the names and descriptions start running together."

"Not to me," she informed him crisply. "Each and every one of the buildings are different. Like people," she added.

The way she said it, he knew she wasn't trying to sound high-handed or find fault with him. She meant it. It was almost as if every fire had a separate meaning for her.

Ethan had a feeling that the fire inspector he'd initially felt that he'd been saddled with had more than one outstanding secret in her closet. He meant to find out how many and what they were, although, for the life of him, he couldn't clearly state *why* he was so determined to do this. Why he wanted to unravel the mystery that was Kansas Beckett.

But he did.

Chapter 8

They were getting nowhere.

Five days of diligently combing through ashes, testimonies and the arrest records of felons who had a penchant for playing with fire hadn't brought them to any new conclusions, other than to reinforce what they already knew: that there were some very strange sociopaths walking the earth.

Their lack of headway wasn't for lack of tips. What they did lack, however, were tips that didn't take them on elaborate wild-goose chases.

With a frustrated sigh, Ethan leaned back in his chair. He rocked slightly as he stared off into space. The lack of progress was getting to him. The latest "person of interest" he was looking into turned out to have been in jail when the fire spree initially started. Which brought them back to square one.

Again.

"I'm beginning to feel like a dog chasing his own tail," he said out loud, not bothering to hide his disgust.

Kansas looked up from the computer screen she'd been reading. "I'd pay to see that," she volunteered.

Closing her eyes, Kansas passed her hand over her forehead. There was a headache building there, and she felt as if she were going cross-eyed. She'd lost track of the number of hours she'd been sitting here, at the desk that had been temporarily assigned to her, going through databases that tracked recent fires throughout the western states in hopes of finding something that might lead to the firebug's identity. Every single possibility had led to a dead end.

There had to be something they were missing, she thought in exasperation. Fires that could be traced to accelerants just didn't start themselves. Who the hell was doing this, and when was he finally going to slip up?

Noting the way Kansas was rubbing her forehead, Ethan opened his bottom drawer and dug out the container with his supply of extra-strength aspirin in it. In the interest of efficiency, he always bought the economy size. He rounded his desk and placed the container on top of hers.

The sound of pills jostling against one another as he set the bottle down had Kansas opening her eyes again. She saw the bottle, then raised her eyes to his. "What's that?"

"Modern science calls it aspirin. You can call it whatever you want," Ethan told her, sitting down at his desk again. Because she was looking at the oversize bottle as if she wasn't sure what it might really hold, he said,

"You look like you have a headache. I thought a few aspirins might help."

Picking the bottle up, Kansas shook her head in wonder. "This has *got* to be the biggest supply of aspirin I've ever seen."

"We get it by the truckload around here," Dax told her as he walked into the room, catching the tail end of the conversation. He raised his voice slightly to catch the rest of the task force's attention. "I suggest you all take a few with you."

Kansas swung her chair around to face Dax. A leaden feeling descended on her chest. There could be only one reason why he was saying that. "Another one?"

"Another one," Dax confirmed grimly. "Just got the call."

Ethan was on his feet, grabbing his jacket and slipping it on. "Where?"

"Down on Sand Canyon," he answered. "The place is called Meadow Hills."

Kansas stopped dead. She recognized the name instantly. "That's a nursing home," she said to Dax, but even as she said it, she was hoping that somehow she was wrong.

She wasn't.

Dax nodded, holding a tight rein on his thoughts. He was not about to let his imagination run away with him. "Yeah."

Kansas shuddered, trying to curtail the wave of horror that washed over her. She couldn't get the image of terrified senior citizens out of her head.

"What a monster," she muttered.

"It's still in progress," Dax told them as they all hurried out the door. "Luckily, the firefighters got there quickly again. They've been a regular godsend. They had a lot of people to clear out, and I'd hate to think of what might have happened if they'd delayed their response even by a few minutes."

Kansas said nothing. She didn't even want to think about it, about how helpless and frightened some of those older residents of the convalescent home had to feel, their bodies immobilized in beds as they smelled smoke and then having that smoke fill their fragile lungs.

Another wave of frustration assaulted her, intensifying the pain in her head.

"Why can't we find this bastard?" she cried, directing the question more to herself than to any of the men who were hurrying down the hall along with her.

"Because he's good," Ethan answered plainly. "He's damn good."

"But he's not perfect," she shot back angrily.

"That's what we're all counting on," Dax told her.

Reaching the elevator first, Kansas jabbed the Down button. When it failed to arrive immediately, she turned on her heel and hurried over to the door that led to the stairwell.

Ethan was quick to follow her. "Running down the stairs really isn't going to make that much of a difference," he told her, watching the rhythmic way her hips swayed as she made her way to the door. "In the long run, it won't get you there any faster."

Kansas didn't slow down. Entering the stairwell, she started down the stairs, her heels clicking on the metal steps.

"I know," she tossed over her shoulder. "I just need to be moving." She hadn't really meant to share that. What was it about this man that seemed to draw the words out of her? That seemed to draw out other things, too? "It makes me feel as if I'm getting something accomplished."

"We're going to catch him," Ethan told her with quiet affirmation once he reached the bottom step and was next to her.

She looked at him sharply, expecting to see that he was laughing at her and being condescending. But he wasn't. He looked sincere. Which either meant that he was or that he was a better actor than she'd initially given him credit for.

Kansas went on the offensive. "You don't really believe that."

"Actually," he told her, "I do." They went down another flight, moving even faster this time. "I just don't know how long it's going to take. The more fires there are, the more likely it is that he's going to trip up, show his hand, have someone catch him in the act. *Something,*" he underscored, "is going to go wrong for him— and right for us."

Reaching the first floor, Kansas hurried to the front entrance. Not waiting for the others, she pushed it open with the flat of her hand.

"Meanwhile, the bastard's turning Aurora into a pile of ashes."

"Not yet," Ethan countered. They were outside, but she was still moving fast. Heading toward his car. He kept up with her. "I take it that you don't want to wait for the others."

"They'll meet us there," she said, reaching his vehicle.

His keys in his hand, he hit the remote button that disarmed the security device. Getting in, he shook his head. "Ever have a partner before?" he asked Kansas.

She got in and buckled up, tension racing through her body. She was anxious to get to the site of the fire, as if her presence there would somehow curtail any further harm the fire might render.

"I don't have one now," she pointed out glibly. As far as she was concerned, "temporary" didn't count.

The look Ethan gave her did something strange to her stomach. It felt as if she'd just endured an accelerated fifty-foot drop on a roller-coaster ride.

"Yeah," Ethan corrected, "you do. Better adjust," he advised mildly.

Mild or not, that got her back up. "And if I don't?" she challenged, unconsciously raising her chin as if silently daring him to take a swing.

"It'd just be easier on everyone all around if you did. We're all after the same thing," he reminded her not for the first time. "Nailing this creep's hide to the wall."

She began to retort, then thought better of it. The man was right. This was her frustration talking, not her. Taking a deep breath, she forced out the words that needed to be said. "You're right, I'm sorry."

He gave her a long glance. Had she just apologized to him? That wasn't like her. "Don't throw me a curve like that," he told her, and she couldn't tell if he was serious or not. "I'm liable to jump the divider and crash this beautiful car."

She noticed that he put the car first. The man really was enamored with this cream-colored machine, wasn't he?

"Very funny," she cracked. "I admit I have a tendency to go off on my own, but it's just that I'm so damn frustrated right now," she told him. Then she elaborated: "We should have been able to find him by now. *I* should have been able to find him by now."

"No, you had it right the first time," he said quietly. "*We* should have been able to find this sicko by now."

She was out of ideas and her brain felt as dry as the Mojave Desert. "What are we doing wrong?"

"I don't know," he admitted.

There was a long moment of silence, and then he became aware of Kansas suddenly straightening in her seat. He was beginning to be able to read her. And she'd just thought of something. He'd bet money on it.

"Talk," he told her. "What just suddenly occurred to you?"

So excited by what she was thinking, she could hardly sit still. But she answered Ethan's question with one of her own. "Do we have any footage of the crowds that gathered around to see the outcome of these fires?"

"*We* don't, but I'm sure the local news stations do. This is the kind of story that they live for." With each fire, the coverage became that much more intense, lasting that much longer. He'd never known that so much could be said about any given topic. The media were in a class by themselves.

She didn't care about the press. Reporters who earned a living focusing on people in possibly the worst moments of their lives had always struck her as annoying at best. At worst they were vultures. But right now, they could unwittingly provide a useful service.

"Do you think we can get our hands on some of that footage?"

He personally couldn't, but he figured Dax could. Or, if not him, then certainly the chief of Ds could. "Don't see why not." It didn't take much to figure out where she was going with this. "You think our fire-bug's in the crowd?"

She never liked committing herself, even though her answer was yes. "Worth a look."

Ethan nodded. "I'll ask Dax to requisition as much footage from each fire as is available. If he can't, the chief can. I'll tell him it's your idea," he added, just in case she thought he might be tempted to steal her thunder.

Because O'Brien was being magnanimous, she could return the favor, all the while reminding herself not to let her guard down. That would be a mistake.

"*Our* idea," she corrected. "We were brainstorm-ing. Kind of."

Ethan grinned. "You just might make it as a team member yet, Kansas."

"Something to shoot for," she allowed. Although she damn well knew that by the time she'd adjusted to being "one of the guys," or whatever O'Brien wanted to call it, she'd be back at the firehouse, working on her own again.

It might, she couldn't help thinking as she stole a side glance at Ethan, actually take a little adjusting on her part to make the transition back.

Who would have ever thought it?

When they arrived at the site of the newest fire some fifteen minutes later, chaos had settled in. The rather small front lawn before the nursing home was completely littered with vintage citizens, many of whom, despite the hour, were in their pajamas and robes. A number were confined to wheelchairs.

She saw several of the latter apparently on their own, deposited haphazardly away from the fire. One resident looked absolutely terrified. There weren't nearly enough aides and orderlies, let alone nurses, to care for or reassure them.

As she started toward the terrified, wild-eyed old woman, Kansas's attention was drawn away to the almost skeletal-looking old man who was lying on the grass. There was a large and burly firefighter leaning over the unconscious resident, and she could tell from the fireman's frantic motions that the old man's life hung in the balance.

Kansas held her breath as the firefighter, his protective helmet and gloves on the ground, administered CPR. He was doing compressions on the frail chest and blowing into the all-but-lifeless mouth.

A distressed nurse was hovering beside the firefighter like an anemic cheerleader, hoarsely giving instructions as he worked over the senior citizen.

"Now that's really odd," Kansas muttered under her breath.

Before Ethan could ask her what she meant, Kansas was already working her way through the crowd and over to the scene. By the time she reached them, the firefighter had risen unsteadily to his feet. His wide face was drawn and he was clearly shaken.

"I lost him," he lamented in disbelief. The anguished words weren't addressed to anyone in particular, but more to the world in general. It was obvious that the towering firefighter was berating himself for not being able to save the old man. "I lost him," he cried again, his voice catching. "Oh, God, I lost him."

With effort, the nurse dropped to her knees. Steadying herself, she pressed her fingers against the elderly man's throat, searching for any sign of a pulse. She didn't find it.

The nurse sighed, shaking her head. Her next words confirmed what had already been said. "Mr. Walters is gone." Looking up at the fireman, in her next breath she absolved him of any blame. "You did everything you possibly could."

"I didn't do enough," the firefighter protested. He looked defeated and almost lost.

"Yes, you did," the nurse said with feeling. She held her hand up to him and the distraught firefighter helped her to her feet. "Don't beat yourself up about it. It was Mr. Walters's time."

The next moment, a reporter with one of the local stations came running over to the firefighter and the nurse. His cameraman was directly behind him. Thrusting his microphone at the duo, the reporter began firing questions at them, ready and willing to turn this tragedy into a human-interest sound bite in a blatant attempt to be the lead story of the hour tonight.

Kansas noted that the firefighter looked even more anguished than he had a few moments earlier as he began to answer the reporter's questions.

She glanced over toward Ethan, who had caught up

to her again. "What do you make of that?" she murmured in as discreet a voice as she could manage and still be heard above the din.

Ethan wasn't sure where she was trying to go with this. "He's obviously someone who takes his job to heart." He saw the number on the engine and knew that she'd come from that fire station. "I take it that you don't know him."

Kansas shook her head. "He came to the house just when I got promoted to investigator. I hang out at the firehouse, but I have my own office, do my own thing. They answer the calls, I only go if arson's suspected." She pressed her lips together. "I'm really not part of that whole firefighting thing anymore."

Ethan detected something in her voice. "Do you miss it?"

He had a feeling he knew the answer to that no matter what she said. He was prepared for her to say something dismissive in response. He'd come to learn that she was nothing if not a private person. Ordinarily, that would be a signal for him to back off.

But she intrigued him.

"Sometimes," she murmured in a low voice, surprising him. "Other times, I feel I'm doing more good as an investigator. Or at least I was before this lunatic showed up, setting fire to everything in his path and driving me crazy. Us," Kansas amended quickly. "Driving us crazy."

Thinking in the plural was harder than she'd realized. It was really going to take practice.

Ethan grinned, appreciating the effort she was making. He couldn't help wondering if she was just turning over a new leaf or if she was doing this solely because of what he'd said earlier.

"You're coming along, Kansas. You're coming along."

She had no idea why his approval didn't incense her. Why it had, oddly enough, the exact opposite effect. Maybe she'd been breathing in too much smoke these last few years, she theorized.

About to say something flippant about his comment, Kansas stopped as she became aware that the rest of the task force had just joined her and Ethan.

The moment they had, Ethan went to Dax and she knew without having to listen in that he was making the request for the available footage of the last dozen fires. She couldn't help smiling to herself as she made her way over to the two men.

They looked alike, she caught herself thinking. Both dark, both good-looking. On a scale of 1 to 10, they were both 10s. With Ethan possibly being a 10.5.

And what did *that* have to do with the price of tea in China? she upbraided herself. She needed to stay focused and not let her mind wander like this.

When she was within earshot, she heard Dax ask her partner, "You think he stuck around to watch the fire department try to save the buildings?"

"The minute Kansas said it, it made sense. I'm sure of it," Ethan told Dax vehemently. "He wouldn't be able to resist. This is like an opiate to him. It's too much of a draw for him to pass up."

"Okay," Dax agreed. "I've got a few connections. I'll see what I can do."

"I've got a smartphone," Ethan suddenly remembered as Dax began to walk to his car.

Youngman looked at him oddly. "As opposed to what, a stupid phone?"

"No, you idiot," Ortiz, years younger than the veteran detective, berated his partner in disgust. "He means he's got a video camera in it."

Ethan was already putting his phone to use, panning the surrounding area and committing the image to film. It was a very simple act. He sincerely hoped it would help in capturing what was turning out to seem like a very complex perp.

"I believe this comes under the heading of 'be careful what you wish for,'" Dax announced the following morning as he walked up to Kansas's desk and deposited a huge carton. The carton was filled to the brim with videotapes.

She had to rise from her chair in order to see inside the box. "What's all this?" she asked.

"These are the tapes you asked for," he reminded her. "This is all footage from the fires."

"All these?" she asked incredulously, having trouble processing the information. There was an incredible amount of footage to review, she thought with a sinking feeling.

"No. That's only a third. Youngman and Ortiz are bringing the other two boxes."

She groaned as she took out the first tape. It looked as if her eyes were about to become tread-worn.

Chapter 9

"What are you doing?" Kansas asked in surprise.

On her feet, she'd picked up the first box of tapes that Dax had gotten for her to review. Braced for hours of incredible boredom, she was about to head to the small, windowless room where a monitor, coupled with a VCR, was housed. Her question, and the surprise that had prompted it, was directed toward Ethan, who had just picked up one of the other boxes and was walking behind her.

"Following you," he said simply.

She immediately took that to mean that he thought she needed help transporting the tapes. It was inherently against her nature to allow anyone to think she wasn't capable of taking care of herself in any fashion.

Kansas lifted her chin. He was beginning to recognize that as one of her defensive moves. He really needed to find a way to get her to be more trusting, Ethan thought.

"I can carry them."

"I'm sure you can," he told her in an easygoing voice, but he couldn't help adding, "Probably with one hand tied behind your back." He gave her a weary look. "For once, why don't you just accept help in the spirit it's offered? This isn't any kind of a covert statement about your capabilities. I just thought I'd help you with them, that's all."

Kansas felt a flush of embarrassment. She supposed she was being a little paranoid. She was far more accustomed to put-downs than help. It hadn't been easy, even in this day and age, getting accepted in her chosen field. It was still, for all intents and purposes, mostly an all-boys club. Female firefighters and female arson investigators were a very small group, their authority and capabilities challenged almost at every turn.

"Sorry," she murmured in a small voice as she resumed walking. "Thank you."

Ethan nodded. "Better." Grinning, he fell into place beside her as they went down the hall. "I thought I'd give you a hand viewing them. There're two monitors in the room and two sets of eyes are better than one."

She hadn't realized that there were two monitors, but even if she had, she wouldn't have expected anyone else to volunteer for the tedious job of looking for the same face to pop up somewhere within every crowd shot of the various fires.

She stopped walking and looked at him in astonishment. "You're actually volunteering, of your own free will, to help me go over the tapes?"

Arriving at the room, he shifted the box to one side, balancing it on his hip in order to open the door for her. He stepped back and allowed her to go in first. "I think if you play back the conversation, that's what I just said."

Walking in, she deposited the box on the long, metal-top table that served as a desk. Both monitors with their VCRs were on it.

"Why?" she asked, turning to face him.

He put down his box next to hers. "Because that's what partners do, and like I said, for better or for worse, we're temporary partners." He pulled out his chair and sat down. "The sooner we get done with these, the sooner we can move on to something else. Maybe even catching this guy," he added.

Considering the way she'd treated him, O'Brien was being incredibly nice. She wondered if it were a mistake, letting her guard down just a little. She didn't like leaving herself open. But verbally sparring with him after his offer of help didn't seem right, either.

"Thank you," she finally said. "That's very nice of you."

He took out the first tape. The writing on the label was exceptionally neat—and small. An ant would need glasses to read it, he thought.

Ethan gave her a glance. "Remember that the next time you want to take my head off."

She supposed she had that coming. She hadn't exactly been the most easygoing, even-tempered person to work with.

"It's not your fault, you know," she murmured, sitting down. "The way I react."

"Never thought it was," he answered glibly. Ethan paused, waiting. But she didn't say anything further. So he did. "Okay, whose fault is it?"

Again, Kansas didn't answer right away. Instead, she seemed to be preoccupied with taking tapes out of the box and arranging them in some preordained order on the long, narrow table that they were using. It was a balancing act at best. Most of the space was taken up by the monitors. She remained silent for so long, Ethan decided she wasn't going to answer him.

And then she did.

"My husband's," she replied quietly. "It's my husband's fault."

Ethan stared at her. To say he was stunned would have been a vast understatement. His eyes instantly darted to Kansas's left hand. There was no ring there, which caused another host of questions to pop up in his head. Men didn't always wear a wedding ring. Women, however, usually did. But she didn't have one.

"You're married?" he asked, the words echoing in the small room.

"Was," Kansas corrected him. "I *was* married. A long time ago." She took a breath, because this wasn't easy to admit, even to herself, much less to someone else. But he was still a stranger, which in an odd way made it somewhat easier. "Biggest mistake of my life."

The statement instantly prompted another thought. "He abused you?"

The moment the words were out of his mouth, Ethan felt himself growing angry. Growing protective of her. The only other time he'd ever felt that way was when his mother had told them about their father. About being abandoned by the only man she'd ever loved, which to him represented abuse of the highest degree.

"Not physically," Kansas was quick to answer. Which only led him to another conclusion.

"Emotionally?"

She laughed shortly, but there was no humor in the sound. "If you call bedding the hotel receptionist on our honeymoon emotional abuse, then yes, Grant abused me emotionally." And broke her heart, but she wasn't about to say that part out loud. That was only for her to know, no one else.

She knew that kind of thing couldn't just happen out of the blue. A guy didn't become worthless scum after he pledged to love, honor and cherish. The seeds had to have been there to begin with.

"You didn't have a clue what he was like before that?"

Yes, she supposed, in hindsight, she had. But she was so desperate to have someone love her that she'd disregarded any nagging doubts she had, telling herself that it would be different once they were married.

Except that it wasn't. It just got worse. So she'd ended it. Quickly.

Kansas shrugged carelessly. "I was in love and I made excuses for him."

Ethan looked at her for a long moment. She didn't strike him as the type who would do that. Obviously he was wrong. His interest as well as his curiosity was piqued a little more.

"If he came back into your life right now," Ethan asked, selecting his words carefully as he continued unpacking tapes and lining them up in front of him, "and said he was sorry, would you take him back?"

Kansas regretted having said anything. He was asking a question that was way too personal, but she couldn't blame him. This was all her fault. She'd opened the door to this and O'Brien was doing what came naturally to him—prying. And besides, the man *was* being helpful to her. She supposed she owed him the courtesy of an answer.

"That depends," she said tentatively.

He raised a quizzical brow. Definitely not what he would have expected her to say. He decided to push it a little further. "On what?"

And that was when he saw the lightning flash in her eyes. "On whether or not I could find a big enough barbecue skewer to use so that I could roast him alive."

Now *that* he would have expected to hear, Ethan thought, doing his best to keep a straight face. "I had no idea you were so bloodthirsty."

"I'm not," she admitted after a beat, "but he wouldn't know that—and I'd want him to sweat bullets for at least a while."

Ethan didn't even try to hold the laughter back. "How long did you stay married?" he asked once he finally sobered a little.

Kansas didn't answer him immediately. She hadn't talked about her short stint as a married woman to anyone. In a way, it almost felt good to finally get all this out. "Just long enough to file for a divorce."

That, he thought, explained a lot. "Is that what has you so dead set against the male species?" he asked, voicing his thoughts out loud.

"Not all of it," she corrected. "Only the drop-dead handsome section of the species." Her eyes narrowed as she looked at him. "Because drop-dead handsome guys think they can get away with anything."

She was looking at him as if she included him in that small, exclusive club. But there was no way to ask her without sounding as if he had a swelled head. Ethan opted for leaving it alone, but he couldn't resist pointing out the obvious. "You can't convict a section of the population because one guy acted like a supreme jerk and didn't know what he had."

"And what is it that you think he had?" The question came out before she could think to bank it down. Damn it, he was going to think she was fishing for a compliment. Or worse, fishing for his validation. Which she didn't need, she thought fiercely. The only person's validation she needed was her own.

"A woman of substance," Ethan told her, his voice low, his eyes on hers. "You don't just make a commitment to someone and then fool around."

No, he's just trying to suck you in. He doesn't mean a word of it.

"And you, if you make a commitment, you stick to it?" she asked, watching his eyes. She could always tell when a man was lying.

"I've never made a commitment," he told her honestly. "It wouldn't be fair to have a woman clutching to strings if there weren't any."

Why was her breath catching in her throat like that? This was just talk, nothing more. There was absolutely no reason for her to feel like this, as if her pulse were just about to be launched all the way to the space station.

Shifting, trying to regain her bearings, her elbow hit one of the tapes and sent it falling to the floor. She exhaled, and bent down to pick it up. So did Ethan. They very narrowly avoided bumping heads.

But other body parts were not nearly so lucky. Stooping, their bodies brushed against one another, sending electric shock waves zipping through both of them at the same time. Kansas sensed this because just as she sucked in her breath, she thought she heard him do the same, except more softly.

When their eyes locked, the circuit seemed absolutely complete. Rising up, his hands on either side of her shoulders as he brought her up to her feet, Ethan didn't think his next move through, which was highly unlike him. What he did was go with instincts that refused to be silenced.

Ethan bent his head, lightly brushing his lips against hers. And then he savored a second, stronger wave of electricity that went jolting through his system the moment he made contact.

He would have gone on to deepen the kiss, except that was exactly the moment that Dax chose to walk in with the third box of tapes.

Dax looked from his cousin to the fire department loan-out. It didn't take a Rhodes scholar to pick up the vibes that were ricocheting through the small room. The vibes that had absolutely nothing to do with the apprehension of a firebug.

Clearing his throat, Dax asked a nebulous question. "Either of you two need a break?" His tone was deliberately mild.

Ethan glanced at her, then shook his head. "No, we're good," he assured Dax.

Yes, he certainly is, Kansas couldn't help thinking. Even a mere fleeting press of his lips to hers had told her that.

She was definitely going to have to stay alert at all times with this one, she thought. If she wasn't careful, he was going to wear away all of her defenses in the blink of an eye without really trying.

This was not good.

And she didn't know if she believed him about not making any false promises. He sounded convincing, but it could all be for show, to leave her defenseless and open. After all, she didn't really know the man.

But she knew herself.

It wasn't in her to play fast and loose no matter how much she wanted to. She wasn't the kind who went from man to man, having a good time with no thought of commitment. If she succumbed to this man, it would be a forever thing, at least on her part. And she already knew that there was no such word as *forever* in O'Brien's vocabulary.

"Good." She seconded Ethan's response when Dax turned his gaze in her direction.

"I'd send you a third pair of eyes." He addressed his remark to both of them, then waved at the equipment they were going to be using. "But there are only two monitors to be had."

"That's okay, Dax," Ethan answered for both of them. "We'll manage somehow."

"I'll hold you to that," Dax promised. Then, with a nod toward Kansas, he left the room, closing the door behind him. The lighting in the windowless room went from soft to inky.

It felt to Kansas that she'd been holding her breath the entire time. She stared at the door as if she expected it to open at any moment.

"Do you think that he saw us?" she asked Ethan uneasily.

"If he had, he would have said as much." There was no question in his mind about that. "Dax doesn't play games. None of the Cavanaughs do. They're all straight shooters."

She laughed softly, shaking her head. "That puts the lot of them right up there with unicorns, mermaids—and you."

He grinned at her. "Always room for more."

What did that even mean? she wondered. Was O'Brien just bantering, trying to tease her? Or was there some kind of hidden meaning to his words? What if he was saying that he and she could—

Stop it. Don't be an idiot. That's just wishful thinking on your part. How many Grants do you need in your life before you finally learn? We come into this world alone and we leave it alone. And most of us spend the time in between alone, as well.

"I'll have to get back to you on that," she told Ethan.

"Fair enough," he commented. And then he looked back at the piles of tapes. "We'd better get to work before Dax assigns us a keeper."

She merely nodded and applied herself to the task at hand.

And tried very, very hard not to think about the firm, quick press of velvet lips against hers.

* * *

"So?" Dax asked when Ethan and Kansas finally returned to their desks two days later and sank down in their chairs. They had brought in the boxes of tapes with them and deposited them on the floor next to their desks.

Ethan groaned, passing a hand over his eyes for dramatic effect. "I may never look at another TV monitor again."

There was only one way to take that comment. Disappointment instantly permeated the room. "Then you found nothing?"

"Nothing," Ethan confirmed. "Except that a lot of people could stand to have complete makeovers," he quipped.

Dax looked over toward the fire investigator. "Kansas, have you got anything more informative than that for me?"

She really wished she did. After all, looking through the crowd footage had been her idea. "No, I'm afraid not. Neither one of us saw anyone who turned up at all the fires—or even half of them," she added with an impatient sigh. "Because a lot of the fires took place in close proximity, there were some overlaps, the same people turning up at more than one blaze, but they definitely didn't pop up at enough fires for us to look for them and ask questions."

Dax didn't look as if he agreed with her. "How many overlaps?" he pressed.

"One guy turned up four times," Ethan interjected. Dax looked at him, listening. "Another guy, five. But five was the limit," he added. "Nobody showed up more than that."

Ethan opened his bottom drawer, looking for the giant bottle of aspirin. Finding it, he took it out. Then, holding it up, he raised an inquiring eyebrow in Kansas's direction.

Kansas nodded, the motion relatively restrained because of the headache that was taking over. Shaking out two pills, Ethan leaned over and placed them on her desk, along with an unopened bottle of water that seemed to materialize in his hands. She didn't know until then that he usually kept several such bottles on hand in his desk.

"So here we are again, back to square one," Ortiz complained, looking exceedingly frustrated. "No viable suspects amid the known arsonists and pyromaniacs, no firebug hanging around in the crowd, bent on watching his handiwork, secretly laughing at us."

Youngman added in his two cents. "Only good thing is that, except for that old man the other day, there haven't been any casualties at these fires."

Dax pointed out the simple reason for that piece of luck. "That's because the fire department always turns up quickly each and every time. Don't know how long that lucky streak's going to continue."

"Yeah, lucky for the people involved," Youngman commented, picking up on the key word. "Otherwise they'd most likely be being referred to in the past tense right about now."

Kansas began to nod, then stopped as Youngman's words as well as Dax's words replayed in her head.

When they did and the thought occurred to her, she all but bolted ramrod straight in her chair.

Ethan noted the shift in her posture immediately. She'd thought of something, something they hadn't covered before. It surprised him how quickly he'd become in tune to her body language.

He told himself he was just being a good detective. "What?" he pressed, looking at Kansas.

She in turn looked around at the other three men on the task force. "Doesn't that strike anyone else as strange?" she wanted to know.

"What, that the fire department turned up at a fire?" Ortiz asked, not following her. "It's what they do." His puzzled expression seemed to want to know why she was even asking this question. "You of all people—"

But Ortiz didn't get a chance to finish.

"No," she interrupted, "the fire department turning up early. Each and every time. Doesn't that seem a little odd to anyone? It's the same firehouse that answers the call each and every time, as well." And it was her firehouse, which made her pursuing this line of questioning even worse.

"There're only two firehouses in Aurora," Dax pointed out. "These fires are taking place in the southern section."

She was well aware of that fact. And aware that in many towns, there *were* no fire departments with firefighters who were paid by the city. Instead, what the townships had were dedicated volunteers who responded to the call whenever it went out, no matter where they were and what they were doing. Aurora was lucky to have not one but two firehouses charged with nothing more than looking out for their citizens.

But these early responses were definitely a lot more than just happy coincidences. Something was off here.

"I know that. But getting there in time to save everyone, the odds start to rise against you when the number of occurrences goes up. And yet, each and every time, the fire department is practically there just as the fire starts."

Dax looked at her sharply. "What are you getting at, Kansas?"

She took a deep breath before saying it. And then she forced the words out. "That maybe whoever is setting these fires is one of the firefighters."

Chapter 10

Her statement had gotten all four detectives to sit up and stare at her. Frustration and exhaustion were temporarily ousted.

"Do you know what you're saying?" Dax asked her incredulously.

Kansas nodded grimly. "I know *exactly* what I'm saying. But what other avenues are open to us?" She didn't want to think this way, but it had been a process of elimination. "The way I see it, it *has* to be one of the firefighters."

What she was suggesting was something no one wanted to think about or seriously consider.

"This is your own house you're pointing a finger at," Dax reminded her, clearly trying to wrap his mind around what she was saying.

The anguish was evident in her voice as she answered him. "Don't you think I know that? Don't you think that I wish there was some other answer?"

"What makes you think *this* is the answer?" Dax persisted.

Telling him it was a feeling in her gut would only have the detectives quickly dismissing the idea. As far as they were concerned, she was the "new kid." And the new kid wasn't allowed to have gut feelings for at least a couple of years. So she cited the clinical reference she'd read about the condition.

"It's the hero syndrome," she replied simply.

Scratching the eight or nine hairs that still populated the top of his head, Youngman looked at his partner, who offered no insight. Youngman then looked at her.

"And the hero syndrome is?" he wanted to know.

To her surprise, Ethan took over just as she was about to explain. "That's when someone arranges events in order to come running to the rescue and have people regard him—or her—as a hero," he told the others. "Or like a nurse might fiddle with a patient's medication, making them code so that she can rush in with defibrillator paddles to bring them back from the brink of death. People like that get off playing the hero. It makes them feel important, like they matter." Finished, Ethan looked at Kansas. "That's what you mean, right?"

He explained it better than she could, she thought. Had he come across this before? "Right."

Dax seemed to be turning his cousin's words over in his head before asking his next question. "And just which of these firefighters do you think is capable of something like that?"

She wished it was none of them, but she simply couldn't shake the feeling that it had to be.

"I don't know," she told Dax honestly. She was aware that all four pairs of eyes were on her, with perhaps Ethan's being the kindest. "Look, I hope I'm wrong, but if I am, then we're back to that damn square one again."

That suggestion was obviously more to Ortiz's liking. "It could still be a pyromaniac who just hasn't made the grid yet," he pointed out.

Ethan shot down his theory. "That's why Kansas and I just spent all those hours going over the news footage, looking for a face that might keep cropping up in the crowd shots. There wasn't any. The most hits we got were five." He repeated the information he'd already delivered once.

"So maybe these actually *were* just accidental, random fires," Ortiz suggested hopefully. "That kind of thing *does* happen around here."

"Then how do you explain the accelerants I found?" Kansas asked quietly.

"I forgot about that." Ortiz's shoulder slumped and he seemed to slide down a little farther in his chair. "I can't."

"You know those firefighters better than any of us," Dax pointed out, turning toward her again. Crossing his arms before him, pausing for a long moment, he finally asked, "How do you suggest we get started?"

When in doubt, go the simple route. Someone had once said that to her, she couldn't remember who. But she did remember that she'd taken it to heart and it had helped her see things through.

"Same way we'd get started with any suspects we're

trying to rule out," she told the prime detective on the case. "Call them in and interview each of them one at a time."

Ortiz shook his head. "They're not going to cooperate," he predicted.

"They might," Ethan theorized. The others looked at him curiously. "If we ask the right questions, we should be able to get some idea of what's going on."

"Right questions," Ortiz echoed. "Such as?"

She'd already started forming them in her head. "Such as if they remember seeing anyone suspicious in the vicinity when they arrived. Or if they saw anything suspicious at all—coming, going, while they were there. Anything." She took a breath. This was the million-dollar question. "And if they thought that any of the other firefighters behaved with undue valor."

"You're going to question their bravery?" Ortiz asked in astonishment.

"Exactly," she answered.

Youngman shook his head, evidently foreseeing problems. "That'll make their radar go up immediately."

"We've got five interview rooms." Dax volunteered a fact they all already knew—with the exception of the fire investigator. "We divide and conquer and keep this under wraps."

"For as long as it takes to interview the first five firemen," Ortiz pointed out glumly. "After that, all hell's going to break loose. They'll talk."

Broad shoulders rose and fell. "Still better than nothing," Dax commented.

"I don't like this," Youngman protested. "Those guys risk their lives, running into a burning building when any sane person would run in the opposite direction as fast as they could—and now we're pointing fingers at them? Accusing them of actually *starting* the fire?"

"Not at *them,* at *one* of them," Kansas insisted.

Youngman frowned, clearly not won over. "I can't believe you just said that. You know how united those guys are. You focus on one of them, the rest close ranks around him, forming an impenetrable wall that's next to impossible to crack."

She pressed her lips together and nodded. "Yes, I know."

The older detective shifted in his seat, making direct eye contact with her. "And when they find out this is your idea," he predicted, "they're not going to be very happy."

She knew that, too. But she refused to let that dictate how she did her job. "Nothing I haven't encountered before," she replied quietly, bracing herself for what was to come.

Ethan was perched against her desk, leaning a hip against the corner. He had been observing her for a few minutes and now finally commented: "You know, if you shrug your shoulders just the right way, that big chip you're carrying around could very possibly fall off."

If there was something she hated more than criticism, she couldn't remember what it was. "I don't *have* a big chip," she insisted.

Ethan lifted his right shoulder in a timeless, careless shrug. "Then it's got to be the biggest dandruff flake I've ever encountered," he assessed.

Swallowing an exasperated sigh, she ignored him

and instead looked at Dax. "I don't *want* to be right about this."

He could see by the look on her face that she was telling the truth.

"I know you don't," Dax commiserated. "For the time being, why don't you and Ethan re-canvass the areas of the last few fires, knock on the same doors, see if any of the stories have been altered this time around."

She saw through the suggestion. "I appreciate what you're trying to do, Detective Cavanaugh, but I really don't need to be shielded. I don't break. It's my suggestion, so I can handle my end of it."

Dax couldn't hide his concern. "I'm thinking about when this is all over and you have to go back."

So was she…for about a second. Why borrow trouble? It would be there waiting for her once this was over.

"I appreciate that, Detective, but I really can handle myself. Captain Lawrence is a fair man, and I don't really interact with the men on any sort of a regular basis anymore anyway." Kansas didn't realize at first that she was smiling as she looked around the squad room. "Not like I do here."

Dax allowed himself a small smile as he nodded. "All right, then. Since this involves possibly getting on the fire department's bad side, let me just run this by the chief of Ds and see what he has to say about it." He looked around at the task force. "When he gives his okay, who wants to inform Captain Lawrence?"

She began to say that she would, but she wasn't fast enough. Ethan raised his hand and beat her to it. "I will."

"Hope you're up on your self-defense classes," Ortiz murmured.

Kansas swung around to look at her partner. "It's my idea. I'll do it." He began to say something, but she held up her hand to silence him. "They won't hit me. You, they just might."

Dax laughed. "She's got a point," he said to his cousin.

Ethan wasn't going to argue with him—and he knew better than to argue outright with her.

"Fine," Ethan compromised. "We'll both go."

He was adamant on that point. There was no way he was going to let her walk into the firehouse with this new twist like some lamb to the slaughter. Whether she liked it or not, he was her partner for the time being, and that meant he intended to have her back at all times.

Kansas waited until Dax left to talk to his father. "I don't need a keeper," she informed Ethan indignantly, keeping her voice low.

"Yeah, you do, but that's an argument for another day," he retorted. "Besides, we send you alone, we look like a bunch of chickens hiding behind a woman." He shook his head. "Ain't gonna happen."

She inclined her head. Much as she wanted to argue with him, she could see his point. "I didn't think of it that way."

And neither had he—until just now.

But Ethan merely nodded in response and kept his satisfied grin to himself.

Brian looked at his son thoughtfully. Dax had laid out the theory that Kansas had come up with and that

Ethan had backed as succinctly as possible. Finished, his son waited for a comment.

Instead, Brian gestured for him to take a seat. Once Dax did, he asked for his opinion. "So what do you think of this idea?"

Dax knew that this was a giant step they were taking, one that didn't allow for any backtracking. And if they were wrong, there was going to be hell to pay. There might be hell to pay even if they were right. No one took being a suspect well, and this would cause at least a temporary rift between the police and the fire departments.

All that considered, Dax said, "I think they might be on to something. We've followed up all the so-called tips that have been coming in from the public hotlines, and all we've done is go around in circles." He sighed. "And meanwhile, buildings keep being burned. After each fire, we haul out all the usual suspects, all the firebugs out on parole and the known pyromaniac wanna-bes and come up with nothing. They all make sure that they've always got an alibi."

"And the media footage?" Brian asked. It had taken a bit of persuading on his part to secure that from the various local stations. "Did that show up anything?"

Dax shook his head. "Different faces at different fires. If this firebug's doing it to get a rush, he's got some remote hook-up going to view the sites, because he's not showing up in the crowds."

They had no choice but to pursue this new avenue, Brian thought. They were out of options. "I'll talk to Captain Lawrence. Go ahead and question the firefight-ers. Just try to do it as delicately as possible," he cautioned, though he was fairly confident he didn't really have to. Dax had a good head on his shoulders. All the younger Cavanaughs did. "I don't want some yahoo getting it into his head to turn this into a feud between the Aurora police department and the fire department."

Dax was already on his feet and crossing to the door. "Don't worry, we'll do our best to be discreet," he promised.

"Oh, and, Dax?" Brian called out just as his son was about to walk out.

Stopping, Dax looked at his father over his shoulder. "Yes?"

"How's Ethan coming along?" This was the first time that Dax was working with the other detective, and Brian was curious about the way things were going between them. As a family, the three O'Briens and the Cavanaughs were all still getting accustomed to one another.

And that didn't even begin to take in the curveball that Andrew had thrown him the other week. That, Brian knew, was still under wraps as far as the rest of the family was concerned.

Dax grinned. "Just like you'd expect, Chief. Like a born Cavanaugh."

Brian nodded his head. "Good to hear." He had equally good reports on Kyle and Greer. At this point, it seemed as if the only one of them who had ever disappointed the family had been Mike, who'd ultimately never managed to conquer the demons he lived with. "Keep me apprised of the way the questioning is going," he requested. "And give me a holler if you need me," he added, raising his voice just before his son went down the hall.

Dax raised his hand over his head as he kept going. "Absolutely."

Brian crossed to the door and closed it. He knew that Dax wouldn't be coming to him with any problems. He'd raised them all to know that family was always there for them if the need arose but that they were expected to stand independently on their own two feet if at all possible. None of his sons, nor his daughter, had ever disappointed him.

And neither, he thought now, had Lila's four kids, whom he'd regarded as his own even before he and Lila had exchanged vows.

All in all, he mused, getting back to the report he'd been reading just before Dax came in, he was one hell of a lucky man.

Arms crossed before his barrel chest, covering the small drop of ketchup that recalled lunch and the fries he'd had, Captain John Lawrence was one frown line short of a glare as he regarded the young woman who'd spent the last four years assigned to his firehouse.

"What do you want to talk to them for?" he asked suspiciously, grinding out the words.

The smile on his lips as he'd greeted her and the detective she'd walked in with had quickly dissolved when she'd made her request to interview each of his men. Eyes the color of black olives shifted from Kansas to the man standing beside her and then back again, waiting.

Kansas tried again. She'd been the object of Lawrence's displeasure before, when she'd first been assigned to him. In time, she'd won him over. It looked now as if all her hard work and dedication had just been unraveled in the last couple of minutes.

"We're hitting a dead end," she explained patiently, "and we're hoping that one of them might have seen something that we didn't."

"They were kind of busy at the time," he pointed out. Lawrence didn't bother trying to mask the sarcasm in his voice.

"We appreciate that, Captain Lawrence," Ethan said respectfully but firmly. "But you never know what might help break a case. Sometimes the smallest, most inconsequential thing—"

Impatient, Lawrence waved a hand at him, dismissing the explanation. "Yeah, yeah, I know the drill— and the drivel," he added pointedly. He looked far from pleased. Just as it seemed that he was going to be stubbornly uncooperative, the captain grudgingly said, "If you really think it can help the investigation, I'll send them over to talk to you." He looked at Kansas and his expression softened, but only slightly. Ethan could see that she had fallen out of favor. With any luck, it was only temporary. "You want everybody?"

She gave him a little leeway. "Everybody who was on call for the fires."

The disgruntled expression intensified. "That's everybody."

"Wasn't it just one shift?" Ethan asked innocently. Most of the fires had taken place under the cover of twilight or later.

"They overlapped," the captain answered coldly. His attention was back to Kansas. "Okay with you if

I send just three at a time—barring a fire, of course," he added cynically.

Ethan ran interference for her, determined to take the brunt of the captain's displeasure. "Of course," he said. "Goes without saying. The fires always take precedent."

There was something akin to contempt in the captain's dark eyes as they swept over him. "Glad you agree," Lawrence finally commented. And then he asked Kansas, "Tomorrow okay with you? Most of the guys you want to talk to are off right now. It's been a rough few days."

In Ethan's opinion, it had been a rough few months. And besides, it was getting late anyway. He and Kansas were both off the clock and had been for the last half hour. Lawrence had kept them waiting almost an hour before he "found" the time to see them.

"Tomorrow's fine," Ethan answered. Leaning forward, he shook Lawrence's hand. "Thanks for your cooperation." He managed to say the words with a straight face.

"Hey, we're all on the same team, right?" It was hard to tell whether Lawrence was being serious or sarcastic, but Ethan was leaning toward the latter.

"Right," Kansas agreed.

It had earned her a less than warm look from the captain. She was in the doghouse and she knew it. It was obvious that the man was annoyed with her because she hadn't been able to somehow spare him what she was sure Lawrence saw as a major inconvenience.

She was equally sure that he didn't realize that his men were under suspicion at the moment. Because if he had known, he would have said as much. Most likely at the top of his lungs while liberally sprinkling more than a few choice words throughout his statement. Lawrence wasn't the kind to keep things bottled up and to himself. If he was angry, *everyone* knew he was angry. They also knew about what and at whom. The man didn't believe in sparing feelings.

Taking their leave, Kansas and Ethan walked out of the fire station. Once outside, she turned to him and said, "You should have let me do the talking."

He'd done the brunt of it for a very simple reason. "You've got to come back here. I don't. I wanted Lawrence to think of me as the messenger in all this. When he realizes what's going on, he's not going to be a happy camper," Ethan predicted. "I don't want him taking it out on you."

Kansas looked at him, curbing her natural impulse to shrug off any offers of help and declare that she could take care of herself. If pressed, she would have to admit, if only to herself, that it was rather nice to have someone looking out for her. It was something she'd really never experienced before.

Her lips curved in a half smile as she said, "I guess chivalry isn't dead."

Smiling in response, Ethan lead the way across the parking lot to his car.

The fact that she'd accepted his help had him deciding to venture out a little further. He watched as she got in, then got in himself. His key in the ignition, he left it dormant for a moment and turned toward her.

"Feel like getting some dinner?" he asked her, then added, "We're off the clock."

A couple of weeks ago, she would have turned him

down without a moment's hesitation. A couple of weeks ago, she *had* turned him down, she recalled.

But that was then, and this was now. And she really didn't feel like going home and being by herself. Not after the captain had just looked at her as if she were a leper.

"Sure, why not?"

He'd learned not to declare victory with her until he was completely certain of it. "You realize I don't mean a drive-through, right?"

Her smile widened. "I realize."

He found he had to force himself to look away. Her mouth could look very enticing when it wasn't moving. "Good. We're on the same page."

Not yet, she thought, a warmth slipping over her. But she had a feeling that they were getting there.

Chapter 11

"You look like you could use a friend," Ethan commented as he sank down into his chair across from Kansas.

It was the end of yet another grueling day of interviews. For the last two days, he and Kansas had been questioning the firefighters who had been the first responders to each and every fire under investigation. The firefighters who, for the most part, she had once worked with side by side.

The interviews, as she'd expected, had not been a walk in the park. At best, the men were resentful and growing steadily more begrudging in their answers. At worst, the responses bordered on being insulting, hostile and verbally abusive. And Kansas, because she was considered one of them—or had been until now—had caught the worst of it.

It took her a moment now to realize that O'Brien was

talking to her. And then another moment to replay in her head what he'd just said.

"I could use a drink," she countered, closing her eyes and leaning back in her chair. Every muscle in her shoulders felt welded to the one next to it, forming knots the size of boulders. "And a friend," she added after a beat.

If he was surprised by the latter admission, he didn't show it. "I might have a solution for both," Ethan proposed. The comment had her opening her eyes again. "We're off duty." Technically, they'd been off for the last twenty minutes. "What do you say to stopping by Malone's?"

"I still have these reports to finish," she protested, indicating the daunting pile of files sitting in front of her on the desk.

Getting up, Ethan leaned over their joint desks and shoved the files over to the far corner.

"We're off duty," he repeated. Then, to make his point, he rounded their desks, got behind her chair and pulled it back so that she was actually sitting in the aisle rather than at her desk.

She looked over her shoulder at him. "What's Malone's?" she wanted to know.

Ethan took her hand, urging her to her feet. She had no choice but to acquiesce. "A haven," Ethan answered simply.

"A haven that serves drinks," Kansas amended in amusement.

"That's what makes it a *good* haven," he explained, a whimsical smile playing along his lips.

He'd become acquainted with Malone's the day he

became a detective. One of the other detectives invited him along for a celebratory drink in honor of his newly bestowed position. Malone's was a local gathering place, more tavern than bar. Detectives of the Aurora police force as well as various members of their family gravitated there for no other reason than to just be among friends who understood what it meant to be a police detective or part of a detective's family.

On any given evening, a healthy representation of the Cavanaughs could be found within the ninety-year-old establishment's four walls. He, Kyle and Greer had discovered that shortly after they'd discovered their new identities. Coming to Malone's helped bolster a sense of camaraderie as well as a sense of belonging.

"Are you up for it?" he prodded.

"If I say no, you won't give me any peace until I surrender." It wasn't a question, it was an assumption. O'Brien had definite pit bull tendencies. She could relate to that. "So I guess I might as well save us both some grief and say yes."

Ethan grinned, looking exceedingly boyish. He didn't come across like someone to be reckoned with—but she knew he was.

"Good conclusion," he told her. He watched her close down her computer. "I can take you," he volunteered. "And then later I can bring you back to your car."

The last interview had gone exceptionally badly. Tom Williams, a man she had once regarded as a friend, had all but called her a traitor. She was feeling very vulnerable right now, and the last thing she wanted was to be in a car with Ethan when she felt like that. Major mistakes were built on missteps taken in vulnerable moments. If she hadn't felt so alone, she wouldn't have fallen for Grant like that.

"Why don't I just follow you and save you the trouble of doubling back," she countered.

"No trouble," he assured her, spreading his hands wide. The look on her face didn't change. "Have it your way," he declared, raising his hands up in mock surrender. "I'll lead the way." She had her purse, and her computer was powered down. He looked at her expectantly. "You ready?"

Kansas caught her bottom lip between her teeth. She supposed that one drink couldn't hurt. But one, she promised herself, was going to be her limit.

"Ready," she echoed.

It was a good plan, and had she stuck to it she would have been home at around the time she'd initially planned. In addition, there would have been plenty of time to get a good night's sleep. But she strayed from the path within the first fifteen minutes of arrival.

Because she'd felt as stiff as a rapier and really wanted to loosen up a little and fit in, she'd downed the first drink placed in front of her instead of sipping it. Ethan's cautionary words to go slow—something that surprised her—were ringing in her ears as she ordered a second drink. Maybe she'd ordered it *because* he'd warned her to go slow and she was feeling combative.

After facing what amounted to blatant hostility all day, being here, amid the laughter of friendly people in a warm atmosphere, was the difference between night and day. Reveling in it, she consequently let her guard down as she absorbed the warm vibrations of the people around her.

An hour into it, as more and more people filled the tavern, she turned to Ethan and whispered, "I can't feel my knees."

He hadn't left her side the entire time and had warned her against the last two of the three drinks she'd had. He looked down now, as if to verify what he was about to say. "They're still there," he assured her.

"I'm serious," she hissed. She didn't like this vague, winking-in-and-out feeling that had come over her. "What does that mean?"

This time he looked at her incredulously. She was serious. Who would have thought? "You've never been drunk before?"

"I'm drunk?" Kansas echoed, stunned. "You sure?" she questioned.

Suppressing his grin, Ethan held up his hand, folding down two fingers. "How many fingers am I holding up right now?"

Kansas squinted, trying her best to focus. Her best was not quite good enough. "How many chances do I get?"

He had his answer. "Okay, Cinderella, time for you to go."

Kansas tried to take a deep breath and began to cough instead. She was feeling very wobbly. "I don't think I can drive."

"No one was going to let you," he assured her. His tone was friendly but firm. He would have wrestled the keys away from her if he'd had to. "C'mon, let's go outside for some fresh air," he urged, slowly guiding her through the crowd.

She found that she had to concentrate very hard to put one foot in front of the other without allowing her knees to buckle. "I'd rather go somewhere more private. With you." Those were the words in her head. How they'd managed to reach her tongue and emerge, she really wasn't sure.

He nodded toward the room behind them teeming with people. "Right now, outside *is* more private. And I'll be coming with you. I'll be the one holding you up," he told her.

"Good," she said, "because I'm not altogether sure I can manage to do that on my own," she confessed. The second the words registered with her brain, she asked, "What did you put in my drink?"

"I didn't put anything into your drink," he told her, shouldering a path for her as he kept his arm around her waist. He caught Kyle looking his way—and smiling. "Could be that having three of them in a row might have had something to do with your knees dissolving on you."

Having made it to the front door, he pushed it open and guided her over the threshold. Once outside, he moved over to the side and leaned her against the wall in an effort to keep her upright and steady. He had the feeling that if he stepped back, she'd slide right down to the ground.

He was close to her. So close that his proximity worked its way into her system, undermining every single resolution she'd ever made.

God, he was handsome, she thought. Jarringly handsome.

"You know, you're just too damn good-looking for my own good."

She would have never said that sober, he thought. Ethan couldn't help the grin that came to his lips. "I'll remember you said that. You probably won't want me to, but I will." He put his arm up to hold her in place as she began to sink a little. "Take a deep breath," he instructed. "It'll help."

She did as he told her, which was when Ethan realized that his supporting arm was way too close to her chest. As she inhaled, her breasts rose, making contact with his forearm.

All sorts of responses went ricocheting through Ethan.

"Maybe not quite so deep," he suggested.

She was very aware of the contact. And equally aware of what it was doing to her.

"Why?" she asked, cocking her head as she looked at him, her blond hair spilling out onto his arm like soft fairy dust. "Am I getting to you, Detective O'Brien?"

She has no idea, does she? he thought. "You need to sleep this off," he informed her.

Her eyes were bright as she asked, "You're taking me home?"

"Yes." And then, to make sure that there wasn't any confusion about this, he added, "Your home."

Kansas sucked in another deep, deep breath. "'Kay," she agreed glibly.

Weaving one arm around her waist again, Ethan began to usher her to his car. While trying to maneuver, Kansas got the heel of her shoe caught in a crack in the asphalt. She kept moving, but the shoe didn't, and she wound up dipping forward. Sensing she was about to fall, Ethan tightened his hold around her waist, dragging her closer against him.

For one second, their faces were less than a measurable inch away from one another.

And the next second, even that was gone.

Giving in to the moment and her weakened state of resistance, Kansas kissed him. Not lightly as she had in the kiss they'd previously shared, but with all the feeling that Ethan had stirred up within her. The alcohol she'd consumed had eroded her defenses and melted the distance she'd been determined to keep between herself and any viable candidate for her affections. Kansas wrapped her arms around his neck as she leaned into his very hard body. Leaned into the kiss that was swallowing them both up.

For a single isolated moment in time, Ethan let himself enjoy what was happening. Enjoy it and savor it because almost from the beginning, he'd wondered what it would be like to *really* kiss this vibrant woman who had for reasons that were far beyond him been thrust into his world.

Now he had his answer.

The kiss packed a wallop that left him breathless… and wanting more. Definitely more.

Which was when the warning flares went up.

This wasn't just something to enjoy and move on. This was something that created intense cravings that would inevitably demand to be filled.

As heat engulfed his body, he knew he had to tear

himself free—or else there very likely would be no turning back. And if he was going to make love with this woman, it was *not* going to be because her ability to reason had been diluted by something that came out of a bottle marked 90 proof.

Expending more self-control and effort than he ever had before, Ethan forcibly removed her arms from around his neck, broke contact and took a less than steady step back.

Bewilderment crossed her face. How could she have been so wrong? It was only because she was still inebriated that she had the nerve to ask, "You don't want me?"

He heard the confusion and hurt in her voice. "Not on my conscience, no."

His keys already in his hand, he pointed them toward his car, pressed the button and released the locks a second before he gingerly turned her toward his vehicle. Ethan opened the door and then very carefully lowered her onto the passenger seat. When she merely sat there, he ushered in her legs, shifting her so that she faced forward.

Hurrying around the back of the car, Ethan got in on the driver's side.

"You don't want me," she repeated in a soft, incredulous voice that was barely above a whisper. "God, I'm such an idiot," she upbraided herself.

Sticking the key in the ignition, he left it there and turned toward her. Maybe it was safer to have her think that, but the hurt in her voice was more than he could live with.

"Look, on a scale of one to ten, wanting you comes in at fifteen," he told her. "But I want you because *you* made the decision to be with me. I don't want you making love with me because the decision was made for you by your alcohol consumption."

She stopped listening after the first part. "Fifteen?" she questioned as he started the engine.

"Yeah," he bit off, frustration eating away at him. There were times he wished he wasn't such a damn Boy Scout—even if his reasoning was dead on. "Fifteen."

Kansas took a deep breath, smiling from ear to ear with deep satisfaction. Sliding down in her seat, she stretched like a cat waking from a long, invigorating nap in the sun.

She had the grace of a feline as well, Ethan thought, trying—and failing—to ignore her.

She slanted a coy glance at him. "I can live with that."

He only wished he could.

But he was going to have to, he lectured himself. He had no other choice.

The most intense part of her buzz had worn off by the time Ethan made the turn that brought them into her garden apartment complex.

Her knees, she noted, were back, as were some of her inhibitions. But there was something new in the mix as well: surprise steeped in respect.

Ethan could have easily taken advantage of her temporary mindless condition. She'd all but thrown herself at him. Had he been anyone else, he could have very easily taken her to the backseat of his car and had sex with her, then crowed about it later to his friends.

That he didn't left her feeling grateful—and feeling something more than just simple attraction.

There was nothing simple about what was going on inside her.

The emotion was vaguely familiar, yet at the same time it was as new as the next sunrise. And she had no idea what to make of it, what to do about it or where to go from here. It was all just one great big question mark for her.

That, and an itch that all but begged to be scratched.

"Where can I park the car?" he asked her as they drove past a trove of daisies, their heads bowed for the night.

"Guest parking is over there." She pointed to a row of spaces, some filled, some not, that ran parallel to the rental office just up ahead.

Ethan took the first empty spot he came to. After pulling up the hand brake, he put the car into Park and turned off the engine. Getting out, he rounded the rear of the vehicle and came around to her side. He opened the door and took her hand to help her out.

She placed her hand in his automatically. The semi-fog around her brain was lifting, enabling her to focus better, physically and mentally. When she did, she had to squelch her initial impulse to just get out on her own and she took his hand, allowing him to help her. She knew she needed it.

There was something comforting about the contact, about having someone there with her, that she couldn't deny. That she *had* been denying herself, she thought, ever since she'd run from her disastrous, abbreviated marriage.

She raised her eyes to his as she got out. "Thanks," she murmured.

His smile was slow, sensual and instantly got under her skin. "Don't mention it."

Instead of getting into the car again as she'd expected, Ethan remained at her side. Nodding toward the array of apartments, he asked, "Which one is yours?"

"Number eighty-three," she told him, pointing toward the second grouping of apartments.

As he began walking in that direction, Ethan took her arm and held on to it lightly. He was probably worried that she was going to sink again, she thought. Kansas took no offense. How could she? Her limbs had been the consistency of wet cotton less than half an hour before. He was being thoughtful.

And getting to her more than she cared to admit.

Reaching her door, he waited until she took out her key and unlocked it.

"You going to be all right?" he asked.

The words "of course" hovered on her lips, straining to be released. It was the right thing to say. What she would have normally said.

But instead, what came out was, "Maybe you should walk me in, just in case."

Her eyes met his and there was a long moment that stretched out between them. A moment with things being said without words.

And then he inclined his head.

"All right."

Chapter 12

The second Kansas stepped across her threshold into her apartment, she felt her adrenaline instantly kicking in. It raced madly to all parts of her at once, sounding a multitude of alarms like so many tiny Paul Reveres riding in the night. Her whole body went on alert—not in waves, but simultaneously.

The feeling intensified when she heard the lock click into place as Ethan closed the door behind him.

This is it, she thought. *Time to fish or cut bait, Beckett.*

She wanted to fish. Desperately.

Damn it, Ethan thought as a warmth undulated through his body, why was he doing this to himself? Why was he testing himself this way? He should have just ushered Kansas in, politely said good-night and then gotten out of there.

For every moment he hesitated, every moment that

he *didn't* do the right thing, it became that much harder for him to walk away.

But as much as he wanted her—and until this very moment he had no idea that he could possibly *ever* want a woman this much—he couldn't allow himself to act on that desire. He had a sister. If someone had taken advantage of her in this kind of a situation, he would have cut the guy's heart out and served it to him for lunch. Just because he was on the other side of this scenario didn't make it any more excusable for him to take advantage of the woman.

"So, if you're okay, I'll be going," he said, fully expecting his feet to engage and begin moving back to the door.

But they didn't move. They seemed to remain glued in place.

Kansas looked up at him. How could she be getting more beautiful, more desirable by the second? It wasn't possible.

And yet...

"But I'm not okay," she said.

The drinks she'd had at Malone's were probably getting to her stomach, Ethan guessed. "What's wrong? You feel sick?" He should have never brought her there, he upbraided himself.

"That wouldn't be the word I'd use," she answered, moving closer to him, dissolving the tiny distance between them until there wasn't space enough for a heartbeat.

As she began to put her arms around his neck, Ethan stopped her, catching her wrists and bringing her arms down again. He saw confused frustration crease Kansas's brow.

"In case you haven't noticed, Detective," she told him, "I'm throwing myself at you."

"Oh, I've noticed, all right." He'd been acutely aware of everything about her from the first moment. "And at any other time, I'd be more than happy to do the catching."

Her eyes narrowed as she struggled to understand. She took his words at face value. "What's wrong with Thursdays?"

He laughed softly, shaking his head. "There's nothing wrong with Thursdays. There's something wrong with taking advantage of a woman." He appealed to her because he really needed help if he was going to do the right thing. He couldn't do it on his own. He was only human. "Kansas, you're not thinking clearly. You're probably not thinking at all," he amended.

Otherwise, he reasoned, she wouldn't be acting this way. The Kansas he'd come to know wouldn't have thrown herself at a man. She would have skewered him if he even attempted anything.

Kansas took a breath, absorbing this. Men like O'Brien weren't supposed to exist. Everything she'd ever learned pointed to the fact that they didn't. And yet, here he was, sounding as noble as if he'd just ridden in on a charger with Lancelot.

No, with Galahad, she silently corrected herself, because Lancelot lusted after the queen, but Galahad was purity personified.

Looking Ethan squarely in the eye, she said, "Give me a calculus problem."

Just how hard had those three drinks hit her? "What?"

"A calculus problem," she repeated. "If I solve it, will that prove to you that my brain is functioning? That it isn't in a fog and neither am I? I admit the drinks hit me hard at first," she said before he could bring it up, "but the effect didn't last, and believe me, that 'I can touch the sky' feeling is long gone." Although, she thought, it had served its purpose. "While it lasted, it let me say what I couldn't say stone-cold sober. That I want to make love with you."

Pausing for a moment, she looked up at him. Every breath she took registered against his body, against his skin.

"Don't you want to make love with me?" she asked as the silence stretched out between them.

Oh, God, did he ever. "You have no idea," he told her, feeling as if the effort to restrain himself was all but strangling him.

The smile that slipped over her lips in almost slow motion drew him in an inch at a time. Trapping him so that he couldn't turn back, couldn't cut loose. Couldn't tear his eyes away.

She rose up on her toes. "Then educate me," she whispered, her lips all but brushing against his as she spoke.

He was just barely holding on to his self-control. The next second, as the promise of her mouth whispered along his, his self-control snapped in two, leaving him without any resources to use in the fight against his reactions.

Instead of doing the noble thing and protesting, or

saying anything about the way she was going to regret this, Ethan pressed his lips against hers and kissed her. *Really* kissed her.

Kissed her so deeply and with such feeling that he was instantly lost.

All he could think of was having her. Having her in the most complete, satisfying sense of the word and steeping himself in her until he wouldn't be able to tell where he ended and she began.

The kiss went deeper.

Yes!

The single, triumphant word echoed over and over again in Kansas's brain even as she felt her body melting in the flames that his mouth had created within her. This, this was the connection she'd missed, the part of herself she had struggled to pretend didn't exist, the part of her that hadn't been allowed to see the light of day. It broke free and filled every single space within her.

Everything within Kansas hummed with a happiness she hadn't known was achievable.

But as that feeling of happiness, of absolute joy, progressed, all but consuming her, Kansas swiftly came to realize that this really *wasn't* the feeling she'd hoped for.

This was more.

So very much more.

Before this, any kind of happiness she'd experienced with Grant amounted to little more than a thimbleful in comparison. This "thing" she was feeling was like an ocean. An all-encompassing, huge ocean. And she was swimming madly through it as the current kept sweeping her away, taking absolutely all control out of her hands.

She was at its mercy.

And she loved it!

She felt Ethan's breath on her neck, making her skin sizzle.

Making her want more.

And all the while the very core of her kept quickening in anticipation of what was to be. What she *hoped* was to be.

She struggled to hold herself at bay, struggled to savor this for as long as she could. For as long as it went on. Because something told her that these conditions would never be met again. This was a one-of-a-kind, one-time-only thing. Like the sighting of a comet.

And then, just like that, Ethan was no longer kissing her. His lips were no longer grazing the side of her neck, rendering her all but mindless. Ethan had drawn back, cupping her face in his hands as he silently declared a time-out.

Confused, with shafts of disappointment weaving through her, she looked at Ethan quizzically. "What?" she asked breathlessly. Had she done something wrong? Turned him off somehow?

"Last chance," he offered.

She shook her head, not understanding. "Last chance for what?"

"For you to back out." He held his breath, waiting for her answer. Praying she'd say what he wanted her to say.

It came in the form of a soft laugh. The sound all but ricocheted around her small living room. "Not on your life."

He couldn't begin to describe the urge he felt just then.

"Okay, just remember, I gave you a chance. You asked for this," he told her, his voice gruff.

"I know," she managed to say before her lips became otherwise engaged.

The next moment, his mouth was back on hers, kissing her senseless as his fingers got busy removing the layers of her clothing that were between them.

He began with her jacket, sliding it down her arms. The garment was followed by her cherry-red tank top and her white skirt. With each piece of clothing he removed from her, the heat encircling her intensified. And his breathing grew shorter, she noted, as a haze began to descend over her brain.

Refusing to be passive, even if she was being reduced to a mass of fiery yearning, Kansas started to remove his clothes, as well. As she worked buttons free, took down zippers, she felt as if her fingers were clumsier at this process than his were. But then, it wasn't as if she was altogether clear-headed right now. Or experienced at doing this kind of thing.

They achieved their goal at the same time.

Clothes commingling in a pile on the floor, their bodies primed and aching, he swept her into his arms as if she weighed no more than one of the reports that she'd left abandoned on the desk at the precinct.

"Where's your bedroom?" he asked in between pleasuring her mouth with bone-melting kisses.

"At the end of the hall," she answered with effort.

Because her lips had been separated from his during this short verbal exchange, Kansas framed his face with her hands, held his head in place as she raised up her mouth to cover his.

He almost dropped her. But that was because she was so effectively weakening his limbs.

Bringing her into her bedroom, he placed her on the bed, joining her without breaking rhythm. Ethan began kissing her with even more passion.

He made her forget absolutely everything, especially the glaring looks and thinly veiled derogatory remarks she'd received from this afternoon's collection of firefighters.

Nothing else mattered. Not her past, not the lonely isolation of her childhood, nor the emptiness of her short-lived marriage to a narcissist. All that mattered was sustaining this incredible feeling that was crescendoing through her.

Because of him.

In response to him, her own kisses became more passionate, more intense. Each place that Ethan touched, she mirrored the gesture, sweeping soft, questing fingertips over his tantalizingly hard body. Glorying in the way he responded to her, the way he moved. The sound of his moan drove her crazy.

She saw that she could arouse him even more with just a touch—just the way he could her. The thought of exercising that kind of control over him was mindblowing. She felt like an equal, not just like a receptive vessel. That was the moment that this completely transcended anything she'd ever experienced before.

Thinking that she was at the highest level she could reach short of the final one, she discovered in the next moment that she was wrong.

She all but lost the ability to snatch a thought out of the air when Ethan began to trace a hot, moist path to her very core, first with his hands and then, very swiftly, with his lips.

Suppressing a surprised gasp, Kansas was barely able to breathe as she rode the crest of the all-consuming climax Ethan had just produced within her.

She arched and bucked, desperate to absorb the sensation and keep it alive for even so much as a heartbeat longer. But when it left, leaving her convinced that she'd experienced the best that there was, Ethan's clever mouth brought another wave to fruition.

And then another. Until she cried out something unintelligible. Whether she was asking for mercy or for more, neither one of them knew.

But suddenly, there he was, over her, pressing her deep into her bed as he slid his hard body along hers, activating yet another host of sensations until she was completely convinced that she had somehow just vibrated into an alternative universe where pleasure was king and nothing else mattered. Ever.

Breathing hard now, trying vainly to draw in enough air to sustain herself, Kansas parted her legs and opened for him.

And cried out his name as she felt him enter.

The music suddenly materialized in her head, coming from nowhere.

The dance began slowly, building quickly.

A waltz developed into a samba, then the tempo went faster and faster until the final moment with its satisfying dispersion of mind-numbing sensations echoed within them both.

It was like New Year's Eve when the clock struck

midnight and confetti came raining down, accompanied by cries of good wishes and happiness.

Gradually, she became aware of clinging to Ethan, became aware that her arms were still wrapped tightly around his back and that her body was still arching into his even though he was on top.

She became aware as well that his breathing was just as short as hers.

And aware, most of all, that she didn't want this very special moment to end. Didn't want to exchange what she was feeling for reality, where guilt and vulnerability and, most of all, disappointment resided, ready to rain on her parade.

But the moment linked itself to another and then another until finally, the descent came, slowly rather than rapidly, but it came. And it brought her down with it.

She felt Ethan shift his weight off her and realized that he'd been propping himself on his elbows the entire time they'd made love to spare her being oppressed by his weight.

That was when she recalled having trouble breathing when Grant made love with her. Grant always allowed his full weight to press against her, against her lungs, after he'd satisfied himself. Once he'd actually fallen asleep and had gotten angry at her for waking him up. He claimed not to remember the incident when he was awake the next day. And because she loved him, because she wanted him to love her, she'd believed him.

Or said she had.

They weren't the same kind of men at all, he and Ethan, she realized. Maybe there really were two different kinds of men. The good ones and the bad ones.

No, don't do that. Don't go there, she warned herself sternly. *You're just going to start hoping and setting yourself up for a fall. You fell once, crashing and burning, remember? That should be enough for anyone, including you.*

She felt Ethan's smile before she saw it.

Turning her head to look at him, Kansas saw that she was right. He was smiling. Grinning, really. Was he laughing at her, enjoying some private joke at her expense?

She could feel herself withdrawing. "What?" she demanded.

His smile seem to soften, or maybe that was wishful thinking on her part, a way for her to save face in her own eyes.

"You, Kansas," he told her, "are just full of surprises."

She could feel her defenses going up, and just like that, she was ready for a fight. "Meaning?"

"Meaning I don't think I've ever actually been blown away before." He stopped as if he was thinking, trying to remember. But there was no need to think, really. Because he already knew. "No, never blown away. Until now." He combed his fingers through her hair, looking into her eyes. Despite everything, all those defenses she thought she'd just hastily thrown up, she felt herself melting. "You really can make the earth move, can't you?"

What she wanted to do was lean into his touch. But she knew the danger in that. Instead, she rebuffed his words. "You don't have to flatter me, O'Brien. We already made love," she pointed out.

"I don't *have* to do anything at all," he told her. "I tend not to, as a matter of fact. Kyle's the family rebel, but that doesn't mean that Greer and I just fall docilely into step, doing whatever we're told, following all the rules just because they're rules." His smile deepened as he looked at her, thoughts cropping up in his head that he was not willing to share yet—if ever. "You, Beckett, are a force to be reckoned with. But I already kind of figured you would be."

He was doing it again, she thought, he was breaching her soul. But somehow the sense of alarm that should have accompanied that realization was missing. "Oh, you did, did you?"

He traced a light, circular pattern along the back of her neck and managed to send shivers down her spine. "Yup."

"Is that because you think you're such a red-hot lover?" she asked, doing her best to sound sarcastic. But her heart just wasn't in it. Her heart was elsewhere. Hoping…

"No," he answered seriously, his eyes holding hers. "It's because I'm a pretty good judge of people."

"And does this ability to correctly judge people help you guess what's going to come next?"

"Sometimes," he allowed.

"Okay," she challenged, "what's going to come next now?"

She could feel his smile getting under her skin as it spread over his lips. "Surprise me," he whispered.

Funny how a whisper could send such shock waves through her system, she thought. "That," she informed him as a sexy smile curved her lips, "is a downright dangerous challenge."

"Oh, God, I certainly hope so."

Then, before she could comment on his response, Ethan pulled her to him, his mouth covering hers. Silencing her the best way he knew how.

It was the best way she knew how...as well.

Chapter 13

There had to be something. *Something,* Kansas insisted silently as she sat at the desk that, after more than a month of being here, she'd begun to regard as her own. She felt as if she'd been reexamining files forever.

It was late and everyone on the task force had gone home long ago. She'd even sent away Ethan, who had remained after the others—including the two extra detectives the chief had given them—had left, trying to do what he could to make the tedious process go faster. But another case he'd been working on had required his attention as well, and consequently he'd gotten next to no sleep in over two days.

He was beginning to resemble death walking, she'd told him, insisting that he go home. Ethan had finally given in about ninety minutes ago, leaving the precinct after making her promise that she'd only remain another few minutes.

A "few minutes" had knitted themselves into an hour, and then more. She was still here.

But there was nothing waiting for her at home, and she felt far too wired to actually get any sleep, so she reasoned that she might as well stay and work. At least if she was working, she wouldn't be tempted to call Ethan, suggesting a really late dinner. That was, at best, thinly veiled code for what she knew would happen.

It wasn't the thought of dinner that aroused her. It was the thought of sitting opposite Ethan in a setting where she didn't have to remain the consummate professional. Where, mentally, she would count off the minutes before he would reach for her and they would make love again.

After that first night together, there had been several more evenings that had ended with their clothes being left in a heap on the floor and their bodies gloriously entwined.

And with each time that they made love, she found that instead of finally becoming sated, she just wanted more.

Always more.

At least if she was here, embroiled in what was beginning to look like a futile hunt, she couldn't do anything about getting together with Ethan. Superman or not, the man did need his sleep.

As for her, Kansas thought, she needed to be vindicated, to prove to herself that she hadn't all but destroyed her hard-won career with the fire department on a baseless hunch.

She was right, Kansas silently insisted. She could feel it in her bones. She just needed to find something, that one elusive, tiny trace of something or other that would finally lead her to the person who was responsible for setting the fires.

But so far, it didn't look as if she was going to get anywhere. All the firefighters who had responded to the various alarms seemed to be above reproach. There were no citations, no disciplinary actions of any kind in their personal files.

The only unusual notation that she'd come across was the one in Nathan Bonner's folder. He was the firefighter who had come on the job after she was no longer an active member of the team. The captain had inserted a handwritten note that said the man was almost too eager, too ready to give 110 percent each and every time. The captain was afraid he was going to burn himself out before his time. Otherwise, he was excellent.

She sighed, leaning back in her chair, staring at the screen and the database that she'd been using. Her methodical review had been eliminating suspects one by one until, instead of at least a few left standing, there was no one. From all indications, this was a sterling group of men.

They probably didn't even cheat on their taxes, she thought, disgruntled. Too bad. When all else failed, the authorities caught racketeers and career criminals by scrutinizing their taxes. Income tax evasion was the way the FBI had brought down the infamous Al Capone. Her mouth curved at the irony in that. When in doubt, check out their tax forms.

She sat up, straight as an arrow, as the thought registered.

Why not?

She'd tried every other avenue. Maybe she *could* find something in their income tax forms that she could use. At this point, Kansas was desperate enough to try anything.

Pressing her lips together, she stared at the screen, thinking. Trying her best to remember. When she was in college, before she'd thought that the world began and ended with Grant, she'd gone out with a Joe Balanchine. Joe had an ingrained knack for making computers do whatever he needed them to do. Trying to impress her, he'd taught her a few things, like how easy it was to hack into files that were supposedly beyond hacking.

"Here's hoping I can remember what you taught me, Joe," she murmured.

It took her several unsuccessful tries before she finally managed to scale the electronic cyberspace walls and hack into the system. When it finally opened up, allowing her to access federal and state income tax data, Kansas felt almost giddy with triumph.

She realized that she should have taken that as a sign that maybe it was time for her to go home and get some sleep, approaching this from a fresh perspective tomorrow morning. But again, she was far too wired to even contemplate going to bed. If she went home now, she'd spend the night staring at the ceiling.

Or calling Ethan.

The latter thought had her chewing on her lower lip. When had that become the norm for her? When had sharing moments large and small with Ethan become something she looked forward to? This was dangerous ground she was traversing, and she knew it.

But right now, she was far too happy with this latest success to care.

With the firefighters' Social Security numbers at her fingertips, she arranged them in ascending numerical order. That done, she quickly went from one file to another, using the seven-year window that had once been the standard number of years an audit could go back and hold the taxpayer culpable for any errors, unintentional or not.

Employing a general overview, she went from one firefighter's file to another.

And one by one, she struck out.

She couldn't find a single suspicious notation, a single red flag that an auditor had questioned. There weren't even any random audits.

The euphoria she'd previously experienced faded as dejection took hold. Her eyes swept over the tax forms of the second-to-last firefighter, the numbers hardly penetrating.

This had been her last hope. Her last...

"Hello," she murmured to herself, sitting up. "What's this?"

Blinking a few times to make sure she wasn't seeing something that wasn't there—or rather, not seeing something that was, she focused on Nathan Bonner's file.

"So you *do* have a skeleton in your closet," she said to the screen, addressing it as if she were talking to Bonner. The likeable firefighter's returns went back only three years. The same amount of time he'd been with the Aurora fire department.

According to the form he'd filled out when he joined

the department, he had transferred from a firehouse in Providence, Rhode Island. She recalled seeing copies of glowing letters of recommendation in his file. But if that were the case, he would have had to have worked at the firehouse there. And earned a living. Which necessitated filing a tax form.

And he hadn't.

Kansas went through the records a second time. And then a third. There were no returns filed from that period.

Maybe it wasn't Rhode Island. Maybe it was somewhere else. She did a search, using just his name and inputting it into each state, one by one. A Nathan Bonner, with his Social Security number, finally turned up in New York City. With a death certificate.

She sat back, staring at the information. Nathan Bonner died in a car accident in January of 2001. He was seventy-five years old at the time. The Social Security number and month and date of birth all matched the ones that Bonner had claimed were his.

Wow.

"Nathan Bonner" was a fraud, she thought, her heart launching into double time. This was it, this was what she was looking for. Bonner was their firebug. He had to be. She didn't know why he'd gone through this elaborate charade or what else he was up to, but he was their man. She was sure of it.

Excited, she grabbed the phone receiver and was inputting Ethan's cell phone number. He had to hear this.

The phone on the other end rang four times and then Kansas heard it being picked up. She was almost breath-

less as she started talking. "Ethan, it's Kansas. Listen,
I think that—"

"You've reached Ethan O'Brien's cell phone. I can't
talk right now, but if you leave your—"

"Damn it!" Impatience ate away at Kansas. Was he
sound asleep? She heard the tone ring in her ear. "Ethan,
it's Kansas. If you get this message, call me. I think I
found our man." Why hadn't she gotten the number of
his landline? At least when she left a message, if he was
anywhere in the area, she stood a good chance of waking him up by talking loudly.

Biting off an oath, she hung up.

She contemplated her next move. Everyone liked
Bonner. He was friendly and outgoing and appeared
to take an interest in everyone around him. He was always willing to listen, always willing to go catch a beer
at the end of the day—or lend money to tide a brother
firefighter over to the next paycheck.

If she suggested that he was behind the fires, the
rest of the house would demand her head on a platter.
There was no way anyone was going to believe her
without proof.

Okay, if it's proof they wanted, proof they were going
to get. She hit the print button, printing everything she'd
just read. She'd need it to back her up.

Once that was done and she had collected the pages
from the mouth of the printer, she tried calling Ethan
again. With the same results. She hung up just before
his voice mail picked up.

Frustrated, she deposited the papers she'd just printed
into a folder. She wanted Ethan to see this. The sooner
the better. He was, as he'd claimed, her partner, and he

needed to see proof that she was right. That he hadn't just backed her up only to have her take a dive off a cliff.

Humming, she got her things together and left the squad room.

She barely remembered the trip to Ethan's apartment. She'd been there only twice before. Once to return his cell phone that first night—and once when he'd brought her to his place after taking her out for dinner and a movie.

Her mouth curved. Just like two normal people. That night they'd made love until they'd fallen asleep, exhausted, in each other's arms.

Excitement raced through her veins, and it was hard to say what was more responsible for her getting to that state—the fact that she was convinced that she'd found their firebug or that she was going to Ethan's apartment to see him.

By her calculation, Ethan had gotten about two hours' sleep if he'd gone right home and straight to bed. A person could go far on two hours if he had to, she reasoned. God knew she had. More than once.

And she *knew* Ethan wouldn't want her to wait until morning with this.

Pulling up directly in front of his apartment, taking a slot that she knew had to belong to someone else who, conveniently, was gone at the moment, she jumped out of her car. She didn't even bother locking the doors. She'd move the car later, but right now she had to see him.

Kansas headed straight for his door. It took everything she had to keep from pounding on it. Instead, she just knocked on his door as if this were nothing more than just a social visit instead of one that ultimately was a matter of life and death. They needed to catch Bonner before he set off another device.

When no one answered her knock, she knocked again, harder this time. Hard enough to hurt her knuckles.

"C'mon, c'mon. Wake up, Ethan," she called, raising her voice and hoping that it carried through the door. Just as she was about to try to call him on her cell again, thinking that the combination of pounding and ringing phone would finally wake him, the door to his apartment opened.

"Well, it's about time that yo—"

The rest of the sentence froze on her tongue. She wasn't looking at Ethan. She was looking at a woman. A gorgeous blonde with hypnotic eyes.

She felt as if someone had punched her in the stomach. Just the way she'd felt when she'd walked in on Grant and the hotel receptionist.

Stunned speechless, Kansas took a step back. "I'm sorry, I must have made—"

That was when she saw Ethan approaching from the rear of the apartment. Where the bedroom was located. He was barefoot and wearing the bottom half of a pair of navy blue pajamas. The ones he kept at the foot of his bed in case he had to throw something on to answer the door at night, he'd told her.

"—a mistake," she concluded. "I've made a terrible mistake. I'm sorry to have bothered you," she told the woman coldly. Kansas turned on her heel and hurried away, leaving the woman in the doorway looking after her, confused.

She heard Ethan call her name, but she refused to stop, refused to turn around. She was too angry. At him. At herself.

And too full of pain.

Damn it, it had happened again. She'd *let* it happen again. How could she have been naive enough, stupid enough to think that Ethan was different? That he could actually be someone who was faithful? It was inherently against a man's religion to be faithful, and she should have her head examined for thinking it was remotely possible.

Getting into the car, she didn't even bother securing her seat belt. She just started the car and put it into Drive.

Kansas felt her eyes stinging and she blinked several times, trying to push back her tears, fiercely telling herself that she wasn't going to cry. He wasn't worth tears.

No strings, remember? You promised yourself no strings. Strings just trip you up, she told herself. *What the hell happened?*

"Kansas, stop!" Ethan called after her.

She deliberately shut his voice out. All she wanted to do was get away.

Now.

She should have never come here—no, she amended, she *should* have. Otherwise, how would she have ever found out that he was just like all the rest? Deceitful and a cheat. Better now than later when she—

Kansas swallowed a scream. Keen reflexes had her swerving to the left at the last minute to avoid hitting him. Ethan had raced after her and had managed, via some shortcut he must have taken, to get right in front of her. He had his hand on her hood in an instant, using himself as a human roadblock.

Her heart pounded so wildly it was hurting her chest. Had she gone an instant quicker, been driving an instant faster, she wouldn't have been able to swerve away in time.

Angry as she was at him, she didn't want to think about that.

Had it not been so late, she would have leaned on her horn. Instead, she rolled down her window and shouted, "Get out of the way."

"Not until you tell me what's wrong with you," he ground out between teeth that were clenched together to keep from giving her a piece of his mind.

"Nothing anymore," she declared, lifting her chin in what he'd come to know as sheer defiance. "Now get the hell out of the way or I'll run you over. I swear I will," she threatened.

A movement in her rearview mirror caught her eye. The woman who'd opened the door was hurrying toward them. Great, that was all she needed. To see the two of them together.

"Your girlfriend's coming," she informed him, icicles clinging to every syllable. "Go and talk to her."

"What the hell are you talking about?" Ethan demanded. "What girlfriend?"

Did he think that if he denied any involvement, she'd fall into his arms like a newly returned puppy? "The one who opened the door."

He looked at her as if he was trying to decide if she'd

lost her mind—or he had. Glancing behind the car for confirmation, he told her, "That's Greer."

Was that supposed to make her feel as if they were all friends? "I don't care what her name is. Just go to her and get out of my way." She gripped the steering wheel as if she intended to go, one way or another.

The woman he'd just referred to as Greer peered into the passenger-side window. In contrast to Ethan, she looked calm and serene. And she had the audacity to smile at her.

The next moment, she was extending her hand to her through the opened window. "Hi, we haven't met yet. I'm Greer. Ethan's sister."

Had her whole body not been rigid with tension, her jaw would have dropped in her lap. "His what?"

"Sister," Ethan repeated for her benefit. "I told you I had one."

A sense of embarrassment was beginning to shimmer just on the perimeter of her consciousness. She valiantly held it at bay, but the feeling of having acted like a fool was blowing holes in her shield.

"You said you were triplets," Kansas protested. "She's a blonde. She doesn't look like you—"

"And I thank God every day for that," Greer interjected with a very wide grin. A grin that made her resemble Ethan, Kansas thought, chagrined. "I'm going to go, Ethan. Thanks for the pep talk, I really appreciate it." She looked from the woman behind the wheel to her barefoot brother. "I didn't mean to wake you," she apologized. About to walk away, she stopped and added, "By the way, you're right," she told her brother, amusement in her eyes. "She really is something." And then she nodded at her. "Hope to see you again, Kansas."

For a second, Kansas was silent, watching the other woman walk to her car. "She knows my name?" she asked Ethan.

"Yeah." His expression gave nothing away.

There was only one reason for that as far as Kansas knew. "You told her about me."

Ethan shrugged carelessly. "Your name might have come up." And then a smattering of anger returned. "What the hell is all this about?" he wanted to know.

As embarrassing and revealing as it was, Kansas told him the truth. She owed him that much for having acted the way she had. But it wasn't easy. Baring her soul never was.

"For a minute, I thought I was reliving a scene from my past," she confessed.

His eyes narrowed. "Involving your husband, the idiot?"

Kansas pressed her lips together before nodding. "Yes."

"I'm not him, Kansas." He wondered if he would ever get that through to her. And what it would do to their relationship if he couldn't.

It wasn't in her nature to say she was sorry. For the first time, she caught herself wishing that it was. But the words wouldn't come no matter how much she willed them to. Saying "I know" was the best she could do.

"Good. Now go park your car and come back inside." He looked down at the pajama bottoms. "I'm going to go in before someone calls the police to complain about a half-naked man running around in the parking lot, playing dodgeball with a car."

The moon was out and rays of moonlight seemed to highlight the definition of his muscles. The term "magnificent beast" came to mind. "I don't think they'd be complaining if they actually saw you," she told him.

His eyes met hers. Again, she couldn't tell what he was thinking—or feeling. "It's going to take more than a few words of flattery to make up for this."

"Maybe when you hear why I came in the first place, you'll find it in your heart to forgive me." Mentally, she crossed her fingers.

"We'll see," he told her, making no promises one way or another.

Turning away, Ethan hiked up the pajama bottoms that were resting precariously on his hip bone, threatening to slip, and started back to his apartment.

Kansas sat in her car, watching him walk away, appreciating the view and trying not to let her imagination carry her away.

It was a couple of minutes before Kansas started up her car engine again. Her other engine was already revving.

Chapter 14

"Do you really think that little of me?" Ethan demanded, his voice controlled, the second she walked in. "So little that you just assume that if I'm with another woman, it has to be something sexual? That I have to be cheating on you?"

"No, I don't think that little of you," she answered, raising her voice to get him to stop talking for a moment and listen. "I think that little of *me*." He looked at her, confused, so she elaborated. "I'm not exactly the greatest judge of character when it comes to the men in my personal life. I try not to have a personal life because…because…" The words stuck in her throat and her voice trailed off.

"Because you're afraid of making a mistake?" he guessed.

She shrugged dismissively, wanting to be done with

this line of discussion, and looked away. "Something like that."

Ethan threaded his fingers through her hair, framing her face with his palms and gently forcing her to look at him. When she did, he brought his mouth down to hers and kissed her with bone-melting intensity.

After a very long moment, he drew back and asked her, "Does that feel like a mistake?"

Kansas's adrenaline had already launched into double time, threatening to go into triple. Everything else was put on hold, or temporarily forgotten.

The only thing that mattered was experiencing heaven one more time.

At least one more time, she silently pleaded with whoever might be listening. Because tomorrow would come and it might not be kind. But she had today, she had right now, and she desperately wanted to make the most of it.

"Ask me again later," she breathed. "I'm too busy now."

And with that, she recaptured his lips with her own and slipped off for another dip in paradise's sun-kissed waters.

He lost no time in joining her.

It wasn't until dawn the next morning, as Kansas woke up by degrees in his arms and slowly started removing the cobwebs from her brain, that she began thinking clearly again.

"What was it that you came here to tell me?" Ethan wanted to know, bringing everything back into focus for her.

Kansas raised herself up on her elbow to look at this man who, however unintentionally, kept rocking her world. From his expression, he'd been watching her sleep again. The fact that he hadn't woken her up with this question, that he'd waited until she'd opened her eyes on her own, just reinforced what she already knew to be true—the man was completely devoid of any curiosity.

Unlike her.

She needed to know everything. Public things, private things, it made absolutely no difference. She had always had this incredibly insatiable desire to know everything.

As for him, if the information wouldn't help him crack a case, he could wait it out—or even have it just fade away. It appeared to be all one and the same to Ethan.

"It's about Nathan Bonner—" She saw that there was no immediate recognition evident in his expression when she said the name. "The firefighter who was giving that old man from the nursing home CPR. The old man who died," she added.

It was the last piece that had the light dawning in his eyes.

"Oh, him, right."

Playing with a strand of her hair, he was completely amazed that he could be so fiercely drawn to a woman. In the past, his usual M.O. was to make love with someone a couple of times—three, tops—and then move on, deliberately shunning any strings. But he didn't want to move on this time. He wanted to dig in for the long haul.

That had never happened to him before.

"What about him?" Ethan asked, whispering the question into her hair.

His breath warmed her scalp and sent ripples throughout her being. If this wasn't so important, she would have just given in to the feeling and made love with him. It was a hell of a good way to start the day.

But this had to be said. Ethan needed to know what she had discovered. "He doesn't exist."

Ethan looked at her, somewhat confused. "Come again?"

"Nathan Bonner doesn't exist," Kansas told him, enunciating each word slowly—then quickly explaining how she'd come to her conclusion. "He didn't even exist seven years ago. There're no federal income tax forms filed except for the last three years. If you go back four, there's nothing. No driver's license, no tax forms, no credit cards. Nothing," she emphasized.

Ethan stopped curling her hair around his finger and straightened, as if put on some kind of alert. Kansas had managed to get his undivided attention. "Hold it. Just how did you get hold of his tax records?"

A protective feeling nudged forward within her. Kansas shook her head, even though she knew her response frustrated him. She couldn't tell him how she'd gotten the information.

"If I don't tell you, the chief can't blame you," she told him. "Or kill you." Then, because he was staring at her intently, obviously not pleased with her answer, she sighed. It wasn't that she didn't trust him. She didn't want him blamed. But he had to know that her information was on the level. "I hacked into his files. His and a few others'," she confessed.

For a second, she looked away and heard him ask in a quiet voice, "How many are a few?"

She thought of hedging, then decided against it. "All of them," she said quietly.

He'd never been this close to speechless before. "Kansas—"

"I was looking for something we could use," she explained, afraid he was going to launch into a lecture. "I didn't expect to find that Bonner was just an alias this guy was using." The moment he disappeared off the grid, she started hunting through old tax returns, trying to match the Social Security number. Her dogged efforts brought success. "He got his identity off a dead man."

That kind of thing happened in the movies, not real life. Ethan cast about for a reasonable explanation. "Maybe he's in the witness protection program."

The suggestion took some of the wind out of her sails.

"I suppose that could be one possibility." She rolled the idea over in her mind. Her gut told her it was wrong, but she knew she was going to need more than her gut to nail this down. "Do you know anyone in the marshal's office?" she asked him. "Someone who could check this out for us?"

Ethan grinned in response. She was obviously forgetting who she was talking to. "I'm a Cavanaugh by proxy. If I can't find out, someone within the family unit can."

There were definite advantages to having a large family beyond the very obvious, she thought with a mild touch of envy. "You're going to need a search warrant," she added.

"*We* are going to need a search warrant," he corrected.

"No," she contradicted him in a deceptively mild voice that made him decidedly uneasy. "Technically I can search his place, warrant or no warrant. Some people might see that as breaking and entering, but if I find anything incriminating, it *can* be used against him."

Ethan knew that look by now. It was the one that all but screamed "reckless." He had a feeling that it was probably useless, but he had to say this anyway. "Don't do anything stupid, Kansas."

The expression she gave him was innocence personified. "I never do anything stupid."

It took all he had not to laugh. "I wouldn't put that up for a vote if I were you." Throwing back the covers, he got up and then held his hand out to her. "C'mon, let's shower."

Taking it, she swung her legs out to the side and rose. "Together?"

Ethan paused for a second just to drink in the sight. Damn, he wanted her more each time he was with her. "It'll save time," he promised.

But it didn't.

Within an hour, they were at the firehouse. Together they confronted the captain with their request.

The veneer on the spirit of cooperation had worn thin and there was definite hostility in Captain Lawrence's eyes as he regarded them. The brunt of it was directed at Kansas.

"Bonner? You've already questioned everyone here once. Why do you want to talk to him again?" Lawrence demanded impatiently. The question was underscored with a glare. Before either could answer, the captain said, "He's one of the best firefighters I've ever had the privilege of working with. I don't want you harassing him."

Ethan took the lead, trying once again to divert the captain's anger onto him instead of Kansas. After all, she had to come back here and work with the man as well as the other firefighters. A situation, he thought, that was looking more and more bleak as time wore on.

"We just want to ask him a few more questions, Captain. Like why there's no record of him before he came to the firehouse. And why he has the same Social Security number as a guy who died in 2001."

If this new information stunned him, the captain gave no such indication. He merely shrugged it off. "That's gotta be a mistake of some sort," he replied firmly. "You know what record keeping is like with the government."

"Maybe," Ethan allowed. "But that's why we want to talk to Bonner, to clear up any misunderstanding."

"Well, you're out of luck." Lawrence began to walk to his small, cluttered office. "I insisted he take the day off. He'd been on duty for close to three weeks straight. The man's like a machine. We've been shorthanded this last month, and he's been filling in for one guy after another."

"Isn't that unusual?" Ethan challenged. "To have a firefighter on duty for that long?"

"That's just the kind of guy he is," the captain pointed out proudly. "I wish I had a firehouse full of Bonners."

"No, you don't," Kansas said under her breath as Ethan asked the man for Bonner's home address.

The look that the older man slanted toward her told Kansas that her voice hadn't been as quiet as she'd initially thought.

Less than twenty minutes later they were walking up to Bonner's door. The man without an identity lived in a residential area located not too far from the firehouse where he worked. The ride to work probably took him a matter of minutes.

Ethan rang the doorbell. It took several attempts to get Bonner to answer his front door.

When the firefighter saw who was on his doorstep, the warm, friendly smile on his lips only grew more so. Kansas would have wavered in her convictions had she not read the files herself. The man looked like the personification of geniality.

"Sorry," he apologized. "I was just catching up on some Z's. I like to do that on my day off. It recharges my batteries," he explained. "Come on in." Opening the door all the way to admit them, he stepped to the side. "Sorry about the place being such a mess, but I've been kind of busy, doing double shifts at the firehouse. We're short a couple of guys, and since I really don't have anything special on my agenda, I volunteered to pick up the slack. The pay's good," he confided, "but it leaves my house looking like a tornado hit it."

"I've seen worse," Kansas told him as she looked around.

Actually, she thought, she'd lived in worse. One of the foster mothers who had taken her in, Mrs. Novak, had an obsessive-compulsive disorder that wouldn't allow her to throw anything out. Eventually, social services had come to remove her from the home because of the health hazards that living there presented.

But for all her quirkiness, Mrs. Novak had been kinder to her than most of the other foster mothers she had lived with. Those women had taken her in strictly because she represented monthly checks from social services. Mrs. Novak was lonely and wanted someone to talk to.

"What can I do for you?" the firefighter asked cheerfully.

"You can tell us why you're using a dead man's Social Security number," Kansas demanded, beating Ethan to the punch. She slanted a quick glance in his direction and saw him shaking his head. At any other time, she might have thought that her partner looked displeased because she had stolen his thunder. But not in this case. Ethan wasn't like that. He wasn't, she had to admit, like any of the other men she'd worked with. Maybe he thought she should have worded her statement more carefully.

Too late now.

"Oh." The firefighter cleared his throat, looking just a tad uncomfortable. "That."

The response surprised Kansas. Her eyes widened as she exchanged a glance with Ethan. Was Bonner, or whatever his name was, actually admitting to his deception? It couldn't be this easy.

"Do you care to explain?" Ethan prodded, giving him a chance to state his side.

The firefighter took a breath before starting. "All my

life I wanted to be a fireman. I was afraid if they saw my record, they wouldn't let me join."

"Record?" Ethan asked. Just what kind of a record was the man talking about? Was he a wanted criminal?

"Oh, nothing serious," the firefighter quickly reassured them. "I just got into trouble a couple of times as a teenager." In his next breath, he dismissed the infractions. "Typical kid pranks. One of my friends took his uncle's car for a joyride. I went along with a couple of other guys. But he didn't tell his uncle he was taking it, so his uncle reported the car stolen and, you guessed it, we were all picked up.

"I tried to explain that I hadn't known that Alvin was driving without his uncle's blessings, and the policeman I was talking to thought I was giving him attitude." He shrugged. "He tried to use his nightstick, and I wouldn't let him hit me with it. I was defending myself, but the judge in juvenile court called it assaulting an officer of the law." And then he raised his hand as if he were taking a solemn oath. "But that's the sum total of my record, I swear on my mother's eyes."

Ethan supposed that could be true, but then, since it could all be explained away, why had he gone through this elaborate charade?

"That doesn't exactly make you sound like a hardened criminal," Ethan pointed out.

Bonner looked chagrined. "I know, I know, but I was afraid to risk it. I didn't want to throw away the dream."

"Of rushing into burning buildings," Ethan concluded incredulously. Most people he knew didn't dream about taking risks like that.

"Of saving lives," the other man countered, his voice and demeanor solemn.

That seemed to do it for Ethan. He rose to his feet and shook the firefighter's hand. "Sorry to have bothered you, Mr. Bonner."

Ethan glanced at Kansas. She had no choice but to rise to her feet as well, no matter what her gut was currently screaming.

A bright smile flashed across the firefighter's lips. "No bother at all," Nathan assured him. He walked them to the front door. "I understand. It's your job to check these things out. In your place, I would have done the same thing. That's why this city gets such high marks for safety year after year," he said, opening the door for them.

The minute they were alone, as they walked to his car, Ethan said to Kansas, "It all sounds plausible." Before she had a chance to comment, his cell phone began ringing. Taking it out of his pocket, he flipped it open. "O'Brien. Oh, hi, Janelle. How's that search warrant coming?" He frowned. "It's not? Why?" He said the word just as Kansas fired it at him in frustrated bewilderment. His response was to turn away from her so he wouldn't be distracted. "Uh-huh. I see. Okay. Well, you tried. I appreciate it, Janelle. Thanks anyway." With that, he terminated the call.

Kansas was filling in the blanks. "No search warrant?"

He nodded, shoving the phone back into his pocket. They were at the curb and he released the locks on the car's doors. "That's what the lady said. Turns out the judge that Janelle approached for the search warrant had his house saved from burning to the ground last year by guess who."

Kansas sighed. "Bonner."

He gestured like a game show host toward the winning contestant after the right answer had been given. "Give the lady a cigar."

She opened the passenger-side door and got in. "The lady would rather have a search warrant."

"Maybe we can find another way to get it," he told her, although he didn't hold out much hope for that. "But maybe," Ethan continued, knowing she didn't want to hear this, "it's as simple as what Bonner or whoever he really is said. He didn't want to risk not being allowed to become a firefighter because he was a stupid kid who went joyriding with the wrong people."

Kansas stared off into space. "Maybe," she repeated. But he knew that she didn't believe that for a moment.

The rest of the day was mired in the same sort of frustrating tedium. Every avenue they followed led nowhere. By the end of the day Kansas was far more exhausted mentally than physically. So much so that she felt as if she were going to self-combust, she told Ethan as he parked his car in her apartment complex.

Ethan grinned seductively. Getting out of his beloved Thunderbird, he came around to her side of the car and opened the door.

"I have just the remedy for that," he promised, taking her hand and drawing her toward the door.

She hardly heard him. "Maybe if I just go over—"

He cut her off. "You've gone over everything at least twice if not three times. Anything you come up with now can keep until morning. Right now," he whispered into her ear, "I just want to get you into your apartment and get you naked."

That did have promise, she mused, her blood already heating. "I take it your girlfriend canceled on you," she deadpanned.

"Don't have a girlfriend," he told her, and then added, "Other than you," so seriously that it took her breath away.

"Is that what I am?" she heard herself asking, her throat suddenly extra dry. All the while a little voice kept warning her not to get carried away, not to let down all her barriers because that left her far too vulnerable. And she knew what happened when she was too vulnerable. Her heart suffered for it.

"Well, you're certainly not my boyfriend," he answered, his eyes washing over her warmly.

"I don't think they really use that word anymore," she told him. "Girlfriend," she repeated in case he didn't understand which word she was referring to.

"I don't really plan to use any words, either—once I get you behind closed doors."

He saw what he took to be hesitation in her eyes and gave it his own interpretation. She was thinking about the case, he guessed. It was going to consume her if he didn't do something about it.

"It's the best way I know of to unwind," Ethan assured her. "Do it for the job," he coaxed. When she looked at him in confusion, he explained, "This way, you'll be able to start fresh in the morning. Maybe even find that angle you've been looking for."

The man could sell hair dryers to a colony of bald

people. "Well, if you put it that way...you talked me into it."

Slipping his arm around her waist, he pulled her to him. "I had a hunch I would."

Chapter 15

Kansas couldn't let go of the idea that she was right, that Bonner, or whatever his real name was, was the one who was behind the fires.

For a while, as Ethan made love to her, she hadn't a thought in her head—other than she loved being with this man and making love with him.

But now that he was lying beside her, sound asleep, she'd begun to think again.

And focus.

And maybe, she silently admitted, to obsess.

She just couldn't let go of the idea that she was dead-on about Nathan Bonner. Furthermore, she was afraid that he had a large, packed suitcase somewhere, one he could grab at a moment's notice and flee.

If he hadn't already.

She desperately wanted to look around his house, and, more important, to look around his garage. If she were part of the police force, the way Ethan was, her hands would be tied until that search warrant materialized—and that might never happen.

But she wasn't part of the police force, she thought, becoming steadily more motivated to take action. She was part of the fire department—a situation she had more than a sneaking suspicion might not be the case very soon. But right now she was still a fire investigator. And as such, she could very easily look around, turning things over to the police if she found anything the least bit incriminating. It was her job to prevent fires from starting.

Granted, entering Bonner's garage was technically, as she'd said to Ethan, breaking and entering, but if she found what she thought she would find, she sincerely doubted that she'd be charged with anything.

Even if she was, it would be worth it if she could stop this man from setting even one more fire.

Very slowly, moving an inch at a time so as not to wake Ethan, she slipped out of bed. Once her feet were finally on the floor, she quickly gathered up her scattered clothes and snuck out of the room.

Entering the living room, she left the light off and hurried into her clothing. With her purse in one hand and her shoes in another, she quietly opened the front door and eased herself out. Closing the door behind her took an equally long amount of time. The last thing she wanted to do was wake Ethan up. She knew that he would immediately ask where she was going.

She couldn't tell him the truth because he would stop her, and she didn't want to lie to him. Sneaking out like this allowed her to avoid either scenario.

Kansas quickly put together a course of action in her head while driving to the house of the man she now regarded as the firebug. She couldn't very well knock on his door and ask to see his garage. He was within his rights to refuse.

Her only option was not to give him that opportunity.

She'd noticed, as she and Ethan had left the man's house, that the garage had a side entrance as well as the standard garage doors that opened and closed by remote control.

Her way in was the side door.

More than likely, the door was locked, but that didn't pose a deterrent. Picking a lock was exceedingly simple if you knew what you were doing. And she, thanks to one of the foster kids whose path had crossed hers, did.

Because there was no traffic in the middle of the night, she arrived at her destination fairly quickly. Parking her vehicle more than half a block away from Bonner's house, Kansas made her way over to the one-story stucco building, keeping well to the shadows whenever possible.

Bonner, she noted, wasn't one of those people who left his front porch lights on all night. The lights were off. That worked in her favor, she thought, relieved.

Within a minute and a half of accessing the garage's side door, she'd picked the padlock and was inside the structure.

Taking out a pencil-thin, high-powered flashlight, Kansas illuminated the area directly in front of her. She was extra careful not to trip over anything or send something clattering to the finished stone floor.

There was no car inside the garage, no car outside

in the driveway, either. Maybe he was gone, or on call, she thought. Either way, she still wasn't going to take any chances and turn on the lights.

That, however, did slow down any kind of progress to a crawl. It wasn't easy restraining herself this way, considering the impatience drumming through her veins and the fact that the garage was easily a packrat's idea of heaven. There were boxes and things haphazardly piled up everywhere. Looking around, she sincerely doubted that any vehicle larger than a Smart car could actually fit in the garage.

Rather than go through the preponderance of boxes, she decided to start with the shelves that lined opposite sides of the structure, methodically going from one floor-to-ceiling array to another.

Twenty minutes in, she got lucky.

Hidden beneath a tarp and tucked away on a bottom shelf situated all the way in the rear of the garage, conveniently behind a tower of boxes, she discovered some very sophisticated incendiary devices.

Several of them.

"Oh, my God," she whispered, feeling her insides begin to shake. He wasn't planning on stopping. There were enough devices here for him to go on indefinitely, she realized.

Setting down her flashlight, she angled it for maximum illumination on her find and took out her camera. Holding her breath, Kansas took one photograph after another. This was definitely the proof she needed to convince the captain that he had a rogue firefighter on his hands.

"I'm really sorry you found those, Kansas."

Surprised, she bit down on her lower lip to keep from screaming. She shoved the camera quickly into her pocket before she turned around. When she did, she found herself looking up at Nathan Bonner. His genial expression was gone and he looked far from happy to discover her here.

"You can't do this," she told him. "You can't use these devices. You're liable to kill someone."

He waved away her protest. "No, I won't. I'm an expert on handling these things. Nobody's going to get hurt."

He couldn't believe that, she thought. But, looking into his eyes, she realized that all the dots were not connecting. He had no idea of the kind of havoc that he could bring down on a neighborhood if things went awry. He was too focused on what these fires would accomplish for *him*.

"Like no one was supposed to get hurt at the nursing home?" she challenged.

The firefighter looked genuinely stricken that she should think that he had somehow failed the deceased man. "That was his heart, not the fire."

Was the man that obtuse? "But the fire brought on the heart attack," Kansas cried.

The firefighter didn't seem to hear her. Instead, he grabbed her in what amounted to a bear hug, pinning her arms against her sides. Caught off guard, she desperately tried to get free, doing her best to kick him as hard as she could. But, although she made contact several times, he gave no indication that any of her blows hurt.

"You're going to tire yourself out," he warned. And

then he shrugged as he carried her over to an old, dilapidated office chair. It had rusted wheels and its green upholstery was ripped in several places. Each rip bled discolored stuffing. "Maybe it'll be better that way for you."

A cold chill ran down her back. "Why?" Kansas demanded.

"If the fight goes out of you—" he slammed her down onto the chair, and the impact vibrated all the way up through the top of her skull "—you'll go that much quicker."

She thought she picked up a note of regret in his voice, as if he didn't want to do what he was about to do. "You're not talking about letting me go, are you?"

"No, I'm not."

She struggled, straining against the rope that he was wrapping around her as tightly as if it were a cocoon. Using the rope, he secured her to the chair. "I thought you said you planned these things so that no one would get hurt."

"I do. But all those fires have to do with my coming to the rescue. I can't come to your rescue. You made it so I can't come," he told her with a flash of anger just before he applied duct tape over her mouth. "This isn't my fault, you know. It's yours. If you hadn't come around the firehouse, snooping like that—if you hadn't accused me—" his voice grew in volume "—you could have gone on living. And I could have gone on fighting fires. Rescuing people. It's what I'm good at, what I *need* to do." His eyes glinted dangerously. "But you want to spoil everything. I can't let you go now."

For a moment, he stood over her, a towering hulk

shaking his head. "You women, you always spoil everything. My mother was like that, always telling me I'd never amount to anything. That I was just some invisible guy that people looked right through. She said no one would ever notice me."

The angry look changed instantly and he beamed. "Well, she was wrong. They notice me, the camera people, they notice me." His hand fisted, he hit the center of his chest proudly. "People are grateful to me. To *me*." And then he sighed, looking down at her. "But I really am sorry it has to be like this."

And then, as she stared, wide-eyed, he was gone, using the side door. She heard him put the padlock back on the door.

He was locking her in.

She'd deal with getting out later, Kansas told herself. Right now, she needed to get untied from this chair. Somewhere along the line, the unbalanced firefighter had learned how to execute some pretty sophisticated knots.

Maybe there was something she could use to cut the ropes on the workbench.

But when she tried to move her chair over, she discovered that the wheels didn't roll. The rust had frozen them in place. She wasn't going anywhere.

Desperate, Kansas began to rock back and forth, increasing the momentum with each pass until she finally got the chair to tip over. The crash jolted through her entire body right down into her teeth. But it also did what she'd hoped. It loosened the ties around her just the slightest bit, giving her enough slack to try to work herself free.

But as she struggled and strained against the ropes, she realized that she smelled something very familiar.

Smoke.

It registered at the same time as the crackling sound of fire eating its way through wood. The entire garage was unfinished, with exposed wood on all four sides. A feast for the fire.

Panic slashed through her.

Kansas forced herself to remain calm. Panic would only have her using up her supply of oxygen faster. Filling her lungs with smoke faster.

The ropes are loosening, she told herself. *Stick with the program, Kansas.*

Straining against the ropes, she kept at them relentlessly. The rope cut into her wrists, making them bleed. She couldn't stop, even though she was getting very light-headed and dizzy. Even though her lungs felt as if they were about to burst.

Finally, her eyes stinging, she managed to get one hand partially free. Hunching forward, she bent her head as far as she could. At the same time, she stretched her fingers to the breaking point until she managed to get a little of the duct tape between two of her fingertips. The awkward angle didn't let her pull as hard as she wanted to. But she did what she could.

It seemed as if it was taking forever, but she finally got the tape off her mouth.

She could have cried. Instead, she screamed for help, hoping that someone would hear her. She screamed again, then stopped, afraid that she would wind up swallowing too much smoke if she continued. Using her teeth, she pulled and yanked at the ropes until she got them loose enough to pull her wrist free.

But all this struggling was getting to be too much of an effort for her, all but stealing the oxygen out of her lungs. She was losing ground and she knew it.

Damn it, she wasn't ready to die. Not now, not when it looked as if things might really be going right for her for the first time.

Why had she sneaked out? Why hadn't she told Ethan where she was going? Left him a note, woken him up, something? Anything.

She was going to die and he was never going to know how she felt about him. How she…

Kansas was winking in and out of her head. In and out of consciousness.

The smoke was winning.

She was hallucinating. She thought a car had just come crashing through the garage doors. But that was only wishful thinking. Just like thinking that she heard Ethan's voice, calling her name.

If only…

Her eyes drifted shut.

"Goddamn it, woman, you are a hard person to love," Ethan cried, trying to keep his fears banked down as he raced to her from his beloved Thunderbird, which he'd just embedded in the garage door in an effort to create an opening. He got to her chair-bound body on the floor. There wasn't time to undo her ropes so he lifted her, chair and all, and carried her and it out onto the front lawn.

Just in time.

The next moment, the shingled roof over the garage

collapsed, burying the two-car garage in a shower of debris and flames.

Focused only on her, Ethan began cutting her free. Her eyelashes fluttered and then her eyes opened for just a second. His heart leaped into his throat. She was alive!

"Kansas, Kansas, talk to me. Say something. Anything. Please!"

He thought he heard her murmur, "Hi," before she passed out.

When she came around again, she was no longer bound to a chair. Instead, she was strapped to a gurney. The gurney was inside an ambulance.

Its back doors gaping open, she could see what was left of Bonner's house. The fire was pretty much out, the embers winking and dying. The fire truck had arrived with its warriors in full regalia, ready to fight yet another fire. It wasn't much of a fight. The fire won before finally retreating into embers.

"Idiot."

Kansas smiled. She could recognize Ethan's voice anywhere.

Turning her head, she saw him sitting beside the gurney. She let the single word pass. "He did it, Ethan. He did it for the attention. He wanted to play the big hero and have everyone say how wonderful he was."

"You were right."

"I was right." She let out a long sigh, exhausted. If Ethan hadn't come when he had… "How did you know where to find me?"

"Because I know how you think," he told her, torn between being angry at her and just holding her to him to reassure himself that he'd been in time, that she was alive and was going to remain that way. "Like some damn pit bull. Once you get an idea in your head, you don't let go. When I woke up to find you gone, I just *knew* you were at Bonner's house, trying to find something on him any way you could." He looked over at the ashes that had once been a house. "Looks like if there was any evidence, it's gone."

It all came back to her. The fear, the fire and everything that had come before.

"Not necessarily," Kansas told him. He looked at her quizzically. "I took pictures." She touched her pocket to reassure herself that the camera she'd used was still there. It was. "You find him, Ethan, we can convict him. He won't burn anything down anymore." Her voice cracked as it swelled in intensity.

He began to nod his head in agreement, but then he shook it instead. "Never mind about Bonner. I don't care about Bonner." Everything she'd just put him through—the concern, the fear, the horror when he first heard her scream and realized that she was inside the burning garage and he couldn't find a way to get in—came back to him in spades. He could have lost her.

"What the hell were you thinking, coming out here in the middle of the night, poking around an insane man's garage?"

Her throat felt exceedingly dry, but she had to answer him, had to make him understand. "That he had to be stopped. That you couldn't do this because the evidence wouldn't be admissible, but I could because I wasn't bound by the same rules as you were." She stopped for breath. Each word was an effort to get out. Her lungs ached.

He looked at her incredulously, still wanting to shake her even as he wanted to kiss her. "And getting killed never entered you head?"

She smiled that smile of hers, the one that always made him feel as if his kneecaps were made of liquid gelatin. "You know me. I don't think that far ahead."

Meaning she gave no thought to her own safety. He thought of the first night he met her. She'd run into a burning building to rescue children.

Ethan shook his head. "What am I supposed to do with you?"

The kneecap-melting smile turned sexy. "That, Detective, is entirely up to you."

He already had a solution. One he'd been contemplating for the last week. "I suppose I could always put you in protective custody—for the rest of your life."

Had to be the smoke. He couldn't be saying what she thought he was saying. "And just how long do you figure that'll be?"

He took her hand in his, still reassuring himself that she was alive, that he'd gotten to her in time. "Well, if I make sure to watch your every move, maybe the next fifty years."

Okay, it wasn't getting any clearer. "Are you saying what I think you're saying?"

"The way your mind works, I never know," he admitted. "What is it you think I'm saying?" When she shook her head, unwilling or unable to elaborate, Ethan decided it was time to finally go the whole nine yards and put his feeling into words.

"Okay, maybe I'm not being very clear," he admitted. Leaning in closer so that only she could hear, he said, "I'm asking you to marry me."

A whole host of emotions charged through her like patrons in a theater where someone had just yelled "Fire!" Joy was prominently featured among the emotions, but joy was capped off by fear. Fear because she'd thought herself safe and happy once before, only to watch her world crumble to nothing right in front of her eyes.

She never wanted to be in that position again. "How about we move in together for a while and see how that goes?"

That wasn't the answer he was hoping for. "You don't want to marry me?"

Her first reaction was to shrug away his words, but she owed it to him to be honest more than she owed it to herself to protect herself. "I don't want another broken heart."

"That's not going to happen," he told her with feeling. "You have my word." He held her hand between both of his. "Do you trust me?"

She thought of how he came riding to her rescue—literally. A weak smile curved her mouth. "I guess if I can't trust the word of the man who just messed up the car he loves to save my life, who can I trust? You really sacrificed your car for me," she marveled.

"It doesn't kiss as well as you do," he told her with a straight face.

"Lucky for me."

"Hey, O'Brien." Ortiz stuck his head in, then saw

that Kansas was conscious. "How you feeling?" he asked her.

"Like a truck ran over me, but I'll live," she answered.

The detective grinned and nodded his approval. "Good." Then he got back to what he wanted to say to Ethan. "We caught him," he announced triumphantly. "Dispatch just called to say that Bonner was picked up at the Amtrak station, trying to buy a ticket to Sedona. Seems that the machine rejected his credit card." He was looking directly at Ethan when he said the last part.

By the look on Ethan's face, Kansas knew he had to have something to do with the credit card being rejected. "Just how long was I out?"

Ortiz withdrew and Ethan turned his attention back to her. "Long enough for me to get really worried."

"You were worried about me?" She couldn't remember the last time anyone cared enough to be worried about me. It was a good feeling.

This was going to take some time, he thought. But that was all right. He had time. Plenty of time. As long as he could spend it with her. "I tend to worry about the people I love."

She struggled to sit up, leaning on her elbows. "Wait, say that again."

"Which part?" he asked innocently. "'I tend'?"

"No, the other part."

"'...to worry about'?"

She had enough leverage available to be able to hit his arm. "The last part."

"Oh, you mean 'love'?" he asked, watching her face.

"The people I love," she repeated, her teeth gritted together.

"Oh?" He looked at her as if this were all new to him. "And who are these people that you love?"

Why was he toying with her? "Not me. You!" she cried, exasperated.

"You love me?" Ethan asked, looking at her in surprise and amazement.

"Of course I love you—I mean—" And then it hit her. "Wait, you tricked me."

He saw no point in carrying on the little performance any longer. His grin went from ear to ear. "Whatever it takes to get the job done."

She was feeling better. *Much* better. "Oh, just shut up and kiss me."

This he could do. Easily. Taking hold of her shoulders to steady her, he said, "Your wish is my command."

And it was.

Epilogue

Andrew Cavanaugh's house was teeming with family members. All his family members. The former chief of police hadn't merely extended an invitation this time, as was his habit—he had *instructed* everyone to come, telling them to do whatever they had to in order to change their schedule and make themselves available for a family gathering.

When his oldest son had pressed him why it was so important to have everyone there, Andrew had said that he would understand when the time came.

"Anyone know what this is about?" Patrick Cavanaugh asked, scanning the faces of his cousins, or as many as he could see from his position in his uncle's expanded family room. There seemed to be family as far as the eye could see, spilling into the kitchen and parts beyond.

Callie, standing closest to her cousin, shook her head. "Not a clue."

Rayne moved closer to her oldest sister, not an easy feat these days given her condition. Rayne was carrying twins whom she referred to as miniature gypsies, given their continuous restless state.

"Maybe he's decided, since there're so many of us, that we're forming our own country and seceding from the union," she quipped. Rayne laced her fingers through her husband's as she added, "You never know with Dad."

Kansas looked at Ethan and briefly entertained the idea—knowing that the Cavanaugh patriarch celebrated each family occasion with a party—that this might be because she and Ethan were engaged. So far, it was a secret. Or was it?

"You didn't tell him, did you?" she whispered to Ethan.

Ethan shook his head, but the same thought had crossed his mind, as well. If not for the way the "invitation" had been worded, he wouldn't have ruled out the possibility.

"From what I hear," he whispered back, "there's never a need to tell the man anything. He always just seems to know things."

They heard Brian laugh and realized that the chief of detectives had somehow gotten directly behind them. "Despite the rumors, my older brother's not a psychic," Brian told them, highly amused.

This was the first opportunity Kansas had had to see the man since Bonner's capture. In all the ensuing action, she hadn't had a chance to tell him how grateful she was that he had come to her aid. Rescuing obviously ran in the family, she mused.

Turning around to face Brian, Kansas said, "I really want to thank you, Chief, for putting in a good word for me with the Crime Scene Investigation unit."

"All I was doing was rubber-stamping a very good idea," he told her, brushing off her thanks.

Brian had been instrumental in bringing up her name to the head of the unit. He'd done it to save her the discomfort of going back to the firehouse and trying to work with people who regarded her with hostility because she'd turned in one of their own.

Seeing her smile of relief was payment enough for him. "Thank *you* for agreeing to join the CSI unit. They're damn lucky to have you," he told her with feeling. "Hopefully, you'll decide to stay with the department after Captain Lawrence comes to his senses and asks you to reconsider your resignation."

Kansas shook her head. She sincerely doubted that Captain Lawrence would ever want her back. He all but came out and said so, commenting that he felt she would be "happier someplace else." And he was right. She felt she'd finally found a home. In more ways than one.

"You have nothing to worry about there." Things had gotten very uncomfortable for her within the firehouse after Bonner was caught and arraigned. Everyone agreed that Bonner should be held accountable for what he'd done, but the bad taste the whole case had generated wasn't going to go away anytime soon. And it was primarily focused on her.

Transferring to another fire station wouldn't help. Her "reputation" would only follow her. She would always be the outsider, the investigator who turned on her own. She'd had no choice but to resign. The moment she had, like an answer to a prayer, Brian Cavanaugh had come to her with an offer from the Crime Scene Investigation unit. The division welcomed her with open arms.

"Good. I know I speak for all the divisions when I say that we look forward to working with you on a regular basis."

About to add something further, Brian fell silent as he saw his older brother walk into the center of the room. He, along with Lila and Rose, were the only other people who knew what was going on—if he didn't count the eight people waiting to walk into the room.

This, Brian thought, was going to knock everyone's proverbial socks off.

"Everybody, if I could have your attention," Andrew requested, raising his deep baritone voice so that he could be heard above the din of other conversations. Silence swiftly ensued as all eyes turned toward him.

"What's with the melodrama, Dad?" Rayne, his youngest and a card-carrying rebel until very recently, wanted to know, putting the question to him that was on everyone else's mind.

"No melodrama," Andrew assured her. "I just wanted all of you to hear this at the same time so I wouldn't wind up having to repeat myself several dozen times. And so no one could complain that they were the last to know." He was looking directly at Rayne as he said it.

"Repeat what several dozen times?" Zack called out from the far end of the room.

Andrew paused for a moment, then, taking a breath, began. "First of all, I think you should all know that your grandparents had four sons, not three."

"Four?" Teri, Andrew's middle daughter, echoed, stunned. "Where's the fourth one?"

"Let him talk," Janelle counseled.

"Good question," Andrew allowed. "The son your grandparents had after Mike and before Brian only lived for nine months. Your grandmother woke up one morning to find that he had died in his sleep. What you also don't know," he continued, raising his voice again as snatches of disbelief were voiced throughout the room, "was that, for weeks after she first came home from the hospital, your grandmother kept insisting that they had switched babies on her. That Sean—that was the baby's name—wasn't *her* Sean. Nobody really paid attention to her, thinking she was just imagining things." He paused again to let his words sink in before he came to the most incredible portion. At times, he still didn't feel as if it was real.

"Recently, people—like your uncle Brian—have been coming up to me, asking me why I was ignoring them when they encountered me on the street. Other than thinking maybe I had an early onset of dementia—"

"Never happen," Rose told him fiercely, threading her arm around her husband's waist.

Andrew grinned down at the wife he'd gone to hell and back to find, bringing her home after everyone had assumed she was dead. "Anyway," he told the others after planting a kiss on his wife's forehead, "I started my own investigation into this so-called doppelgänger people were seeing. Long story short—"

"Too late," Brian deadpanned.

Andrew ignored his brother. "It turns out that your grandmother was right, which will teach the male segment of this family never to doubt their women's instincts. I won't bore you with details—"

"Also too late," Brian commented loud enough for everyone to hear.

Andrew slanted his brother a patient, tolerant glance. "Right now, I would like to introduce you to the end result of my investigation. Everyone, I'd like for you to meet your uncle Sean—oddly enough that's what the people who raised him called him, too—and his seven kids…your cousins."

The silence within the family room was deafening as eight more people walked into the room. Each and every one of them blended in perfectly with the people who were already there.

It would have been difficult to tell them apart.

"We really *could* start our own country," Ethan murmured, remembering what Rayne had said earlier.

"I don't know about our own country," Kansas whispered in his ear, deciding that the time was right to tell him, "but we have gotten started on a family."

He looked at her sharply. "Are you—?"

She grinned broadly at him. "I am."

He couldn't begin to describe the joy he was experiencing. "*Now* will you marry me?"

Her eyes sparkled. "You bet I will."

If she was going to say anything else, it would have to wait. Because Ethan scooped her into his arms and kissed her. And he intended to go on kissing her for a very long time to come.

* * * * *

REQUEST YOUR FREE BOOKS!
2 FREE NOVELS PLUS 2 FREE GIFTS!

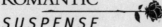

ROMANTIC
SUSPENSE

Sparked by Danger, Fueled by Passion.

YES! Please send me 2 FREE Harlequin® Romantic Suspense novels and my 2 FREE gifts (gifts are worth about $10). After receiving them, if I don't wish to receive any more books, I can return the shipping statement marked "cancel." If I don't cancel, I will receive 4 brand-new novels every month and be billed just $4.49 per book in the U.S. or $5.24 per book in Canada. That's a saving of at least 14% off the cover price! It's quite a bargain! Shipping and handling is just 50¢ per book in the U.S. and 75¢ per book in Canada.* I understand that accepting the 2 free books and gifts places me under no obligation to buy anything. I can always return a shipment and cancel at any time. Even if I never buy another book, the two free books and gifts are mine to keep forever.

240/340 HDN FEFR

Name	(PLEASE PRINT)
Address	Apt. #
City	State/Prov.	Zip/Postal Code

Signature (if under 18, a parent or guardian must sign)

Mail to the **Reader Service:**
IN U.S.A.: P.O. Box 1867, Buffalo, NY 14240-1867
IN CANADA: P.O. Box 609, Fort Erie, Ontario L2A 5X3

Not valid for current subscribers to Harlequin Romantic Suspense books.

Want to try two free books from another line?
Call 1-800-873-8635 or visit www.ReaderService.com.

* Terms and prices subject to change without notice. Prices do not include applicable taxes. Sales tax applicable in N.Y. Canadian residents will be charged applicable taxes. Offer not valid in Quebec. This offer is limited to one order per household. All orders subject to credit approval. Credit or debit balances in a customer's account(s) may be offset by any other outstanding balance owed by or to the customer. Please allow 4 to 6 weeks for delivery. Offer available while quantities last.

Your Privacy—The Reader Service is committed to protecting your privacy. Our Privacy Policy is available online at www.ReaderService.com or upon request from the Reader Service.

We make a portion of our mailing list available to reputable third parties that offer products we believe may interest you. If you prefer that we not exchange your name with third parties, or if you wish to clarify or modify your communication preferences, please visit us at www.ReaderService.com/consumerchoice or write to us at Reader Service Preference Service, P.O. Box 9062, Buffalo, NY 14269. Include your complete name and address.

HRS11B

HARLEQUIN®

SYTYCW SO YOU THINK YOU CAN WRITE

Harlequin and Mills & Boon are joining forces in a global search for new authors.

In September 2012 we're launching our biggest contest yet—with the prize of being published by the world's leader in romance fiction!

Look for more information on our website,
www.soyouthinkyoucanwrite.com

So you think you can write? Show us!

*In the newest continuity series from Harlequin®
Romantic Suspense, the worlds of the Coltons and their
Amish neighbors collide—with dramatic results.*

*Take a sneak peek at the first book, COLTON DESTINY
by Justine Davis, available September 2012.*

"I'm here to try and find your sister."

"I know this. But don't assume this will automatically ensure trust from all of us."

He was antagonizing her. Purposely.

Caleb realized it with a little jolt. While it was difficult for anyone in the community to turn to outsiders for help, they had all reluctantly agreed this was beyond their scope and that they would cooperate.

Including—in fact, especially—him.

"Then I will find these girls without your help," she said, sounding fierce.

Caleb appreciated her determination. He *wanted* that kind of determination in the search for Hannah. He attempted a fresh start.

"It is difficult for us—"

"What's difficult for me is to understand why anyone wouldn't pull out all the stops to save a child whose life could be in danger."

Caleb wasn't used to being interrupted. Annie would never have dreamed of it. But this woman was clearly nothing like his sweet, retiring Annie. She was sharp, forceful and very intense.

"I grew up just a couple of miles from here," she said. "And I always had the idea the Amish loved their kids just as we did."

"Of course we do."

"And yet you'll throw roadblocks in the way of the people best equipped to find your missing children?"

Caleb studied her for a long, silent moment. "You are very angry," he said.

"Of course I am."

"Anger is an...unproductive emotion."

She stared at him in turn then. "Oh, it can be very productive. Perhaps you could use a little."

"It is not our way."

"Is it your way to stand here and argue with me when your sister is among the missing?"

Caleb gave himself an internal shake. Despite her abrasiveness—well, when compared to Annie, anyway—he could not argue with her last point. And he wasn't at all sure why he'd found himself sparring with this woman. She was an Englishwoman, and what they said or did mattered nothing to him.

Except it had to matter now. For Hannah's sake.

Don't miss any of the books in this exciting
new miniseries from Harlequin® Romantic Suspense,
starting in September 2012 and running
through December 2012.